The Things That Always Were

Solla Carrock

Running Girl Press

Portland, Oregon

2013

First Printing

First Published in 2013

Copyright 2013 Solla Carrock

Printed in the U.S.A.

Published by

Running Girl Press

Portland, Oregon

info@runninggirlpress.com

Front cover painting: *Girl With White Dog* by Solla Carrock

ISBN 978-0-9888292-3-7

Acknowledgments

Thanks to the Dangerous Writers Group and the Portland Novel group of Carol Collier, Leanne McLennon and Mark Anderson for reading, editing, advice and support.

And special thanks to:

Kamela Bremer who was especially generous with her time and her criticism.

My daughter, Erin, for her editing and years of emotional support.

Several members of LibraryThing who read the novel and gave their responses, especially Anna Shook, Brent Higgins and Andrew Stancek.

The Things That Always Were

These are the things that always were: Mama, Daddy, my big brother Danny, my little sister Renee. Mama said I was born in St. Charles, Missouri. She said we moved to Yakima when I was one year old, but Yakima was all I remembered. Yakima was part of the things that always were.

I remembered my baby brother Sammy coming home from the hospital with Mama, me sitting way back on the couch when Mama laid Sammy in my lap. But now it seemed there never was a time without Sammy. Sammy was one of the things that always were.

The photo album held a picture of a small house on a dirt plot, and written on the back, "Danny and Annie, St. Charles, 1952." Danny stands beside me as I crawl on the dirt, and Mama sits on the porch steps. But I only knew the white house in Yakima. At the corner lot on the other side of the street was the green two-story house and the great big tree that grew up past the second story. This tree was the perfect climbing tree because its branches started low enough to the ground so I could reach my arms around the lowest branch and pull myself up into the first fork of its trunk. At least I could when I was five and allowed to cross the street.

One day I climbed that tree so high. I put my arms around the low branch, lifted my legs and wrapped them around the branch, pulled myself over onto the top, scraping my legs and the undersides of my arms a little on the bark. The tree trunk, so sturdy where I leaned my back when I rested, was part of the things that always were. I stood up, wrapped my arms around the tree trunk, then reached up for another branch. I stepped on a knob of the tree, then another branch. The branches were closer together towards the top but some of them were not so strong, so I just rested my foot on the part right next to the trunk to keep my foot from slipping and used my hands to pull myself up.

Danny came into the corner lot. I watched him from the high branches. He walked from the sidewalk, over the tiny hill and under my tree, then started over to the sawed off tree trunk. The top of Danny's head was round and smooth, fuzzy crew cut, and his T-shirt was a patch of white. Danny stopped at the tree trunk and turned slowly around, all the way around, looking.

"Annie," he yelled.

"Danny," I called, "Danny, I'm up here." I wanted him to see me so far up.

Danny walked back under the big tree and tilted his chin up, looked at the lower branches, tilted more to see higher up, still not high enough. Danny's eyes opened wider when he finally looked up high enough to see me, but he just said, "Mama wants us home for lunch now."

I looked down, and it was so far. I couldn't see the next place to put my foot. I said, "I don't remember how to get down."

"Mama wants us now." Danny tipped his head back so his face was almost flat on top of his white T-shirt and walked around the tree. "Ok," he said, "around the trunk, just a little to the right, move your right toe down there."

Grasping the trunk tightly, I moved my right foot from the safe branch and stretched it out to the right, feeling with my toe.

Danny said, "Just a little further down."

My toe found the knob.

"Ok," Danny said. "Move your arm down to the branch on your left."

I did it.

"Now you can reach the next branch with your left foot."

In the middle of moving to find the branch I remembered

how to get down the tree, at least my arms and legs remembered.

Danny said, "Okay, .."

I said, "I can do it now."

Danny said, "Just step.."

I said, "I know how."

When we got home Mama asked what took us so long and Danny told her. Mama said I wasn't allowed to climb that tree anymore.

But I kept right on climbing that tree.

Danny never told.

#

These are the things that always were: Mama, Daddy, Danny, Renee, Sammy, Yakima, the white house, the big tree on the corner lot, my body remembering how to climb down the big tree and Danny never telling.

The white house was part of the things that always were, and the new kitchen that Daddy built. Daddy added the new kitchen and a bedroom to the white house. Then you could run from the kitchen, to the dining room which used to be the kitchen, to the living room, to the hall, past two of the three bedrooms, to the bathroom, then out the new bathroom door to the kitchen again. We didn't do that when Mama was there. Just when Daddy was alone with us, like one evening while Mama worked the evening shift at a grocery store in Walla Walla. Daddy cooked us hamburgers and they smelled so good and I was so hungry, waiting for Daddy's hamburgers. Danny and I chased through the house, around and around again. Danny had left his bow from his bow and arrow set, wedged between the bathtub and the toilet, so every time on my way around I jumped over the bow. Except one time I forgot to jump, tripped on the bow, fell forward and hit my chin on the bathtub.

We were out of big Band-Aids, so Daddy put little ones on

my chin. The blood seeped out from the little Band-Aids, so Daddy put more little Band-Aids on my chin, about ten or fifteen little Band-Aids. All the little Band-Aids on my chin moving up and down while I ate the hamburger that Daddy made that tasted so good.

Then Mama came home and yelled at Daddy and took me to the emergency room at the hospital.

These are the things that always were: Mama, Daddy, Danny, Renee, Sammy, Yakima, the white house, the big tree on the corner lot, running through the house when Mama wasn't there and Daddy putting all the little Band-Aids on my chin and Mama yelling at Daddy about all the little Band-Aids.

The white picket fence, the new kitchen that Daddy built, the back porch and the swing set and slide and sandbox that Daddy made, and how we all rode out to the sand works to pick up the sand to pour in the sandbox, in the black car with the running board, the black car that was part of the things that always were.

The sand in the sandbox was like the sand on the beach in the summer where we went for vacation. Danny and I built sandcastles and tunnels. The wet sand clung to our arms, got under our fingernails.

You have to stick in your arm as far as you can to make a proper tunnel, and the other person digs from the other side until that moment when you break through, a finger hole first, then, if you stretch as far as you can, and he stretches, you can clasp each other's hand. My hand. Danny's hand. The tunnel is finished then, or it collapses.

These are the things that always were: Mama, Daddy, Danny, Renee, Sammy, Yakima, the white house, the big tree on the corner lot, Mama yelling at Daddy, the black car with the running board, the sand, Danny's hand, my hand.

Part One: Summer 1959
1 Leaving Yakima

Daddy came by today. He drove up in the car that used to be our car, but now I guess it's just his car, or maybe his car and us kids' car, but I don't think it's Mama's car anymore. Daddy walked through the gate, up the path and on to the front porch. He knocked on the door, even though it was only the screen door closed so actually he rapped on the woodwork, even though he could see right through and knew we could see him too. He looked through at us, and he knocked on the woodwork.

"Come on in, Clifford," Mama said, and I wondered how she saw, because she was staring out the kitchen window over the sink, out into the back yard, though it didn't seem like she was looking at anything in particular back there.

Daddy walked through the living and dining room, into the kitchen. He took a look through the kitchen window too, so I looked too, but it was just the backyard, the swing set, the sandbox, the sun reflecting off the tin of the slide, and way in the back the trees between our yard and the empty lot, nothing different, nobody strange in our yard, and then Daddy looked away, so I did too, but Mama didn't. Daddy wore his station uniform, all white and greasy. He'd have a clean one for his next day of work, but after work his uniform was always smeared here and there with grease. Just like his hands were scrubbed clean except around his fingernails where the grease never came out.

Daddy just stood there and looked at Mama. He seemed about to say something, but he didn't. Mama stared out the back window, then she looked down at the box she was packing. Her hands kept moving even when she looked out the window. She didn't look at Daddy, but I expect she saw everything, just like she saw

Daddy standing at the front door even though she wasn't looking that way.

Mama said, "We're trying to get packed Clifford." She didn't stop packing when she said this. She filled boxes with kitchen stuff, cleaned out drawers. She had stacks of newspaper lying on the kitchen table, and she'd pick up a sheet and wad it up with anything she'd pack, or use the paper to wrap something up.

Daddy said, "Well, what're you going to eat? Don't tell me you're cooking in the middle of all this. I could take them out for some dinner. You'd have that much less to worry about."

"We've got peanut butter." Mama said, and she said it in a way so I knew we'd go if Daddy could just talk a little longer without fighting. She was just saying that we were doing fine, just fine, whether he took us to dinner or not, but she wasn't saying she wouldn't let him.

"Save it for the train," Daddy said. "They charge an arm and a leg for a hot meal on a train. Kids'll have their fill of peanut butter on a three day trip to Springfield." He took off his hat and played with it. I liked those hats, like soldier's hats, only white. Uncle Lou had a soldier hat like that when we visited him once in Missouri.

"I guess they will," Mama said.

"How about it kids? You want to go out to eat at A & W? Annie, Danny?" Daddy asked.

I nodded my head, and Danny said, "Can we Mama?" Renee came over to stand by Mama, and Sammy just went right on playing with his toys like he had before, only he was also singing "root beer, root beer," so I expected Daddy to call him the Cornball Kid like he did sometimes, but Daddy didn't.

"Go ahead," Mama said, and turned back to packing. Us kids, even Renee who didn't always want to come with Daddy, all followed him out to the car, the car that wasn't Mama's car any more.

Daddy walked through the dining room, and as he passed the freezer he looked at it. I sucked in my breath a little, but he didn't say anything, not like the last time, when he'd said, "Barbara, I wish'd you told me you were getting a divorce. I'd of never bought that freezer on time."

It made Mama angry and I was glad he didn't say anything about that freezer again. I wanted A&W root beer, and I wanted Daddy, one more time at least before we left for Missouri. We weren't taking the freezer to Missouri, or any of the furniture, just what could be packed in boxes and sent on a train, and Mama wrapped everything up carefully so none of it would break, so I didn't know what would happen to that freezer that Daddy was buying on time.

#

Daddy drove us out to the A&W. Usually we just got root beer, but Daddy told us they had hamburgers too, and he asked us what we wanted on the way so we'd be ready when the carhop girl came to take our order. Danny wanted a burger with fries. "Can I have a large root beer?" he asked Daddy.

Daddy said yes, Danny could, and I asked could I have a large one too, and said I wanted a burger and fries. Daddy smiled at me and said I could have a large one. But Sammy and Renee, he told them that he'd get them a medium instead of the baby size they usually got, and if they wanted more he'd get them another. Sammy and Renee wanted a burger and fries too.

Up ahead on the left was the A&W's big sign showing a mug of frothy root beer. Daddy slowed down, waited a minute for a car going the other way to get past, and then turned the car into one of the empty spaces of the parking lot. The lot was mostly empty and almost right away a carhop girl came out to take our order, so it was good that Daddy had already asked us what we wanted.

The carhop girl wore black shorts and a white blouse and a little white apron, which was what they always wore, and she also had white tennis shoes, and white anklet socks folded down into cuffs. She wore her hair in two pigtails and bangs, with the A&W hat perched up on her head just behind the bangs, and held in place with bobby pins. The carhop girl had a turned up freckled nose and she skipped out to the car, not really skipping but bouncier than just walking, all cheerful, just like the A&W carhop girls always did.

"What can I get you?" the carhop girl asked, pulling out her little pad and a pen from the back pocket of her shorts. Daddy told her what we wanted and she wrote it all down. She smiled when he said that his two older kids were getting so big, they thought they'd like to try a large root beer this time. Actually, Daddy smiled first, and she smiled back at him, then she looked back down at her pad and kept on writing.

After Daddy paid her and she left with our order, Daddy turned in his seat so he could see Danny in the front seat, and me and Renee and Sammy in the back. I sat right behind Daddy, behind the driver's seat, and he turned way around so he could look at me too. Daddy said, "Well, in a few more days, you'll be seeing your Grandma and Grandpa Keenan, and your Uncle Ted, and Aunt Sharon. Guess you'll be glad to see them all again."

Danny said, "Sure, Daddy." I wasn't too clear on who Uncle Ted was but Aunt Sharon had come out to Yakima once to visit.

Daddy turned away. He looked out the window, then at the dashboard. His arms rested on the steering wheel. His hands squeezed the rim then let it go. He lowered his eyes and it seemed like he stared at the hump in the floor between the two front seats, but that wasn't anything to look at. Finally, Daddy turned back to us and he smiled and said, "Well, I hope you have a good time with your grandparents." Then he didn't say anything more, and neither did we, and a little bit later the carhop girl came back.

This time she carried an orange tray, with five mugs of root beer and two white paper bags on it, and when he saw her coming Daddy hurried to roll up his window part way, just a few inches so the tray could set on the window right. The tray had these hooks that settled right over the window. Daddy tried to help the car hop girl, but she didn't really need help. Then she pulled some change out of her pocket, and she laid it on the tray along with the order form, and she said, "Here's your change, Sir," and skipped away.

Daddy handed us our hamburgers and our fries. We set them in our laps, and we reached out again, and this time he handed us each our mug of root beer. Root beer from A&W is the best root beer. The glasses are so cold, the glasses get mist on them, like in winter when you can write on the car window with your finger, only Mama always says not to. The root beer has thick foam on the top, and when you hold the root beer your fingers make marks on the fogged up sides of the glass, and you hold it by the handle as soon as you can without spilling, because it is so cold.

Daddy gave me my root beer first, a big mug just like his, and said, "Be careful now." I had set my burger and fries in my lap so I could take the root beer with both hands. The thick mug was kind of heavy, and he didn't let go until he was sure I had it. I set it down carefully on the car seat, but even after I set it down, I held it by the handle so it wouldn't spill on the seat of the car, the car that wasn't Mama's car any more. Then Daddy handed a mug to Renee. He was slow about it and made sure she had a good hold on it too before he let go. When he came to Sammy, he decided that Sammy better come up in the front seat between him and Danny, and then they both could help Sammy with his root beer and his food. So Danny opened his door and came back and opened Sammy's door. Sammy got out and went up into the front seat, and sat in the middle, and got to put his feet up onto the hump in the floor, so that they weren't dangling off the seat because his legs were so short.

Danny had Sammy's burger and fries, so Daddy handed Sammy his medium sized mug of root beer. You could tell it was a lot for Sammy to hold, so Daddy kind of helped him guide the mug to his mouth. After Sammy took a long foamy swallow of it, Daddy said, "Here, I'll keep it on the tray for you and you can tell me when you're ready for another drink." Then Danny gave Sammy his burger to hold and put his fries down where Sammy could reach them.

Daddy said, "You doing okay back there?" to me and to Renee, and I said yes and Renee said yes. Then we all just ate and drank, and every once in awhile Daddy helped Sammy take another drink of his root beer. Then Daddy turned back round in his seat so he could see all of us, way around so he could even see me around behind him, and Daddy had tears coming from his eyes. I saw them. He opened his mouth to say something. Then he had to cough a couple of times before he could talk, then he said, "I never thought she'd take you kids away from me." Daddy was crying and I never saw him cry before, then he reached over to the tray for his root beer and he took a drink of it like that would help him stop crying, but it didn't. I wasn't crying, not really, but my eyes were all misted like the mugs with the root beer and when I looked out it was like looking through fog on a window.

2 The Train

"Come on," Danny said to me on the train. "Let's see what's in the other cars."

"Now just you wait a minute," Mama said. "Let's just get settled in here before you two go gallivanting up and down the train. I could use a little help. Annie, here, stick this suitcase up under the seat ahead of you." She handed the suitcase up over the seat back. I shoved it hard under the seat ahead, then turned back to see if there was anything more that she wanted so I could do it quickly and be off with Danny.

Mama stood in the middle of two facing seats arranging things around Sammy and Renee. They'd sit together so Mama could watch over them, but Danny and I had a seat up ahead.

Sammy looked out the window, while Renee stayed close to Mama. The train moved ahead with a little jolt and Renee grabbed at Mama's dress. Mama reached a hand out to steady her. Danny stood a little into the aisle, and I stayed right next to him. While the train jolted ahead I tried to see if I could keep my balance without having to put a hand on the back of the seat. The train vibrations came up through my legs, shaking. Then the train's movements smoothed out. Renee let go of Mama's dress and Mama moved her hand away.

Danny and I didn't sit because we were waiting to go. Mama lifted a suitcase up into the overhead bin, and set a smaller suitcase on the other seat. She opened it up to show Sammy his teddy bear and three little cars. Sammy drove one of the cars along the edge of his seat. It was a blue metal pickup with some of its paint scraped off.

"Chug, chug, chug," Sammy said.

"It's not a train, you silly," Renee said.

"I think I can. I think I can," said Sammy.

That made Mama laugh. "It can be a train if he wants," she said.

"It's an engine," Sammy said.

Danny moved closer to Mama. "What would you like me to do, Mama?"

"Well, I guess there's really not much you can do," Mama said. "You're not tall enough to reach the luggage bins."

"I could hand things to you." Danny stood up really straight and looked like he had nothing else in the world to do but help Mama, nothing in the world he'd rather do. He had on a short sleeve white shirt, open at the neck, and his gray, corduroy school pants because Mama said he might as well get some wear out of them before he outgrew them and no sense saving them because it wasn't likely the new school would have the same kind of uniform. His hair was combed with the part really straight and the front hair to the side of the part kind of combed back and fluffed up, the way it was when Mama helped comb it for church.

Mama said, "Yes, you could do that, but I could probably do it just about as easy myself. I got you all some traveling games down in that suitcase Annie put under the seat. Don't you want to take a look at them before you go exploring the train?"

Danny said, "I think I'd like to do that first thing when we get back," and he grinned at Mama with his mouth open grin. Danny was so handsome. Sometimes Mama would say, when Danny was all dressed up for church or for something else that you get dressed up for, that she sure had a handsome boy. And it was true. My brother was so handsome.

Mama smiled back at Danny, said, "Well, go ahead then, but remember what car we're in."

"Come on," Danny shouted, like I hadn't heard it all, didn't know we had to go before she changed her mind. I hurried after him, but we didn't run. We walked because we knew that Mama would be mad at us if we ran in the aisles. She would tell us to sit ourselves down in our seats and that we could sit there the whole trip if we didn't behave ourselves. When we made it through the door, a light swinging door, then we were safe.

But we weren't anywhere yet, because this was just another compartment like ours, full of seats, some facing, some straight ahead, people in most of them, wide windows with hardly any space between them, so the view from one joined into the view from the next, so you didn't just see the view to the side, but could look way ahead at what was coming. Ahead was flat and brown with blowing sagebrush and telephone lines. Already we were outside of Yakima, far from the train station.

If you looked straight out to the side, the telephone poles zipped past, but if you looked ahead, you could see them coming for a long time and then they didn't seem to rush by so fast.

"This is our first train ride," Danny said.

"I know that," I said.

The next door was a heavy metal one with a doorknob. Danny had to push hard to get it open. Then I had to push it hard to hold it open long enough to get through. As soon as the door opened, the noise of the wheels on the tracks grew loud, and then louder still when I stepped into the doorway. There was just a little space and then another door. The walls on the side weren't solid. There were windows in the walls, one to each side, so little you could just look straight through, not ahead or behind, and everything outside rushed past those windows so fast.

I stood on the door ledge, not wanting to step down. The floor rattled and on the other side of the little room the wall that showed between the floor and the bottom of the door showed sometimes more, sometimes less. Danny didn't slow down. He ran across the little space and opened the next door, so I hopped down. The floor shook and rattled, but I stepped across fast, and up onto the other door ledge where Danny held the door open for me. Quickly I stepped onto the solid floor. Then Danny let the door close.

Quiet.

It was dark here, a hallway with doors along the sides. "What do you think this is," I asked Danny.

"I think it's the sleeping cars," Danny whispered. "They have them on TV sometimes. Inside they have bunk beds against the wall."

"How come we don't have one?"

"I think they're only for rich people." Danny said.

"But where are the porters? Don't they always have porters knocking on the door and checking to see that everything is okay?" I asked.

"No," Danny said. "The man has to stick his head out of the compartment and say, '"Oh, Porter'. Then the porter comes to see what he wants, and then the man has the porter bring something for the beautiful woman."

"Oh yeah, that's right. What do you think would happen if we said, 'Oh, Porter.'"

"We might try it if we had some money. The man always gives money," Danny said.

"How come the man always gives the money?" I said. "If we had money I would want to be the one to give it."

"It's always the man," Danny said.

"That's not fair," I said.

"Well, we don't have any money anyway, and if we called, the porter might tell us to go sit down."

The next car held lots of tables and chairs, and at the far end had another swinging door. Just then a man pushed through. He had a tray with some dishes on it and he wore blue creased pants, a blue jacket with gold buttons on the cuff and a white shirt. He had a cap. He laid out dishes on one of the tables. The tables were all covered with long white tablecloths. Nobody else was in the dining car. I wondered if we should be there. The man tugged at the tablecloth to straighten it, then raised his eyes up level with Danny. The man said, "The first dinner call will be in about an hour."

"Ok," Danny said. "We'll come back then."

"Yes Sir, young man." The man set down some cups.

Danny started back.

"Do you think we'll eat there?" I said.

"Maybe."

#

We went back and told Mama that the first dinner call was in about an hour.

"I know, but I brought some chicken for our dinner tonight. We'll be eating in the dining car tomorrow. Are you hungry?" Mama said.

"No, not yet." Danny said. I slid over to the seat by the window and pulled out the suitcase with the games. Danny watched from the aisle seat as I opened it up.

"Look at this," Danny said. It was a metal board with checkers and backgammon. The checkers were brown and cream with magnets on the bottom. Danny picked up the metal board and a picture of Superman showed underneath.

"Hey, comics," I said.

"There's two each," Mama said, "but then you can read the other person's."

"Thanks, Mom," said Danny.

"Yeah, thanks, Mom," I said.

We got magic slates too, the gray pad that you press the red wooden pencil into to write, but it doesn't have lead, then you lift the film part to erase it. Also new crayons and coloring books. Trains are cool.

We played checkers first, then read one comic. Danny's was *Superman*. I read *Archie and Veronica* and Renee had *Richie Rich*. After dinner we drew on our slates and I looked out the window. We were in the mountains and sometimes it looked like we were right out in the air. I knew there were really tracks under the wheels, but it felt like nothing held us up.

It got darker. Mama showed us how to lay our seats way back to sleep. She got us blankets and pillows.

"You can turn on the light if you want to read," Mama said.

I did, and read my other comic, then I turned the light off and laid back. The whole train was dark, but some people still had their lights on. The light reflected off their windows and off other windows. At some places the outside showed and at others only the reflections of the lights and the people inside the train. Sometimes I could see the inside and the outside at the same time, and reflections of the person sitting at the window along with reflections of the people on the other side of the train. The reflections of the people on the other side of the train made them look like they were riding high up close to the ceiling. I looked out my window. At first it all looked dark, then I saw some places that were a little less dark. Those places turned into the sky, and I realized we were still in the mountains, with light places of sky between peaks, cloudy sky, no stars. I tried to look down and saw only dark. Sometimes I thought I could see bushes to the side. I tried to see tracks up ahead, but I couldn't. We seemed to be rushing ahead into nothing.

The train shifted into a curve and my body slid closer to the window. I leaned my head on the window next to my seat and closed my eyes.

I lean my head on Becca's shoulder in the back seat of the black car with the running board. Only it doesn't have its top. It's open like a convertible. The day is clear and the sky bright blue. Becca is my best friend. Becca's wearing a white sweater. Her hair is in pigtails. I hold her hand. "I'm so glad to see you," I tell her. We travel up a road which winds around a mountain. The mountain face is to our right. Sometimes the face next to the road is so high I can't see anything else. Other times there is a ledge before the mountain rises up, and I can see more even on that side. On the left, across a valley, I see other peaks. Something happens. I'm not in the car beside Becca. I'm up here in the cliffs, leaping from peak to peak, running along, easy, like skipping. The car's down below, moving on that little road winding around that mountain over there. Now I'm back in the car, no, I never left. I finish the sentence I was saying to Becca, and we laugh. When Becca laughs I see her two front teeth that stick out a little. She's wearing a light spring dress, so I see her skinny legs, her knobby knees. Of course, I've always been here, sitting beside Becca. I never left her, never will. I'm leaping again. I'm so free, so light up here running along the tips of the mountains. I don't worry about falling. I could never fall. Becca is talking to me. "Yes," I say, "we'll be friends always, best friends."

#

When I woke it was light outside and we weren't in the high mountains anymore. It looked like country, bushes, trees, tall grass, wet from dew or rain. I got out of my seat, crawled over Danny to the aisle.

"Are you awake already?" Mama asked me. She opened her eyes halfway through the sentence.

"I have to go to the bathroom." I said.

"Okay, then come on back and try to sleep a little longer."

The bathroom was in the next compartment, just on the other side of the swinging doors. I didn't stop there. I went straight on to the second door, the heavy door, turned its knob and pulled as hard as I could. I stuck my foot in when I got it open a little ways. Afraid someone would hear the noise and come and tell me I couldn't go that way by myself, I slid my shoulder into the space, braced my back against the door jamb and pushed out against the door with both my arms to open it farther. I felt the vibration under my feet on the door jamb. I got the door open just enough to slip through, and let it close, almost all the way.

Then I stepped down, onto the floor of the little room between the railway cars. I let the door close the rest of the way. I stood there on the floor, felt the rattle, felt the floor shift up and down, heard the loud squeal and rattle of the train wheels on the track. Out one of the little windows, so little you couldn't look anywhere ahead of the train or anywhere behind but just straight through, everything whirred past so fast. The wheels on the track went round and round so fast. Everything rattled, I'm rattling, bumping up and down, hard to stand up, move back and lean back against the other wall. That wall shakes, feels like canvas, not quite solid, stretches tight then goes loose, but I lean against it anyhow, lean back looking all the time out that little window, out at everything, all of it blurred together, everything passing by so fast.

3 Divorce

Mama stopped going to church after we moved from Yakima to Missouri. In Yakima we went every Sunday because Protestants could miss sometimes but Catholics never could. In Missouri we never went to church except once when Mama let some friends of hers take us to theirs, and then Mama didn't come. It wasn't a Catholic church we went to and I didn't know if a not Catholic church counted for going to church, but I didn't think it did, and I knew for sure when they did the communion that I wasn't supposed to do it, not even if the crackers and grape juice they were handing around really was the body and blood of Christ and I wasn't sure whether it was or wasn't.

Halfway through the Mass - but it wasn't a Mass - the priest - but he wasn't a priest - said the kids could go to their Sunday school classes now. So we went too, Danny and Renee and Sammy and me, when the Sunday school teacher called out our ages. I was in a class separate from any of them and that's where I got the pamphlet that I read in the back of the car on the way home.

The pamphlet said that divorce was a sacrilege, that it was an abomination in the eyes of God.

The Catholic church had sacrilege too. The priests and nuns said "sacrilege" sometimes. Like when Sister Mary Olivier told us about the martyrs who wouldn't step on the cross, because stepping on the cross was a sacrilege. So they were burned at the stake, and St. Lawrence was roasted on a grid iron. After he roasted for awhile St. Lawrence said, "You can turn me over now. I'm done on this side." That showed he had a sense of humor. That's what Sister Mary Olivier told us.

I just hadn't known that Mama and Daddy committed a sacrilege, and I wanted to ask Mama if it really was, if it was a

Catholic sacrilege, but I never asked. I left the pamphlet in the back seat of the car.

#

Being divorced was like that day in first grade after I had waited and waited for Sister Mary Olivier to say that it was time to go to the bathroom and get a drink of water, but she never did, not that day. School was almost out when Sister Mary Olivier noticed the puddle spreading from under my desk out into the aisle and asked, "What's that? Where's that coming from?" So everyone looked and saw the puddle and where it was coming from.

I wanted to hide, but I couldn't leave my desk without permission.

Then all the other kids were gone for the day and Sister Mary Olivier stood by my desk, saying, "Annie, why didn't you tell me you had to go to the bathroom?" She said it more than once. All the time I could see the puddle, still spreading out, getting closer to Sister Mary Olivier's heavy black shoe and I hoped the puddle wouldn't reach.

Then the janitor came in with the big metal bucket on wheels with the wringer, and the smell that reminded me of when people threw up.

When the janitor came Sister Mary Olivier backed away from my desk, and even though she hadn't given me permission the bell had rung, so I slipped out. The wood of the seat of my desk was wet, spongy and rough. The wood rubbed my leg and caught my underpants, so I had to jerk to get out of the desk.

No, actually, divorce was more like the days after that when everybody knew I'd wet my pants at school and I was the only one that did in the first grade. Divorce was like once in second grade at recess when this girl, who wasn't even in my class, sat down next to me on the blacktop, and leaning against the concrete school building, said to me, "You're the girl who wet her pants in school last year."

So even leaving Yakima, leaving my best friend, Becca, still there was one thing. In the new school, nobody would know about me wetting my pants. I wouldn't be ashamed.

Except for being divorced.

In the new school, in the third grade, in Missouri, being divorced was Mrs. Deaver calling me up to her desk to pick up my arithmetic paper after she checked my answers, just like she called up all the other kids, only Mrs. Deaver saying, "Sit down for a minute," in her soft voice.

Mrs. Deaver saying, "You're doing very well in arithmetic. In fact, you're doing very well in all your work. You must have come from a good school."

Me saying, "Yes, I went to St. Paul's school in Yakima."

Mrs. Deaver was a nice teacher. She never yelled. She had light brown waved hair and smooth gray wool skirts and blouses with collars made of soft material that never wrinkled.

"Why did you leave Yakima?" she asked.

"I'm not sure exactly, " I said.

Mrs. Deaver waited for me to figure it out.

"My grandparents live here," I said.

"My father's still in Yakima, " I said, but I didn't mean to say that.

She looked at me, her face very still, listening to me carefully like grownups usually didn't, only I didn't want Mrs. Deaver to be listening to me so carefully just then.

"He's staying for awhile because he has a job there. He'll be coming later," I said.

Mrs. Deaver said, "I see."

She pressed her hand down her leg, smoothing her wool skirt, like it was bunched up or had a wrinkle in it, but it didn't. "Well, I'm sure he's very proud to have a daughter like you who does so well in school."

She picked up a pencil then and she wrote right on the top of my arithmetic paper. It was upside down to me but I still could read it, "Good work." Then Mrs. Deaver said, "Go ahead and take a seat now."

#

One of those Sundays when we didn't go to church, Mama drove us out to a farm to meet a man she'd met who lived out there with his two kids, a boy Danny's age, a girl my age. Mama turned the blue Plymouth that she'd bought soon after we'd arrived in Missouri into the long drive, the car churning up dust. Out in a field by the side of the road some long grasses shook, then a girl ran out. Her hair, short and straight, chopped off evenly at the bottom, flew back, she ran so fast. Her skinny legs flew like scissors opening and closing.

We drove closer to the house, white with some old chairs sitting on the big front porch. Mama stepped up the two little stone steps onto the wooden porch, opened the screen and knocked on the front door.

A tall thin man with short dark brown hair opened it. He pulled the door back further and smiled.

"Hi, Barbara." He wore bright new jeans and a long sleeve flannel shirt with the sleeves rolled up past his elbows. His arms looked almost as long and skinny as the legs of the girl running and running in the field.

"Hi, Sam," Mama said. She spoke quietly like on the first day in a new school, but even though her mouth didn't smile, it looked full and pink and happy. Mama was pretty.

Sam reached out a hand and Mama took it. Sam pulled her towards him and Mama let him, but before she got all the way to him she stopped and turned to half-face the rest of us coming in the door. She said, "These are my kids."

Sam squeezed Mama's hand before he let it go. Then he reached to shake Danny's hand, saying, "Pleased to meet you. You must be Danny." Sam turned half around then and called out, "Tim, come and meet our visitors."

Tim's hair was exactly the same straight brown as his father's. His eyes were the same soft brown. He didn't seem especially tall though, about my size, and he wasn't skinny like his father and sister.

Sam squatted down on one knee to take Renee's hand and say hello. He got back up before he took mine. His eyebrows came closer together when he smiled at me and said, "Annie, right? You must be just about my daughter's age." He turned around. "Tim, have you seen your sister?"

Tim said, "She took off as soon as she heard their car." Tim shook his head slowly and shrugged his shoulders up and down before he looked right at me and said, "Heather's real shy."

His father laughed, "Maybe she'll come back before you leave." He turned to say hello to Sammy, but Sammy leaned back against Mama's leg and held her dress instead. Sam said, "I guess she's not the only shy one."

Mama said, "Oh, that won't last long." She put her hand on Sammy's head and took pieces of his hair between her fingers, until Sam motioned toward her purse, "Here, let me take that."

Mama had to take her hands off Sammy's head in order to take the purse off her arm and when she did Sammy came over by me. Mama handed the purse to Sam. He took it with one hand and took Mama's hand with the other. When he pulled her close, this time Mama didn't pull away.

Sam said, "Tim, why don't you show our visitors around the farm?"

On the road to the pasture, Tim said, "I could show you our bull. Our bull is friendly. It's the cows you have to watch out for. We have some mean cows. But the bull's gentle."

Tim, Danny and I walked together with Renee and Sammy following behind. Tim said, "We can get in over there," pointing to a place in the fence where the lowest string of barbed wire was a little higher. "Come on." He grabbed my hand and I ran with him. He dropped my hand to hold up the bottom string of barbed wire, his fingers between two barbs. "Here," he said, "duck under so it doesn't catch you."

So I got on my belly and crawled under.

"That's the way," Tim said.

Danny had reached us by then. Tim held the wire, while Danny, Renee and Sammy crawled under. After that Danny held it up for Tim to come through. Tim jumped up and brushed off his shirt, white for Sunday or for visitors. He tucked it back into his pants as he gazed around the pasture, finally pointed a long ways away. "There's the bull."

I didn't walk so fast as before, but Tim slowed down to let us catch up, and reassured me, "This is a nice bull." We headed toward the bull in a bunch. The grass of the pasture felt cool.

"Here he is," Tim said. He petted the bull. The bull's horns dipped toward the ground as he lowered his head to eat the grass. I moved next to Tim.

"Here, feel how soft he is," Tim took my hand and put it over on the side of the bull. The bull was brown and white, white on its face, brown on its head and the outside of its ears, brown on its side, but with specks of white, and white on the bottom of its side as it got closer to the bull's belly. Tim moved the flat of my hand down the side of the bull, then left my hand there. It was like having your hand against a wall. Only this wall moved just a little back and forth every time the bull breathed. When the bull stopped biting off the grass and swallowed I felt it on the bull's side. I patted the bull in little strokes because I didn't want to move too far from where Tim had placed my hand. I didn't know how the bull would feel about it.

Sammy petted the bull, right near the bull's stomach because that was where he could reach. The bull didn't do anything. So I moved my hand lower to pat the softest white fur next to the bull's belly.

Danny stepped up to my left. Even Renee came then, and touched the bull on its side. The bull just chewed on the grass.

Tim said, "You see, the bull's gentle, just like a cow. Except our cows are mean. I could pull his tail and he wouldn't do nothing." But Tim didn't pull the bull's tail. "The cows would though. They'd kick. Our cows are mean."

So we stayed away from the cows on the way to the barn. The barn sat way up next to the fence on the part of the pasture that was nearest the house. From the outside the barn looked about the same size as the house, but once we got the big wooden doors pulled open and went inside the ceiling was so high up it looked even bigger. The cow stalls where the cows got milked were lined up on either side of a big trough filled with grain. No cows were there now but a couple of stalls had short stools inside. The barn smelled like manure and the grain had a grassy smell.

Tim showed us the buckets for milking, and the milking cans, big and silver, that the buckets of milk were poured into, and the ropes and halters on the wall. He led us around a wall that went nearly all the way across the barn into a second room. Tim pointed to the back. "There's another room back there with hay and stuff. It opens on the other side so the cows can be brought straight in for the night."

The room we were in was filled with stacked-up bales of hay. On one side the bales were stacked like a staircase so you could climb up on them to the top. Next to the hay staircase was a wooden crib, about two feet high, like a big sandbox filled up with loose hay instead of sand. Tim jumped up onto the staircase of hay and climbed almost to the top of the stack then he jumped out over the crib and turned his body so he landed flat on his back, right in the middle of the loose hay. He lay there with his arms and legs all spread out and his eyes closed.

Tim didn't look hurt but I wondered if he could be. Then he opened his eyes, looked at me and grinned. "You want to try it?"

"Yes," I said. I climbed up just the same as he had. I jumped way out in the air, turning my body to be spread out flat just the same as Tim did, only then wondering if the hay was thick enough. But I landed on my back the same as Tim had. The hay felt soft, not like the bull's hide, but soft to land in, pushing back a little springy like a mattress but softer than that, not as packed, dry and pokey when you touched it with your finger. I laid there resting until Danny shouted, "Get out of the way!"

He stood high up on the layer next to the top of the hay mountain in his blue jeans and white T-shirt, short blondish brown hair, blue eyes. I wanted to lay looking up at him, but if I did he would be mad, so I rolled over on the hay until I had rolled to the edge, then I pulled my legs over onto the ground and stepped out.

Sammy and Renee climbed up the bales of hay while I followed after. Each bale came to Sammy's waist and he had to grab the bale and pull his legs up on it. I helped by pushing up on his bottom while he pulled. Several rows before the top Renee stopped, "I'll jump from here."

I put my hands on Sammy's shoulders to make sure he waited until Renee was out of the crib. I told him, "Jump way out, Sammy."

Sammy landed right in the middle of the hay on his bottom.

This was all right, not like rides at the fair that you had to pay for. We could do it all day. Sammy climbed out at the edge of the crib. I went up to the very top of the mountain of hay and jumped out. There was no way to be hurt, just jumping out free like that into the air, lying there in the hay, smelling the hay smell; watching Danny help Sammy climb the bales. Tim by the side of the crib, not jumping anymore, just watching, looked at me lying in the hay.

"Come on," he says, and reaches out his hand. I roll over to him. He puts his arm under my back, and lifts. I'm just as big as he is so I use my feet to help him get me up. I step on the board on the side of the crib and then down on the ground. Tim's arm is still around me just for a moment before I start back up the bales of hay.

#

Danny stood by the wall next to the other room of the barn. He motioned us over, shushing with his finger. "They're kissing in there," Danny said. He pointed to a crack for me to look through.

Hay was stacked up in there just like in the jumping room, staggered like rows of bleachers. Mama and Sam sat about half way up, his arm around her, and Mama leaning back against him with her eyes closed, but they weren't kissing. Maybe they'd get married and we'd be able to move out to this farm.

Tim asked, "What are they doing?"

I said, "They're just sitting there now."

Danny shook his head, "Well, they were really smooching away earlier." He sat on the ground and leaned back against the wall between the two rooms. Tim sat down too and I sat beside him.

"It'd be great if they got married," Tim said.

"Yeah, maybe," Danny said, slowly, so I wondered if he was thinking about Daddy. "But who knows what grown ups will do."

#

Mama sat on the living room couch in a skirt like one of Mrs. Deaver's skirts. She wore a soft lilac blouse. Her hair looked the way it did when she put the hairspray on it, everything in place.

She said, "Kids, get some nice clothes on. Sam is bringing Heather and Tim into town and we're all going out to a movie."

It was getting dark by the time an old smoky blue gray pickup truck parked in front of our house. I watched out the picture window. Tim got out the passenger side while the engine was still running, waited for Heather then slammed the door shut. The weather had turned cold. Both Tim and Heather wore coats with scarves around their necks. Heather had a furry round hat with a tie under her chin, but Tim's head was bare and the wind blew his hair. The truck engine died. A truck door slammed. Sam followed Tim and Heather up to our front door.

I would have opened the door, but Mama hurried ahead of me, so she was already there when they knocked.

"Come on in, kids," Mama said. They came over to me and Danny.

"Hello," I said to Tim, and then I turned to Heather and said hello to her too. She was the girl who was my age, and she said hello back even if she was shy.

I said, "You can take your coats off."

But Mama said, "Actually, we're going to go ahead to the movie now, so why don't you and Danny and Renee get your coats on and help Sammy with his."

We rode in our Plymouth to the movie but Mama let Sam drive. Renee sat in the middle up front. Mama held Sammy in her lap, so just the four of us older kids sat in the back seat, Heather at the left window, me next to her, then Tim, then Danny. It helped keep us warm to be so close together in the car before it heated up. Nobody said anything with the grownups there in the front. All of us pressed together in the chilly dark.

The car barely got warm before we reached the theater. Sam parked the car while Mama and the rest of us waited in line to get the tickets. Tim stood next to me. His coat came open so I could see his gray sweater underneath. It matched his dress pants, soft gray, like his eyes were soft brown. He looked sharp dressed like that.

"Are you cold?" Tim asks me and when I nod yes, he puts his arm around me for a moment. But Mama has the tickets now and Sam has come. We go into the theater. We follow the grownups but only Renee and Sammy sit with them, the rest of us sit in the row behind them. Danny goes in first, and Tim follows him, but when he does Tim reaches for my arm to make sure that I am in the seat beside him. Heather comes after me. The lights are already dimmed. I move my hand over towards Tim's seat and he takes it and holds it next to him. Tim holds my hand through the opening music. The movie starts and he's still holding my hand. In the middle of the movie he's still holding my hand, and I ask him, I whisper, "Are your parents divorced?"

"Yes, " Tim whispers back.

4 West Plains

Just a few days after Christmas, Mama told us to dress in our Sunday clothes, we were going for a ride. She wore her black dress with a belt and high heels. When we all got in the car, Danny asked to sit up front and Mama said he could. She said she had to talk to a priest at the rectory in West Point. Maybe that was why we were dressed up.

"What are you going to talk to the priest about?" Danny asked.

"I'll tell you about that later," Mama said. She said it in her quiet voice, serious quiet.

When we reached West Plains, Mama drove the car into a dirt driveway next to a church and a long white building that must be the rectory. She turned the car off and rested her arms on the steering wheel, her eyes straight out ahead.

She turned halfway round in her seat. "You stay here in the car. It shouldn't be too long."

It was winter but the sun shone, and the car was warm. Danny rolled his window down a crack.

I said, "Want to go in the front, Sammy?"

He nodded so I lifted him and kind of rolled him over the seat. Sammy sat in Mama's seat and pretended to drive.

We were in the middle of a big dirt lot. The lot and the church and the rectory were the only things on the block. Nobody walked by our car. No cars even drove by on the street. The nearest house was across the street where we couldn't really see it. We hadn't brought any games to play. I leaned against the car door and listened to Sammy make noises like he was driving.

"I wonder what she's talking to the priest about," Danny said. He leaned back against his car door, his eyelids closing. I felt sleepy too.

"Maybe she'll tell us when she comes back," I said.

"Maybe," Danny said. "I just don't understand why she couldn't have gone to see a priest in Springfield. Why did we have to drive all the way down here?"

I couldn't answer that. First Mama stops going to church, and then we drive for a couple of hours for her to see a priest. I didn't want to think about it. I leaned against my car door and let my eyes close. Danny and Renee must have done the same, because I heard Sammy's voice but no one else's.

A long time later I heard a door close, then the crunching sound of steps on gravel. Mama came to the car, the priest beside her. He wore a black cassock and looked young to be a priest. On the passenger side of the car, he looked in the open window at Danny.

"Hello, son. What's your name?" the priest said, holding out his hand.

Danny shook the priest's hand and said, "Danny."

"What grade are you in, Danny?"

"Fourth."

Sammy scooted from behind the steering wheel and stood on the seat, holding on to Danny's shoulder.

"And how are you, young fellow?" the priest asked, but Sammy just sucked on his fingers. The priest didn't seem to mind. Renee rolled down her window and the priest talked through it to Renee and me.

It was strange to see a priest after all this time. Even at St. Paul's the priests hardly ever spoke to you. Mostly just the nuns did. The priests talked for a few moments on some special occasion, like when we practiced for our first communion.

This priest asked each of us what grade we were in school, except Sammy, since he was only three.

When Renee told the priest she was five he patted her shoulder and said, "You sure are big for a five year old." Everybody said that about Renee and me, except with me they said I sure was big for an eight year old.

"Well, I'm glad to meet you all," the priest said. He walked to the driver's side where Mama stood by her car door. The priest said, "You have four fine children there."

He took Mama's hand then, and shook it. He held her hand while he looked straight at Mama. Mama bent her head down and looked away.

"Thanks so much for your help."

The priest said, "It will be all right." He let go of Mama's hand and headed back towards the rectory.

We heard the rectory door close.

Mama got back in the car.

Mama turned around in her seat and her voice came out hard quiet, angry quiet, "What do you mean by not saying 'Father' when you talk to a priest?"

Mama looked at Danny first. Danny straightened up in his seat and his face got red. Mama looked at me. My face felt hot and I wondered how I could have forgotten. Only last year I was in second grade in St. Paul's school and now I was already forgetting how to be a Catholic.

Mama said, "Do you want him to think you are rude children who haven't been brought up properly?"

I shook my head no.

Danny said, "We're sorry, Mama. We'll remember next time."

Mama turned back around. She turned the key and pressed on the gas pedal. Danny lifted Sammy back up over the seat and I helped him slide the last way over into the back so he didn't fall.

Mama got the car started and drove out of the gravel parking lot, the tires churning on the gravel. For a long time Mama just drove, looking straight ahead, her hands tight on the steering wheel.

Mama talked, in a quiet voice again, serious quiet. Renee and I leaned up against the front seat to hear. She said, "I'm going into the hospital soon. It's for something called a nervous breakdown. The doctor says I need a long rest."

I never heard of a nervous breakdown. Danny didn't look like he'd heard of a nervous breakdown either. His face didn't look red anymore but he didn't move, his arms, his legs, his face, everything, completely still. Renee closed her eyes. Her blue eyes gone, all of her was pale, her face, her blond hair, big light curls that you could see through. Renee opened her eyes again and laid her head down on the back of the front seat.

Mama said, "You'll be staying with the family of the man who drives the bus for the Catholic school, the Willises, and you'll go to Catholic school again. The Willises have kids too, a boy who's ten, and a girl who's thirteen. Plus they have three older boys who take care of their farm in Ava.

"You'll be able to live on a farm." Mama said that like a question and she looked away from the road over to Danny for the answer. She said, "The boy's name is Danny too. That might be a little confusing." She smiled at my brother, but not an all the way smile, more like a smile she would finish if Danny smiled back.

But Danny didn't smile back.

Mama looked ahead at the road.

Danny said, "How long, Mama?"

Mama didn't answer right away. She lowered her head a little, then raised it back up. She opened her mouth like she was going to talk, then closed her mouth and swallowed. Her hands stopped holding the steering wheel so tight.

"About six months, maybe a little longer," Mama said. "The doctor can't say for sure."

Danny turned his head towards his window, leaned his forehead on the glass, shut his eyes, opened his eyes, and turned his head back to face Mama.

Danny said, "That's summer. Will you be out by Renee's birthday and my birthday?"

July 7th, July 11th.

Mama said, "I don't know for sure. I think so. I hope so." Her hands held tight to the steering wheel, but she wasn't angry at Danny. Her voice wasn't angry.

Danny whispered, "Sammy's birthday?"

August 8th.

Mama said, "Almost certainly before Sammy's birthday."

Six months, maybe a little longer.

Renee sat back down in her seat and scooted back, her legs out straight. She rested her arm on the window ledge, laid her head on her arm, and Renee didn't look so big for her age.

Mama drove for a while. Then she glanced at us before she fixed her eyes back on the road.

She said, "You kids will behave for the Willises, won't you?"

It was like when she went to beauty school, and Uncle Ted, Mama's youngest brother, babysat us. We told her Uncle Ted was mean to us, and Mama said she'd try to find a new babysitter, but there wasn't really much choice. We just had to put up with him.

The only choice was whether to cause Mama trouble or not.

"And you'll remember to call the priest 'Father,' now, won't you?"

"Yes," I said.

"Yes," Renee said.

"We will," said Danny.

"You'll watch out for the littler kids, won't you?" she asked Danny and me.

"Of course we will, Mom," Danny said.

He answered for both of us.

5 Sammy

It wasn't just because Mama told us to watch out for the little kids that I looked out for Sammy. It was because Sammy was mine to take care of.

This is how I knew that Sammy was mine to take care of. Not when he first came home from the hospital all covered up with a baby blanket, Mama holding him against her shoulder with her big hand, fingers spread out over his back and bottom. Daddy coming after with Mama's suitcase and the diaper bag.

Mama sat down on the couch, lowered Sammy from her shoulder to her lap and lifted the blanket off his head. Sammy's head was covered with light colored hair. His eyes were closed and tiny blue veins showed right through the skin of his eyelids. But that wasn't when I knew.

Before we said anything, Mama lifted her finger to her lips. "Shh," she said, "He's asleep."

"Can we hold him?" I whispered. I leaned against the couch so I could look at him.

Renee leaned against the couch too, on the other side of Mama, touching Mama's leg. Danny sat on the big chair. Renee touched Sammy's blanket about where Sammy's foot would be.

Mama said, "Don't wake him," not in an angry voice but Renee moved her hand away and put it in the little pocket of her pedal pushers. So I couldn't touch Sammy then.

Danny said, "Does he sleep all the time?"

Mama's mouth started to smile, then she held it back, but it made her face fill out soft. She said, "No, not all the time, but newborn babies do sleep a lot at first." Mama's eyes went soft too when she looked at Danny. I started to ask again if we could hold him but then Mama turned her soft eyes to me.

She said, "You'll be able to hold him after supper when he wakes up. All of you will be able to hold him."

After supper I watched TV and waited for Mama to be ready. Mama washed the dishes first. Then she walked through the living room to the hallway, so I thought maybe she was going to get Sammy, but she came back and sat down with us to watch the rest of the Huckleberry Hound show. When the show was over she went to the TV and turned it off. I thought she would go then and get the baby out of his crib, but she didn't.

She turned on the lamp that stood on the end table between the armchair and the couch and she turned off the dining room light, before she sat down in the armchair. The light from the living room lamp made a big round warm spot on the couch and the carpet.

Mama said, "You kids all sit up there on the couch. Then I'll go get your baby brother." Danny sat on the end near the lamp, closest to Mama. I sat next to him, and Renee sat next to me.

"Scoot way back," Mama said. I scooted back, so my legs were straight because my knees didn't make it to the edge of the couch, so they couldn't bend. My feet stuck out over the edge a little. Renee's feet barely made it to the edge of the couch. Even Danny's legs stuck straight out. His legs were longer than mine, because he was six and I was still four.

Even though I scooted all the way back on the couch, and so did Danny and Renee, Mama came up to Danny, then to me, then to Renee to make sure. When she came to me she kind of lifted me up and scooted me back even more, so I sat up real straight against the back of the couch, the ridges of the couch material against my legs.

Then Mama went to get the baby.

Sammy was so small.

Mama sat back down in the big chair, underneath the lamp with its warm light. She let the blanket fall off Sammy a little bit. Then I could see the little nightgown he was wearing, and his little fists. He moved his fists just like boxing, but slow, with his eyes closed. He pressed his eyelids tight together, then it looked like he was trying to open his eyes, but he didn't quite get them open. He let his arms rest on the blanket for a bit, and stopped trying to open his eyes. I thought he was fast asleep again, but then he started the whole thing over.

It was so warm, the way it was dark but the light shone on my little brother, and on the light brown carpet in front of the couch, and the light wasn't too bright.

Mama said, "Now, I'm going to hand him over to each of you, and I want you to get ready. You bend your arm like this," she showed us how her arm was bent underneath Sammy's head, "and you hold up the baby's head with your arm."

Mama waited. When she saw that Danny and I and Renee were all looking at her, Mama said, "That's important, to hold up the baby's head."

Mama laid her other hand on the side of Sammy away from her body, and said, "With your other arm hold him securely in your lap."

I got all ready, my arm bent just right for his little head to go into, ready to use my other arm to put on his leg or his side to hold him up against me.

Mama bent over the couch. She held Sammy out to set him into Danny's lap. When she bent over underneath the lamp, the lamp light shone on her, on her hair, on her housedress, lit her up warm like the warm spot on the rug. Mama set Sammy down in Danny's lap, but she didn't let go until she checked Danny's arm holding the baby's head, his other arm, over the baby, made sure Sammy couldn't fall off Danny's lap. Then she sat back down in the armchair. I wanted it to be my turn, but the longer Danny's turn was, the longer my turn would be, so I didn't say anything. I waited, thinking all the time that I would get to hold Sammy that long too. I would get to hold him for a long time. I didn't talk, and nobody else talked either. I watched Sammy in Danny's lap, but that still wasn't when I knew.

When I knew was when Mama lifted Sammy off Danny's lap and put him on my lap instead. I had my arm all ready to hold his head, but then his head was really there in my arm. I was holding him. It was Mama arranging my arm, picking up my other hand, and putting it down on Sammy's side and feeling Sammy's plastic pants on my leg where the nightgown had scrunched up, smelling the baby powder smell and feeling his skin on my skin. I had to concentrate on what I had to do, with my arm bent for his head, with my other arm going around him. Now he was in my lap where I could see him clear, see his little fingers, his little feet and toes, and he was everything. He was so little, but he was so big, and somehow I could hold him.

That was when I knew that Sammy was mine to take care of.

#

Sammy was three now that we were staying with the Willises. Sammy still wet the bed at night.

The things that happened to Sammy at the Willises because he was three years old and he still wet the bed at night were: the strap, the creek, the green food coloring, and the last, worst thing.

Mrs. Willis always said, "Every day I pray to God your parents will get back together."

Like that one winter day when it was so cold outside that only snow would get you out in it, and there wasn't any snow. All of us kids were in the living room, not Shirley Willis, who was 13, and acted like a grown up, but Buddy Willis (he'd volunteered to go by

Buddy and let my brother be Danny) and all the rest of us.

Mrs. Willis entered the room and tossed a cushion from the couch onto the wood floor. She breathed loudly as she lowered herself onto the cushion, and arranged the wide bottom of her big housedress around her. Mama's house dresses were brighter colored, and not so big. Sometimes Mama wore slacks, but Mrs. Willis never did.

Mrs. Willis's eye settled on Sammy on the floor next to her wiggling the loose button eye of his teddy bear. If I looked at someone as long as Mrs. Willis did, Mama would be telling me to stop staring.

Mrs. Willis glanced just for a moment at Buddy on the couch, then longer at Danny. Both of them leaned over the coffee table working on homework. She looked at Renee and me, playing jacks on the wood floor. I was teaching Renee, "Cherries in a basket," a new game I'd learned at school. Mrs. Willis's eyes stayed the longest on Renee. Renee laughed when the jack she tossed went over her hand instead of in it and the ball bounced away. Renee's dimples showed when she laughed, her curly hair bounced up and down with her.

Mrs. Willis breathed in and out even more loudly until Buddy Willis, my brother Danny, and Renee all looked at her. Mrs. Willis said, "Such nice children. Not a day goes by that I don't pray to God for your parents to get back together."

Mrs. Willis wrapped her arm around Sammy and pulled him up next to her. Sammy leaned his head against her arm, then climbed up in her lap.

"Sammy was so cute today," Mrs. Willis said, which was the second thing that Mrs. Willis always said. "We were watching TV while I ironed, and a commercial came on with a car driving by and he just kept saying, 'Mama's car. Mama's car.' And he'd look up at me and say, 'See, Mama's car.' He said it the whole time the commercial was on."

"He says the cutest things," Mrs. Willis said, "I should write them all down for your mother." She put her hand on Sammy's head and pressed it up against her.

#

The Willis farm didn't have enough beds for us all. Renee, Sammy and I slept on the floor of the living room in our sleeping bags. I slept in my clothes. One morning I woke in the middle of a dream of going to the bathroom. I woke up cold, my jeans wet.

There was only a small damp spot on my sleeping bag, so I rolled it up to hide the wet spot. I tied the cord around it so it wouldn't unroll. I got my shoes and socks and jean jacket on as quickly as I could and headed for the outhouse because I still had to go and I didn't want to be caught with wet pants. Mr. Willis spanked me with a belt once when I had wet pants.

After the outhouse, I walked around the chicken coop a couple of times, then farther down the path to the pig pen, and around the pig pen. The dirt made a crunching sound of wet dirt that froze in the night. My pants felt damp still so I couldn't go back in, I headed toward the house to get out of the wind and stood with my back to a wall.

The screen door bounced on the wood frame when Larry came out the kitchen door. The tallest of the Willeses' three grown sons, Larry had a long, lanky cowboy sort of look, good looking and friendly.

I pressed back against the house to make sure the back of my jeans didn't show.

Larry said, in his friendly voice, "Hey Annie, if those pants are wet, they'd probably dry a lot faster inside by the wood stove."

Larry's grin filled his whole face, but I didn't tell him he was right about my pants. Larry seemed nice, but I didn't know if he really was. His brother Ben was nice. Ben wanted to be a priest, and he talked seriously to me. But Larry just joked. I didn't go back inside until my pants were dry.

When I did go in Mrs. Willis was laying Sammy's sleeping bag over the backs of two chairs next to the wood stove. She laid his wet pajamas over the back of another chair.

"What a mess," Mrs. Willis said. "What a stinking mess."

#

And then, besides "Every day I pray to God your parents will get back together," and "Sammy was so cute today," Mrs. Willis said "Wetting the bed is a filthy habit," and "Your poor mother shouldn't have to be changing sheets and doing laundry every morning after she gets out of the hospital."

But not until summer did she start saying how three, almost four, was old enough to stop wetting the bed. Mrs. Willis said she'd have to have Mr. Willis use the strap on Sammy when he wet the bed so she could break him of the dirty habit.

I woke early one morning, but hadn't left my warm sleeping bag. Mrs. Willis came into the living room and knelt beside Sammy, still asleep. Mr. Willis waited by the bedroom door. Mrs. Willis reached inside Sammy's sleeping bag. When she took her hand out, she shook her head back and forth a couple of times as if exasperated, "He's wet again."

Mr. Willis wasn't as big as Daddy, not even as big as Mrs. Willis. He was more the size of Uncle Joe with a wiry kind of body like Uncle Joe had, but he walked right over to Sammy's sleeping bag, reached in, took hold of Sammy under Sammy's arm and yanked him up off the ground with one hand, while he used the other hand to pull the sleeping bag off Sammy. He still held Sammy up in the air while he pulled Sammy's pajama bottoms down and off and tossed them on the floor.

Sammy's eyes opened, but he looked confused like he didn't know what was going on or where he was. Then he saw me and reached out his hand.

I scrambled out of my sleeping bag. I wanted to grab Sammy away from Mr. Willis, but I couldn't. If it was another kid hurting my brother it would have been my job to protect him, and I would have protected him, but Mr. Willis was a grownup.

Mr. Willis still held Sammy under Sammy's arm, one handed, and carried him that way over to the other side of the living room by the fireplace. He set Sammy down on the floor.

There wasn't a fire in the fireplace. There never had been while we were there, but there were knickknacks on the mantle, and on a hook on the side of it hung a strap which was really three leather straps twisted together at the top to form a handle. Mr. Willis turned Sammy so he had a grip on Sammy's shoulder with one hand, and with his other hand he reached for the strap. He lifted it off its hook and without stopping pulled his arm way back, then swung the strap hard against Sammy's butt. Sammy squealed and jumped up off the floor. Maybe he wasn't all the way awake until then. Sammy pulled away from Mr. Willis, but Mr. Willis didn't let go of Sammy's shoulder and he swung that strap back again and hit Sammy's butt again while Sammy cried and tried to get away. Where the strap hit, where each of the straps hit, a bright red raised line showed on Sammy's skin.

Renee crawled out of her sleeping bag to stand by me. She didn't ask what was going on. Mr. Willis hit Sammy with that strap again and Sammy squealed and twisted and stretched as far as he could away from Mr. Willis and reached out his arm again, reaching and pulling away from Mr. Willis toward me. The muscles in my legs tightened, but I couldn't move. My arm reached out to Sammy, but only made it to Renee's hand beside me. I held it tight, too tight so I made myself loosen my fingers. Then that strap hit Sammy again and Renee's hand clenched mine too, way too tight.

Mrs. Willis moved beside us and her voice came out like nothing special was going on, just the way she always talked. "He looks so cute and sweet," she said, like she always did. "It breaks my heart to have to spank him like this."

Mrs. Willis laid her hand on Renee's shoulder. Renee's fingers got tight on mine again and I could feel her arm get stiff. She moved closer to me. That wasn't far to move but Mrs. Willis took her hand off Renee's shoulder.

Renee didn't look at Mrs. Willis and I didn't look, but Mrs. Willis went right on talking, talked faster even. "Wetting the bed is a filthy habit," she said. "We have to break him of it before your mother gets out of the hospital and has to clean up after him every morning."

But Mama wouldn't want this.

We wouldn't look at Mrs. Willis. But our mouths didn't open. Our voices didn't make the words to say that Mama wouldn't want this.

Sammy's hand didn't reach out now. He just pulled away while Mr. Willis pulled him back to hit him again with the strap.

Mrs. Willis talked like she didn't see what Renee and I saw. "Yes, you just have to spank them, no matter how cute they are. Why when I used to go see the convicts in the penitentiary, man after man would tell me, 'I wouldn't be here now if only my mother had spanked me more.' "

Then I knew she was pressing her lips together like she did, but I didn't look.

"You won't catch me making that mistake," Mrs. Willis said.

Mr. Willis hit Sammy with that strap again and again and

Sammy squealed each time, tried to get away from Mr. Willis and the strap each time. Until Mr. Willis finally let his arm with the strap drop to his side and let go of Sammy's shoulder, then hung the strap back up on the hook on the side of the fireplace. Sammy moved toward me and Renee. My legs walked towards Sammy and my arm reached out to him, Renee right beside me. But Mrs. Willis hurried past. She reached Sammy, wrapped both her arms around him and hugged him up against her so I couldn't even see Sammy anymore.

"My poor boy," Mrs. Willis said.

Our legs, Renee's and mine, stopped walking. My arms dropped to my side with nothing to do.

Mr. Willis walked away from the fireplace. When he noticed Renee and me standing there he stopped walking. He put his hands in his overall pockets. Mr. Willis never talked on and on like Mrs. Willis. He hardly talked at all.

"It doesn't hurt as much as it looks like," Mr. Willis said.

6 The Creek

I woke early. I could barely make out even shapes at first, but soon things began to come clear. Usually if I woke this early I went back to sleep. Sometimes I'd try to stay awake to hear the roosters crow for the first time in the early morning. When the roosters wake up they are supposed to say, "Cock a doodle doo." But really they say, "Er er er er."

When I first heard the roosters say, "Er er er er," at my Grandma and Grandpa's farm, I wondered why they didn't say, "Cock a doodle doo," if there was something wrong with those chickens.

Then when I heard the roosters at the Willis farm say, "Er er er er," I decided that I just didn't get up early enough to hear the "cock a doodle do." I decided that the roosters only said that the first time they crowed in the morning, that special time when they first saw the sun rising up golden.

So I'd try to stay awake long enough to hear that first crow.

But no matter how early I listened, the roosters just said, "Er er er er."

Now I had a different reason to wake early.

If Mrs. Willis didn't have to bother with the sleeping bag and Sammy's wet clothes, she didn't always tell Mr. Willis to give Sammy a licking with the strap. In the early morning sometimes, when you are awake, but not quite, still tired, you tell yourself it's not morning yet. You don't have to get up, and you sink back down into sleep. Now I'd tell myself in my half-sleep, Get up. Get him up. If Sammy wasn't wet, I could get back in.

If he was wet, get him out of his sleeping bag. Hang it up on the line outside before Mrs. Willis woke and came out in the living room.

"Wake up Sammy," I said.

Sammy was a bump snuggled in the middle of his sleeping bag, with the top of the bag covering his head. He didn't wake up.

I knelt down beside him next to the leg of the dining room table where he'd scooted during the night. I reached inside the bag for his shoulder and shook it a little. Then Sammy woke up and his eyes opened up wide, real wide. He sat up fast, like he couldn't get away from the strap but he could get himself ready. The lids of his eyes relaxed when he saw me. He laid back down and closed his eyes, almost like he'd never been awake. But he opened them again, "What?"

The bag smelled, but it could have been the old wet smell.

"Are you wet?" I whispered, and Sammy nodded.

"I'm sorry," Sammy said. His eyes looked so blue, and his face so white with his hair curled up away from his forehead.

So I said, "It's alright."

But it wasn't and we had to hurry. "Let's get you changed before Mrs. Willis gets up."

Sammy scooted out of his sleeping bag while I got the clean clothes out of the dresser. His wet pajamas clung to his bottom and his legs. I unsnapped the top from the bottoms, pulled it over Sammy's head. The top was wet too on the edges with the snaps, and I didn't like to touch it but I had to.

I pulled down the bottoms, rolled them down where they were wet and pulled off the stocking feet, the pajamas going inside out. Sammy stuck his legs into the clean underpants. I pulled them up, then put one of his little t-shirts on him, forcing the neck hole to stretch down over his head. Then he stuck one of his hands up through the sleeve, then his other hand through the other sleeve and it was hard because his shirt was too tight. The pants were easy to get on. Then his shoes and his socks, and maybe he was safe because

Mrs. Willis wouldn't want to undress and dress him again.

Maybe he still wasn't safe.

The handle of the living room door that led to the porch and the yard was hard to turn, and the screen door lock was up high and the hook stuck in the round hole when I tried to push it up and out.

That's when I heard the door between the kitchen and the outside open, and I jabbed at the hook, one last try, hard so I hurt my hand. It still didn't come free. But it wasn't Mrs. Willis. Larry and Kevin walked in from the kitchen, both of them in the dirty jeans and boots they wore to walk in the mucky barnyard on their way to the barn to milk the cows. Both of them wore flannel shirts, but they looked different in them. Kevin looked covered up, Larry's shirt lay on him, loose, the sleeves not reaching to the end of his long arms.

Cows have to be milked really early in the morning. I don't know why.

When it is still dark out. Before the roosters wake up and are supposed to say, "Cock a doodle doo," but really say, "Er er er er."

Larry took a long step over to me by the door. His jeans, stiff at the knee with dried mud, made a noise when he walked and the dry mud cracked. He lifted the screen door hook out of its hole. "There you go," he said, all friendly, like Larry was always friendly.

Larry looked at the sleeping bag I had dragged over by the door and the wet pajamas I'd laid on top of them. He still smiled, with that fresh, wide awake look, and Larry's voice still sounded like he just heard a joke or knew a joke, but Larry said to Kevin, "Looks like that boy wet his bed again."

He said, "Guess if he wets it again, we're just gonna have to try and cure him by throwing him into the creek."

I couldn't tell if he meant it. His face never changed.

Kevin, dark, brought together his dark eyebrows that were bushy and almost met in the middle, and said, "I reckon so." Kevin didn't have a joking voice and his voice sounded like it always did, a little slow like the words had trouble coming out. Not many words did come out of Kevin. Mostly he only talked when Larry talked to him.

Larry still smiled, like he was joking, but maybe he wasn't joking.

He could mean in the shallow part of the creek.

Sammy couldn't swim.

Maybe Larry only meant to throw him in then fish him right back out.

But maybe he meant to throw Sammy into the deep water and leave him to make it back to shore or not.

Even if he was kidding, I knew for sure now that Larry wasn't nice.

Kevin walked to the dining room table and picked up a couple of biscuits from a plate left over from dinner. He tossed them to Larry. Larry caught them, one in each hand. Kevin picked up two more, took a bite of one and headed back to the kitchen. Larry followed. When he reached the doorway he turned back around, "See you all later," and grinned like everything was fine and there was nothing to worry about.

Maybe there wasn't.

Except Mrs. Willis would wake up any time now. As I heard the door from the kitchen to the outside close again, I pulled the sleeping bag with the pajamas on top out onto the big wide porch. I carried the sleeping bag bunched up in my arms out to the clothes line first, trying to keep it up off the dirt, but I couldn't lift it all up over the line and keep it out of the dirt at the same time. One end dragged while I tossed the other up over the line, then pulled it down on the other side. So I brushed and hit at it with my hand like beating on rugs to get the dust off.

The pajama tops and bottoms I hung up with clothespins.

Back inside Sammy still stood where I left him with his too tight red shirt and his blue corduroy pants. He said, "Are they going to throw me in the creek?"

Sammy breathed in, but I didn't hear him breath out again. He looked up at me like I knew the answer, like I could tell what grown ups might do. He blinked his eyes like you do if someone moves their hand fast to hit you, if you're surprised.

"I don't know," I said, "but try really hard not to wet the bed."

"I'll try really hard," Sammy said, but it wasn't like there was anything he could do to stop himself from wetting the bed while he slept.

#

When I found Sammy wet again the next morning, I got him out of bed and dressed before Larry and Kevin came in from milking. I took Sammy over to the couch next to the picture window and pulled it out a little way from the wall. "Hide back here, so Larry and Kevin can't find you."

Sammy got into place and leaned against the wall. The couch back was slanted so it didn't have to be out too far to leave Sammy room to sit. Once I lined it up with the wall it looked almost like when Sammy wasn't hiding behind it.

"Be quiet unless I talk to you," I whispered into the gap behind the couch.

"Ok."

I could barely see him sitting back in the dark. I arranged the blanket that hung over the back of the couch so a piece of it hung down the side and covered part of the gap. Then I had to leave him to get his clothes and the sleeping bag up on the line before Larry and Kevin came in. The wet things would make them think about

Sammy wetting the bed.

"I'll be back in just a minute. Try not to move or make any noise."

"Ok," Sammy said, and I left.

When I came back inside there was still no one else in the living room but Renee still asleep in her sleeping bag. She lay on her stomach so all I could see were the curls on the back of her head and one arm sticking out.

I scooted Sammy's bag of toy soldiers through the gap under the blanket, but not his cars because I was afraid he'd forget and make car noises.

"Here's your toy soldiers," I said. "Remember to be quiet."

Sammy said, "Ok," then he was quieter than I ever thought he could be. Either he was so scared, or he just knew how important it was. He didn't look so scared. Maybe he just trusted me to keep him from being hurt. That made me hold my breath until I remembered to let it go.

I went into the kitchen to make him a peanut butter sandwich, then handed that to him through the gap too.

Finally I went to the bookshelf for Book Eight of the *Book of Knowledge*. That was my reason for sitting on the couch, and I got right in the center, so maybe anyone who came in would sit somewhere else entirely and not accidentally discover Sammy.

Like I always did I opened the book to the *Book of Stories*. Like I always did when I passed up the *Book of Science*, with its planets and shiny rocks and cross sections of earth, I thought it looked so interesting that I would read it next just as soon as I finished all the volumes of the *Book of Stories*.

Still, no one else came in the living room, so I got up on my knees and turned around to look over the back of the couch. There was only a little space at the top between the wall and the couch but

I could kind of see Sammy just sitting there quiet with one of his soldiers in his hand.

"Are you ok?" I asked.

Sammy tilted his head back to look up at me, "Yes," he said. And he sounded ok, not scared or anything.

"You might have to hide there all day," I said.

"Ok," Sammy said.

Then I was afraid someone would come in and catch me so I sat back down.

#

Renee woke after awhile. She got dressed and rolled up her sleeping bag. Then she came over and sat down on the couch beside me while she brushed her hair.

"Where's Sammy?" Renee asked.

I put my finger up next to my mouth and nodded my head at Mrs. Willis's bedroom door on the opposite wall.

Renee put down the brush and scooted back on the couch. She leaned her head against the back of the couch then turned it a little towards me.

"What," she whispered.

"He's hiding behind the couch," I said.

Renee got up on her knees and looked down through the crack, then she sat back down. She said, "I think he's asleep."

"Good," I said. "Then he'll be quiet."

"Why is he hiding?"

"Larry said he was going to throw Sammy in the creek if he wet the bed again," I said.

"Maybe he was joking," Renee said, and she bounced her foot on the couch.

"Yeah," I said, "but I don't know. Sammy can't swim."

"I know," Renee said. She started brushing her hair again.

Her hair had a lot of tangles.

Renee said, "I'll go outside and play over by the woods. Then if someone asks where Sammy is you can tell them you think he's somewhere outside with me."

"That's a good idea," I said. "Mrs. Willis will probably ask when she gets up."

Renee scooted off the couch, and set her hairbrush back on the dresser that we shared for our clothes. She picked up her doll and a baby blanket from the top of the dresser.

I said, "Make a sandwich. You might get hungry."

So she did, then she left, going out the kitchen door because she had trouble with the living room door too.

#

Mrs. Willis got up late and I told her I already ate so I didn't have to eat the oatmeal. Mrs. Willis asked me where Sammy and Renee were, so I said Renee took her doll outside to play somewhere and Sammy went with her.

"But not you," Mrs. Willis laughed. "You'd probably read day and night if we let you." I don't know why she thought that was funny.

After her breakfast Mrs. Willis left to pick beans from the garden. When she returned she went downstairs to the basement to do laundry. Other people came in and out, but no one stayed long. Buddy and my brother came downstairs together from their bedroom upstairs but they went outside right after they ate. Shirley came down and made up a lunch to take to her father in the field. Mr. Willis must have gone out before I woke up.

Nobody came into the living room past the doorway. Nobody came anywhere near the couch.

At lunchtime I made myself two peanut butter sandwiches. Only Shirley and Mrs. Willis sat in the kitchen.

Shirley said, "You must be hungry today." Shirley was always nice. She always wore dresses and her long hair was always combed. Shirley looked smoother and cleaner than anyone else.

Mrs. Willis said, "Must be all that reading Annie's doing. Really works up an appetite." She laughed. "That right?

"I guess so," I said. "I am really hungry today."

"Maybe you didn't eat enough at breakfast," Mrs. Willis said. "We'll have to make sure you get more oatmeal in your bowl tomorrow." She knew I hated oatmeal.

"No, I had plenty," I said, and Mrs. Willis laughed again. Her big housedress shook when she laughed. Even Shirley smiled. When Shirley smiled she kind of looked like our old babysitter in Yakima, the nice one with the freckles and turned up nose.

I took my sandwiches over to the couch and I laid one of them between my knees so it was hidden under the book when I lifted the big heavy *Book of Knowledge* up into my lap. If I kept very still I could still hear their voices.

Shirley said, "Mama, I want to show you my painting."

Once a week Mrs. Willis drove Shirley to her painting teacher's house. Sometimes when Shirley painted she'd let me use the leftover oil paints after she finished.

"My teacher says I'm getting almost good enough to be a professional. She thinks I could start selling my paintings pretty soon."

When Mrs. Willis talked to Shirley, you could think Mrs. Willis was a nice person. "That's so nice, dear. I'm so proud of you."

When I heard their steps on the stairs I went to the side of the couch and moved the blanket out of the way. Sammy had his toy soldiers all lined up on the floor beside him.

"Sammy," I said, "Here's a sandwich."

Sammy reached for the sandwich. He took a bite.

"You're real good at being quiet," I said.

"I know," Sammy said, and he leaned back against the wall. Then I could hardly see him at all except for his hair and his face.

I moved the blanket back in place and got back up on the couch, back to "Big Klaus and Little Klaus." What would I do when Sammy had to go to the bathroom?

I heard Larry and Kevin come in for lunch, moving around in the kitchen, and I hoped they'd stay in there. But Larry walked into the living room and up to the couch. Kevin followed after him.

Larry took a bite of his sandwich and said, "Say, where is everyone, anyway?" He looked around the room but there was no reason that he should look behind the couch. I didn't hold my breath. I made myself keep breathing in and out.

"Mrs. Willis went upstairs with Shirley," I said.

"Yeah, well, how about that little guy? Where have he and Renee gone off to?"

Larry put his hand on the back of the couch, but there was no reason for him to look behind the couch. Larry leaned some of his weight on his arm but I didn't look to see if his hand made the blanket move on the back of the couch.

My eyes stayed right on my book, and I didn't think Larry heard my breath stop, then start up again. I said, "They went outside somewhere. I'm not sure where exactly."

Kevin said, "They'll probably show up when they get hungry."

I said, "I think they took sandwiches."

"Making a day of it, huh," Larry said, and walked over and sat down in the window seat on the other wall. Kevin sat down beside him. Kevin put his feet up on the cold wood stove.

Larry said, "Good book?"

I said that it was.

Larry said, "Sure is a nice day today. It's a shame you're wasting all that sunshine sitting in here on the couch all day."

"I want to read my stories," I said, but I couldn't remember the last sentence I read so I tried to find it to read it over again.

"Nothing stopping you from bringing the book outside," Larry said.

I said, "It's cooler in here."

Larry leaned back against the window, crossed his arms and spread his feet out on the floor. He said, "Well, I can see there's no convincing you. Must be something mighty special about that couch."

I had to make myself breath out before I could talk. "It's comfortable."

Larry laughed and said, "Well, Kevin, you and I don't have the luxury of sitting on a comfortable couch all day. We'd better get back out there and give Dad a hand."

Kevin said, "I'm ready." He walked back into the kitchen with Larry behind him. I heard them opening cupboard doors and turning the water faucet on and off.

I thought they'd leave then, but Larry came back into the living room, and Kevin came behind him, both of them carrying a bottle of water, Kevin with another sandwich. Larry walked up to the couch again, but he stopped before he reached it.

Larry said, "Say, Kevin, you know, We've got a lot to do today and I kind of feel sorry for the little guy. What do you say we don't throw him in the creek after all."

Kevin finished chewing, said, "All right by me."

Larry smiled at me, but I didn't smile at him. Larry smiled at Kevin, and Kevin smiled back at Larry.

So probably they knew that Sammy was behind the couch.

Maybe they'd been kidding all along.

I still didn't tell Sammy he could come out from behind the couch. I didn't think it was a trick, but it might be.

Mainly I didn't want to hear them laugh when Sammy came out.

I didn't want Sammy to hear them laugh, didn't want him to hear the sound of Larry's voice that always sounded like he knew a joke. But I didn't what the joke was, and Sammy didn't know.

So I waited until they were gone, until past when they were gone, until they were maybe halfway out to the field where Mr. Willis had been working all morning, out in the sun and the wheat or the corn.

Then I told Sammy he could come out now, that nobody was going to throw him into the creek.

At least not this time.

7 The Visit

Rice with sugar on it slid down my throat fast, so I didn't have to taste it. It didn't glob up like the oatmeal that I had to force down bit by bit.

Mrs. Willis said something. "Your daddy's coming to visit," I thought she said, but when I looked up she just stared at her plate, like she hadn't said anything special. She sat on the couch in the living room. The food was set out on the table, but people spread out in the living and dining room. Sammy ate at the table, and I sat beside him, and so did Renee. My brother and Buddy usually got their food quick and snuck off someplace secret and alone, but they hadn't left yet and my brother turned towards Mrs. Willis, his head still and listening.

But Mrs. Willis loaded up on another forkful of black-eyed peas, kept munching, until I thought I misheard her about Daddy coming, and moved my fork around in my rice, getting ready to shove down another bite. Luckily they didn't force me to eat the black-eyes peas like they did the oatmeal every morning because I'd have to chew those and taste that horrid taste longer while I tried to swallow.

But then Mrs. Willis said, "Two thousand miles, all the way from Yakima, Washington, to see you," and I knew I heard right. Then she looked at Danny, me, Renee and Sammy, like she was checking to make sure we appreciated how far Daddy was coming to see us.

I sat still, but inside shouted, *say it, say it, when? Coming when?*

Then she said, "He expects to be here sometime on Sunday." Today was Thursday – three more days.

So after dinner while Renee and I dried the dishes that

Shirley Willis washed, Daddy drove in his black car with the running board, on the way to Ava, Missouri to the Willis farm.

All day Saturday, while Mrs. Willis mopped the floors and Renee and I helped Shirley Willis scrub the woodwork with rags dipped in hot soapy water and Pine Sol, Daddy drove closer and closer.

Saturday night while I lay in my sleeping bag on the dining room floor next to Sammy and Renee, Daddy drove, or slept in his car, or maybe stopped at a motel, ready to start off again early in the morning to see us in Missouri.

Sunday morning, when I woke up, I didn't stay in the sleeping bag a few more minutes like I usually did. I sat right up.

Renee's sleeping bag didn't move so I reached over and found her shoulder through the thick bag. I jiggled her shoulder and a corner of the sleeping bag flopped up and down on her cheek. When the corner hit her cheek she squinched her eyes, then opened them.

"Renee," I said.

"What," Renee said.

"Daddy's coming today."

Renee pulled her legs up under her, then she sat up on her knees with the sleeping bag still all around her. She rubbed her eyes. Renee reached over and tapped Sammy's shoulder.

Sammy lay half out of his sleeping bag with his head on the bare wooden floor. His cheek had a ridge on it, a mark made by the zipper of the sleeping bag, and his mouth was half open.

"Sammy," Renee said, and pushed his shoulder.

Sammy's eyes opened all of a sudden, bright blue, but then they shut all the way again.

So I got out of my sleeping bag and rubbed his back, and kept saying, "Sammy, Sammy," until he finally opened his eyes again.

Sammy said, "Is Daddy here?"

"Not yet, but we're going to go outside to wait for him," I said.

By the time Sammy had on his striped T-shirt, Danny came downstairs with Buddy. Buddy jumped over the last three steps like he always did, landing hard on the floor. My brother sometimes jumped over three, sometimes made it over the last four steps. Four today. He stumbled just clear of Buddy at the bottom.

Danny said to me and Renee and Sammy, "Let's go wait for Dad."

We headed through the kitchen to get outside but Mrs. Willis stood by the stove stirring oatmeal, in one of her Sunday house dresses, the big one with a light gray pattern on white, the color of oatmeal.

Mrs. Willis said, "Have some breakfast before you go out."

Danny started to say something, his mouth opened, then he saw her face with her lips pressed together tight like she wasn't going to hear any arguments and Danny closed his mouth.

So there was nothing to do but stop and watch her dish up bowlfuls of oatmeal, those big, solid white China bowls like in a diner Daddy took us to once when he took us out on Sundays, after the divorce. That day with Daddy in the diner the heavy white bowls made my cheerios taste better, special being served up in a restaurant, but it never worked with the oatmeal.

Danny said, "We'll eat it outside, so we can look out for Dad at the same time."

"And lose all my bowls and spoons outside?" said Mrs. Willis.

"We won't," Danny said, his hand on the back door, waiting to turn the knob. "We'll bring them all back in. I'll make sure of it."

Mrs. Willis held the wooden spoon that she used to dish out the oatmeal up in the air next to her. Finally, she set it back down in the pan. "Ok," she said. "Make sure you do."

With all of us waiting together like that I wouldn't be able to slip off to the pigpen to dish my oatmeal out to the pigs, but it was worth the oatmeal to see Daddy.

#

Midafternoon, burning hot, we'd been waiting since morning, inside for lunch, then outside waiting again. We leaned up against the wall of the barn which had a good view of the dirt road that wound between the barn and the house, and also had a little bit of shade, a little bit of grass, not much. Mostly it was all dust around the house and the barn. Only over in the fields, not the planted fields, but fields between wooded patches, was there green, long grass, and small trees, patches of blackberries and gooseberries on the edges of the clearings.

Danny, Renee, Sammy and I, and even Buddy Willis sat next to the barn waiting for Daddy.

"There's his car!" Danny said.

I didn't see anything but a little dust flying way far off.

Danny stood up, pushing himself up with his hands in the dirt, then brushed his hands against his jeans. He pulled his white T-shirt out and used it to rub at his hands. He jerked his head to move the hair out of his face back into place parted to the right, and when that didn't work, used his right hand to wipe it out of his eyes.

"Sure is something," Buddy said. He'd stood up too and now placed his flat hand above his eyes to keep the sun out. "Something is kicking up dirt out there."

Just what are you doing here, Buddy Willis. This is my Daddy.

But Buddy went on acting just like he owned my Daddy,

owned the wait while he drove up the road.

"Yeah," Buddy said, "What kind of car did you say he drove, a black Studebaker?"

My brother nodded.

Buddy said, "Yeah, that looks like a Studebaker, rides low, kicking up dust."

Renee and Sammy stood up and looked down the road too. Renee pushed her curly hair back and put her hand up over her eyes the way Buddy did.

She said, "I can't see it. Where is it?"

So I took her finger and used it to point to the swirls of dust that Buddy said was Studebaker dust, and said, "There, do you see it now, where the dust is?"

"Kind of," Renee said, staring very hard with her blue eyes. So I showed her again.

"Oh, yeah," Renee said. Her fingers clenched the bottom of her white blouse. The blouse was too short so there was a space between it and the top of her red shorts.

"Me too," Sammy said.

Sammy was heavy but I could pick him up if he wrapped his legs around my middle and if I braced my leg so he rested on my hip. I had to lean him out a little to keep his head from bumping mine and it made my right arm tired holding onto him that way.

I pointed with my left hand. "See there," and this time it was more than a patch of dust, it was something black and maybe tires.

"Daddy's Studebaker!" Sammy shouted, and he jiggled up and down so it made my arm even tireder to hold him.

Danny ruffled Sammy's blond, reddish tinted hair. He took Sammy from me and lifted Sammy up onto his shoulders. "Now you can really see good," Danny said. Sammy laughed.

"Should be here in another couple minutes," Buddy said.

Obviously.

The black car with the running board drove slow past the barn and pulled up on the other side of the road in front of the house. All of us moved towards the car. Buddy ran. My brother didn't run, because of Sammy on his shoulders, but he walked fast. Renee and I kept up with him, all headed up to the driver side door, Daddy's door.

Mrs. Willis must have heard the car sounds because there she came out the kitchen door, through the yard and around the car to Daddy's door before anyone but Buddy could make it. Buddy reached the door just in time to stand beside Mrs. Willis.

I could see part of Daddy's face, his brown hair, an eyebrow with a blue eye underneath, but Mrs. Willis hid the rest of him.

"Well, hello there, Mr. Mills. Can I call you Clifford? Sure is good to meet you, Clifford."

She reached in the open front window for my Daddy's hand so he couldn't get out of the car, but sat there with his head turned towards her. He shook Mrs. Willis's hand.

"Pleased to meet you." Then Daddy turned his eyes away from her to us coming up to the car now, but Mrs. Willis didn't move to let him out.

"Well, you've had a long drive," Mrs. Willis said.

We stopped just behind her. Danny lifted Sammy down from his shoulders.

"I sure have," Daddy said. He took the keys out of the ignition and pulled up the lock on the door. He wore a short sleeve shirt and his arms were tanned brown and hairy. Daddy pushed the car door open enough to get out, so Mrs. Willis moved back. Daddy got out of the car then slammed the door shut.

All morning waiting for Daddy, half the afternoon, now Mrs. Willis stood between us and Daddy. We couldn't push past her to get to him. We had to wait longer, just look at him, until Mrs. Willis was done.

"You must be tired," Mrs. Willis said. "Let's get your things and I'll show you to your room."

Daddy looked around Mrs. Willis, at us, but Mrs. Willis still didn't move out of the way.

Daddy went to the back of the car and opened the trunk. Danny got next to him, and pulled Sammy along, before Mrs. Willis and Buddy made it to Daddy's other side. Renee and I moved close. Daddy reached into the trunk for his suitcase, tan colored with silver latches.

Mrs. Willis put her hand on it, "Here, my son can get that for you."

Daddy didn't let go. "Just a minute," he said.

Mrs. Willis moved her hand away.

Daddy pushed the button to loosen the latch of the suitcase, and opened the lid. He moved his hand through the folded up shirts and pants, feeling for something. He got it with one hand and set it down on the other, a soft brown leather pouch with a drawstring, his fingers wrapped around the bottom of the pouch like holding a softball. Daddy undid the knot of the drawstring one handed to pull the pouch open. He turned away from the trunk and looked at us kids.

Danny let go Sammy's hand, stood up very straight when Daddy's eyes landed on him.

Daddy reached into the pouch and pulled out a coin. He showed it to Danny, then he held it up and showed it to the rest of us.

"See, kids. Silver dollars."

Daddy reached for Danny's hand, took Danny's hand in his own bigger hands. He spread Danny's hand out, palm up, and put the silver dollar in it. Daddy reached back in the bag and brought out more silver dollars which he added to Danny's hand, until Danny cupped his two hands together to hold them, then pulled up the bottom of his T-shirt to make a pouch to hold all the silver dollars.

Daddy's face was brown and a little bit red on his nose and one side. His voice started out loud, then got softer.

"They're for you kids," Daddy said. "I've been saving them ever since you left. Every time a customer at the service station paid me with a silver dollar I put it away to bring to you."

Daddy blinked his eyes like you do when you are trying to stay awake.

He said, "There's thirty-two of them there."

Daddy put the drawstring pouch on top of the coins. Danny held the coins in the pouch of his T-shirt up against his body with one arm, so he could use his other hand to put the silver dollars back in the bag.

Daddy said, "You see, I thought about you every time I got a silver dollar."

Mrs. Willis leaned against the back fender right next to Daddy.

"Well, isn't that nice," she said. "Would you like me to take care of all that money for them?"

Mrs. Willis reached her hand out around Daddy, towards Danny and the silver dollars. Danny put in the last shiny silver dollar and tied up the drawstring.

Daddy backed up against the fender getting out of the way of Mrs. Willis's arm.

Mrs. Willis's finger just touched the bag. Danny moved it out of Mrs. Willis's reach.

"I'll take care of it," Danny said. He stuffed the bag into his jeans pocket, part way in, pushed at the part that hung out of his pocket to get it the rest of the way in.

Mrs. Willis moved back away from the fender so she could get closer to Danny, but Daddy stopped leaning on the fender then and stood up straight so he was still between Danny and Mrs. Willis.

"That's an awfully lot of money for a ten year old boy to take care of," Mrs. Willis said to Daddy. "Are you sure you wouldn't rather have me put it away for him?"

Daddy put his hands in his pockets, shoved them way down. He didn't look at Mrs. Willis, but down at the dirt. He lifted his head back up.

"That's okay," Daddy said. "Danny can take care of it."

Mrs. Willis pulled back her hand but her eyes stayed on Danny a little longer.

The bag of silver dollars was a big bulge in the pocket of Danny's jeans.

Daddy closed his eyes together again, then opened them back up. Little wrinkles around Daddy's eyes. Daddy didn't use to have little wrinkles around his eyes.

Daddy glanced over at Danny, then turned around and looked at Renee and me and Sammy like there was something else he meant to say or do.

"Hadn't we better be getting you to your room," Mrs. Willis said.

Daddy turned back around to the trunk of the car, shut the suitcase lid and pressed the latches shut. He started to pick up the suitcase, but Mrs. Willis said, "Here, my son can take that."

Danny reached over for the suitcase. "I can get it," he said.

Danny walked kind of funny on the way to the house with the big suitcase bumping against his leg, the big bulge in his pocket.

Inside the front door, Mrs. Willis motioned Daddy to the stairway. "I've fixed you a room upstairs. Let's get you all settled in."

Buddy followed my brother who strained to lift the big suitcase up a step. Renee, Sammy and I started up after Daddy and Mrs. Willis. But Mrs. Willis turned to face us, "The rest of you kids just wait downstairs. Your Daddy will be back down in a little while."

All we could do was watch their backs until the stairway was empty, stayed empty.

"I'm thirsty," Sammy said. Then I realized how hot and thirsty I was too. I let the cool water run from the faucet awhile before I filled three glasses. The water felt good after the morning and afternoon out in the sun.

From the dining room we could watch the stairway door. I took a sip of my water then balanced the cool glass on my leg. My hair felt damp. Sammy and Renee looked just as hot. I leaned back against the couch.

The sound of steps came down the stairway, but the footsteps didn't sound like Daddy, but slow and heavy like Mrs. Willis. There weren't any other footsteps.

Mrs. Willis closed the stairway door and stood with her hand on the doorknob. Her head bent down and her brown hair looked damp. She started towards the living room and just at the door she raised her head so she saw us. She stood up straighter.

"Clifford is just taking a bath and having a little rest before dinner."

He was supposed to come right back down. She said he would.

We stayed on the dining room chairs.

Mrs. Willis looked impatient. Her voice sounded angry. "He drove straight through all the way from Yakima," Mrs. Willis said. "Didn't even stop at a hotel at night, just got a few hours sleep by the side of the road. You surely can understand that he needs a couple of hours of sleep."

So we had to go outside and look for something to do like we usually did on the days when Daddy wasn't here.

But Daddy was here.

#

Food at the Willises' was, most of the time, oatmeal for breakfast, milk with the cream skimmed off because they sold the cream, peanut butter - Mrs. Willis mixed it with coffee to make it last longer - at lunchtime, white rice with sugar on it, black eyed peas or green beans for dinner. Greens sometimes. Greens were the worst, worse than the oatmeal, worse than the rice with sugar on it which slid down your throat quick.

Sometimes we'd have good food when Shirley would make something sweet and Renee and I helped her. Chocolate, or blackberry cobbler or gooseberry pie if we picked the berries. One time Shirley took us all out looking for roots for real root beer. Then she made it and it tasted good, but not like root beer.

Tonight there was fried chicken, green beans, potatoes and gravy.

Mrs. Willis had arranged enough chairs around the table for everyone. She put Daddy on one side next to Danny. I sat across from Daddy with Sammy and Renee. The Willises, Mr. and Mrs. Willis, the three older Willis boys, Larry, Kevin and Ben, Danny and Shirley Willis sat on both sides of us and at the ends.

"Um Um," Larry said, "This sure looks good."

"Just the thing after a hard day's work in the field," Kevin said. "You ever do any farm work, Clifford?" Kevin and Buddy were both dark, but Kevin had bushy eyebrows that met in the center.

Daddy dished up some chicken, taking just a little, not a lot like he did at home in Yakima. The little wrinkles around his eyes were gone. Maybe they were just from being tired.

"Grew up on a farm," Daddy said. "My folks still have a place near Salem, Missouri. Did some sharecropping in St. Charles when I worked in the Ford plant near there, but I couldn't make much of a go of it."

"What'ya say, you mean these city kids got some farming blood in them after all?" Larry laughed.

Daddy smiled so the little wrinkles around his eyes came back. He squeezed Danny's shoulder. "They sure do. They come from a long line of farmers. Danny and Annie were born while we lived on that farm in St. Charles."

I was born on a farm. Wish I'd known that when Shirley and Buddy went on and on about city kids and farm kids, talking about city kids like we were helpless. Wish I'd known I wasn't such a city kid after all.

"Well, Clifford," Larry said, "What say you come swimming in the creek with me and Ben and Kevin after dinner. What the heck, we could even take the two boys along if you think they could keep up with us."

Larry didn't say anything about me coming along. Two boys, meaning Danny and Buddy, not Sammy, for the second boy. Maybe Daddy would say that I could come too. Danny was older, but he wasn't much older, just one year and four months older. And I could swim. I waited for Daddy to say, "Sure, and Annie can come along too."

"Sure," Daddy said, "I'd like that."

#

After they'd gone and I'd helped Shirley with the dishes, I read stories in a chair where I could see the road to the creek through the living room window. It was nearly dark when they came, all bunched together and something odd about the way they walked.

When they were nearly at the edge of the porch I could see they were all gathered around Daddy, holding onto his arms, holding him up while he stepped along.

Buddy broke away from the group up the front porch steps. He flung the front door open wide. Out of breath so it was hard for him to talk. "He got stung by hornets."

I went to hold the screen door open but before I could, Buddy stepped back out on the porch and held it like that was the most important job in the world.

Mrs. Willis ran out from the kitchen, wiping her hands on a dishtowel, "Who got stung by hornets?"

"Mr. Mills did," Buddy, said from the porch. "He ran into a nest of them. They got all over him before he got away."

I'd never been stung by hornets but they were worse than bees and I'd been stung by bees, the sting like a flu shot when the needle has gone in easy, but then the medicine reaches the vein, and you'd forgotten how much it can hurt. Mama said when I was a baby I'd been stung by a swarm of bees so she always had me brush the bees away because she said once you were stung by a lot of bees you never got stung again.

The three older Willis boys, Danny and Daddy all came in a clump, up the steps onto the porch. Daddy's eyes were puffy and mostly closed.

Ben, the kind one who wanted to be a priest, said, "We're just about there, Clifford."

Danny said, "Yeah, Dad, we're just about there."

Larry and Kevin had their arms around Daddy's back, holding him up, while Ben and Danny walked on the outside with Daddy's arms resting on their shoulders. Daddy held his head down. He moved his legs like it hurt him, and like he didn't think his legs would hold him up.

Inside Larry said, "Better let Kevin and me take him up. There's not room enough on the stairs for all five of us."

Ben touched Danny on the shoulder and Danny dropped back. But he followed a step behind Kevin and Larry. He reached his hand like he wanted to pat Daddy's back, but didn't because it might hurt.

Ben went up last.

At the bottom of the stairs Mrs. Willis called up, "I'll make some baking soda paste."

For a long time the sound of their steps was on the stairs, feet stepping then dragging up each stair, more steps in the hallway upstairs, then a door opening. From the dining room I heard a spoon scrape the sides of a China bowl. Ben came back down and Mrs. Willis handed him a bowl of pasty white baking soda. He went back up.

After awhile Larry, Kevin, Ben and Danny all came down.

"How is he?" Mrs. Willis asked. She had an apron on over her gray dress.

"Well, we got him to bed," Larry said, "but he's feeling pretty miserable."

Ben said, "The stings are on his head and face and neck mostly. Some on his arms, and on his back where they got into his shirt." Ben touched my shoulder, "He'll be a lot better in a few days."

#

Daddy didn't get up until the next afternoon. Then he sat on a chair on the end wall of the living room. He had a blanket wrapped around him, one of the scratchy kind. Daddy's eyes barely opened. His face was a mix of red swollenness and white that might have been the baking soda paste.

He didn't look like Daddy. He seemed like a strange person,

so I told myself this was Daddy, Daddy stung by hornets. I walked closer, but not very fast.

"Daddy," I said. "Are you feeling any better?" I stopped at the wood stove.

Daddy tilted his head up so the slits where his eyes barely opened on the bottom were looking at me and it looked like he was trying to open them up further but he couldn't. Then Daddy tried to open his mouth, moving his lips apart, but they were so swollen that even after he moved them they were still together. He kept trying. I wished it weren't so hard for him, but also I just wanted to hear Daddy's voice. Finally, he said, "Yes." I think it was "yes," but his voice didn't sound like Daddy's voice. Then Daddy stopped trying.

In front of Daddy on the coffee table sat a cup of coffee and a plate of eggs and toast. Daddy hadn't eaten much of the food, but he picked up the coffee cup and held it in his hands. He moved it up against his lips and tilted it. I couldn't tell if he got anything to swallow or not.

I decided that talking wasn't such a good idea so I went over to the bookcase and got book eleven of the *Book of Knowledge*. The couch by the window was close enough to see Daddy and hear Daddy, but not so close that anybody had to talk.

Mrs. Willis appeared, not in her special Sunday gray house dress any longer, just an everyday one, and her hair wasn't combed as nice as it was the day before. She picked up the plate of eggs and toast.

She said, "Now Clifford, you really should try and eat something. I cooked up the eggs and toast special for you."

Daddy didn't try to work his mouth open. He pulled the edges of his blanket to get it tighter around him. He moved his coffee cup to his lips and sipped it.

Mrs. Willis stood there for a minute. Her face was always

puffy like Daddy's was now, only not quite as much, but now, right around her mouth it puffed up a little more. Her face didn't look like it hurt though.

"Well," she said, swirling the skirt of her house dress as she turned away.

#

The next day passed and the next and the next just the same with Daddy in a chair with the blanket wrapped around him, barely moving in all that time. Mrs. Willis kept telling Daddy he should be eating more. Sammy and Renee came right over to the edge of the living room, looking at Daddy, and sometimes at me on the couch, but they never went over to Daddy. I think he was too strange for them.

Danny brought fresh coffee, and held it up to Daddy's lips so Daddy could sip it easier. Daddy took three or four sips before he stopped. Then Danny set the coffee cup down on the table by Daddy.

The shape of Danny's eyes when he was serious was just the same shape as Daddy's eyes when they weren't all swollen up with hornet stings, a little narrow like almond shapes.

Danny said, "Anytime you want some more coffee, Daddy, I can help you drink it."

#

The evening before Daddy had to leave I came in from outside, through the living room door. Daddy still sat in his spot in the big chair, but his face didn't look quite so bad. It wasn't so puffy. His eyes opened more. The eyes that looked out looked like Daddy's eyes.

I couldn't tell if he saw me. Maybe he was still too sick to talk.

I stopped before I reached the couch.

If I didn't look beneath his eyes then his face was Daddy's

face, just a little swollen so there was no sign of those little wrinkles around his eyes that came when he was tired or laughing.

But he wasn't laughing. He probably wasn't tired.

I walked over to the coffee table.

Daddy lifted his head. His head seemed heavy so it was a struggle for him to lift his head. He looked up at me. His lips moved apart a little.

"Hi, Annie," Daddy said. It was like his swollen lips and tongue had to force the words out. "How are you doing?"

"I'm fine," I said. "Do the hornet stings still hurt?" I stepped from the coffee table to right in front of Daddy.

"Not so bad." Daddy looked like he tried to smile but his face didn't move much. Daddy's short black hair, the shape of his eyes, just the same as in Yakima. The way he said, "Annie," slower but still the same, saying who I was.

Then it was like when we wrote letters to Mama, and the first lines were easy, "Dear Mama, How are you? I am fine." Then I'd stare at the paper wondering what else to say. I knew there were things, lots of things that I would have said to her during the day if she were there, but staring at the paper I couldn't remember them.

What else could I say here to Daddy?

Maybe, if he said something else, even my name one more time then I'd remember all the things to say.

But he didn't. His head dropped back down.

Nothing came out of me either. I waited for something. Then I reached over to Daddy's knee where I didn't think he'd been stung, and stroked the scratchy blanket with my finger.

#

Back in Yakima before the divorce, at night before we went to sleep was the time that Daddy came in our bedroom, after Mama, to give us a kiss and hug good night. After Daddy came was when it was really time to go to sleep. Even though we didn't have a bedroom, even though we didn't have a bed, if not for the hornets Daddy might have knelt down beside our sleeping bags and said good night.

I scooted down in my sleeping bag, even my head, to shut out the living room light. This was the last night that Daddy was here with us. Tomorrow Daddy would be in the black car with the running board driving farther and farther away from us.

#

Next morning I woke to voices, Daddy's voice came from the table near where I slept. I grabbed for my shoes and socks, then my jean jacket off the hook by the door. It was chilly. Then I rolled up my sleeping bag and set it against the wall out of the way.

Larry, Ben and Kevin sat on the bench on one side of the table. Mr. Willis, Daddy and Danny sat on the other. Larry stopped in the middle of a bite of pancake, "Thought you'd never wake up, sleepy head."

Daddy turned around to see me, "Surprised anyone can sleep through all the racket we're making." His eyes got wrinkles around them when he smiled, his face barely swollen at all now. He said, "Thought I'd wait awhile before I woke you to say goodbye, let you get your rest. It's pretty early in the morning."

"Chickens are barely up," Kevin said. "Cows are waiting to be milked though." He stepped out from the bench.

"You want to get up here and have some pancakes with me?" Daddy asked.

I got up in Kevin's place, right across from Daddy. Kevin took his plate away to the kitchen and brought me back some silverware and a clean plate with a pancake on it.

"Here you go, fresh off the griddle," Kevin said, then he went back out to the kitchen and the door opened and shut as he left for the barn.

Daddy said, "Can I help you with that?"

I didn't need help but I said yes, so Daddy buttered the pancake and poured syrup over the top.

Mrs. Willis brought a whole plate of pancakes, so Daddy put another one on my plate, "Here, we'll get you one for later."

Daddy ate two more pancakes himself, so he'd gotten his appetite back.

Mr. Willis slid his thumb along the edge of the bib of his overalls and tapped the bottom of his empty mug on the red checked plastic tablecloth. He said to Larry and Ben, "You boys through? We'd best be milking those cows too and getting out to the field."

He slid off the edge of the bench, turned to Daddy and said, "It's been good to meet you, Clifford. Sorry you had that run in with those hornets." He held out his hand and Daddy shook it. Larry and Ben followed Mr. Willis out the door.

At the door Larry said, all cheery like, "You take care of yourself now, Clifford." But Ben just said, "Bye, Clifford," before he pulled the door closed.

Daddy rested his arms on the table. In a quiet voice like he was still being careful not to wake anyone, he said, "Maybe we could get the other kids up now."

Danny shook Sammy awake. I woke Renee and helped her roll up her sleeping bag. Daddy went to the kitchen to check on pancakes for Renee and Sammy. Danny helped Sammy get his clothes on and rolled up his sleeping bag. For once, Sammy's clothes looked dry.

Daddy came back from the kitchen with plates, the top plate filled with pancakes and silverware. He put butter and syrup on pancakes for Sammy and Renee and cut Sammy's pancake up into bite size pieces.

We were all here, Daddy, Sammy, Renee, Danny and me, everyone but Mama. Mrs. Willis stayed in the kitchen, so there were no Willises.

Daddy didn't eat anymore. Instead he watched us eat. He had his hand on the handle of his coffee cup but he didn't pick it up to drink.

Daddy said, "Shouldn't be long now before your mother comes to get you. Hope it won't be this long before I get to see you all again. Sorry I didn't get to do too much with you."

Danny put his hand over on Daddy's arm. "It's ok, Dad. It wasn't your fault."

Daddy wiped his forehead with his arm. "I know," he said. "It's just that I planned to do so much with you. I took all the vacation that I had."

Sammy rubbed his eyes. "Daddy going back to Yakima?" he asked.

Daddy said, "Yes, I've got to take off here in just a little bit. I have to get back to my job."

But not quite yet. We all kept eating, with sounds of forks scraping the plates, and cups of milk picked up and put down. The darkness through the kitchen window was less dark now. Daddy drank coffee and watched us eat. Just us, together.

As we each finished eating Daddy stacked up our plates in a pile with the used silverware on top.

Sammy didn't finish his. "You want the rest of his?" Daddy asked Danny.

Danny shook his head no, and his hair fell across his forehead.

Daddy stacked Sammy's plate along with the rest, on the top of the stack.

Daddy waited for Danny and Sammy to get up off the bench,

then pushed it back away from the table to make a space for himself to stand up. He wiped his hands on his pants legs.

"You kids want to walk me out to my car?" he asked. "Better get your jackets."

Daddy walked like it didn't hurt him anymore. I held Sammy's hand. Daddy's suitcase sat next to the doorway between the dining room and the kitchen and Danny picked it up. Renee came last. Daddy stopped at the kitchen.

Mrs. Willis washed dishes at the kitchen sink.

Daddy put his hand on the table. He coughed.

Mrs. Willis turned away from the sink.

Daddy rolled down the sleeves of his shirt. He said to Mrs. Willis, "I want to thank you for your hospitality."

Mrs. Willis dried her hands on a dishtowel. She took a couple of steps towards Daddy.

Daddy backed up one little step then held still.

Mrs. Willis said, "Well, you're welcome, Clifford." She smoothed down her apron, then brushed a hand up against her hair. She said, "I just hope you and your wife can work things out so you can get back together with these kids here before long. Not a day goes by that I don't pray for it."

Daddy's mouth started to open, but he closed it and just shook his head. Daddy reached for the door.

Outside when we reached the gate, Daddy knelt down on the walkway. Danny set down the suitcase. Daddy waited for the rest of us to come around him.

He said, "You kids know, don't you, that the divorce is final. Your Mom and I aren't married anymore."

"We know, Dad," Danny said. He put his hand on the suitcase handle.

"So you aren't letting Mrs. Willis get your hopes up." Daddy looked at me.

Maybe my voice sounded softer than I meant it to. "No, Daddy," I said, but I had been. Mrs. Willis always said how she prayed for them to get back together.

"That's good," said Daddy. "But I'll see you again when I can."

It was getting light. Dew lay on the ground and on the black Studebaker parked up next to the back fence where Daddy had left it. Daddy unlocked the driver's side door. He opened it and sat sideways on the seat with his feet outside. He stuck the car key into the ignition. He lifted his feet into the car, pressed his feet on the pedals and turned the key at the same time. The car started right up. Daddy turned back to us.

"Got to warm it up for awhile," he said.

Sammy let go my hand, went to Daddy and grabbed his knee. "My Daddy," he said.

Daddy picked Sammy up into his lap. He reached an arm around Sammy to the keys and turned the car off. Then he just kept both arms around Sammy.

"Don't go to Yakima, Daddy," Sammy said.

"I've got to go," Daddy said, "but I'll miss you." Daddy kissed Sammy on the top of his head.

Danny said, "We'll miss you too, Dad."

I said, "Yeah."

Daddy reached for my hand and pulled me close to him. He reached again to bring Danny and Renee close too and he hugged us all together. Daddy kissed me and his cheek rubbed against mine, all scratchy like Daddy's cheek always was. Then he seemed my Daddy again, all the way my Daddy.

"Danny, Annie," he said, "Now you know you're the oldest, so you watch out after the younger two, ok?"

"We will, Daddy," I said. "We always do."

"That's good," Daddy put his hand around my head and pulled it into his shirt. His shirt was soft, but his chest was hard.

"Kids. I've got to get going now." We moved away a little bit from him. Daddy handed Sammy over to Danny to hold, then he pulled his feet back in the car and turned the key again.

We moved further back. Daddy shut the door. He rolled down the window so he could talk to us, his right hand holding the steering wheel, left elbow resting on the window opening.

"Your Mom will be coming for you soon," Daddy said. "But don't forget that she's been in the hospital and she'll be needing your help too."

Danny put Sammy down on his feet in front of him.

"Don't worry, Dad," Danny said. "I'll remember. We'll all remember."

Daddy's voice sounded sad, "I know you will."

"Bye, kids," Daddy said. He had the little lines around his eyes when he smiled, but he looked sad. He drove the car up past the house, then around so it pointed in the other direction towards the road. As he drove past us he slowed down, held up his left hand and waved. We waved back. We stood watching the car, the black Studebaker, as it got farther and farther away. It was getting light and I could still see it a long ways away. This time it didn't churn up any dust.

#

Later that morning I hunted for Danny. I'd just seen Buddy headed to the pigpen with table scraps, so I knew my brother would be alone.

I didn't usually go in the barn. It didn't have a loft you could climb up to like Grandma and Grandpa Mill's barn. It didn't have piled up bales of hay like a castle, and loose hay in a crib at the bottom that you could jump into like the barn of Mama's old boyfriend.

I opened the big barn door part way, went inside and pushed it closed. There were rows of empty stalls - the cows were out to pasture. Against the wall on the right were hay bales, stacked in rows several bales high, except the front row which was two high along most of it, a single bale high along part of it. Danny sat there on one bale of hay, leaning back against another.

Danny just sat there, not doing anything.

I sat down by Danny. He moved over to give me a little more room. He pulled his legs up on the bale and wrapped his arms around them. But he didn't say anything.

"Danny," I said, "show me the silver dollars."

Danny stood up and brushed the loose hay off his jeans. He walked to one wall of the barn, to a place that just had the bales two high against it. He pulled one bale off the other. Danny looked towards the barn door and listened before he dragged the bottom bale out from the wall. He brushed away some loose hay so I could see the hole dug in the ground and the bag of coins lying in the hole. The leather bag was dusty with little pieces of hay stuck to it.

He pulled out the bag, brushed it off and stuck it in his pocket, not all the way in. He put the loose hay back over the hole, then moved both bales back. He sat back down, set the bag on the bale between us and undid the drawstring. He pulled the opening of the bag apart so the bag was a flat piece of soft leather, a pile of silver dollars in the center.

Danny picked up one of the silver dollars, rubbed it, then held it between his thumb and a finger.

"Here," he said, and I held out a hand.

Danny laid the dollar in my hand.

I closed my hand over the silver dollar, warm from Danny's rubbing.

Danny said, "Every time Daddy got a silver dollar, he thought about us."

"I know," I said. I sat out there a long time in the barn on the bale of hay beside Danny, holding tight to the silver dollar.

8 The Big Green Stain

Danny and I ate oatmeal at opposite ends of the long kitchen table. The oatmeal lay in a lump in the heavy white bowl in front of me on the red and white checked plastic tablecloth.

Between us Mrs. Willis held Sammy on her lap. He tried to eat, but Mrs. Willis interrupted him, twirling his hair around her thick fingers, or putting her arms around him and pulling him up against her so he couldn't move his arms to fill his spoon.

Sammy didn't complain. He'd lean back, wait for her to let go, then reach out with his spoon to get another bite. Sammy reached for his milk in the little white tin cup and Mrs. Willis put her hand on the cup to help him guide it to his mouth.

"He's so sweet," Mrs. Willis said. "I hate spanking him." She scooted around on the bench like she was trying to get more comfortable, then rested an elbow on the table.

Danny paused his bite, spoon in his hand, raised his brows up and down at me when Mrs. Willis wasn't looking.

Mrs. Willis said, "We have to break him of it now, or it'll be a bad habit that he has all his life." She grasped Sammy's head in her hand, pressing her thumb and fingers into his cheeks, and turned his head around to look at her. "Now, tell me you're going to do your best to stop this bedwetting. Do you promise me now?"

Sammy stopped chewing, until Mrs. Willis loosed her hold on his cheeks. He swallowed what he had in his mouth, then said, "I promise."

"That's my boy," Mrs. Willis said. She put her hands on both Sammy's shoulders and pulled him into her dress. She bent her head down over his head so only her brown hair showed.

This time I raised my eyebrows.

Mrs. Willis let Sammy move again. Her eyes flickered over

at the coffee pot on the stove, then back at Sammy. "You know, if you keep wetting the bed, your wee wee is going to turn green and fall off."

She said that in a regular tone of voice, like she was barely interested, and her face didn't have any kind of expression to it. It was as if she'd said she liked bacon with her eggs better than ham.

So Sammy didn't seem to understand what she'd said at first. Then he did. He stopped eating and looked up at Mrs. Willis, like he expected her to say something else to explain herself. But she didn't say anything, so Sammy just shook his head back and forth, back and forth. It wasn't true.

"Yes, it's true," Mrs. Willis said. "Everyone knows that peeing in your bed makes your wee wee turn green."

Sammy dropped his spoon into his bowl and he kept shaking his head "no." Sammy's mouth was open a little and his face looked stretched like he might cry. He looked at Mrs. Willis as if waiting for her to get serious and tell him it didn't really happen that way, that she was just joking.

Mrs. Willis pressed her lips together, so her cheeks puffed out. She nodded her head up and down, shaking it so her brown hair bounced up and down. "Yes, it will," she said.

#

Something woke me early next morning, while it was still dark, a light, Mrs. Willis with a flashlight. Mr. and Mrs. Willis both stood over Sammy's sleeping bag. Mrs. Willis shined the flashlight down on him. Mr. Willis had already dressed in his flannel shirt, overalls and boots, but Mrs. Willis still wore a long pink nightgown.

She unzipped Sammy's sleeping bag and turned back the cover.

"He's wet again." She laid down the flashlight right next to Sammy so it shone on him still, and pulled down his pajama bottoms. Sammy didn't wake up. He lay there with the sleeping bag turned down and his pajama bottoms down nearly to his knees so his penis was showing. Mrs. Willis squatted. She had something in her hand, something little and squarish, and she sprinkled something from it onto Sammy's penis. In the light of the flashlight, it looked dark green. Mrs. Willis rubbed it around on Sammy's penis with her fingers. Sammy's penis and Mrs. Willis's fingers both turned green.

Mr. Willis shoved his hands deep into the pockets of his overalls.

Mrs. Willis pulled Sammy's pajama bottoms back up. "That ought to scare him dry." She wobbled on her feet a little and reached a hand out to the floor to steady herself. Then she turned up Sammy's sleeping bag and zipped it back up.

Mr. Willis nodded, but didn't say anything, then walked out to the kitchen. I heard the back door open and close, and the noise of his last tug making sure it was all the way shut.

Mrs. Willis picked up the flashlight, pressing it on the floor as she got up so the light bounced on the walls. She winced just before she straightened up. She went into the kitchen while I watched with my eyes barely open so she wouldn't see I was awake. I couldn't see her in the kitchen but I heard her running water and imagined her washing the green food coloring off her hands. Then drying her hands on the dishtowel and all the green coming off, the big green stain of Mrs. Willis.

I heard her before I saw her come back into the dining room. She walked close to me so I pressed my eyes shut until she passed by. Then I watched her from the back, as she paused before each step like it hurt to put her foot down, her body rocking first one way then the other. She turned the doorknob of her room and stepped inside. Then I heard the noise of the springs of Mr. and Mrs. Willises' bed when she laid back down.

At least Sammy hadn't woken up. At least he hadn't been scared. At least Mr. Willis hadn't used the strap on him.

#

The pillow wasn't under my head when I woke again, only the hard floor and the sunlight bright in my eyes. Mrs. Willis squatted over by Sammy's sleeping bag where I was supposed to be before Mrs. Willis woke up to find him wet again. Now I could just watch from my sleeping bag.

But Mrs. Willis talked in a friendly voice. "Here, let's get those wet pajamas off of you." She put one arm around his middle to hold him up while he lifted his legs up for her to pull the pajamas off.

Mrs. Willis laid his wet clothes in a pile and said, "Let me get you some nice dry clothes." She walked across the room to the dresser and pulled out underpants and shorts and a red T-shirt. Her knees didn't seem to be hurting her any more.

The fabric of her long skirt clung to her knees with each step back to Sammy, naked next to his sleeping bag. All of a sudden Mrs. Willis stopped. She looked straight down at Sammy penis.

"Oh my," Mrs. Willis said, "What is that?"

Sammy looked down at his penis too to see what she was staring at.

Mrs. Willis said, "Why, look at that! Your wee wee is turning green."

Sammy stared at his penis. He didn't say anything. He looked at it, then he looked up at Mrs. Willis, and shook his head, "No." Then he looked down at his penis again.

Mrs. Willis said, "If you don't stop wetting the bed, it won't be long before it falls right off."

Mrs. Willis hummed while she pulled Sammy in front of her, and had him lift up his legs so she could get his underpants and his shorts on him. She hummed while she pulled the T-shirt down over his head, the T-shirt I should have already put on Sammy before Mrs. Willis could even wake up and find him wet.

She still hummed while she carried the sleeping bag out of the living room door and laid it over the clothes line outside, then came back in and picked up Sammy's wet pajamas. She hummed while she tossed them down the basement stairs to add to the laundry she'd do with the wringer washer in the basement.

While Mrs. Willis hummed, Sammy stood next to the dining room table. Then he pulled out a chair and just sat in it. But I couldn't say anything to him about what happened in the night, not with Mrs. Willis there.

All through this Renee slept on. Danny was probably still upstairs asleep in Buddy's room.

When Mrs. Willis called Sammy into the kitchen then to get his oatmeal, Sammy walked like he thought something might break. He was so little.

I got up then, too late.

On the bench against the wall, I had to eat the oatmeal that morning because Mrs. Willis stayed in the kitchen. I couldn't slip outside and feed it to the pigs.

Mrs. Willis helped Sammy pour milk on his oatmeal. All the while Sammy ate, Mrs. Willis kept saying things like she'd seen it happen before, some little boy that wouldn't stop wetting the bed, first his penis turned green, then it started shriveling up, and finally it dried up completely and fell off.

I gulped down the oatmeal as fast as I could because I didn't want it all dry and lumpy in my mouth. I tried not to hear Mrs. Willis, when I couldn't even tell Sammy what I saw until I could get alone with him.

Sammy took a bite of the oatmeal and chewed on it. Then he

looked up at Mrs. Willis who still talked about some other little boy she knew whose penis had turned green. Lucky for him, she was saying, he'd learned his lesson before it was too late and stopped wetting the bed before his penis had actually fallen off.

Sammy stopped chewing the oatmeal, then started again. He chewed like his teeth hurt and he had to be careful. Chewed and chewed, but it didn't look like he ever swallowed.

The doorknob from outside turned and Kevin walked in. Larry came behind him.

Larry said, "Good morning," in his wide-awake voice, looked at me and at Sammy, said, "You sleepy heads finally getting up." He turned to Mrs. Willis, "Got some of that oatmeal for me?"

Mrs. Willis said, "Plenty for everyone."

Larry went to the cupboard, handed a bowl to Kevin, got another for himself and used the wooden spoon to dish up some of the oatmeal out of the pan. "Mm mm," he said, like he actually liked the stuff.

Mrs. Willis bowed her head down a little, shook it, and said, "Poor Sammy."

Larry said, "What's wrong with Sammy? The little fellow looks all right to me."

"Oh, no," Mrs. Willis said. "His wee wee was green this morning, from all his peeing in the bed."

Larry said, "Oh my gosh. That is serious. Guess it won't be long now before it falls right off."

Sammy swallowed the big lump of oatmeal. His eyes were wet, and he shouted, "No it won't fall off." Sammy's eyes closed and I could see the tiny blue veins that showed right through the skin of his eyelids before he opened them again.

Larry wiped the back of his hand across his forehead. He said, "Well, I guess it will alright if you don't stop wetting that sleeping bag of yours. Isn't that so, Kevin?" Larry sat down on the bench so it moved and scraped the floor.

Kevin said, "Sure enough. Fall right off." He got his oatmeal and sat down at the table next to Larry.

Mrs. Willis said, "That's just what I've been telling him."

Sammy looked over at me and I felt what he didn't say, "Annie, is it true?" But I couldn't say anything in front of Mrs. Willis, couldn't even shake my head. With Larry and Kevin there, one of them would be sure to see me. So I stared down at my bowl.

#

After breakfast I offered to bring the slop down to the pigs. The slop jar was full of left over scraps of food, mostly oatmeal, and it smelled terrible. I asked Sammy if he wanted to help me.

Outside in the air the smell of the slops wasn't so bad. Sammy reached over with his little hand to help me carry it. So I held it out with one hand so the bucket hung between us. It was harder to carry that way and I couldn't hurry like I wanted to get away from Mrs. Willis, far enough away so no one would surprise us by coming outside while I told Sammy.

I tried to walk fast. Sammy hurried to keep up, but I couldn't keep it up, I slowed down. I said, "This sure is heavy. It's nice to have a little brother to help me carry things."

Sammy smiled and he lifted up on the handle like he was trying to carry more of it for me. I tried to lift up too so the metal handle wouldn't dig into his hand.

We didn't talk until I dumped out the slops in the food trough at the corner of the pigpen and set the slop bucket down. I sat down on the ground on a little grassy hill and Sammy sat across from me. I told Sammy I never heard of anyone's wee wee ever falling off because they wet the bed. I never heard of it happening even once. They were just making it up to scare him.

Sammy said, "Then why is my wee wee turning green?"

So I told him about Mrs. Willis putting on the green food coloring. But I wondered if I should have told him. Maybe he'd worry like I worried: if they'd do that, what else might they do?

So I said, "It's just another of their jokes, Sammy, like the creek."

Sammy sat on the ground across from me. He put his shoes up to touch my shoes, the flat of his shoes against my shoes.

I said, "You remember how Larry and Kevin said they were going to throw you in the creek, but they never did it?"

Sammy nodded. His face relaxed back into my round faced, curly-haired little brother, holding his hands out to me.

"Don't tell them I told you," I said.

I reached for Sammy's hands and leaned back while he leaned forward, leaned forward while he leaned back, there on the grassy spot on the hill. Leaned forward, leaned back, next to the pigpen on the Willis farm and the smell of the slops that the pigs ate. Until Sammy laughed, laughed so hard his hands let go of my hands, and we both lay back spread out flat on the grass.

9 Snakes

Buddy found the first snake. He'd gone with Danny, up ahead of Renee and me, and he found the snake by nearly stepping on it by the side of the creek. The snake slithered off into the shallow water of the creek just past the place where the creek bed twisted around a tree on a high bank, the tree's roots holding the bank together. The water opened up into a wide stretch and spread out into shallows on the left bank where we walked along going upstream. All I saw was a flash of brown, but Buddy claimed he got a good look and it was a cottonmouth for sure. Said he was lucky he didn't get a leg full of poison.

My brother Danny said, if Buddy had been bit, he had his pocket knife with him and he'd seen in the movies how you sliced into the bite and sucked out the poison, and he would have done it to save Buddy from a slow painful death.

"Reckon I'm glad I don't have to count on you to save me from a slow painful death," Buddy grinned, a smirky grin, then shoved my brother in the direction of the creek. Danny stumbled to the edge of the water, the creek water just washing over the toes of his tennis shoes.

Buddy always tried to lord it over my brother. Maybe felt like he needed to, to let everyone know he was older, eleven instead of ten. The two of them were pretty much the same size. If anything, my brother was a little taller. Other than that, they didn't look anything alike, Buddy tanned dark with brown hair, my brother light with blondish hair and freckles just like the rest of us Mills. Buddy claimed his tan was a result of being a farm kid, out in the sun doing chores, not some coddled city kid. I thought it had more to do with how his mother and father were dark complected and ours weren't, cause he sure didn't do a whole lot of work that I could see.

My brother got his balance back and gave Buddy a shove, but Buddy was ready for it, his legs apart to keep his balance, and it wasn't a serious shove anyhow. By the time Renee and I caught up with them they'd stopped shoving and were arguing whether this was a good place to swim.

The two of them always made a game of finding the absolutely best place to swim. Sometimes we'd spend more time finding the place than swimming. Only on really hot days like today did they settle for the first place that looked any good at all.

Up ahead the water was too deep and the current too fast, for Renee anyway. Being only six, she couldn't swim yet. None of us was supposed to go in over our waists without grownups around. Course we did anyway, but not over our chests, and not in the swift current.

This stretch was so wide the water probably didn't go much above our knees, but the day was so hot I figured we'd stay here awhile, so I put down my towel, took off my tennis shoes and waded in. Renee and I wore our shorts and shirts to swim. They'd dry on the way back.

Renee followed me out nearly to the opposite bank. Trees with high shading branches grew all along the edge of the grassy bank but too high above the water for us to climb up to them. Near the high bank the water flowed deep enough to lie down in. The creek bottom felt like silt on my toes, so I floated face down and reached down to put my fingers into it, the water cool on my face.

By the time I came up for air the slow current brought me a long ways downstream and nearly back to the dirt shore. Renee still stood where I had started. She splashed herself with water and looked towards me. The water looked more inviting further downstream, deeper and narrower, but not too deep or too fast.

The boys must have decided to stay because they pulled their jeans off, leaving the swim trunks that had been underneath. I walked past them on my way back to Renee.

Before I reached her I passed a big stick in the water. I headed over to pick up the stick, something to stir up the silt. I stepped closer.

The stick moved.

One end came towards me, stopped, jerked back, and swam away in the opposite direction.

Snake number two.

It was gone before I started to be afraid.

My left leg shook, just at my left knee. It felt like it wouldn't hold me, so I picked it up to stop it. Then I ran to the shore.

"A snake," I shouted. My leg shook again and my breath went faster than it should have from that little run.

Renee splashed through the water behind me, stepping high like she didn't want to leave her feet down in that creek water. "I saw it," she said. "It could have bitten you."

"Where?" asked Danny. He pulled his jeans the rest of the way off and got to his feet.

I pointed. My breath came slower, almost normal.

Danny stood up straight, almost on his toes, and shielded his eyes with his hand against his forehead, looking just past us upstream.

"What color was it?" asked Buddy.

"Brown," I said, "I thought it was a stick."

"Some stick," said Buddy, pulling the cord of his swimming trunks tighter.

"It looked just like a stick," Renee said. "It lay in the water, then Annie came and it swam away." Renee's wet shorts clung to her, but her red T-shirt was only wet on the bottom edge.

"Did it open its mouth?" Buddy asked. "If it opened its

mouth it could have been a water moccasin. Normal snakes can't bite you under water, but water moccasins can. It probably wasn't a water moccasin, though, probably wasn't even poisonous, not like a cottonmouth."

I tried to remember. When it moved its head towards me did it open its mouth? I tried to picture it, and it seemed like I might have seen its mouth open just a little. I might have almost been bit by a water moccasin.

"I'm not sure," I said. "It might have opened its mouth. Did you see its mouth, Renee?"

Renee looked at me like she was trying to tell whether I wanted the snake to have opened its mouth or not, then she shook her head that she hadn't seen. I wondered whether a water moccasin was more poisonous than a cottonmouth, but didn't ask. Buddy would have an answer. The thing about Buddy was that he knew about everything, and he sounded so sure. I didn't always believe he knew what he was talking about, but since I knew almost nothing about snakes, there was no disputing him.

Buddy slapped his thigh and said, "Well, it seems to me that this creek is turning into a downright dangerous place to be, what with all these snakes. I say we put an end to some of them."

Most of the ideas that Buddy had were about hurting something, mostly me, but I kind of favored his idea about the snakes.

"Let's cool off some first," my brother said. He kicked at his tennis shoe.

"With all those snakes around?" asked Buddy.

Danny walked to the edge of the creek then into it and upstream for a ways in the shallow water, looking down at the water the whole time, then turned around and walked back, still looking down at the water. His legs, skinny and white, looked more bare than they usually did. Renee's eyes stayed on Danny, and she didn't look away until Danny stepped out of the creek and came back to us.

Danny looked at Buddy. He said, "I don't see any more snakes. We've been swimming here all summer without being bothered by snakes. Probably it was just a coincidence that we saw two of them today. Probably neither one of them was poisonous."

He reached down for a pebble, a good flat one, twirled halfway round to the creek and did a quick jerk with his wrist. The pebble skipped on the water, one, two three, up again in a half arc, then dropped straight down into the water.

Buddy moved another little rock with his toe, but he didn't pick it up. He said, "Maybe the last one wasn't poisonous, but that first one was a cottonmouth for sure." He looked down at the ground, at the little rock, at his toe, then back up at my brother's face.

My brother said, "May have been poisonous, but it had sense enough to get out of the way when it saw you coming." He grinned his mouth-open grin at Buddy, the one with all his teeth showing, and Buddy grinned back.

Buddy picked up the little rock and didn't even try to skip it because it wasn't the right shape, just threw it hard into the water a couple of feet off shore. He said, "That's right, none of them better show their ugly heads with me around."

Danny said, "So, we'll keep an eye open when we're walking near the edge over here, and stay away from the bank on the other side. That's the only place snakes might be. We'll be safe enough." Danny caught Renee's eye when he said that. Then he said to Buddy, "Afterwards we'll go hunting for snakes."

"Ok," Buddy said.

"It looks better for swimming down there," I said, and pointed downstream where the water deepened and was shaded by trees on the higher bank.

"It does look better," Danny said. He picked up his tennis shoes and jeans, turned to Buddy and said, "Let's try it out. Bound to be deeper than this is."

"Sure, why not," said Buddy.

We waded down to the next section of the creek, dropped our clothes on the shore, and waded out to the deeper place near the opposite bank, but not too near. The water was just exactly deep enough to swim without scraping the bottom. Overhanging trees shaded the best part of it and kept the sun from burning down. I floated on my back and paddled while I looked up through the tree branches, at the light scattered through the leaves. I dipped my hands and kicked now and again. It didn't take much to keep me afloat.

"Let's remember where this spot is," I said.

"It's the best yet," said my brother. He stood in the middle of the pool, the water up to his chest. With his hand turned to the side so just the edge of it dipped into the water, he splashed Buddy. The water lifted up like a wave. Buddy and my brother always tried to see who could make the biggest wave that way, just like they skipped the rocks to see who could make the most skips.

"Sure is," said Buddy, and splashed him back, but my brother dove under water. He swam over to Buddy, lifted him up by one leg and dunked him into the water.

Renee moved away from them, closer to me. But I swam in water too deep for her, so I paddled closer to her.

"It's so cool here," Renee said. She ducked under water and came up with her hair wet. Part of it hung in her face. She pulled it back.

"Want to sit on the bottom and have a tea party?" Renee asked.

We tried to dig our feet into the soft dirt of the bottom to keep us down a little longer, but we only stayed at the bottom a few seconds, pretending to drink our tea before we bobbed back up. Renee came up before me, then back down, her hair floated upwards as she came down.

I stood up, then squatted back down. "How is your tea?" I asked underwater, moving my mouth with little bubbles coming out.

Renee said, "What, what?" I could tell from her mouth but I couldn't hear her. She cupped her hands upwards and tried to pull herself back down. It didn't last. We both went up.

"What did you say?" Renee asked me.

"I said, "How is your tea, Madame Preshire?" Mama used to call Renee that sometimes, when the three of us were doing something special like baking apple pies. Renee and I got to help roll out the dough, then Mama finished it. We pressed the pieces of dough into the pie dishes, or over the cut up apples and cinnamon for the top crust, and we poked the holes in the crust with a fork.

"How about a piece of pie with your tea, Madame Preshire?" I asked, and reached to grab Renee's hands, so we went down together.

"How about a piece of pie with your tea?" I asked again underwater.

I watched Renee's mouth answer, "Yes, please."

Then we had to come up for air.

"That was fun," Renee said.

"Delightful," I said. "And the pie was so delicious."

Renee laughed. She jumped up and down in the water.

The boys were ready to hunt snakes. Shoes back on, the boys carrying their rolled up jeans, we headed back upstream.

Buddy said, "Try to find a big rock to smash the snakes with, maybe some smaller rocks to throw."

I picked up a few smaller rocks, gave a couple to Renee. I wasn't going to get close enough to pound a snake with a big rock.

Renee took the rocks from me, closed her hands around them, then used the inside of her elbow to wipe her hair out of her face. Her barrette had come out. Mama would have been wanting to trim Renee's bangs about then.

"How are we going to find any snakes anyway?" Renee asked.

Danny swung his tennis shoes by their tied together laces. A piece of wet hair fell down over his forehead. "We'll look under rocks and stuff," he said, "and any place where there are long grasses or tree roots growing in the creek."

"There's probably a lot over there hiding under that bank." Buddy pointed. He reached down for a flat stone and skipped it across the creek. One skip, two, not a good one.

Buddy looked all up and down the shore before he walked to a big rock about six inches across, partly stuck in the ground. He put both his hands on it to work it free.

"Careful," Danny said. "It might have something under it."

Buddy jerked his hands away. Danny went away from the shore to some brush and came back with two small tree branches. He handed one to Buddy, who wedged the stick underneath the rock, then pressed down on the end of the stick until the rock came free. He poked with his stick until the rock turned upside down.

Nothing, not even a roly-poly bug on the bottom of the rock, or in the dirt underneath.

My brother picked up a baseball size rock and Buddy got a few smaller ones. We walked upstream.

Every boulder the boys saw in the water, they poked under with their sticks.

Snake number three swam away from the roots of a tree that

grew next to the creek. Buddy scared it out when he hit the roots with his stick, then he caught the snake up on the stick and slung it over onto the bank. Danny ran close to it and threw his baseball rock at the snake's head. The snake lay still, its head smashed.

"Watch out," Buddy said, "It may not be dead." He threw his own rock at the snake and hit it just under its head. He smashed the snake's whole body with the end of his stick.

"Guess that'll do it," Buddy said.

Snakes four and five came from under rocks. The two boys killed snake four the same way as snake three, one of them slinging the snake out of the water with his stick, the other going after it with rocks and his stick to smash it, but snake five got away.

Snake six coiled beside a rock, not under. Danny got snake six with one throw of his baseball rock, smashing it flat just under its head and Buddy used his stick to finish it off.

A couple more and it began to seem easy.

Renee and I threw our rocks at one of them. We didn't pick up any more stones once the first two were gone. We weren't good shots, so we watched the boys trample the snakes.

"Guess those snakes won't be bothering us any more," Renee said.

Up ahead, Buddy raised his stick in the air. "I reckon not," he said.

Renee moved closer to me, whispered, "Do you think any of those snakes were poisonous?"

"I don't think so," I said, "Mostly snakes aren't. Mostly they like to keep away from humans anyway. I read that somewhere."

Renee said, "You never know, though." She stayed well away from those snakes even now that they were dead.

"Yeah," I said, "You never know."

We walked quite a ways further without finding any more

snakes. Danny picked up a few smooth stones and practiced skipping them on the water. Buddy did the same.

Renee said, "Can't we stop now? Maybe all the snakes are dead."

Danny said to Buddy, "It'll soon be time to head back, and we need another swim to cool off before we go."

"Okay," Buddy said, "just one more snake."

Now they checked every possible place a snake might be. They found snake number nine in a clump of tall grasses that grew out of the water. Buddy got it on the very tip of his stick. At first I was afraid he'd lose it and we'd have to keep going until he found another, but my brother got his stick under it too, and together they flung the snake over onto a rocky place on the shore. The snake didn't move. It was small and dark brown. Maybe it hit a rock on its way down. It didn't look like it would hurt anyone, but Buddy ran over and hit it with his stick a couple of times. Then he picked it up with the tip of his stick, laid it on a flat rock, then hit it again and again until the snake was smashed flat. That snake was dead for sure.

#

This time we took just a quick dip to cool off. I dove down under the water and stayed until I was out of breath, trying to take away the hot sun. Renee and the two boys did the same, staying under water to make it last. Danny got out first. Renee and I followed. Buddy floated on his back a moment longer then ran to catch up.

The cool of the swim didn't last long. A walk through some trees, then bushes, then the dusty road and alfalfa fields on either side of us and we were hot again.

We reached a spot where two big trees made some shade on the road. Buddy stopped. Danny sat down on the knobby root of one of the big trees. The two of them whispered and Renee and I waited to see if they would tell us what it was about.

Buddy walked out in the middle of the road and looked all around. You could see all the way to the house from there but it was so far away you could only make out the house, not see any people outside, if there were any. In the other direction lay fields and woods with no one out in the fields and no tractor or car or wagon in either direction on the road.

Buddy said, "We'll pull down our pants if you pull down yours."

Danny got up from the tree root and brushed off his jeans, "That's right. We will if you will."

Renee looked at me to see what I wanted to do. So I said, "Ok."

Renee said, "Ok" too.

Buddy, Renee and I moved closer to the side of the road.

"You first," I said.

Buddy unsnapped his jeans. He pulled down the zipper, and slipped the jeans down to his knees. He looked over at me. So what, just his swimming trunks showing.

My brother started working on his pants too. Danny got his pants unsnapped, unzipped and slipped down to his ankles before Buddy made another move. Then, both at once, the two boys slipped their fingers into their swimming trunks and pulled them down below their knees.

Danny's skin was all white there, and even Buddy's skin was lighter brown than the rest of him. Danny's penis just kind of curled up next to his body down there, but Buddy's poked out a little.

"Your turn," Buddy said.

Renee glanced at me again. I didn't see any sense in fooling around. I put my hands inside the elastic of my shorts and underpants, and used my thumbs to pull them down to my knees.

Renee did just what I did. Then I gazed again at my brother and Buddy. The two of them stared at us, too. We all stood there looking.

Then Buddy turned around in a circle, stopping at the point where his butt was turned toward Renee and me. His butt was lighter too where the swim trunks had been. I turned around too. The shorts at my knees made it hard for me to turn. Danny and Renee's butts were both really white.

There wasn't much to see really.

Buddy made a circle of his left thumb and pointer finger, then put the pointer finger of his right hand through the circle that he had made. He moved his right finger back and forth, into and out of the circle, over and over again.

Renee glanced me as if to ask what is he doing that for and I shrugged because I didn't know. The two of us kept watching Buddy.

He moved towards me. His penis, his thing, stuck out a little more. It looked like a little snake. I hoped he wasn't going to try to touch me with his thing. Buddy moved slowly with little steps because his jeans had fallen down to his ankles. If he got much closer I'd move away so his penis wouldn't touch me but now I watched Buddy and his sticking out thing and wondered what he planned to do. Buddy took another step.

"Stop!" my brother shouted.

Danny shouted like grownups shouted. You did what they said. You knew you'd better.

Buddy stopped. He stepped backwards a step.

My brother Danny pulled up his underpants, then his jeans, zipped and snapped them. He looked at Buddy and Buddy pulled up his underpants and jeans and zipped and snapped them too.

Renee and I did the same.

I would have liked to look at the boys a little longer, but I'd seen everything.

"You'd better not tell anyone about this," said Buddy. "If you do, we'll tell on you too and we'll all get a licking."

"We won't tell," I said.

#

But after dinner when Renee and I dried the dishes that Shirley washed, Renee made the sign that Buddy had made, making a circle of her finger and thumb on her left and moving the finger of her right hand in and out of the circle.

"What's that mean?" she asked Shirley.

Renee didn't know that asking about the sign was telling.

"Who made that sign?" asked Shirley. Her face was red and her lips pressed together.

"But what does it mean?" asked Renee.

"Who made the sign?" asked Shirley.

"Buddy did," Renee said.

Shirley dried her hands on a dish towel, "I'm going to tell my parents."

"But what does it mean?" insisted Renee. Shirley shook her head and walked out of the kitchen.

Mr. Willis shouted from the living room, "Renee! Annie! Get out here."

Shirley stood by Mr. Willis, with Danny and Buddy a couple of feet away.

Mr. Willis said, "Show me that sign you made."

Renee made the sign again.

I said, "But we weren't making it."

Buddy said, "Yes, you were. You did it just the same as us."

I said, "We did not. We didn't even know what it meant." I expected Shirley to say something then.

But Shirley shook her head and went back into the kitchen

without saying a thing. Maybe she'd already told Mr. Willis. Maybe she knew it wouldn't make any difference.

Without saying anything, Mr. Willis went into the bedroom.

Buddy pointed out the picture window back towards the road and shook his head no. He stared hard at me and at Renee and sliced across his neck with the edge of his hand, which I took to mean that we would be dead if we said anything about what we'd done on the way home, but I didn't know if he meant that he would do it or Mr. Willis would.

Back from the bedroom, Mr. Willis took the strap down from its hook on the side of the fireplace.

He whipped the boys first. He made them pull their pants down and whipped them on their bare bottom while Renee and I watched and waited for our turn. Neither of the boys cried, and I didn't cry, even though it hurt just as much as it looked like it hurt.

Even Renee didn't cry. She stood there with her shorts down, fists tight and eyes closed, while the straps snaked around her bottom marking her pale skin with streaks of red.

10 The Last, Worst Thing

We almost never had fruit to eat at the Willises' until one summer day we drove to the house of Mrs. Willis's friend to pick peaches. Then we had boxes and boxes of peaches to eat, all sweet and firm and juicy. Boxes of peaches still remained when the peaches turned a little too sweet, a little mushy. There were still peaches left when the peaches had brown spots you had to eat around, when eating even one left you feeling a little bit sick.

But usually it was her friend, Mrs. Dupre, who came to visit Mrs. Willis. They always played cards together.

Mrs. Willis set up a green plastic folding table in front of the fireplace in the living room, and two dark brown metal folding chairs on either side of it. Right away Mrs. Dupre lowered herself into one of the chairs gingerly like she had to make sure she didn't hit too hard. She said, "Oh, it's nice to get off my feet."

Mrs. Willis moved the floor lamp closer to the card table, then went into her room for the deck of cards that she handed to Mrs. Dupre.

Mrs. Dupre put her thumbs on the inside ends of the two stacks of cards. She shuffled them together but then somehow she lifted the cards up in an arc before they came together into one stack with short slapping sounds.

Her fingers weren't like the rest of her. They were long and slender and they moved too fast for me to follow what they were doing from over on the other side of the living room. Still, I didn't come closer.

From the other chair, Mrs. Willis watched Mrs. Dupre's fingers, like she couldn't stop watching like I couldn't stop. She had her metal chair pulled away from the table and she leaned back so the skirt of her dress spread over her knees and the hem of that skirt didn't move up or down on her leg at all while she watched Mrs. Dupre's fingers.

But after the cards slapped together into their pile on the table, the hem of Mrs. Willis's skirt jerked up and down on her leg. She reached across the table to pat her friend's arm. When she got Mrs. Dupre's attention, Mrs. Willis said with her voice as jerky as her dress, "I think I've come up with something that will finally cure that child of wetting the bed."

"And what would that be?" asked Mrs. Dupre, her smile soft and puffy like Mrs. Willis's smile.

"I've decided to give him a special bath." Mrs. Willis raised her voice, maybe so Sammy would hear, as he played with his toy cars and trucks on the floor near me. "Yes, a special green bath. It'll cure him right away of that bed wetting."

Sammy looked up, but when Mrs. Willis didn't say anything else, he went back to playing with his cars.

Mrs. Willis went into the kitchen, bright from the overhead light. She lifted a roasting pan off a hook over the stove then walked to the right where I couldn't see her, but I heard her set the pan in the sink and turn the faucet on. Water splashed into the pan. The heavy pan scraped the sides of the sink as Mrs. Willis lifted it over to the counter next to the stove. She poured something from a little bottle into the pan. I thought it was the same little bottle of green food coloring she had the other night. She reached to the right. I heard the rattle of silverware in the drawer. She lifted out a large metal spoon with holes in it to stir the water in the pan. After Mrs. Willis placed the pan on the front of the stove, over two burners, she turned the flame of the gas burners all the way up.

When she returned to the card table, Mrs. Dupre handed her the cards. Mrs. Willis dealt, skimming the cards off the top, one for Mrs. Dupre, one for her, one for Mrs. Dupre, one for her. Both of them picked up their cards. Neither talked while they looked them over.

While they played, they spoke in whispers I couldn't hear.

Mrs. Dupre chuckled at something Mrs. Willis said, and the bulge at her stomach shook.

The green water heated on the stove.

Mrs. Willis and Mrs. Dupre picked up cards, laid down cards, looked at their cards, dealt new hands.

On the floor, Sammy punched on a pillow to make a mountain with hills and valleys for his toy cars. He knelt down next to the pillow mountain and skidded the yellow car down into a crevice. His other hand sped the tow truck over for the rescue, backing it to the edge to let down the hook. Sammy's finger was the hook dragging the car back up onto the mountain road.

Mrs. Willis shuffled the deck and handed the cards to Mrs. Dupre. She pointed over to Sammy so Mrs. Dupre looked over.

Mrs. Willis said, "Look how big he's getting."

Mrs. Dupre looked and nodded, then went back to dealing the cards.

Mrs. Willis said, "It's going to be kind of a tight fit to get him into that pan for his bath."

"Just as long as his bottom fits," Mrs. Dupre said.

Mrs. Willis laughed. She pressed her fist into her mouth to stop laughing. She looked over her fist at Mrs. Dupre, and both their bodies shook trying to hold their laughter in.

Mrs. Willis got up. "I'll just go check on it," she said.

At the stove, she lifted one end of the roasting pan. I heard water sizzle against the hot metal pan.

Mrs. Willis said, "It's almost ready now."

But the water was already too hot for a bath.

My foot was burned once in water that sizzled like that. Just before I jerked my foot out of the hot water I could see the little pieces of skin peeled off and floating away from my foot.

Mrs. Willis couldn't mean to put Sammy in that pan. Why would she do that?

But she went to Sammy. "Almost time for your bath." Mrs. Willis picked up the pillow and all of Sammy's cars. Sammy kept his eyes on his cars until she set them down on top of the dresser he shared with me and Renee, then he relaxed. Mrs. Willis tossed the pillow on the couch then squatted down beside him, and he let her take off all of his clothes, lifted each foot when she told him to so she could pull off his shoes, then each pant leg, then his underpants.

"Are you ready to be cured of your bed wetting?" Mrs. Willis asked him. Sammy nodded his head.

Mrs. Willis called over to Mrs. Dupre, "He says he's ready to be cured. Guess, he'll be cured all right."

"Guess he will," said Mrs. Dupre. "If anything will cure him that will." She dealt the cards slowly, one for Mrs. Willis, one for her.

"He looks a lot littler without his clothes, doesn't he?" Mrs. Willis said. "Guess he'll fit in the pan after all."

She pushed on the floor with her hands to raise herself up to her feet, took slow steps over to her chair. She arranged her dress, picked up her cards one at a time, moved her lips together, then apart.

Sammy moved closer to me.

The bandages on my burnt foot had to be changed every day. The dead skin had to be cut off. When I wore shoes again, they were special canvas shoes to let my hurt foot breathe.

But Mrs. Willis wasn't going to put just Sammy's foot in the water. She was going to put his whole body in. His whole body scalded with the skin peeling off. Did she mean to kill him? Mrs.

Willis laughed. "Yes, this ought to cure his bed wetting once and for all."

Mrs. Dupre laughed too and it had to be a joke. Both of them laughed and looked at Sammy. Sammy almost laughed too because they laughed. He looked up at me to see if I knew what was so funny, and pulled his eyebrows together puzzled when I didn't laugh.

It had to be a joke.

What if it wasn't?

#

Between Mrs. Willis at the card table and where Sammy stood were about ten steps for Mrs. Willis. Between me and Sammy were two of my steps. Between Sammy and the door from the dining room to the kitchen, maybe six steps, six of my steps, maybe more Sammy steps. Between that door and the door to the outside there were twelve big squares of black and white, white then black, each square one Sammy step.

If Mrs. Willis started to put Sammy in the basin on the stove could I grab Sammy and run?

Should I get him now while she still sat ten steps away?

My body felt like it couldn't move. I wanted to move so I would know if I could. But I didn't want to move because I didn't want to make them wonder what I was up to, not until I was ready and knew just what I was going to do.

What they were going to do.

Sammy, because it was taking so long, stood on one leg and swung the other, while he waited for Mrs. Willis to give him a bath.

But now they both concentrated hard on their cards, like they'd forgotten all about the green water. Mrs. Willis didn't get up again for a long while.

Sammy twirled around with his hands stretched out, getting himself dizzy. Mrs. Dupre tapped Mrs. Willis's shoulder and pointed to Sammy.

Mrs. Willis' chair scraped against the floor as she pushed herself away from the card table. I pictured myself grabbing Sammy's hand, running out the door. But Mrs. Willis walked towards the kitchen, not towards Sammy. She rattled the pan on the stove, then came back out.

Sammy stopped twirling, stumbled and started to fall next to me. I caught him to keep him from falling on the floor. He was heavy on me, but not too heavy. Right then I could pick him up and grab his hand and run, just keep running.

"Almost ready. Let's have another hand." The chair creaked as Mrs. Willis sat down.

Mrs. Dupre and Mrs. Willis didn't talk as much now. They picked up cards, laid them down.

Twenty-seven floor boards between Sammy and the other door from the living room to the front porch.

Mrs. Willis was fat, and probably couldn't run fast. We could reach the door to the outside before she could, but I'd have to turn the doorknob, get the heavy door open, unhook the high hook of the screen door, the one that was hard to get out of the hole. She might reach us before I got both of them open.

If I went through the kitchen to the back door would Sammy realize he had to come along and be fast?

If we got outside, I didn't know how many miles it was to the next farm. We'd never been there. Sammy would be cold outside with no clothes on.

"Get up a minute," I said to Sammy and lifted him off me.

My jean jacket hung on a hook by the outside door. Glad I could move, I pulled the jacket on and went back to my spot near Sammy.

"You cold?" Mrs. Willis asked me.

I nodded, I didn't think I could talk.

"Sammy might be cold too, but he'll warm up soon enough," she said.

About ten minutes later she went back into the kitchen. My legs felt all heavy again like they'd gone into the floor and I'd have to pull them out before I could move. Mrs. Willis took the basin off the stove, her hands covered with thick oven mitts.

The water sizzled.

She took the basin somewhere out of my sight. There were sounds of pouring.

Three Mrs. Willis steps from Sammy if I waited until she came out the kitchen door, if I waited to see what she did.

I moved right next to Sammy.

Go now, start toward the other door now, slow, not obvious. Maybe eight Sammy steps with me holding his hand. I imagined my legs moving, my hand reaching for him.

But my legs and arms didn't move.

Mrs. Willis started back. She reached the kitchen door. *If she comes his way, grab for Sammy's hand, pull him around her, through the kitchen, out the door.*

My hand was ready.

Mrs. Willis looked our way, then looked past us, towards the card table. She walked over and sat down. When she sat she let out a big breath of air. All the time she eased herself down and the metal folding chair creaked with her weight, she let out the long breath.

Mrs. Dupre turned her head toward Mrs. Willis, looked up, then down again, while she arranged her cards in her hand, then back up at Mrs. Willis.

Mrs. Willis shook her head and didn't say anything. Mrs. Dupre waited for her.

"I just couldn't do it." Mrs. Willis picked up her cards from off the table, one at a time, arranging them in her hand. She looked at her cards, then up at Mrs. Dupre, at her cards again.

Her hand all arranged, Mrs. Willis kept her eyes on Mrs. Dupre. Her eyes shone bright and brown in the middle of her puffy white face. She said, "He looked so innocent standing there naked, I just couldn't do it. No," her voice sounded as though she was disappointed in herself. "I poured that water down the sink."

Mrs. Dupre started to say something, then she didn't say it. Her big slow lips came apart then went back together again.

Mrs. Willis caught Mrs. Dupre's eye and smiled at her then the two of them laughed, a long loud laugh, a big joke to them.

I walked around the card table to the dresser on the other side. I took out a pair of pajamas, the ones with the teddy bears. I walked back around the table and I didn't look at the two women.

I took Sammy's hand. "Time to get ready for bed," I said, and led him over to where his sleeping bag was rolled up next to the wall. I unrolled it and spread it out. I pulled his pajamas on him, sat him in my lap to pull the bottoms over his feet, stood him up to pull them up, pulled one arm of the pajama tops over his fingers, up his arm, put his other arm through the other pajama arm. Buttoned them up.

"What about my bath?" asked Sammy.

"No bath tonight," I said.

I turned down the flap of his sleeping bag. Sammy scooted down in it and I zipped it up most of the way. I sat by him next to his sleeping bag, rested my arm on his shoulder. I wanted to hold him in my lap, cradle his head, watch his little hands and feet as he slept. He was mine to take care of but I couldn't take care of him. I couldn't hold him.

I sat there with my arm on his shoulder until he fell asleep.

11 Lost A Lot

We lost a lot at the Willises, but we didn't lose everything.

We lost the money from our allowance that Mrs. Willis kept for us in a jar on top of the refrigerator, but we wouldn't have had all that money anyway if Mrs. Willis hadn't said that we should stop frittering away the dollar a week Mama sent us and start saving up instead for a nice present for Mama when she got out of the hospital.

So instead of lining up all the candy I could buy for 25 cents, a nickel Snickers bar, a big Baby Ruth for a dime, a nickel pack of gum and the rest penny candy, tootsie rolls and jaw breakers, and thinking how I could make it last the whole week; instead of that, all of us watched the dollars pile up in the jar on top of the refrigerator and thought about what we could buy for Mama with the money we had saved so far and what we could buy by the time she came to the Willises to get us. Each time we added our new allowance we counted what was there, fifteen, sixteen, seventeen dollars. A box of chocolates, a necklace, a new purse, a new dress.

The Monday morning after it was seventeen dollars, Mrs. Willis's voice came from the kitchen, "Annie, get up. It's time to get ready for school."

In the kitchen my brother, Danny, and Buddy already sat at the kitchen table on the bench next to the wall, so I sat on the other side. The bare kitchen light hung down over the table and lit up the right side of Buddy's face and the left side of Danny's face. Danny wore his plaid shirt and leaned his elbows on the slick vinyl tablecloth of red and white squares. Mrs. Willis stirred the oatmeal at the stove, but our bowls and spoons and milk were already laid out on the table. Buddy tapped his spoon against his glass full of milk but Danny waited with his chin in his hands.

Mrs. Willis scraped the wooden spoon along the side of the

pan. When she turned away from the stove, the bulb over the table lit up her face. She said, "Did you happen to hear anything last night in the middle of the night, Annie?"

"No, I didn't hear anything." I wished that I had the side of the bench against the wall so I could lean back and rest a little more.

"Oh," Mrs. Willis said, "sleeping down here, I thought you might have." She carried the pan of oatmeal to the table.

Danny lifted his chin out of his hand, "What would she have heard?"

Mrs. Willis scooped out a big lump of oatmeal with the wooden spoon and plopped it into Buddy's bowl. She banged the wooden spoon on the side of his heavy white China bowl to get the rest of the lump to drop. The oatmeal hung from the spoon and finally dropped into the bowl before Mrs. Willis answered. "There was a loud noise in the kitchen like somebody banging around, like they were opening up the cupboards and moving dishes around. I would have thought it would wake up anybody sleeping just in the next room, but I know Renee and Sammy can sleep through almost anything."

She dished up another big spoonful of oatmeal into Danny's bowl. "I came downstairs to see what it was but when I reached the kitchen there was no one there, just one of the cupboard doors open that I thought was shut last night. I looked out the window," Mrs. Willis pointed the spoon in the direction of the window over the sink, "but all I saw was moonlight shining on the frost on the ground. It was probably lucky for me that the robber had already gone. Who knows, he might have had a knife and slit my throat."

Buddy poured some milk on his oatmeal and stirred it with his spoon. "How can you be sure it even was a robber then," he asked. "Maybe a squirrel got in somehow, and made the noise. Maybe you even dreamed it. Someone could have opened that cupboard door after you saw it last."

Mrs. Willis nodded and pressed her lips together. "You know, that's just what I told myself must have happened last night, but then when I came into the kitchen this morning I noticed that jar is gone."

Danny had a spoonful of oatmeal on the way to his mouth, but he set his spoon back down in his bowl and looked up at the top of the refrigerator.

Did she mean our jar? I couldn't see it but it might just be pushed back too far for me to see. Only Danny's face said that there wasn't any jar on the top of the refrigerator.

Buddy said, "What jar?"

Mrs. Willis said, "Why the jar with Danny and Annie and Renee and Sammy's allowance in it." Mrs. Willis reached over the table and put her hand on Danny's shoulder. "I'm awfully sorry, honey. Of course, if I had the money I'd make it up to you, but I just don't. I'm afraid it's gone."

Mrs. Willis took her hand away from Danny's shoulder, dished up my oatmeal and put the pan back on the stovetop. She ran a pan full of soapy water for dishes like nothing had happened.

No necklace, no purse.

Danny put the spoonful of oatmeal into his mouth. He tried to swallow, his throat muscles gulped, but it wasn't going down. I felt the oatmeal lump in my own throat, even though I hadn't started eating.

No dress, no chocolates.

Danny stopped trying to swallow. He chewed on the oatmeal while his eyebrows scrunched down to think. Then he laid down his spoon and finished chewing the bit in his mouth.

"Do you have another jar?" he asked Mrs. Willis.

"Sure I do," Mrs. Willis said, "Do you want to start saving

again?"

"Yes," Danny said, "But this time I'll hide the jar. No robber is going to find it again."

#

We lost the Easter clothes that Mama sent for Easter.

That happened in the summer time when the Willises held an auction in the barn every Saturday night. Mrs. Willis said our Easter clothes were stored up in the loft of the barn and someone must have got up there during the auction and stolen them.

But I didn't lose my stuffed tiger or my favorite doll because I gave those away to the girl whose mother was dying.

I never actually met the girl whose mother was dying. Mrs. Willis took Renee and me along once when she visited the woman who was dying, but she told us to wait in the car so we wouldn't disturb her. We hoped the girl would come out and talk to us or play chase with us in the yard because it was cold just sitting there, but the girl never came out. We couldn't blame her when her mother was dying like that.

Mrs. Willis came back out to the car. She told us that the dying woman wanted to be baptized Catholic, but her husband said, "Over my dead body," and wouldn't let the priest in the house. Mrs. Willis wondered what would happen to that child when her mother was gone and she was left with her heathen father to raise her.

So when Mrs. Willis told me and Renee that it was the girl's birthday but she wouldn't get any presents at all unless we gave her some of our toys, I wanted to give something to the girl whose mother was dying and whose father wouldn't let a priest in the house.

At first I thought that I could give her the new baby doll that I got for Christmas. She would like the new baby doll. It was a nice doll, but it wasn't my best doll. Then I knew that the little girl whose mother was dying needed my best toys. She needed my favorite baby doll, the one I got when I was really little, the baby doll who had to go to the doll hospital once, I'd had her so long; the one with the big painted blue eyes, that didn't open and shut like the eyes of the new baby doll but just stayed open, and with the molded plastic hair; the one I loved the best.

The little girl whose mother was dying needed my favorite stuffed tiger that I slept with every night, the one that was almost as old as my favorite baby doll. My tiger would stay with the girl when her mother was gone

Mrs. Willis looked disappointed when I gave her my toys but I knew the little girl would like them because they were the best.

We lost a lot at the Willises, but I didn't lose my best doll, didn't lose my favorite tiger, because I gave them away.

#

August came, and Mama was coming soon, Mrs. Willis said, two more weeks.

With Mama just coming out of the hospital, Mrs. Willis said, she wouldn't be so strong. It would be hard for Mama to stand up to do a lot of ironing. But guess what, coming into the auction to be auctioned off was a clothes press and if Mama had that she could sit down in front of it and just feed the clothes in between two rollers. The clothes would come out nice and pressed.

Normally the clothes press would be much more expensive but Mrs. Willis thought she could persuade the owner to let it go for the thirty two silver dollars and the other twelve we'd saved again from our allowance, 44 dollars altogether.

It would be such a nice present for our mother and it would make sure she didn't land right back in the hospital again trying to do too much when she wasn't that strong.

A box of chocolates, a necklace, a new purse, a dress.

A clothes press was not the present I planned for Mama.

But according to Mrs. Willis that clothes press would be just the thing to keep Mama out of the hospital. She told us about it again and again.

"What do you think?" Danny asked me.

"I don't know," I said, "but I don't want her going back to the hospital."

We sat on the porch, where we went to talk away from the Willises. Danny slipped away from Buddy more and more, became more my brother again, not one of the boys, now that Mama was coming soon. Danny talked to me again like he had back in Springfield.

Danny scrunched his eyebrows down like he did when he was thinking hard and wrapped his arms around his knees. "I don't know," he said, "I don't know about nervous breakdowns." Danny sat up straighter. "We'll say yes," he said, "when Mrs. Willis asks us again, we'll say yes. We'll get the clothes press."

He was right. I breathed a deep breath. "Yes," I said, "Let's get the clothes press."

But Mrs. Willis didn't ask us again before Mama came two days early.

Danny and I leaned back in the shade of the back porch again after swimming, to stay cool as long as we could and to think about Mama coming; Sammy and Renee were there too. Our first look at Mama was through the criss cross wires of the screen door, criss crossing in front of Mama, some of the crosses lost in the sun glare on the screen, some of Mama lost in the bright glaring sun, but enough left so we saw it was her.

"Mama," Renee shouted and Mama was there, Mama's hair a little different. She wore a dress I hadn't seen before, plain lavender. She pushed the screen door. The door squeaked as it swung open.

Mama stepped through the doorway onto the porch and there she was, the same as when she left us with the Willises.

Sammy said, "Mama" too, and I would have gotten up to run to her, but I was already running, along with Sammy and Renee and Danny. Mama hugged Sammy and Renee both together, then Danny, then me. She sat down on the porch steps. Sammy got into her lap and Renee held onto Mama's knee. Danny and I sat down on the steps on either side of her.

The lavender dress felt soft against my leg. The smell was fresh laundry and Mama's soap. The sun shone warm between the hard of the porch steps and the soft of Mama's leg.

Nobody talked for a long time.

Danny said, "We planned to have a present for you when you came, Mama."

Mama brushed Danny's hair back with her hand, "That's okay."

Danny said, "We were thinking of a new dress and shoes."

"Or candy," Renee said.

"We have $44 dollars saved counting the silver dollars Daddy brought us," Danny said.

Mama's eyes went to something out in the yard when Danny said 'Daddy,' but they came right back to Danny.

Danny turned on the steps so he was facing Mama.

He said, "But Mrs. Willis said it would be hard for you to iron, that you wouldn't be strong after coming out of the hospital. She said we should spend the money on a clothes press for you so you can iron sitting down. The Willises have one for their auction. Would that really be a good present for you, Mama?"

Mama's leg had gotten tighter but now she breathed a long breath and her leg relaxed. Mama loosened her arms from around Sammy so just her hands held him lightly on his stomach. She said,

"Do you know what I'd really like, what would be a really good present?"

Danny moved closer to Mama and said, "What, Mama?"

Mama said, "That money would be just about enough to buy you all some new school clothes, and that would be a really big help to me if we could use it for that. Would that be okay with you?"

Danny said, "Sure, Mama, if that's what you want. But won't you get tired doing the ironing?"

Mama lifted Sammy up a little further back on her lap and said, "Oh, don't you worry about that. I'm a lot stronger than Mrs. Willis thinks I am."

#

Two days later Sammy sat in the front seat of the blue Plymouth next to Mama driving. Renee, Danny and I rode in the back seat where we could see Mama, her arms on the steering wheel. And, out the back window, we could see the big orange U-Haul trailer rolling behind.

Evergreens surrounded us on either side on the mountain road, trees slanted on the mountain above us on the right, and slanted away from us on the left. Dirt and pine needles and green showed all around us. The sun splashed bright through the branches and shadows every so often. Mrs. Willis was far behind. All the Willises were far behind.

For a long time we couldn't see anything up ahead except a small part of the highway before it twisted out of sight, and other cars that drove towards us on the other side of the road.

Then everything opened up, the road up ahead made a large half circle, going to the right then curving back left. In the middle of the half circle the ledge dropped away. Far down below a river flowed through fields with several patches of smaller trees.

Everything was brighter.

The trees stood out separate against the sky. At the tops their thin trunks were blown over far to one side. They snapped back straight as the wind let up. But an instant later the tree tops whipped back and forth slingshot like before the wind bent them steadily forward again. If it hadn't been for the trees I wouldn't have realized the wind was blowing so hard.

But now the car seemed to be sliding to the left, into the oncoming traffic. At the same time the steering wheel twisted to the left. Then Mama's arms held the steering wheel, gripped it so hard her knuckles went white and all the muscles of her arms strained tight. She turned the wheel right and pressed her foot on the brake.

So far no cars came towards us.

Mama's eye in the rear view mirror looked back.

Out the back window the U-Haul trailer went to the right as the car still moved left. Then the trailer stopped and started sliding back to the left as Mama got the steering wheel turned enough to move the car back in its own lane. But the U-Haul trailer kept going left, over to the other lane of traffic, over close to the ledge. Now the steering wheel turned, on its own to the right, and Mama, stronger than Mrs. Willis thought, held it, turned it back left. The car stayed in the right lane, but the U-Haul was still over in the left lane.

Still no cars came.

The U-Haul began to slide right, and now the car was being jerked over into the left lane again, and the steering wheel rotated left. Again Mama stopped it. But the car and trailer still didn't straighten out. Instead they kept on like that. When Mama was able to get the car into the right lane, the trailer would slide over into the left, and the car and steering wheel would go too far to the right. Then Mama would have to grab the steering wheel, and stop it, and start turning it left, to keep the car from heading toward the mountain side and the trailer from sliding into the opposite lane.

Then it would reverse itself. The steering wheel would go left along with the car, and the trailer would be swinging towards the mountainside. Mama had to turn the wheel right to get the car out of the left hand lane.

The U-Haul jerked left again. This time the U-Haul began to tip as it slid, and then tipped completely over on its side. It blocked the lane on the left, but stopped sliding before it reached the ledge. The blue Plymouth, stopped too with a jerk. I slid against Renee and she slid into Danny up against the door. The steering wheel stopped moving. For a minute, Mama's arms still held and turned it. Then she stopped and laid her head down on the steering wheel.

Mama lifted her head and looked at Sammy then at each of us in the back seat, like she was counting us.

Then she looked outside at the trailer, at the corner of it right up next to the ledge.

If I looked away up at the trees the wind still whipped them around, but down here on the road while Mama looked through the back window at the trailer flat on its side, one corner a few inches from the ledge, everything was still.

No cars came from either direction.

No cars did come, not for several minutes, until a policeman rode on a motorcycle from behind us, and put flares all around the trailer.

The policeman didn't write Mama a ticket because there was no way she could have known about that wind coming up so fast and so strong. The policeman stayed to direct traffic until the tow truck came and lifted the U-Haul trailer back upright. As far as Mama could tell there was no damage done.

We lost a lot at the Willises but we didn't lose everything. We didn't lose the U-Haul trailer over the ledge, because Mama, stronger than Mrs. Willis ever thought, kept the steering wheel straight. It wasn't long at all before we were on our way again in the blue Plymouth, the orange U-Haul with all our furniture behind us, the money for our school clothes in Danny's pocket.

12 Back To Yakima

I started looking for Daddy as soon as the car turned onto the road our old house was on. I figured Daddy had stayed in the house while we were away, and he might still be there, at least for a little while. We drove up in the dark blue Plymouth that Mama bought in Missouri, with the big orange U-haul trailer behind it. Sammy sat in the front at Mama's right because he was the youngest and got to sit there most. He was four now because he had his birthday in August, just before Mama got out of the hospital and picked us up from the Willises' farm in Missouri to bring us back to Yakima. I was the only one that didn't have a birthday before she came to pick us up. In November I would be nine, but now our ages were four, six, eight and ten. Danny was ten, Renee was six. Mama was 27.

Danny and Renee sat in the back beside me. We had to change around who got the window, but right now Danny sat at the left side window and I sat at the right. I watched our house as Mama drove the last ways to it up the street, West 76th Avenue. The tires crunched and little rocks pinged against the bottom of the car, as Mama drove up the gravel road. She parked the car in front of the house on the side of the road, pulling up farther to get the trailer parked too. As Mama parked the car I looked for signs of Daddy. No other car parked in the front - that was a bad sign. No one coming out of the front door, hearing the car parking and running out from the living room where he had been waiting for us. He could be busy. Daddy could be fixing things, just one more thing before we arrived. Give him a minute.

Mama said, "We're home, kids." She didn't move. She looked over Sammy's head through the car window at the house. She had to hold her head down a little to look, and part of her hair fell onto her forehead as she tilted her head forward. Her hair was brown, but it had a reddish tint sometimes, like now when the afternoon sun caught it.

The house looked the same. It still had the white picket fence that Daddy built around the front yard, and the cement porch. The door and the screen door were both closed. The curtains were closed over the picture window in the living room so I couldn't see if Daddy sat there in the easy chair, maybe fallen asleep after working so hard the day before to get everything just right before we came. Maybe Mama was waiting for Daddy to come out and say hello, but Daddy didn't come.

Mama leaned over Sammy in the front seat, unlocked his door, pulled on the handle and opened it. She got out herself on the left side, walked around the car and closed Sammy's door after Sammy got out.

I opened my door and got out, and Danny got out of his, because Mama didn't say, get out on the curb side, like she had every time we'd stopped on the trip back. The road was a gravel road and hardly any cars drove down it. We didn't have to worry so much about traffic in Yakima. Renee slid over across the plastic seat and got out on my side, shut the car door after her, but she didn't lock it. Mama didn't say to lock the car door, not in Yakima.

Mama got a key out of her purse, her soft black purse, not the shiny dress up one, to unlock the front door. She didn't knock for Daddy to let us in, but pushed the door open. The living room looked just the same as we left it, the dull green couch under the picture window, with the matching easy chair against the wall to the right and one of the end tables with the lamp in the corner between them. The coffee table in front of the couch, and the big TV, not portable like the one Mama bought in Missouri, against the opposite wall. The beige rug on the floor. On the wall above the TV set a picture of an avenue with lines of trees on both sides getting smaller and smaller in the distance. But Daddy wasn't there. He wasn't there watching the TV turned up loud, so loud he didn't hear the car coming up the gravel road, or the key turning in the lock.

As soon as I could I went out to the back. In the back yard were the swing set, slide and sandbox that Daddy made for us a long time ago, before I was even old enough to go to school, the sandbox filled with sand from the sand works that we had all ridden out in the car to get. I sat in a swing, a board painted white, hung with rope. I put my hands around the rope and pulled back, pumped the swing once or twice to try it out again, then I let it slow down, and leaned way back to look at the sky and back still farther, letting my head hang back loose, to see the upside down row of tall slim trees marking out the boundary of our yard from the empty lot behind it. I stayed that way leaning way back, until the swing settled down to nothing, stayed there even longer, feeling a little dizzy, but not like I could fall off, no, like I'd never fall off, not here, not home, not in Yakima.

On my way back inside I stopped to look at the back porch. Daddy built the porch, shoveling cement out of a cement truck into a frame he'd made, leveling it with a rake and a hoe and a flat tool with a handle. Before the porch dried, Daddy had called all of us kids, had each of us press a hand and a foot into the wet cement, four handprints, four footprints, and below them Daddy wrote with a stick our names, Danny, Annie, Renee, and Sammy, and "1958."

I touched the print of my foot, felt each toe mark separate from the foot, felt the rough concrete on the ball of my foot and the heel. With one finger, I traced over the path of the stick that Daddy had used to write my name, traced every letter A - N - N - I - E. I spread out my hand, put my 1960 hand over the 1958 hand. My fingers spread out way past where my 1958 fingers had gone. I let them spread, didn't try to scrunch them up to match the old shape, because there was no way at all that my 1960 hand was going to fit into 1958.

Part Two: Fall 1960
13 Barely There

Ray, our neighbor, watered his yard with his old green hose. The grass in Yakima where it almost never rained was thick and green because of the water from the Naches River and the Yakima joining here on their way to the Columbia, giving us irrigation water, plenty of it.

When he saw me Ray took one hand off the hose, and brushed his spread fingers back through his short hair. He asked, "How does it feel to be back in Yakima?"

I moved my barefoot toes around in the grass, Yakima grass, cool on the hottest day. I said, "It feels good."

Ray nodded, a nod like, of course. He put a hand in the pocket of his baggy gray trousers. "Yes," he said, "Yakima is the best place to live."

#

Our house, our neighbors still living beside us, even the grass, made me think that Yakima was just the same as when I left. I couldn't wait for the first day of fourth grade at St. Paul's school to see Leslie and Becca.

I'd met Leslie before we ever left Yakima on the very first day of first grade at St. Paul's. His mother brought him. He cried when she was going to leave so she asked me if he could sit in the desk behind me. We played together so much the other kids teased us, *Leslie and Annie up in a tree, k-i-s-s-i-n-g, first comes love, then comes marriage, then comes Annie pushing the baby carriage.*

Every day of first and second grade Leslie walked part way home with us. We parted at the top of a hill by Leslie's house, as Danny and I continued on down. One day Leslie had yelled at me from the top of the hill, "Catch, Annie!" He reached into his pocket for something. He kneeled on the street and rolled it down the hill towards me.

The baby blue boulder and the cat-eyed marble rolled straight to me. The other two marbles, the green and white, and the solid green went to my left and my right, but Danny caught them and handed them to me.

Leslie walked back and forth, a shadow against the sky way up there at the top of the hill. He stopped pacing and stood still in his gray corduroy pants, and short-sleeved white shirt, just like my brother's gray pants and white shirt, but different on Leslie. Leslie not so thin, not so tall as my brother, just looked at me, with eyes that I couldn't see now. When I was closer, his brown eyes went from darker brown near the center to lighter brown around the edges.

I yelled up at him, "Thank you."

Leslie barely nodded his head before turning to walk back the other way, towards his house. But just before he rounded the corner Leslie turned back to me and waved, his arm raised up high against the sky. I waved back with the hand that held all of the marbles until he walked out of sight.

All four of the marbles, big ones, boulders, shooters. The kind you only get one or two of in a pack of marbles.

"Let me see those," Danny said, and held out his cupped hand. I handed him all of the marbles, one at a time, the two he caught and the cat eye and the baby blue. Danny held his shooting hand up against the baby blue, made like he was going to flick his thumb out and shoot it out of his palm, into the street, but he didn't.

Danny said, "Wow, these are good ones. He must have given you his best shooters."

I held out my hand and Danny dropped each of the marbles into my palm; each one dropped with a weight like a stone. I put the baby blue into my shooting hand, and tested out how it would feel to shoot it. Then the solid green, and the green and white, finally the cat-eye. Leslie's best shooters felt just right.

But now, in fourth grade, Leslie wasn't in my class at St. Paul's. When I looked around the playground at recess, I didn't see him anywhere.

Becca was still there out on the blacktop at recess, Becca with the front teeth that stuck out just a little, with the hair so blond it was almost white, but now we didn't walk around the blacktopped playground the whole recess with our arms around each other's shoulders like we had all through second grade. We didn't play at being Pixie and Dixie, the mice from the cartoon.

Becca, with the long skinny legs, with the knobby knees, didn't point to something or someone on the playground, and say, "See that, Pixie," and I didn't answer, "Yes, I see, Dixie."

Instead she was in a different fourth grade classroom from me, and when I asked her to play, Becca said. "I can't. Our teacher won't let us play with kids in other classes."

After I crossed all the states between Washington and Missouri getting back to her, a rule kept us apart. When I cried, she put her arm around me and found another girl to ask, "Would you play with her, because she doesn't have anyone to play with?"

When the girl said yes, Becca was gone.

#

Instead of Daddy, Todd came around, Todd with the big arms and the bulging muscles.

Mostly he just went out with Mama, but once he took us on a picnic. He showed us how to shoot up tin cans with his rifle. He raised up the rifle and looked down its barrel at the cans on the stump. Todd opened up the gun and filled it with bullets then closed it back up again. He raised the barrel up, then slowly lowered it back down, lined it up again and pulled the trigger. His finger took forever to squeeze all the way, but it still made me jump when the gun made a loud sound and one of the tin cans jumped up off the tree trunk and onto the ground. Todd shot again and another can hopped but only fell onto the tree trunk. One more time and all the cans had fallen over.

Todd pointed the barrel down to the ground. He had on a blue T-shirt with short sleeves stretched tight by the muscles in his arms. His blue jeans were tight too. He walked to the sawed off tree trunk and put all the tin cans back up, stacked them, one on top of the other two. Todd rubbed the short hair on his round head and said to Danny, "How about it, sport, want to shoot up some tin cans?"

Danny jumped up from the ground, and wiped his dusty hands on his jeans, slapping them against the denim. He reached out towards the gun, but Todd didn't hand it to him. Instead Todd held the gun, barrel down, while he walked around to the back of Danny. Then he raised the gun up to Danny's arms.

Todd said, "Here, put your left arm here to support the barrel."

Danny did and Todd said, "Okay, put your right hand around the trigger, but don't put your finger on the trigger yet." Todd still used his left arm to support the barrel and had his right arm near the hilt of the gun while Danny moved his hand onto the trigger area and spread his legs apart for balance.

"Good," Todd said, "Now lift the gun up to your eye level and look through the sights down the barrel."

Danny lifted the gun and as he did it Todd moved his hands away so that Danny held it by himself. Danny had to bend his knees then force them straight to hold the gun up on his own. He got it up with the hilt wedged up into his shoulder and his head bent down to look through the sights. The barrel wobbled so Danny had to keep bringing it back to the center and look down the sights again. But then he got it almost still, just a little shaking back and forth.

"Got it?" Todd asked.

"Yes," Danny said.

"Then keep the barrel where it is but raise your head up so the gun doesn't kick back and hit you in the eye when you pull the trigger."

Danny lifted his head up away from the sights. His hair fell across his forehead again, but he didn't jerk his head like he usually did to get it back on top of his head. Instead he moved his head up slowly. I couldn't see his face but I imagined he kept his eyes on the target.

"Good," Todd said. "Now, don't move the barrel, but just put your index finger on the trigger and pull it back as slow as you can."

Danny's finger on the trigger moved back slowly and Danny's arms trembled with the weight of the gun, then there a loud noise burst out and the hilt of the gun came back and knocked Danny's shoulder so he stumbled backwards.

Todd reached out to the gun to steady it and laughed, "She's got a kick doesn't she?" When Todd laughed the top part of his cheeks filled out like apples.

Danny took a step forward and nodded his head, then he looked to the tree trunk at the tin cans but they all sat there just like before.

Todd looked at Danny, then at the cans, "Well, Bud, let's give the other kids a chance and then you can try again." He lifted the gun up out of Danny's arms, holding the barrel pointed up again.

But Mama said, "Annie can try it if she wants, but not the two younger ones," worry in her voice.

So Todd turned to me, "How about it, want to try?" When I nodded yes he held the rifle in his left hand, moved behind me and put his other arm around my shoulder. He moved the barrel of the rifle down and lifted the hilt up close to my shoulder. He helped me get my hands on it like he did with Danny. I could feel his muscles under his T-shirt in his arms and his chest and he had some kind of perfumey smell on his face when he bent down over my head, maybe aftershave, not like Daddy's smell, from the gasoline and grease from the service station and the gritty lava soup that Daddy used to wash grease off his hands and arms.

When Todd moved his hands from the gun, I could barely lift it up to look down the barrel. Todd showed me the two little strips of metal to use to get the target in the center. The barrel of the gun kept dipping down so I had to lift it up and line it up again. Then I pressed the trigger, and I tried to do it slow but the gun was slipping away so I just fired it.

The gun jumped back and hit me hard in the shoulder so I probably would have dropped it except that Todd had hold of it now too. The noise sounded so much louder. My right ear hurt with the noise and my right shoulder hurt where the gun banged into it.

The tin cans stayed just the same.

I never wanted to fire that gun again.

#

Everything was the same in the house, except for the two sets of bunk beds brought back from Missouri, one set for Renee and me, instead of the big double bed we used to share. On the top bunk I dreamed of a planet, a planet covered with thick trees and birds with colored beaks, rich with leaves and birds and color. The leaves felt cool and soft like Yakima grass. I never touched them, but I knew how they felt.

This planet was right next to mine. The two planets came so close they almost touched, maybe did touch, nudged each other, then bumped apart, like balloons might touch then move apart. The planets so close that I could step right over onto the planet of birds, so close I almost did, but first I woke up.

#

Daddy didn't pick us up on Sundays like he had right after the divorce. He didn't come before school started. He didn't show up even after school started. Daddy didn't come at all until my birthday in November.

Becca had made it to my party, and some other girls. All of us had gathered in the dining room to take a turn to hit the piñata with a blindfold over our eyes, when someone knocked at the front door. Mama finished tying the scarf to cover Shannon's eyes, before she said, "Just a minute, girls," and went to the door.

Shannon whacked my brother's bat through the air. Becca and I kept close to turn her back to the piñata and away from the other girls. I didn't notice Daddy until he was right in the dining room, next to me.

Then I didn't notice Daddy so much as Mama, staring at Daddy, her eyes narrower and her mouth pushed together so her lips looked thin.

Daddy wore jeans and a plaid shirt, what he usually wore when he hadn't just come home from work. He had something in his hands that he held in front of him, something made of dark cloth that hung down with his hands grasping it at the top.

When we first came back to Yakima, to our house, I expected to see Daddy in the house because that was where he'd always been. When he wasn't there, and he didn't come, I had to put him out of my mind to keep from wanting him. Maybe that was why Daddy looked so out of place in the white house, in the dining room that used to be the kitchen before Daddy built the new kitchen.

Daddy must have felt it too because he kept his head bent down and shifted his weight from one foot to the other, back and forth, and he held whatever it was in front of him like he wanted to hide behind it.

Seeing Daddy, I had to miss him all over again, want him again. Then be glad to see him.

I started to say, "Hello, Daddy."

But I didn't say it, because Mama spoke first, her voice cold and angry and so low I think only Daddy and I heard her.

She said, "You could at least have wrapped it."

Mama was so angry, but she didn't let it out so my friends could see. She stood still and perfect, but her face was tight and pale now when it had been warm and relaxed. Mama stood up so straight in her good dress, with just a little tremble in the thin calf of her leg.

Mama turned away from Daddy, back to the party.

But Daddy stood there still and he lifted his hands up and away from his body so the dark cloth dropped down all the way, and it was a dress, dark green. He shoved the dress out towards me, and I took it, but Daddy's hands stayed out in front of him like he was still holding onto the present.

I saw the dress but I looked at Mama to see why she was so angry that Daddy brought me a present. But Mama was already tying a scarf on the next girl to hit the piñata.

Daddy said, "Well, happy birthday." He turned around and walked in long, fast steps so he had almost reached the door before I got it out.

"Bye, Daddy," I said. Too late to run after him, and there was my party, and Mama, watching, I knew, though she acted busy with my friends.

Then he was gone, only the dress left in my hands.

The color came back to Mama's face. Her face went back to being the face she had for my friends whenever they were over, the face that smiled. Before Daddy came Mama smiled like she was happy. Now she just smiled.

When I started to set the dress down on the table with the rest of my presents Mama said, "Why don't you take that dress into your bedroom for now and come back for your turn." Her voice sounded the way it did when she talked to my friends or when she talked to me when my friends were there.

So I didn't look at the dress. I ran to my bedroom, tossed it up onto my bed and came back for my turn at the piñata.

#

After the party, after I found places for all my new things in my room, then I climbed onto my bunk and spread out the dress on top of the covers. The dress was so soft that when you laid it down it didn't keep its shape but just made a heap. It was dark green, but not a solid dark green. It was like there were other colors, lighter and darker green and even other brighter colors inside of the dress, just under the surface. But not so you could touch it and say, "This is red." It was just that the red was in there somewhere.

My dress was rich, like the planet of birds.

The next morning when Mama woke us, I said, "I'll wear my new dress today."

But Mama said, "No, you should keep it for good," which meant for church because I wore a uniform to St. Paul's school.

It seemed every time I wanted to wear my dress, Mama would say, "You wore that last week, why don't you wear something different for a change?" So I'd put on something different.

But alone in my room, I'd reach in my closet and feel the soft of the dress, take it out of the closet and hold it near the light to see the colors all there under the surface, so rich, so beautiful, the colors I couldn't quite touch.

#

Then, so quick, before Becca and I found our friendship again, before Yakima was a part of me again, we left for California.

The night before, Mama and our neighbor, Pat, filled up a U-Haul trailer with all our furniture. While our mothers worked, Danny, Renee, Sammy, me and Pat's kids, Steve, Little Bill and Mikey, played hide and seek in the dark. Usually we never got to stay out after dark. Even though it was Christmas vacation it wasn't really cold, not if you ran a lot, not very cold even while we hid and waited for the coast to clear to run for base. In the dark it wasn't so hard to find a good place to hide: flat against the side wall of the house so you blended with it in the dark; standing like a tree between the small trees that separated our back yard from the empty lot behind; laying face down on the slide in the backyard. All kinds of places that didn't work in the day, did work when you blended in with the dark.

Mikey called out, "Allee, allee, all come free!" He'd caught Danny sneaking in. Now the rest of us were home free.

Danny counted, his face flat against the bark of the big tree in the front yard. I could see him from my hiding place behind the bush that grew by the front porch. I knelt there, holding the little branches away from my face. Danny almost finished counting, "..94, 95.." when Mama shouted, "It's time, kids, time to come in."

The twigs of the bush scratched against my face when I climbed out and up onto the cement front porch. I leaned back against the white boards of the house to wait for the others to leave their hiding places. My legs felt achy, growing pains, Mama said. I stretched out my legs and leaned my head back against the hard of the house. The sky was lit up by a half moon and a slight wind blew, so on the corner lot across the street the tall tree waved dark in the wind against the lighter dark of the sky. The light from our living room spilled out of the open door onto the front porch to the dirt road in front of the picket fence where Mama and Pat still packed a few more boxes into the U-Haul. The light inside the U-Haul trailer lit Pat and Mama around the edges, but I couldn't see what they looked like. They were just dark shapes outlined by light.

Mama closed up the trailer. Now Mama and Pat turned into dark shapes without their bright outlines. Sammy, Renee and Danny reached the porch. Steve, Mikey and Little Bill followed Pat next door.

Coming closer to the light of the house, Mama changed from a dark shape to Mama, her eyes tired. She moved her arm and shoulder up and down like she was trying to get a kink out. Then she came on inside for her last night in Yakima.

14 Uncle Gary

When we got into the mountains Mama said, "We're going to stay with your Uncle Gary for awhile in California. And I'll find work. Gary says there are plenty of jobs."

Danny, in the front, leaned against the car door, his legs halfway up on the seat. "I didn't know we had an Uncle Gary."

"Well, he's my half brother," Mama said. "He's Grandpa's son from his first marriage before he married your Grandma. He didn't always live with us, but one year he did when I was about twelve or thirteen."

She scanned the road ahead, "I was always getting into trouble that year and Gary would try to talk me out of doing the things that got me in trouble. But when he wasn't there I was the oldest, and even when he was there it was still me who was stuck with watching the four younger kids and doing a lot of the cooking and cleaning. When I got to be thirteen I just wanted to get away from it all for awhile, even if it did get me into hot water later."

Mama had to give her attention to the road and used both hands to turn the steering wheel on a left hand curve, but all the rest of us stared at her: Mama getting in trouble.

She said, "One day riding home from school on the bus, Gary knew that I planned to go home with my friend, Rebecca, and that I hadn't asked permission. I didn't ask permission because I knew that Dad would say no, that I was needed at home, because that was what he always said."

Mama had her window partly rolled down and a cool breeze whipped through the car, and blew her hair back. The air kept Mama awake. The rest of us had sleeping bags to keep us warm. Mama's arms had goose bumps, but she didn't shut the window.

"So all the way on the bus to my friend's stop, Gary tried to talk me out of it. He told me how angry your grandpa would be and pleaded with me to just come on home, but I wouldn't do it.

"Then next day when I did come home, come to find out that Gary told Dad that my girl friend had asked me to come because her mother was real sick and she needed help taking care of her and her brothers and sisters. Gary told Dad that he'd told me to go ahead and go, he was sure that Dad would want me to go. So even though I could see that Dad was fuming about it, he couldn't actually come out and yell at me that time. Maybe he yelled at Gary the night before for telling me I could go, or saying he did."

Mama shivered then and rolled up her windshield. She said, "Your grandma never liked Gary much. Even your grandpa didn't seem to care much for him, but Gary always had a kind heart. No one else ever tried to protect me."

I hoped she'd talk more about Gary. Instead Mama told us about Great Aunt Lorene, who we'd also spend a night with on the way to Gary's, and about her second cousin, Rita, and Rita's husband, Nick. Rita and Nick lived further south in San Diego. All these new relatives we got just by going to California.

#

Mama had said Gary was staying in a hotel, but when she found the place, it looked like an apartment building. 5B was up two flights of outside stairs and off a balcony. Green paint peeled off the old wood of the stair railings.

On Mama's second knock Gary pulled open the door. He was one of those comfortable looking men in loose pants and a baggy sweater. His brown hair, a little long, hung down on his forehead until he brushed it back with a big soft looking hand.

He didn't look like Mama. His eyes were brown and big and he moved slower.

"Well, hello, Barbara," He put his arms around Mama. Mama

rested, leaning against Gary.

He said, "Good to see you again."

Mama pulled back from Gary and her muscles got that tight look again, like she was carrying something heavy. She said, "We left the suitcases in the car."

"Let me meet your kids," Gary said, "then I'll get the bags."

"Danny can help." Mama motioned to Danny, who grinned his open mouth grin, the one that showed all his teeth. He wiped away the strand of his dusty blond hair that had fallen onto his forehead.

Mama introduced the rest of us, then Gary pulled open the screen door. "Come on inside," he said. "I'm sure you need a cool drink after that long drive."

In the cool dark living room a sofa sat against a long wall, with a big chair next to it. A woman sat at the kitchen table in a chair that faced the living room. Her long red hair was tied back, except some of it was loose and fell down the sides of her head. Her eyes were big, but her eyelids half closed over them. Her eyes and her eyelids together were the shape of almonds.

Gary said, "Come meet my wife, Shari."

Shari opened her half-almond eyes into whole almonds and tilted her head back to look up at Gary.

"Shari, this is my sister, Barbara, and her kids." Gary pointed to Danny, said his name, then mine. I stopped leaning against the wall and stood up straight. "Renee," Gary said, "and Sammy." Like he'd known our names forever, but he just met us.

Every time Gary said a name Shari's eyes flickered in their direction just for a second. She said, "Hi, good to meet you," to Mama, and she said, "Hi, kids." But she wasn't paying attention.

Shari's dress was blue and made of some material softer than Mama's cotton one, so it settled closer on her body. Her hair wasn't really red, just what people call red, really light orange, straight and soft. Her eyebrows were thick in the middle, then arched to a point like someone had shaped them. After she finished saying hello, Shari's eyes went almost shut and she leaned back in her chair. There was blue on her eyelids.

Gary pulled out a kitchen chair for Mama. "Have a seat." He motioned to the rest of us. "The couch is real comfortable if you kids would like to sit down."

Renee and Sammy stayed near Mama, and Danny still leaned against the wall. I sat on the couch so Uncle Gary wouldn't think we didn't like it. Then the other kids all sat down next to me. The couch was comfortable. Gary gave us each our own can of coke, crisply cold.

#

All the days at Long Beach were like summer. Every day we played in the big park next to the apartments. We could get balls or checkers, or make things in the craft cottage. We liked to sit up on the low stone wall around the park, and eat candy we'd bought with change that Gary gave us.

We were up there one day when Gary walked up, "Hey, kids, I'm going to take you to see your grandpa."

"Grandpa's here?" Danny asked.

Gary said, "Yeah, in the summer he sells ice-cream in Missouri. Then in the fall he comes out to California to sell it for a few more months. He'll be here a couple more weeks before he goes back to Missouri. I gave him a call and he said he'd like to see you."

Gary took us to his gray curvy car, all gray inside too. On the way he drove through a McDonald's, 3 million sold, and bought us hamburgers, pop and French fries, which we ate on the way, even Gary, his one hand with the hamburger resting on the steering wheel between bites.

Grandpa stayed in just one room in a hotel, most of it filled up with a big bed, with barely room for the dresser at its foot, or the chair to its side. He sat on the foot of the bed, his gray pant legs creeping up as he sat so his brown socks showed more of his skinny ankles. Grandpa had his same short white hair, big nose and glasses just like when I saw him last in Missouri, but it was different seeing him here instead of sitting in the big green chair in the living room of the house in Springfield, Missouri. He seemed smaller. We all sat down beside him.

Grandpa lifted Sammy into his lap, "How are you, young fella?"

Sammy leaned back against Grandpa's chest. "Fine," he said.

"Well, how about the rest of you?" Grandpa asked. "Life been treating you okay?"

We said yes, because that's what you say when grownups ask you that. You say fine, or you say ok. I guess you'd say the same if a kid asked you that, but kids never do.

Grandpa reached over around Sammy to a drawer knob of the bottom dresser drawer. He had to lean forward to reach it so his left arm wrapped around Sammy to keep him from falling, and the sleeve of his blue shirt slipped up, so the muscles on the inside of his arm stood out. Sammy's head looked like it was getting scrunched under Grandpa's head leaning over into it, but Sammy just moved to one side and waited for Grandpa to get done. Grandpa stopped pulling at the drawer knob and used that hand to scratch his mustache where Sammy's hair had tickled against it. Then he tugged at the drawer knob again.

The drawer started out crooked and got stuck after opening a few inches open. Grandpa grabbed on to the drawer front between the two knobs. He jiggled the drawer and managed to get it straightened out and then pulled straight forward. "Got a little something for you guys in here," he said.

He pulled out a lot of little packages, tossing them onto the center of his bed. Each time he leaned over for more packages Sammy got his head out of the way, and Grandpa stopped to scratch his nose or his mustache.

When Grandpa sat up straight again, Sammy got off his lap and climbed right up next to the packages. They were flat and covered with cellophane so you could see what was inside.

"Each of you can choose one," Grandpa said.

I got up on my knees on the foot of Grandpa's bed, so my shoes stayed off the blanket. Danny walked to the side of the bed opposite Sammy. He barely fit between the bed and the wall.

There were Groucho Marx glasses and mustaches, one of those paddles with a ball attached by a rubber string, a slate with a red wooden pencil, a princess necklace and bracelet, toy handcuffs, a pack of green toy soldiers all posed in different positions with their little molded guns.

Renee picked up the princess necklace and bracelet right away and held it up against her shirt. Maybe she thought I'd want it, but I didn't.

"Take your time," Grandpa said. "Make sure you get just the one you want."

Renee laid the princess necklace down beside her. She reached over to the pile and moved some other packages around, but she kept one hand on the princess necklace and after a little bit she held it up against her shirt again.

Danny picked up each cellophane package, looked at it and set it down in a spot away from the ones he hadn't seen yet. I looked at the packages closest to me then slid them over to Danny. Then I started in on the ones that Danny had laid back down. While we looked, Grandpa pulled out the drawer again, picking through it for packages with something different than the ones we'd seen so far.

Where did Grandpa get so many toys?

I picked out the ball and the paddle. Renee took the necklace. Danny took the Groucho Marx face. We all waited for Sammy to choose.

Finally, he reached out for the bag of little green soldiers. Sammy already had some toy soldiers, but I guess he wanted a whole army. He yanked on the cellophane to pull the sides apart, but Grandpa stopped him. "Why don't you wait and take those out later when you're back home, " he said. "That way they won't get lost."

Sammy opened his mouth. Maybe he was about to tell Grandpa that he wouldn't lose the soldiers, he'd take good care of them, because Sammy always was careful to pick up his toy soldiers and put them back in the little cloth bag Mama had given him. But Grandpa said, "Right now I have something else for you to play with." Sammy closed his mouth and looked at Grandpa to see what it was.

Grandpa leaned way over, almost double, showing the thin hair on the back of his head. He put his hands on both drawer knobs and yanked the drawer way out so the front part of it sat on the floor. He reached to the back and pulled out a big handful of long skinny balloons. "You ever play with balloons like this?" he asked.

I said, "No, not skinny ones like that."

Grandpa handed me one. "See if you can blow that up."

So I put the end of it into my mouth, and blew. The first inch of it filled up with air, but even though I blew and blew I couldn't get the air to go in any further.

"Let me show you how to do it," He took the ends of the balloon between his two thumbs and forefingers and pulled his hands apart. "First you stretch it," Grandpa said.

"See here. You suck the end into your mouth to make a little bubble." Grandpa put the closed end of the balloon into his mouth and sucked until the end of the balloon was filled with a small bubble of air. He held the open end of the balloon closed so that the bubble of air wouldn't escape. Then he put the open end into his mouth, loosened his finger hold on it, and began to blow gently.

The balloon started to fill, first from the open end so there was a fat place at each of the two ends of the balloon and a flat place in between. The new bubble finally reached all the way to the little bubble that Grandpa had made at first and then they joined into one big bubble. At first it was like a really skinny wiener all the way from top to bottom. But once the whole length had some air in it, the balloon got thicker around too. But even when he got done it was still real skinny, not like a regular balloon, and it got really long, about a whole yard long. Grandpa tied the end of it then.

"Now," Grandpa said, "if I twist this just right," he started to twist, and the balloon squeaked so I got ready for the loud noise if the balloon should pop. But it was like the balloon had a weak spot where the air went out and there was a twist instead and now the balloon was jointed into two parts.

Grandpa left that joint alone and started to twist another section of the balloon. When that part twisted at its weak spot, Grandpa looped the balloon around so the two weak spots were twisted together and there was a loop like a head and a little foot at the end of the balloon.

He said, "We need another balloon for this one." So he went through the all the steps again with another balloon. Then he twisted and looped the balloons together until finally it looked something like a dog or maybe a baby deer with a pointy face and a tail sticking up.

Grandpa handed a balloon to Danny then and one to me. I stretched the balloon, and Danny stretched and stretched his balloon for a long time. Then I sucked on the end, until I got the little bubble.

Danny sucked on his end, and then blew on the open end, and already his balloon started to fill up a little.

I put the open end in my mouth and blew but even with all the stretching and the little bubble on the other end, it was still hard. The air came out of my mouth and around the edges of the balloon instead of into it. I pulled the opening wider and stuck it into my mouth again and blew very hard. I kept blowing. I couldn't seem to get the air past the first part of the opening of the balloon. I kept blowing. After awhile the part of my neck just under my jawbone began to ache. While I blew it felt like something might burst in there.

At last something in the balloon gave way and stretched into a bubble in the top part of the balloon. Little by little the full part of the balloon got bigger and bigger moving down until it joined with the bubble at the end.

Grandpa had started balloons for Renee and Sammy. Sammy blew so hard that he blew the balloon right out of his mouth, but he just put it back in again. Renee blew and nothing happened. She tried again, but then she just stopped.

When I got my balloon as full as Grandpa's had been, I asked Grandpa to tie it for me.

He showed me how to do it: wrap the end around two of your fingers, so then you can pull the fingers apart to make a space to put the end through and make a knot. I tried, but it was hard and I lost some of the air and had to blow the balloon up again before I finally got it tied.

Grandpa said he could show me how to make a swan or a hat, so I chose the swan. I twisted the balloon to make the joints, and Grandpa showed me where to twist the joints together. The swan had a beak, a long neck and a circle for a body.

By the time Gary knocked on the door, Danny and I had each made a dog, a swan and a hat, and Grandpa had helped Renee and Sammy blow up their balloons and make a swan and a hat.

Grandpa walked to the door with steps that barely lifted his feet off the floor. He opened the door, but he didn't stay and say hello to Gary. Instead he sat back down on the bottom corner of his bed. He didn't even look at Gary standing on the other side of the screen door.

Gary put his hand on the handle of the screen door, but didn't pull it open. He talked through the screen, "Well, kids, guess I'd better be getting you back home to your mother." He shifted his weight onto his other foot and held his head down so his hair fell forward.

Grandpa picked up Sammy's toy soldiers and handed them to Sammy. He put his hand on Sammy's shoulder and Sammy said, "Bye, Grandpa," then walked to the door with one hand clamping the toy soldiers up against his chest, and the other holding the balloon hat down on his head.

Grandpa said, "Bye, young fella."

Gary opened the screen door for Sammy to come through.

Renee had her princess necklace and bracelet in one hand and her swan in the other. She scooted off the foot of the bed, her shorts moving up her leg. Grandpa reached over and put a hand round her back and under her arm to help her off the bed.

"Bye, Grandpa," Renee said, and Grandpa rubbed his hand back through his white hair that stood straight up. "Take care of that swan, now," Grandpa said.

Danny put his left arm through the gap in his balloon hat and through the hole in his swan. He picked everything else up with his free hands. I got hold of my things the same way. Grandpa said, "Well, it looks like you've got everything under control."

So Danny gave him one of his mouth open grins and said, "We sure do, Grandpa. Thanks a lot for the balloons and for showing us how to make things."

"Yeah, thanks, Grandpa," I said.

Grandpa stared down at the floor, When he lifted his head again his face looked the way grownups' faces look when they're not crying but they might if you weren't there. His voice came out a little shaky. "Well, it's not every day that I get to spend an evening with my grandkids."

Danny and I squeezed past Grandpa's knees on the end of the bed. Grandpa patted Danny's back, then he patted my back as I went by him.

"Bye, Grandpa," I said.

Gary had the door pulled open for Danny and me. He closed the screen door after us, and said right through it, "Well, Dad, we'll be going then."

Gary stood on one leg, then the other again, but Grandpa didn't say anything back. Finally Gary turned away, then ran ahead of us to pull open the back car door.

Before he stepped into the car, Sammy said, "See my hat?"

"Sure do," Gary said. "You make that yourself?"

Sammy pulled the hat down farther on his head, "Grandpa helped."

Gary said, "Looks like a good job to me. Just be sure to hold onto it in the car so the wind doesn't blow it away."

"Ok," Sammy said as he stepped into the car and sat down on the seat. He put one hand over his head and used the other to hold the packet of soldiers up against his chest.

Gary helped Renee up on the door ledge because her hands were both full. She said to Gary, "I made a pink swan."

"That's a nice one," Gary said.

Gary closed the back door after he helped me in. Then he opened the door on the passenger side for Danny. He was back in the driver's seat when the screen door of Grandpa's hotel room opened.

"Grandpa's coming," I said.

Grandpa walked past Gary and around the front of the car over to the front window on the passenger side. Danny rolled down the window. He had his balloons all wedged under the front seat and held there with his feet so his hands were free.

Grandpa had another big handful of balloons, maybe 20 or 30 of them. He handed them in to Danny. "Here, this will give you all something to do over your vacation."

"Thanks, Grandpa," Danny said.

Grandpa looked into the back seat and said, "I probably won't see you again before I go back to Missouri. Take care of yourselves now."

"We will, Grandpa," Renee leaned up against the front seat to see Grandpa better.

Grandpa stooped down and looked through the window at Gary who was leaning forward in his seat with his arms resting on the steering wheel. He didn't have any special expression on his face, but he must have felt Grandpa's glance because he turned Grandpa's way.

Then Grandpa might have said something to Gary, said goodbye, or thanks for bringing them, but his eyes went back to Danny, then to us in the back seat, and what he said then was, "Don't you go growing so fast that I don't recognize you the next time I see you."

"We won't," I said, but how could we stop it? Danny always measured another inch on the yardstick, telling me he was lots taller than me now, but he wasn't, barely at all.

"Ok then, goodbye." Grandpa walked around the car and

back to his room. He walked slowly and hitched up his pants so the cuffs of his pants were up high on his leg and his brown socks showed beneath the gray pants. Gary waited for Grandpa to open his door, step in and close the door again, before he started the car, and the whole time he sat still in the driver's seat, resting his arms on the steering wheel. Then Gary turned around toward the back seat.

"Everybody got a good hold on your balloons?" he asked. "Danny," he said, "I think we better get that window rolled up just in case."

Danny rolled it up.

Gary drove then. When he got the car out on the street, he said, "Seems like you had a good time with your grandpa."

I held my arms around all my balloons. "We did," I said.

Sammy leaned against the car door, pushing his hat down on his head. "We made lots of stuff," he said, "and I got soldiers."

Danny asked Gary, "Are you on vacation like us?"

Gary's eyes watched the road and his big hands twisted the steering wheel to turn left at the corner.

"Not exactly. I left my old job. Now I'm looking for a new one."

Danny said, "What do you do?"

Gary said, "I train elephants."

Wow.

"I'm trying to get a new job training elephants at the San Diego Zoo," Gary said.

I said, "Danny and I rode on an elephant once, at the Seattle zoo." There were seats on top of the elephant, like you see in movies about India with princes. The hairs on the top of the elephant stood straight up. I reached my hand out flat to feel them. They felt stiff, almost as stiff as pins.

Gary looked back and smiled at me and his face got all full

again like when he smiled at Mama. "You did, did you?" he said.

Danny said, "I never even knew we had an Uncle Gary." Danny frowned, got creases in his forehead like he was trying to figure something out. "Mom never told us anything about you."

Gary smiled again but not a smile that filled out his whole face, just his mouth moving like in a smile, and his eyes looking sad, smiling at something that wasn't a surprise.

"I'm not exactly her brother," he said, "We had different mothers, so I'm just her half-brother." He drove for awhile without talking. "Most of the time we didn't live together, just for a month or two at a time."

I felt sad too, for Gary, for Mama. If Gary was my half-brother I'd want him to be my whole brother, like Danny was my whole brother, riding next to me on an elephant with hair as stiff as pins; my brother grown up, the elephant trainer.

#

The next day was the day we were supposed to leave for Rita and Nick's, but instead it was the day of Renee not waking up, lying in her sleeping bag so still she didn't seem to even be breathing. The cloth of the sleeping bag didn't move even the slightest bit as Renee breathed in and breathed out. The big bouncy curls on Renee's head, all matted down and damp, didn't move. Mama called the hospital. Her voice sounded like she wanted to talk fast and loud, but forced herself to be quiet and steady, "Like I already told the other nurse, she's got a fever and I can't get her to wake up. She just lays there."

Finally, Mama drove off with Renee.

#

Mama came up to us on the stone wall, without Renee in her arms, but with wrinkles on the top of her dress where Renee had been. She said, "Renee's going to spend the night in the hospital, but she's going to be okay." Mama looked like her legs were about to not hold her up, like even her purse was too heavy for her to hold right now, but she didn't sit down.

I said, "What's wrong with her?"

"She has pneumonia," Mama said. "She's having trouble breathing, but now she's in an oxygen tent to make it easier, and the doctor is giving her antibiotics to clear up the pneumonia. She's going to be just fine."

Mama breathed in deep and shut her eyes. She held tight to her purse with both hands.

Danny jumped down, his jeans making a noise sliding against the stone. "How long will she be in the hospital?"

"Maybe just for tonight," Mama said. "Maybe two nights. The doctor has to wait and see how the medicine works to bring down her fever."

Sammy scooted to the edge of the stone wall, and Mama set down her purse and lifted him the rest of the way down.

"You want to come up to the apartment with me?" she asked Sammy. He nodded his head and leaned against her, his head about to her waist.

Mama picked her purse back up. "The two of you should come in before too long. I'll make us some dinner in awhile, then I'm going back to the hospital for the evening visiting hours. If Renee's awake she may be scared all by herself in the hospital." Mama looked like she might cry, her lip and her voice shaky, but she didn't. She turned around, holding Sammy's hand, and started towards the stairs.

When they were gone Danny said, "She wanted to take that U-Haul back. Now she's gonna have to pay extra.

"But Renee's going to be all right," he said.

#

We'd gone to bed in sleeping bags on the living room floor

- 152 -

before Mama got back from the hospital. The sound of Mama coming in the door woke me, then Gary said something softly.

It was still dark in the living room, but the kitchen light was on. Mama, Shari and Gary sat at the kitchen table drinking coffee.

Mama said, "I'm not sure how I'm going to handle all this, Renee sick, the hospital bill. I was supposed to get that trailer back tomorrow morning. Now we're going to be charged extra for every day it's late."

Gary put his hand on Mama's arm. He looked at Shari and Shari moved her head, side to side, just one time. Gary's face looked like it was about to crumple up, his lip trembling, but he got it smooth again. I don't think Mama saw Shari shake her head or Gary tremble. Unless Gary's hand on her arm trembled too and she felt that.

Gary said, "It'll be all right, Barbara."

Mama moved her arm away to reach for her purse, so Gary's hand was left there alone. She got a cigarette from her pack and picked up the lighter. She flicked the top up and used her thumb to start the flame.

Gary laid his hand down on the table.

Mama breathed in her cigarette, then moved it away from her lips. She said, "I just don't know how it's going to be all right. All the money I've got saved needs to go for a deposit on a place for us to live." Her hand trembled on the cigarette, "I just don't know what I'm going to do."

#

Renee's breath sounded like scraping.

Mama laid Renee down on the couch. She unrolled her sleeping bag and pulled it up around Renee. Renee never moved but one eye opened when Mama lifted her up to pull the bottom of the sleeping bag under her. When Mama pulled her old pajamas off and put the clean ones on, Renee tried to move her arms to make it easier. Once Mama finished Renee's eyes closed again but the cloth of the sleeping bag moved up and down with her breath, and her breath made a noise like scraping, like dry paper bags rubbing against each other.

Renee came home from the hospital Saturday. The next day, she would need to rest more and the U-Haul place was closed anyway. Monday morning we'd leave for Rita and Nick's.

Mama sent us out to the park to play or, she said, we could sit on the floor and watch TV if we were quiet and didn't bother Renee up on the couch, so I sat there and listened between the noises of the TV to Renee breathing, and sometimes it didn't sound quite like scraping. Sometimes the sound was more regular, easy. Sometimes there was no noise, then I looked to make sure the sleeping bag still moved up and down.

#

Sunday morning when I woke only Mama sat at the kitchen table. She hunched forward in her chair and stared at the wall in front of her. Danny got out of his sleeping bag and took his clothes into the bathroom to dress. I got clean clothes and the hairbrush out of the suitcase.

Danny came out in his jeans and striped red T-shirt, his hair combed, and sat down at the kitchen table. Because there was room now he didn't have to sit on the couch to eat. He asked, "Where's Gary and Shari?"

Mama picked up the coffee cup with both her hands wrapped around it and brought it up to her mouth. She sipped, then she held the cup steady in front of her, her elbows braced on the table.

"They're gone," Mama said.

Gone, but they live here. We're the ones who are supposed to leave.

- 154 -

"Gone?" Danny asked.

"That's right," Mama said, "They just took off sometime early this morning while I was still asleep." Her voice didn't sound angry, it didn't sound sad. It sounded like she was just concentrating hard to say the words.

Danny picked up a little box of corn flakes and opened it up. He went to the fridge for milk and poured some into his snack pack cereal box so he could eat it right out of the box.

"Why would they do that?" Danny asked.

Mama braced her arms under the coffee cup and her hands held it tightly. She moved the cup to her mouth. Then she didn't take a sip but set the cup back down on the table. She set it down with two hands, before she let go and picked up her cigarette from the ashtray.

"I don't know. Maybe Gary thought he'd have a better chance of getting a job in San Diego if he went there to look," Mama said. She sucked on her cigarette and blew the smoke out.

Danny said, "Is that where they went? San Diego?"

"I don't know," Mama said. "They left a note." Mama nodded her chin at a piece of paper on the table. "I don't even know if they paid the hotel bill. I don't know if they paid it through tomorrow, or if they just skipped out and didn't pay at all for the whole time they've been here."

Mama set down her cigarette and picked up the note. She looked at the writing on the front, then turned it over and looked at the back, where nothing was written. She laid it back down.

She said, "Annie, come eat your breakfast now."

After lunch Mama let us stay inside to watch cartoons. She said we'd be going to bed early so we could get up early in the morning before it was light out, because if Gary hadn't paid the hotel bill there was no way that she was going to be able to pay it. She said we could sleep in our clothes tonight and that we should brush our teeth before we went to bed so tomorrow we could just get in the car and sleep on the drive. We'd eat breakfast at Rita and Nick's house in San Diego.

15 The House by the Ravine

The house we moved into after Rita's house sat right in front of a big ravine. The ravine was all dirt and the way down to it like a wide giant staircase that had been carved into the hard earth. You jumped down a few feet to a ledge maybe three feet wide, then down again another few feet to the next ledge. It was like that all the way to the bottom.

So the very first time Mama said, *you kids get out from under my feet, go outside and play*, that's where we went. And way along the length of the ravine, blocks and blocks long, behind other houses, other kids, too, ran up and down the steps.

Inside the house, the couch was set up under the window that looked out to the front yard. Mama put the portable TV up on a little table where Renee could watch it.

On the opposite wall, Mama's double bed took up most of the room.

The bedroom was smaller than the living room. Our twin beds were stacked up in two sets, with the two dressers shoved together at the foot of one bed because the door opened at the end of the other. There was just enough space left to get between the dressers and the bed. We had to stand to the side to pull out the drawers.

At night, one at a time, Danny and I stood between the beds and held onto the railings to pull ourselves up to the top bunk.

Up there in the dark we whispered across the space between the beds. It was like camping out, all sharing one tent.

The other rooms were the bathroom and the kitchen with the table squeezed in.

After dinner Mama washed the dishes and I dried. Her hips almost touched the stove when she stood at the sink. When she needed to get past me to clear more dishes off the kitchen table she had to squeeze around, even though I pressed myself up as small as I could against the counter.

#

Maybe the tiny house was why Mama got angry so much more often. Maybe she worried about money still.

The times that Mama got most angry in the house by the ravine were not on Monday through Friday, because those were school days when we were soon out of her hair.

On those days, we got out clean clothes, each of us, one at a time, from the dresser drawers. We changed in the bathroom and brushed our teeth. After breakfast, Mama would tell Renee and me to brush all the tangles out of our long hair. After awhile she'd come sit on the foot of the bed, next to the dresser with the mirror and help Renee. She brushed Renee's hair shiny and smooth. Then she combed through Renee's hair until every tangle was gone.

Then Mama looked at me, and I wanted to run, but it would only be worse to make her so angry, and anyway there was nowhere to run in the little house.

Instead I brushed very hard with the hairbrush. I brushed from underneath because Mama always said not to just brush the top. I did it as fast and as hard as I could so Mama wouldn't think she needed to give me any help. Maybe she wouldn't think it until the timer she set had gone off and we had to leave for school.

Halfway through my stroke, the brush caught on all my tangled hair. I couldn't pull it through. I pulled the brush out and started over again next to the roots.

Mama said, "Haven't you got those tangles brushed out yet?" She said it like she already knew I hadn't. I didn't know what to say.

She grabbed me hard. Her fingers dug into my shoulder.

She said, "Get over here." But she'd already pulled me over

in front of her knees. She pulled a comb through my hair until the comb was stopped by a big wad.

But Mama didn't stop. She kept pulling and I braced my feet to try to keep from going with the comb and falling over. It hurt, but it didn't hurt as much, her pulling at the big tangle like that, as it did when she got hold of a smaller one that she could actually pull through if she yanked hard enough.

This time the comb didn't break through.

"What is this rat's nest? I thought I told you to brush out those tangles." She gave it one more good yank. I lost my balance then and fell against her knee.

She shoved me away, "You brush that hair again, and don't you just be brushing the hair on the top either."

Even though I wanted to brush the outside of my hair smooth and shiny, however tangled it was underneath, I didn't dare. Mama watched every stroke, and said over and over, "Get those tangles brushed out. Don't just be brushing on the top. Get underneath."

I never got to brush it smooth and shiny.

Then the timer went off. It was time for us to walk to school whether my tangles were all the way out or not.

#

The only thing I didn't like at F-Street school was Social Studies which we read together. All those voices, reading out loud how California didn't have enough water, made me sleepy. I'd rest my head against my arm and stay awake just enough to be ready if it got to be my turn to read.

When I first got to F-Street school, Mrs. Costa told me the class was doing all the problems in the back of the math book, but if I got tired of doing math I could read the books on the shelf at the back of the room, or library books, or I could just rest as long as I was quiet and didn't disturb anyone. Those were the class rules.

I finished all the math problems by the second week.

A cartoonist visited our class. He showed us how to start with a stick figure, then flesh it out, until we had a cartoon person holding a baseball bat, little tremble lines around the knees, ready to swing.

So except for half an hour of Social Studies, I could read the whole day, *Hans Brinker and the Silver Skates*, *Little House in the Big Woods*, *California Public School Sixth Grade Reader*. Or I could fill big sheets of manila drawing paper with cartoon figures of baseball players. I could read about baseball and the fans in Mudville, in "Mighty Casey has struck out." Or about Mary and Laura Ingalls getting red mittens and a stick of peppermint candy for Christmas. Laura Ingalls with her new rag doll. "Did you ever see such big eyes?" Hardly any presents, but they were happy.

All day long, every day, not like at home, no one saying, "Get your nose out of that book and go outside to play."

#

After supper, when Mama and I did the dishes alone in the kitchen, sometimes she talked to me, told me things, friendly, like I was a person to her, like another grownup.

I'd stand by the dish rack waiting for another dish, or dry one from a stack already there. Mama had the dishrag in her hand, rubbing the inside of a pan or a glass. The pull chain light bulb overhead wasn't bright enough to really light up the kitchen once it was dark outside so Mama scrubbed to get the dirt she couldn't see.

One time she said, "I'm going to tell you something, but you have to promise not to tell the other kids."

"Ok," I said. I shifted from one leg to another, my legs tired from standing.

She said, "You have to promise not to tell, because it might not happen, and if it doesn't I don't want to get their hopes up and have them be disappointed."

"I promise," I said. "I won't tell."

"You always were the best at keeping secrets." She turned on the hot faucet to rinse a plate and handed it to me instead of putting it on the dish rack. "Rita and Nick are going to help me out, so I think I may be able to take all you kids to Disneyland."

I stopped drying the plate, I just held it there. "Disneyland," I said, "we might go to Disneyland?"

Mama smiled, even though Mama hardly ever smiled now, and almost never smiled when she looked at me. "Yes," she said, "Disneyland. I hope I can. But remember, I can't promise."

"Ok," I said. I started wiping the plate again. Mama washed another and put it in the rack. Disneyland. Our secret.

#

It wasn't on the days we were invited over to Aunt Rita's that Mama got the most angry, because on those days she'd be in a hurry to get going. She'd help Sammy dress, then brush Renee's hair without telling her first to do it herself. Not even looking at my hair to see if it was still tangled, she'd say, "That's good enough. Go get in the car now."

Aunt Rita's house had so much space: An upstairs I never even saw where Mama had slept with Renee when we stayed there before we got our own house. The big kitchen and dining room joined together and the even bigger living room that had glass doors that slid open out to the patio.

The patio had a picnic table and Aunt Rita had puzzles that we could take out there and put together. She had so much space we could just leave the puzzle out and it would be there just the same the next time we came over.

Beyond the patio, the big yard had a fish pond made of ceramic tile. The bottom was arranged with broken tree branches and big mossy stones. It was filled with ordinary goldfish that you could always see, the orange of them standing out against the mossy green, and with some small tropical fish of blue and green and brown that blended in until you saw them move. There was one big fish with a strange name that Aunt Rita told us to look for. I only saw it once, brown and whiskered, only its head poking out from under a big branch. In the shadows and not moving, it looked more like another branch than a fish.

The whole living room was empty because the grownups always sat together around the kitchen table and drank iced tea. Aunt Rita cooked, or sometimes Mama cooked some new, special California food like enchiladas, all crisp with hamburger and melted cheese. Uncle Nick had been a sailor. Now he told stories about deep sea fishing. Some nights supper was fish that he'd caught. Sometimes the grownups included some friend of Nick's who'd fished with him or been in the Navy. Other times Aunt Lorene came down from Santa Clarita for the day.

Aunt Rita's living room had a whole bookcase full of books and a big comfortable chair that couldn't be seen at all from where the grownups sat at the kitchen table. If Mama came into the living room and saw me sitting in that big chair with a book, she might tell me to go outside, but she'd say it nicer, "Take your book out on the patio to read."

Then she'd turn back towards the grownups at the kitchen table and say, "She'd sit inside and read all day if I let her." I'd hear Aunt Rita and Aunt Lorene laugh, but they laughed in a nice way

#

Danny and Sammy had short hair so they could wash it in the bathtub when they took a bath, but Renee and I had to get our long hair washed in the kitchen sink.

After breakfast, on a day that wasn't a school day, and wasn't a day when we went to Aunt Rita's, Mama washed our hair. Usually

- 162 -

Renee went first. She still had to stand on a chair to reach the sink and be high enough to put her head under the faucet. But I just kneeled on the chair that was sideways against the sink.

Mama made me take my blouse off to have my hair washed so I always hoped that Danny would stay out of the kitchen, but if he didn't there was nothing I could do. Mama never told him to stay out, so I couldn't either.

This time, when Mama got to my hair she was in a hurry to be done. She pushed my head down under the faucet and turned it on. The water came out too hot so I tried to jerk it away, but she pushed it down, holding hunks of the hair on my head. Then she changed the water so it wasn't quite so hot. But already she was mad at me. "Hold still," she slapped at my shoulder.

Her fingers pulled my hair away from my head while she lathered the soap, then she scratched and scratched on my scalp, her stomach pressed into my side.

She shoved my head under the faucet so the soap and the water streamed into my closed eyes and my nose. She pulled apart the strands of my hair to get out all the soap while I tried to hold my breath to keep the water out of my nose. After awhile Mama pulled my head out from under the faucet and tested the hair by pulling on a strand of it. If it squeaked it was rinsed all the way. When it didn't squeak, she shoved my head down under the water again.

Afterwards she rubbed my hair hard with a towel, then wrapped the towel around my head.

She said, "Now, you go in the living room and you take that comb and you'd better comb every single tangle out of your hair."

I did, but first I stopped at the kitchen chair for my blouse.

Mama told us to start with the big end of the comb, where the teeth were wider apart, and once that went through, to change to the small side of the comb and get the smaller tangles out.

I hardly ever made it to the small side of the comb.

Danny turned the TV on, and there was Elmer Fudd with his hat and gun and funny voice. Bugs Bunny, always ahead, munched on his carrot while he waited for Elmer.

Danny sat down on the couch beside Sammy, who was on the floor setting up his soldiers. They didn't have to clear tangles out of their one minute combing hair.

Renee's comb had already caught in her tangles.

I scooted down to the foot of the bed, closer to the couch, so I could see Bugs Bunny better.

Mama's voice came from the kitchen, "Turn that TV set down before I turn it off."

Danny got up, and turned the volume. He sat back down.

"Ah, what's up Doc?"

"Did you see a wabbit?"

"I said, turn that TV down."

Danny scooted to the edge of the couch. "I did turn it down, Mom."

"Then turn it down some more."

He turned it down more. It was hard to hear what Elmer Fudd said, and I leaned forward with the comb in my hand.

"Why aren't you combing your hair?" Mama stood in the kitchen doorway. I saw the comb in my hand on the bedspread, instead of in my hair, so I moved it up to the back of my hair and combed down. Mama still stared angrily at me. I looked down at my legs on the bed while I kept on combing.

Then Mama moved, but she went to the dresser, then to Renee.

She said, "Here give me the comb so I can get some of those tangles out."

When Renee said "ouch" Mama didn't pull so hard. She put

her hand on the strand of hair, on top of where she was combing, so it pulled from there instead of from Renee's scalp.

When she finished she sat down at the foot of the bed, next to the dresser, close enough to reach me. I combed with my eyes part way shut, putting all my attention on my hair, as if that would keep her from reaching over and telling me with her slapping hand that I wasn't doing it right.

Mama said, "You might be able to get some of those tangles out if you opened your eyes and paid attention to what you were doing. If you're not watching cartoons, you're falling asleep. You'd try anybody's patience."

I opened my eyes. I didn't look at Mama. I didn't look at the cartoon. I looked at the long ends of my hair, and I moved the comb down to the ends so I could look at it like I was supposed to look at it.

Mama said, "How many times do I have to tell you to comb all of your hair, not just the top and not just the ends?" and she hit my head with her flat hand when she said "top," and she hit my shoulder when she said "ends." I started to close my eyes again, but I stopped myself. I looked at my knees, and I moved my comb underneath my hair, next to the roots, to comb from the underneath side.

Mama said, "Danny, turn that TV down. How many times do I have to tell you?"

Danny said, "Mama, I can hardly hear it."

Mama said, "Ok, that's it. Turn it off."

Danny said, "Mama."

"Turn it off now!"

He turned it off, then sat back down on the couch. He didn't move. His eyes looked to the corner of the couch.

Sammy watched Danny, but Danny didn't seem to see.

Sammy went back to setting up the rest of the soldiers in his bag.

Mama grabbed my shoulder. She jerked me up off the bed and in front of her. She combed down my hair from the top and when the comb caught on a tangle she just pulled and pulled until the comb went through. I held my head as still as I could, straight against her pull. I tried to close my eyes, to not see, without closing my eyes, to concentrate on keeping my head still while she pulled, and not close my eyes when her pulls made sharp pains at my scalp, hold still and not feel.

It can't last forever.

Finally, Mama pushed me away. She looked at Danny. She said, "Don't you just sit there sulking either."

Then to Sammy, she said, "Pick up those soldiers off the floor. Do you think I have nothing better to do than be tripping over your toys on the floor. Pick them up now or I'll throw them out."

Danny got down on the floor and helped Sammy pick up the toy solders. Renee and I helped too. We got them all back into the bag.

Then we all sat up on the couch. I sat on the far end away from Mama and behind Danny. Danny leaned forward with his elbows on his knees. He stared down at the floor, his face all smooth and quiet like he was not going to say anything. Sammy scooted way back on the couch and he had his bag of soldiers held up against him. He kept opening up his bag, looking inside and touching his soldiers but he didn't take any out. Renee, nearest to Mama, glanced at her, then back at the floor and at her knees.

Mama pulled the comb through her own hair. She had short hair and it just slid through. She said, "You all don't have to just sit there like that."

She looked at us all, but mostly at Danny. Not at me, because I kept my head so Danny's body was between me and Mama's eyes.

If I got up it would be to find a book and I'd have to go past Mama to get it from our room. I stayed where I was. Renee and Sammy looked at Danny because Mama did.

Mama stopped combing. She laid her hand in her lap, in the folds of her dress. Her face got softer and her voice got softer. She said, "You all could play a game together. You could play Monopoly."

Danny didn't look at her or move.

"Or checkers."

Danny kept his elbows on his knees and his head down. He said, "I don't want to play checkers."

Then Mama looked hurt. She lifted up the comb and her eyes got narrow. Her chin trembled until she opened her mouth. "Just get out of my sight, all of you. Get out of my sight. You're nothing but a bunch of little brats. Go outside and leave me alone."

Danny grabbed Sammy's hand and pulled him to the door, the bag of toy soldiers in Sammy's other hand. Renee and I followed behind them. Me last.

I closed the front door.

#

Out of the house, there was plenty for us to do:

Run up and down the ravine.

Check out the empty lot on one edge of the ravine to see if a game of work-up baseball was going on. Two kids up at bat, the rest of us fielding. The really long balls that went off the edge down into the ravine were automatic home runs while the fielders raced down the giant steps to be the first to find the ball.

Climb the tree that was the only green in the front yard of dust. I was the only one that liked to do this.

Go to the park, Grover Cleveland Park, where we could check out balls or giant checkers to play on the checkerboard tables.

We stayed out until we got too hungry. Then the rest of us waited at the park while Danny went home to see if we could have a picnic lunch. He came back with a bag of sandwiches, a jar of Kool-Aid, four plastic cups.

Mama was always in a better mood when we got back, supper cooking, the house clean.

#

When I sat in the big chair at Aunt Rita's house, next to the stairs, I could hear the voices of the grownups in the kitchen. When they talked to each other they were nice. They said, Would you like some tea? Yes, please. Thank you. Let me help you with that.

They told each other stories and when they said something funny, the other grownups laughed, even when it wasn't very funny.

Once, during dinner, Mama spilled her glass of iced tea, but no one yelled at her. Rita just handed her a dishrag and filled Mama's glass again.

Not like one lunchtime when I spilled my glass of strawberry Kool-Aid. It spread out on the table around all the dishes of food. Mama slapped me on the shoulder, "Can't you watch what you're doing?"

Then she said to Rita, "She never pays attention. It's a wonder she doesn't spill everything she touches."

Rita made sympathetic sounds to Mama, shook her head and handed Mama the dishrag.

Mama handed me my plate. "Just take this out on the patio and see if you can eat it without knocking anything else over."

She would never say that to one of the grownups. She wouldn't want to hurt their feelings.

One night, back home again after a day at Rita's, I laid up in my bed in the dark, the whole house quiet. Even Danny was asleep now, even Mama. It must be that grownups just didn't realize that children have feelings like grownups do. If they realized, they wouldn't treat kids the way that they do. They wouldn't say the things they say.

It wasn't that they tried to be mean. They just didn't remember.

I turned over on my side, and kicked down my blanket so only the thin plaid bedspread covered me. I lifted my head and folded my pillow in two so it was thicker under my head.

When I grew up I'd remember that children have feelings just like grownups do. I'd never forget.

My head settled into the pillow. I wrapped my arm around it and closed my eyes.

16 Leroy

Mama washed, I dried. When she squeezed around me to pick up more dirty dishes, she joked, "Annie, either this kitchen is getting smaller, or one of us is getting fat."

I didn't want to say that it was her belly poking out farther and farther.

Then Rita's husband, Nick, and his friend Leroy had helped us move out to the roomier house in Chula Vista, five miles from the Tijuana border.

Aunt Lorene and Rita visited now that there was more space.

Aunt Lorene's lips moved even before she talked, and her wide open eyes seemed to sparkle. It may have been her glasses. She said, "I don't think they're even married."

She sat with Mama and Aunt Rita at the dining room table, while I washed the lunch dishes in the kitchen. Rita set down her coffee cup and both she and Mama leaned towards Aunt Lorene.

Aunt Lorene said, "Gary said he and Shari were married here in California, but I checked all the county courthouses around here, and none of them had any record of it." Her gray hair was pulled back in a bun that bounced while she talked. "I think he just told me that so we wouldn't ask questions, and that they never really got married at all."

Mama took a long drag of the cigarette. "I think she's a drug addict," Mama said.

Rita rested an elbow on the table and put her chin on the palm of her hand. She puffed her cigarette, then laid it back down on the ashtray. "Could be," Rita said, "could be."

Mama said, "They hardly came out of their rooms when we were all staying at your house. I think it was because she was drugged up on something."

Rita said, "That could be."

Mama said, "Though I don't see how they could be so brazen as to come there at all, after they snuck out of the place at Long Beach that way. I still don't know if they paid their hotel bill or not."

Rita said, "Probably not, else why would they have left in the middle of the night without saying a thing to you. And it wouldn't surprise me if Shari was a drug addict. I always thought her eyes looked kind of funny."

"That's right," Mama said. "At Long Beach too, her pupils were so big and she seemed to be off in some dream world, not paying attention to the things around her. She hardly spoke a word to me the whole time."

Lorene said, "That may be why they didn't get married. California requires a blood test. She probably didn't want her drugs to show up."

"Imagine that," Rita said, "Couldn't even stop it long enough to get married."

When Aunt Rita visited they stayed up talking even after us kids went to bed. One night I woke. I could see through the door into the kitchen, Mama leaned over the kitchen counter, head in her hands, her big belly up against the counter. She cried and cried, "What am I going to do?"

"Shh," Aunt Rita patted Mama's back. "Barbara, it's gonna be all right."

#

Nick's friend, Leroy, started coming by.

"He plays with the kids," Mama told Aunt Rita. "Clifford never did that, not when they were little."

Mama got happier when Leroy came over. I didn't know if I liked him or not. He did play catch with us, and carry Sammy around on his shoulders sometimes. But I just wanted him to come to make her happy.

When I was little, before the divorce, when things were still okay, Mama would sing sometimes. Not very often, but sometimes. She always sang in a fakey voice, too high or too low, singing that way, she told us, because she couldn't really sing. She said probably none of us kids would be able to sing either, that bad singing ran in the family. But I liked it when Mama sang.

She hadn't sung in such a long time. But when Leroy was coming over, she didn't yell so much. She didn't sit smoking, stare at the kitchen wall, or yell at us to go outside and stay there. When Leroy was coming, Mama hummed while she worked. I liked to be in the kitchen with her then. It was always in the kitchen when Mama sang.

If Leroy kept coming, if Mama was happy, if I was in the kitchen with Mama when Mama was happy, then I might hear Mama sing again. Then everything might be okay.

#

Mama gathered us kids around her. In her something important voice she said, "I'm going to have a baby."

I said, "A baby," all of us gathered close around Mama, the baby inside her.

She looked at us one at a time, at our eyes, in her pay attention way. "The baby isn't Leroy's," she said. "It's Todd's baby." I remembered Todd, with his gun that banged into my shoulder. Mama said, "Leroy knows it's Todd's baby, but you shouldn't ever mention that because we don't want Leroy to feel bad."

She waited a minute, then asked, "You understand? You'll remember?"

Danny said, "Sure, Mama."

I said yes, Renee said yes, Sammy said yes.

A baby. That was wonderful.

#

The reason they didn't get married in California was because California made you get blood tests. After the blood tests you had to wait three days, and they didn't want to wait. That was the reason for our long drive to Arizona in Aunt Rita's station wagon because Aunt Rita and Aunt Lorene came too. They were the witnesses.

We were all crowded in. Even the air that blew in through the wide open windows was hot.

Once there, Danny, Renee, Sammy and I waited in the car. But it didn't take very long. Afterwards we went to a drive through for lunch and a service station for gas and the bathroom, and then the long, hot ride back, married.

The next day Leroy was on and off the phone all day trying to change the date he had to report back for duty. He talked on the phone and with Mama about emergency leave. Then he made more calls about getting a moving allowance to help us all get to Virginia. His voice went on and on. Waiting. Then talking again. Then he got the emergency leave. He got the moving allowance.

Maybe it would be okay.

17 Maybe I Should have Known

Maybe I should have known how it was going to be from the way that Leroy always stood up so straight and looked like his stomach was sucked tight into his chest. Maybe from the way, when he wore his Navy whites with a T-shirt, his arm muscles bulged out, and from how he showed us that he could turn over the sleeve of his T-shirt to hold a pack of cigarettes in there so he didn't even need a pocket.

Maybe I should have known on Mama's 28th birthday, before they got married, when Leroy came over for the celebration. I was at the kitchen table, still eating my cake, when I heard Leroy's voice out in the living room tell how you let kids know who was boss. You didn't have to be mean. If they misbehaved, you didn't have to spank hard, just hard enough to show them who was in charge. Once they knew that, they would behave. It sounded good, that Leroy didn't think you had to be mean, except I wondered what he'd do if it didn't work, and maybe I should have known that the main thing was showing who was boss. The main thing was being right.

Maybe I should have known when Leroy stayed with us while Mama was in the hospital. When Leroy said, "Wake me at 2 o'clock and make sure I'm really awake," so he could visit Mama and the new baby. Danny tried to wake him but Leroy didn't wake up. Then Danny shook Leroy's shoulder, and Leroy yelled at him to stop it. So Danny stopped, and he waited but Leroy didn't wake up. Danny shook his shoulder again, and that's when Leroy punched Danny in the arm and said if Danny didn't leave him alone Leroy would beat the crap out of him. Danny came out to the kitchen where I was making chili in the pressure cooker that scared me because of the little thing on the top that started shaking so I thought maybe it would explode. And, it could too, if you did it wrong.

Danny said he didn't know what to do. Leroy would really be mad if he missed the visiting hours.

"Turn the TV set up really loud." The portable TV set was on the dresser in the bedroom. "Don't get near him. Then he can't hit you."

I dumped the browned hamburger, chopped onions, tomato, tomato sauce from a can and the beans I'd left soaking overnight into the pressure cooker. I put on the lid, twisted it tight and turned the burner on. Then I went with Danny to the door of the bedroom. Renee and Sammy stopped drawing and came with us. But only Danny went inside.

He turned the TV set up as loud as it would go. Then he ran out, shut the door as he left, and all of us went back into the kitchen because we didn't want to be there when Leroy woke up.

 I had to time the shaking on the pressure cooker so the chili wouldn't over cook. I set the timer on the stove when it started. Renee and Sammy went back to their drawing. Danny read his comic, but he kept looking towards the bedroom door.

There was a slap sound on the door, then Leroy rushed through, with his two black shoes in one of his hands, and I couldn't hear what he said, but it sounded angry. He got to the kitchen. He wore his shirt, not just his T-shirt, but it wasn't buttoned. He stopped in the kitchen and put on one shoe - then the other - and yelled at Danny, "Why didn't you wake me up? And what the hell was that TV doing on so loud?"

But Leroy didn't even wait for Danny to answer, or for me to say that it wasn't Danny's fault. He opened up the door and slammed it behind him.

#

There had been an evening back in Yakima, when I watched this television show. It was the end of a series, maybe "Walt Disney

Presents," one of the classics, and I only saw the last episode. Even so it stuck with me. There was a boy. He wore glasses, but they'd gotten broken and so he had to get around half blind. He was staying with a family who mistreated him. I remembered his blinking. Everyone talked about him as if he was some sort of criminal. Then finally came the day that his parents were coming for him. He got his broken glasses back so he could finally get them fixed. But he didn't look happy or relieved. The people he'd been staying with seemed scared of what he might say, but he told them not to worry that he wouldn't tell and it was almost like he wouldn't because he agreed with them about what he was like, that there was something wrong with him. And I felt a sense of recognition like I knew that something like that was going to happen to me. And I should have known.

Maybe I should have known when I couldn't protect my little brother. Before that I could do anything that I needed to do. I thought I could take care of him, but I let him down. I should have been able to protect him. If I'd been the kind of kid that Mama wanted, maybe I would have been able to protect him.

#

For sure, I should have known on the trip to Norfolk, Virginia, Amy just a week old, all of us crammed into the blue Plymouth. Three kids and the huge white wicker bassinet were in the back. One kid was in the middle of the front seat, with Amy in Mama's lap or asleep in the bassinet. One window had to stay shut despite the heat because of the plastic dry cleaner bag that hung on the door filled with Leroy's dress blues. But we left in the evening so the little bit of air from Danny's side was enough. At first it was nice to sit there and watch the sky get darker, traveling away from lit up buildings until there was just highway, and the stars the only light.

I was tired, but with the bassinet against the window there

was nothing to lean against. Renee and I had to sit up straight and try and lean back against the back seat, stretching our legs out as far as we could to be more like laying down. Sometime in the night we did fall asleep. I know Renee did, because I saw her asleep, and I must have, because I kept waking up, looking out through Danny's window to see the stars and the dark.

The car had stopped when I woke up next, but it wasn't daylight yet. It was that time of the early morning when you could just begin to make out the outline of things in the places outside where the car's headlights weren't brightening it up. Almost always when you see that time of the morning there is something special happening, usually being woken up to travel somewhere, or waking up early from the strangeness of an unfamiliar place like the loft of the farmhouse at Grandma and Grandpa Mill's in Missouri.

Mama held Amy. "Annie, if you're awake reach into the bassinet and get me one of those bottles of formula."

I handed it up to her.

She said, "Leroy, we're going to have to find a restaurant to stop at to warm up the baby's bottle. She's going to realize she's hungry any time now."

Leroy said, "I'll take the next exit and look out for a truck stop. I'm getting sleepy anyway. Maybe I can catch a nap soon."

Mama said, "Just get me some coffee when you go in to get the milk warmed up. Once the baby falls asleep again I can take over driving for awhile."

Amy was making little crying noises by the time Leroy pulled into the truck stop parking lot. When he opened his door, Mama handed him a rolled up diaper and said, "Here, take this dirty diaper and put it in the plastic bag back there. We'll have to wait to wash them the next time we stop at a motel."

Leroy took the diaper with the tips of his fingers and held it away from him on the walk around to the trunk.

Before he got back with the warm bottle Amy was crying for real and Mama jiggled her up and down, saying "there, there, just a few more minutes," and "God, I wish to hell he'd hurry up."

The crying woke up Danny but Sammy and Renee just slept on.

Danny lifted his head off the back door window, "Where are we?"

I said, "I don't know."

Mama heard him. "Someplace in Arizona still."

Danny said, "Arizona, we've already been there. It's only one state over."

Mama picked up the map on the dashboard with one of her hands, while she still jiggled Amy. "Turn on the overhead light."

He flipped it on, and it was too bright then.

"Arizona goes on for quite a ways. Go back to sleep and maybe when you wake up again we'll be in New Mexico, maybe up in the Rocky Mountains."

#

When I woke again we were in mountains, coming down. Roads on mountains always seem so narrow, even if they're two way. Sometimes there's a metal rail on the edge, sometimes just wood, or none at all, like these mountains, which just had a shoulder, not that wide. The dirt was reddish brown, sprinkled with pine needles.

After breakfast we were back on a wide highway, two lanes on each side.

Danny leaned his head against the edge of the window. His hair blew back. It had been awhile since his last haircut. He pointed to a pickup truck in the next lane. "Look," he said, "the license plate. New Mexico, Land of Enchantment."

The backseat was already hot so I was scooted up on the seat, trying to keep a space between me and Renee who was coloring, and between me and the scratchy bassinet.

"Land of Enchantment," I repeated. "Do all the states have nicknames?"

"I don't know," Danny said, "but Washington had one, the Evergreen state, and California's is the Golden State."

"Let's see how many we can find."

All we came up with before lunch was Arizona, *the Grand Canyon State*, and Arkansas, *Land of Opportunity*. Most of the plates were New Mexico, and most of the ones that weren't didn't have anything on them.

After lunch Mama had Leroy move the bassinet up front next to her, because Leroy drove again after his nap. Sammy moved into the back next to Renee. That left me the window but I couldn't open it because of Leroy's dress blues.

We ate supper in the car in a grocery store parking lot, bologna sandwiches. Mama got the bologna and some milk right then because there hadn't been room in the car to take the cooler. After Mama got back from shopping Leroy left to take the bottle into a restaurant to be heated.

When he got back Mama woke Amy to feed her.

Leroy handed Mama the bottle and took the bologna sandwich she handed him. Leroy said, "I don't see why we all couldn't have just gone in and eaten in the restaurant. Makes me feel stupid to be asking for a bottle to be heated when I'm not ordering anything."

Mama said, "You got your coffee, didn't you."

He said, "Even so, they make you feel like you're asking a lot when all you're getting is coffee."

"What are we supposed to do then, stop and spend ten or

twenty dollars every four hours just because we need a bottle warmed?" Mama moved Amy in her lap. "Warm it under the hot water faucet in the restroom then. You know we talked about trying to save from the travel expense money in case we have to stay in a hotel for awhile while we look for an apartment."

Leroy turned around to the steering wheel. "Yeah, yeah, I know," he said. "Sorry, forget I said anything." He laid his bologna sandwich down on the dash and started the car.

Mama finished feeding Amy, then laid her back down in the bassinet.

"Can I make you another sandwich?" she asked Leroy.

Leroy shook his head.

Mama said, "How about anyone else?"

Danny said, "I'd like another."

She made it and handed it to him, then poured the rest of the half gallon of milk into a paper cup and handed that to him too. She said, "Drink this too, it's going to go sour if you don't. And, all of you, be sure and tell me if any of you get hungry again, because we won't be able to use that bologna after tonight. There's no way it'll stay good in this heat."

Then no one said anything and I got sleepy with the quiet and the car moving and leaned back on the seat. My head fell against the window, and I felt the soft padding of the cleaner plastic over the dress blues. I knew I should move but I didn't. My head wasn't going to wrinkle anything.

"What do you think you're doing?" Mama's voice woke me up. Her eyes looked back at me in the rear view mirror, then she turned around, reached over the back of her seat and slapped at me, but only the tips of her fingers got my shoulders.

"Get off those clothes," Mama said.

I sat back up straight.

She said, "I'd better not see you anywhere near them again."

Then I wished I wasn't sitting by the window, that I was sitting anywhere else. Now I'd have to keep myself awake and sitting straight up to make sure I didn't relax anywhere near those clothes. I didn't see why they couldn't have gone in the trunk so the window could be rolled down and at least make a little bit of a breeze, but I couldn't say that to Mama. I couldn't do anything but sit there and wish to not see her eyes in the mirror.

Somehow even sitting up like that I still went to sleep because the next thing it was already dark and Leroy was angry at Renee, saying, "The next time I have to say something to you I'm going to stop the car and give you a spanking." I wondered what she could have done.

Renee scooted way back on the seat. She put her hands together on her lap and sat very still, like Renee was good at.

All of us sat up straight, except Danny who had a door to lean against. We all looked straight ahead at the back of Leroy's seat; all of us quiet. Even Sammy didn't move. It got darker so outside we only saw headlights coming closer on the other side of the highway, and the taillights of the cars in the lane beside us.

It got dark enough and cool enough I could even feel the air moving on my legs like I couldn't when it was so hot during the day. The cool air let me feel separate from the others when before I just felt all crammed in together.

Finally, Renee relaxed. She leaned way back against the seat and stretched out. When she stretched her legs one foot kicked against the back of Leroy's seat. She pulled it back right away and she sat back up straight again.

Leroy didn't say anything, but the car slowed down. He drove it over on the dirt shoulder of the highway, and stopped. He turned around in his seat all the way, and he stared at Renee and his face looked all quiet, a rigid quiet like you are holding all the pieces still.

He said, "What did I tell you?" His voice didn't get loud angry, it was quiet like his face. "Get out of the car." He opened his door and put one leg outside.

Mama said, "Just what are you doing?"

Leroy said, "I'm telling her to get out of the car so I can give her the spanking she deserves."

Mama said, "The spanking she deserves. Why does she deserve a spanking? What about all the things that Annie has done today? What about when she leaned against your clothes and wrinkled them?"

Leroy pulled his leg back into the car and turned towards Mama. "I told her if she kicked my seat again she was going to get a spanking."

Mama said, "She barely touched your seat. At least Renee helps me whenever I ask. She doesn't hold back and do things as slowly as possible like Annie does. Why haven't you given Annie a spanking? If anyone deserves one, she does."

Leroy turned back around to face me. He said, "I thought I told you to be careful of those clothes. Didn't I tell you that those were my dress blues?" Then he waited.

"Didn't I?"

I said, "Yes."

Leroy said, "You get out of this car now."

But I couldn't get out on the dress blues side, so I had to move over Renee and Sammy and Danny to get through Danny's door and out by the side of the highway.

Leroy grabbed my arm and walked me back to the trunk end of the car. He leaned me against the trunk and hit me with his free hand on my butt and my legs as hard as he could with his hand held stiff. But it didn't hurt bad like being spanked with a belt. It didn't hurt that bad at all.

But I should have known how it was going to be.

18 Statues

Mama thumped the cupboard door closed. The faucet handle squeaked as she twisted it on and the water rushed out, then it squeaked in a different way when she turned the water off.

I tried to get my eyes open, and be all the way awake, before she came and grabbed my shoulder, shaking, her voice a loud alarm. She'd rush us, Renee and me, get up, roll up the foam rubber mattress, pull the table out from the wall, put the chairs around it. Hurry up. Do it faster, maybe a slap.

Already it was hot, the sheet sticky on top of me. Renee had kicked her half of it off.

Mama's steps came our way and I got my eyes open, but she walked back to the sink. I pushed back the sheet and sat up, careful not to make any noise. I was still tired. I wanted just a few more minutes to get ready for the day.

Renee moved her arms. She looked all sweaty even in her shorty pajamas, even lying still, her curly hair damp around her face. She wiped her eyes with her arm and sat up.

She might make it before Mama yelled.

Mama turned around from the sink, shouted, "Don't just sit there. Get that mattress out of the way now!"

Renee stood up fast and almost lost her balance stepping off the mattress. I pulled the sheets off the bed and laid them on the floor. Renee got down on her knees at one side of the mattress. I got down on my knees on the other. We rolled it up, tight, the way Mama wanted it, up towards the wall, pushing down on it as we rolled to keep it tight, to keep it from bouncing away loose. Then I held it up against the wall, while Renee went to get the cord to tie around it, two pieces, one for each end.

Mama set the frying pan down on a stove burner. She wore a

lavender colored dress with little flowers on it. The hair around her forehead was wet with sweat and she pushed it away. She unscrewed the cap off a bottle of Wesson oil.

Amy cried in the other room, so Mama put the cap back on the oil. She ran water into the little pan for Amy's bottle, set it on a burner and turned the burner on. The flames shot up and Mama turned the gas down until the fire just reached the bottom of the pan. She took a bottle of formula, already made up, from the fridge and put it inside.

Renee handed me the cord to tie the mattress. Then she held one end of the foam rubber while I tied the other. It kept coming loose, so I pushed it together and tied it up as quickly as I could so Mama wouldn't shout. Then I tied Renee's end too.

From the stove, Mama said, "Can't you roll that any tighter?"

I pulled on the edge of the foam rubber to try to roll it tighter without pulling off the cord I had already tied.

Mama picked up the bottle of formula out of the pan and shook it, put it back down. "Oh, never mind. Just get it out of the way, and pull the table back out. Hurry up now."

Danny was lucky. Sammy was lucky. We were all crowded into this little apartment, until Leroy could find us a new place, but Danny and Sammy slept on a mattress in the living room, next to where Leroy and Mama slept on the couch bed, and Amy slept in the bassinet. They weren't in the way when Mama got up to cook breakfast and get Amy's bottle. They didn't have to get up until they woke up on their own or until Mama called them for breakfast.

Boys didn't have to help with breakfast, didn't have to try to figure out what Mama wanted them to do before she got angry and yelled because they hadn't done it.

Renee picked up one of the sheets. She handed one end to me then took the two corners of the other end, one in each hand. We backed away from each other, so we could pull the sheet tight between us. We moved into the hallway between the kitchen and the living room so we would be out of Mama's way, and we each folded our corners together, so the sheet was folded in half lengthwise.

Renee and I didn't talk while we worked. That way Mama might not say anything to us, and we knew exactly how Mama wanted us to fold the sheet.

We each took the new corners and moved together, so the corners met. Renee took hold of all the corners then and held them up, and I reached down to get the folded end hanging down. We did this again and again until the sheet was folded small with all its edges smooth and even. Then I brought the sheet over to the foam mattress where it stood in the corner, and laid it down on top of one end.

Then we folded up the other sheet.

Renee took hold of one end of the table and I got the other. We lifted it out away from the wall so it wouldn't scrape the floor. The chairs were unstacked and set around the table and Mama hadn't yelled at us again.

My shorts and blouse lay on our suitcase. Renee's clothes were folded up next to mine. I got clean underpants for both of us out of the suitcase, then closed it up and shoved it against the wall, out of the way. Renee and I went into the bathroom to change.

It took just a minute to pull off our pajamas and put on underpants and shorts and a blouse, another minute to brush our teeth. Renee picked up her hairbrush. I brushed my hair underneath, then on top, wanted to brush and brush until it was shiny and smooth.

Renee's reflection looked at me. She said, "I guess we'd better go help Mama with breakfast."

The long mirror over the sink showed two girls stop brushing, hold their hairbrushes still next to their hair. The brushes seemed to get heavier, until the girls in the mirror laid them down on the edge of the sink.

"Yeah," I said, "before she starts yelling for us."

Mama had a diaper over her shoulder now. She picked up the baby's bottle, and shook it upside down towards her left wrist, so a couple of drops shook out of the nipple. She went to the sink and turned on the faucet, holding the bottle under the running water for a little bit. She shook it again onto her wrist, then took the bottle out into the living room.

I looked at the stove and the kitchen counters to see what Mama had planned for breakfast, so I'd know what dishes to get out, but only the frying pan was there. She had probably planned eggs, but now that Amy was awake she might change her mind and have cereal for breakfast instead. Then we would need bowls, and plates would be wrong. Maybe we would have toast, then we'd need the butter dish. Salt and pepper for eggs, napkins. If she cooked potatoes with the eggs, the bottle of ketchup. Mama didn't like it if I put out the wrong thing, or if I didn't put out everything that we needed. Probably eggs, but if she didn't make potatoes, maybe she would just want to use saucers so there wouldn't be so many dishes to wash.

Mama came back into the kitchen, holding Amy in her left arm, and the bottle in her right hand with the nipple in Amy's mouth. Amy was so little her head fit right on Mama's elbow, her bottom right in Mama's hand. Amy's hair was wet too, and she had a rash around her neck, heat rash, Mama said. There'd been a heat wave ever since we got to Virginia, a week ago.

Renee pulled out a chair for Mama, and Mama sat down. Renee always knew what to do. Mama looked at me and frowned. "Don't just stand there. Start peeling some potatoes."

Peeling potatoes was a good job, because it took a long time and I didn't have to try to figure out what Mama wanted, just take out the potato peeler, take out five or six potatoes from the bag, just keep peeling. We never had French fries for breakfast so I knew, once they were peeled I should cut them up for fried potatoes. I peeled them into the sink. Mama fed Amy and told Renee what to put out on the table. It would be all set by the time I got done with the potatoes.

The bottle of formula was empty and Mama took Amy back into the living room. When she returned she walked to the sink and got the dish rag that was folded over the faucet. She rinsed it out and then washed the counter.

She said, "Whoever wiped off this counter after dinner last night did a pretty poor job of it."

But there wasn't any way to peel a potato wrong. Unless I was too slow, so I peeled faster.

Leroy walked in. He had a lit cigarette and Mama handed him an ashtray. He set the ashtray on the table, then turned a chair around and sat, leaning his elbow on the chair back. Even when he leaned like that on the chair back, Leroy looked like he was sitting up straight. He puffed on the cigarette then set it on the ashtray.

Leroy said, "I hope Annie is being more helpful this morning than she was last night."

Mama got eggs out of the refrigerator, got a bowl from the cupboard, started breaking the eggs into the bowl. Each one she hit against the side of the bowl, just once, then pulled the shell apart so the egg fell. Mama said, "About as helpful as she ever is." She said it like I was never helpful. But I always did my best to figure out what she wanted. Why didn't she see that?

After breakfast, I cleared the dishes off the table.

After breakfast was easier to figure out than before breakfast. First you scrape the food off the dishes all onto one plate. Then you scrape that plate into the garbage under the sink. You stack up all the plates, all the bowls that food was in, put the silverware inside the top bowl, and you carry them all over to the counter by the sink.

You come back for the glasses and cups. Then you run water

in the sink, hotter water than you want, hot like Mama likes it to be, put in soap, for a sinkful of soapy water.

Get the dish cloth wet, dip it in, holding it by one corner so the water won't burn your hands. Wait a minute to wring it out so it cools a little bit. Then come over and wash off the table.

You have to wash the table three times, rinsing out the dish cloth in the hot soapy water in between. The first time you just wash all the crumbs off. Wipe the crumbs over to one edge of the table, then push them into your hand where you hold it open part way under the edge. Don't get the crumbs on the floor. The second time you scrub all the dirty spots, the spilled egg yolk spots, hard to get clean spots. The third time you wash all over the table again to get anything you missed the first two times.

Then you wash the dishes, put your hands in the hot water and they burn at first, until you get used to it. Wash a dish, turn on the hot water faucet, only hot to rinse, hold the dish by one edge only, to keep from being burned, but don't drop it. Do the silverware really fast because it stays hot even after it comes out of the hot water. Put the dishes into the dish rack. Turn off the faucet. Don't waste the hot water.

In between the rinse water Mama and Leroy's voices came from the living room.

In California, I used to be glad when Leroy came over and Mama got happy. Waiting in this apartment for Leroy to find us a place to live in Norfolk near the Navy base, Mama seemed always sad and angry. Now when she talked to Leroy sometimes her voice sounded like it did when she talked to me. I couldn't hear what she said now, but I knew it was about finding a house because Mama's voice sounded like that. Maybe she would be happy again, when Leroy found our new place.

I rinsed a dish in cold water, quickly, in case Mama stopped talking and came back into the kitchen.

#

The big tree in the front yard that I could climb into from the top of the concrete porch steps was one good thing about this apartment. The other good thing was it was a block away from the beach, and right next to it, the Virginia Beach Amusement Park with a huge wooden roller coaster. Danny said a kid got killed on it last summer. He heard it from another kid who lived in the apartment house. We only went one time to the amusement park. We had one ride apiece because it was expensive. But after dinner, once the dishes were done, and it started to cool off a little, almost every night we got our swim suits on and went to the beach to swim.

We were going to the beach in a few minutes. We gathered the towels, the diaper bag, blankets.

Everyone had something to carry to the beach. I carried the bassinet. Leroy carried the baby. Even with the bassinet to carry I felt lighter with the day cooling down, and soon I'd be in the water. I hurried to keep up with everyone. Sometimes I'd start thinking about something while I walked, then Mama would yell at me to keep up.

The bassinet of white wicker was big but light, with two long rounded handles on its sides. I held it by one of them and felt like swinging it along beside me while I walked, but I didn't, because Mama would be annoyed. She already had enough to bother her, Amy's heat rash and Leroy's not finding a place for us to live yet. So I didn't swing the bassinet.

When we came to the sand, I took off my flip-flops and put them in the bassinet. I swung my feet along the top of the sand, and felt it on the bottom of my foot before I lowered my toes. Nobody noticed me doing this. I didn't slow down. Sometimes I took a step sideways instead of straight forward, but not very far, so nobody noticed.

Soon I would be in the cool water.

Mama stopped. "Put the blankets down here," she told Danny.

Danny spread one blanket out, and Mama and Renee spread out the other one. I put down the bassinet and took my flip-flops out, then went over to help Danny spread out the other blanket. He picked up two corners and I picked up two corners and we pulled it out tight, then slowly lowered it down on the sand. Danny's arms were thin and taut.

Mama said, "Put the bassinet on the blanket."

She took Amy from Leroy and laid her into the bassinet, on her stomach. Amy was asleep. Mama took the baby blanket that Sammy carried and laid it over the bassinet, leaving a small space on the end where Amy's head was.

"Sit down here and watch the baby while I swim," Mama told me. "You can go in afterwards."

That was okay because I could just sit on the blanket and think about things and look at the baby. No one would tell me to stop daydreaming.

Mama said, "If she cries, don't pick her up. Just give her the pacifier, and if she won't stop crying, call me." She followed Leroy and Renee and Danny and Sammy down to the shore. I watched my brothers' smooth backs, the line of their backbones, the elastic of their swimming trunks; Danny so tall and straight; Sammy running zigzag along the wet sand, jumping in the waves coming in; Renee going slow once she got to the water, sticking her toes in, then wading on in, stopping every time a wave came, standing still until it passed over her.

Far away now, Leroy, my stepfather, stood up in water to his waist, then came back for Sammy, lifted him under his arms and carried Sammy out to the deeper water. He lifted him up when a wave came, so the water didn't go over Sammy's head.

Mama reached them. Renee came after her and jumped up when a wave came. Danny too.

Leroy twirled Sammy around in the water, then handed him to Mama. Then Leroy turned around, daring Danny and Renee to come and get him. Danny reached him, and Leroy picked him up and threw him out into the water. Renee came and Leroy tossed her up too. Danny reached Leroy again, got tossed again.

I couldn't see Mama's face, if she was laughing, if she was happy. Maybe it would be better, with Leroy here. Maybe it would be okay.

Inside the bassinet, Amy's smooth little head, and her little arms and fists stuck out from her undershirt. She sucked on her pacifier even in her sleep. I imagined myself picking her up, and Amy waking up, holding Amy up in front of me, blowing on her tummy, Amy laughing, squealing, looking at me, smiling at me. I reached in the bassinet and stroked the back of her head, even though Mama wouldn't like it because it might wake her up. Just a few weeks ago Amy wasn't in my life at all.

Mama stayed out longer than she usually did. It had started to get dark before she came back up the beach and told me I could go swim now.

Leroy and Danny and Sammy and Renee only stayed a little longer after I came, then headed to shore. Sometimes Leroy was still tossing them into the water when I got to come and play and he'd toss me in too, but not today.

The water nearly reached my shoulders. When a high wave came I jumped into it and floated on it towards the beach, then swam back out and waited for the next one. I felt so cool and light, floating on the waves. After awhile I was tired, but I didn't want to go back, not before Mama sent Danny or Renee to call me.

It was really dark. Usually we left before it got so dark.

I stopped jumping in the waves, just floated on them, letting the waves carry me close to shore. I stood up, the water up to my knees. I'd better get back before it was too dark for them to find me. Maybe they had yelled and I didn't hear.

I walked slowly back and felt heavier as I went along, leaving the waves behind.

Then I looked up to see where the blankets were, and there they all were, Mama and Leroy, Danny and Renee and Sammy, all in a circle, playing with the beach ball, throwing it from one to another. Danny threw the ball to Sammy. Sammy caught it, but tripped and fell backwards down on the sand. Mama laughed.

Mama was laughing.

I ran up the beach to them.

Then I could hear them, not what they were saying, but talking together, laughing together.

I ran, feeling so light looking ahead at them. The beach ball in the air, Mama reached to catch it. She caught it, held it, deciding whom to throw to. Everyone got ready, in case it was them.

Until the moment that Mama saw me.

She stopped laughing. Her face stopped moving. Her smile went away so there was no expression on her face. Then she looked away from me. For a minute, Leroy and Danny and Renee and Sammy still waited for her to throw the ball.

Then they stopped waiting.

Mama's arms got heavy, fell down to her side, and the ball rolled out of them onto the sand.

She said, "I don't feel like playing anymore." Her voice was flat like her face.

I stopped running.

Danny walked over to the blankets, picked up the one that didn't have the bassinet on it, folded it.

My legs walked slower and slower to the blankets. Then they stopped. I just stood there, like in a game of statues, when you've been twirling and twirling around, and now you have to hold yourself as still as you can. Only, I felt like I couldn't move, like I'd been frozen. What had I done to make her hate me so much?

Nobody said anything to me. They didn't act like they saw me. Maybe they thought Mama would turn on them if they came near me. Maybe there was something wrong with me, and they all knew what it was. I stood in the center of where the circle had been, but everyone had turned away from the circle, gathered things together to take home, folded towels, folded blankets. Only I wasn't helping. Soon Mama or Leroy would turn around and see me, yell at me for being lazy.

I looked for something to do, saw a towel lying on the sand, forced myself to take a step, take another step, walk over to it, pick it up, fold it, slowly so I would have time to find something else to do, so if someone looked at me, I was doing something.

Nobody looked at me, but I kept picking things up, because you just have to keep going.

Nobody said anything during all the time we picked things up. Nobody said anything on the walk home. Nobody looked at me. I walked along in the back, carrying the bassinet. I didn't want to swing it, my feet weren't light, but I kept walking, because that's what there is to do, just keep walking, one step after another.

19 The Skate Key

I said, "Please don't tell."

"I have to tell." Renee answered. She walked faster. It was really getting dark now. The streetlights were on. I was the one who kept us late, first roller-skating a little longer, then not remembering where I left the skate key.

"You don't have to tell. We can get another skate key. Mama doesn't have to find out."

"How can we get another skate key without buying another pair of skates?"

I said, "Maybe they sell them separate. People must lose them all the time."

"You lose them," Renee said.

"We just won't go skating again until we get one. She won't find out. We'll go to the school ground tomorrow and look again. Probably we'll find it right away when it's light."

"It was light when we started looking."

Renee always felt bad keeping secrets. Like that time in Yakima when we slid out on the ice on the canal – my idea – and I broke through the ice. Mama wasn't there when we got home. We could have hidden everything from her. But Renee told. I got spanked because I was older, but I didn't really blame her then. It wasn't so bad, only a yardstick.

Only, it was different now. Couldn't Renee understand that it was different now.

"Please, don't tell," I asked again.

"She'll find out." Then I wanted to say, *then tell her you lost it*, because it wouldn't be bad if Renee lost it. Then it would be a small thing. Mama might be a little angry, but she wouldn't look at Renee the way she would look at me. But I didn't ask that. I only said, "Please don't tell," again.

Renee didn't say anything. She pressed her lips together.

"Please don't tell her." She didn't say again that she had to tell.

We climbed up the stairs of the new apartment in Norfolk and opened the door to the bright kitchen with the yellow linoleum. Mama sat at the kitchen table, her hand on the handle of her coffee cup, her cigarette resting on the ashtray. She said, "It's after dark. What are you doing home so late?"

I said, "We left when it got dark." Maybe she'd let it go.

But Renee didn't even wait for Mama to respond. "We were looking for the skate key. Annie lost it."

Mama looked at me the way I knew she would look at me, the way she wouldn't look at Renee if it were Renee who lost the skate key, the way she only looked at me. "It wasn't enough you lost your own skate key, you had to lose hers too."

I tried to make that look go away. "I laid it down where we put on the skates. We probably just missed it in the dark. I could look for it tomorrow."

"You're not going anywhere tomorrow. Now get in your bedroom and get ready for bed."

Renee came after me down the hallway and I moved as far as I could to the right so I didn't touch her. Got my pajamas out from under my pillow and put them on without looking at her. Got in my bed and pulled the covers up over my head, without looking at her.

#

The next night Leroy arrived home late from his weekend duty on the base. Soon after he came into our room. Renee was doing something on her bed and that's where Leroy sat at the foot, turned towards her. I sat on my own bed reading.

"Renee," Leroy said, so Renee faced him and paid attention.

Quickly, Leroy glanced over my way, then back to Renee, so I knew I was supposed to hear, but I kept my eyes on my book the best I could.

Leroy said, "I just wanted to know what present you'd like for being such a good girl this week." Another little glance at me.

Renee's eyes turned away from him, first at the bed, then a quick look at me too, her body all stiff and miserable. I hated her.

Finally, she mumbled, "I don't know."

Leroy's voice stayed bright, "Well, I guess it'll just have to be a surprise then. But you let me know if you think of something. We want you to know how much we appreciate having a good girl like you."

He waited for her to say something more, but the good girl didn't. The good girl stared at her bed and held her little good girl hands in her lap, until Leroy put his arm around the good girl's shoulders for a moment, then left our room.

The good girl looked over at me, but I stared at my book. After a long time, she went back to what she was doing before, and I reread the sentence I'd been on when Leroy came until it had some meaning again.

20 Rolling My Hair

I leaned back in the tub just for a moment sinking into the warm water. I hesitated as the hot water touched a new place on my skin then relaxed into it. The door creaked and I sat up straight.

Mama came in. She looked at me with that look. The what are you doing, whatever it is it's wrong look. I put soap on a washrag, rubbed the bar back and forth on the rag draped over my hand, avoided the moment when I would have to start washing while she watched to see that I did it right, and it wouldn't be right.

Mama was always right. She looked away from me and into the mirror, and it didn't matter if I watched because I couldn't make her wrong. She took her time looking and patting her hair. Then her eyes in the mirror were looking at me, and my eyes looked away quickly before she could catch them. She said, "Well, don't take all day. Don't you know there are other people in this house who want a bath." Looking away from me she used one finger to press a strand of hair back. She fixed the collar of her dress. It was pink with some blue pattern and the pink set off the red in her brown hair.

She set a plastic bag filled with curlers down next to the faucet. "Here, I want you to do something with that scraggly hair of yours. Put it up in these curlers so maybe tomorrow it won't be going every which way around your face. I hate that scraggly look of yours."

"Ok." I didn't know I had a scraggly look. Then I worked myself up to say it, "I don't know how to roll my hair."

Mama looked at me with her nose scrunched up like I started to smell. She picked up a comb from the back of the sink and put a small part in the front of her hair. She separated a small rectangle in the front and combed the hair up straight. She held the hair in one hand, wrapped slightly around her finger. Then she put down the comb and reached for a roller instead. She put the roller on her head next to the hair. Then she moved it along the hair like a brush until it was on the tip of the squared off hair, then she rolled the hair around the curler. When the curler lay next to her head again it was wound tight. She held it against her head while she dug in the plastic bag for a metal clip. She clipped the hair on one end of the roller, then dug for another clip for the other end.

"There," she said, "that's the way you do it, only while it's wet." Then she took out the clips and pulled out the roller, shaking the hair loose, and everything was right about how she shook her hair. Mama picked up the comb and combed her hair back as it had been.

She said, "Don't you be too long about it either," and went out the door.

I lathered my hair up once and rinsed it in the tub. Then I lathered it again, turned on the faucet, more cold than hot. I leaned back on the faucet end of the tub to rinse the soap out. I hung my head back as far as I could to keep the soapy water out of my eyes. My hair was long, almost to the middle of my back. I pulled a strand of it to see if it squeaked, but it didn't so I rinsed it some more. It hurt my neck to lean back like that, but Mama said it left soap if I laid back and rinsed my hair in the tub. If she saw soap in my hair she'd be angry.

Finally the hair squeaked. I pulled the towel off the bar and rubbed and rubbed my hair to get it dry. I pulled the plug, stepped out of the tub and quickly got into my pajamas. I combed and combed my hair to get out the tangles, using the wide toothed end of the comb, then the narrow tooth end.

Then I tried to put in the part, on the left side of my head. I did it like Mama did. I reached to the back of my head with the comb, and with one finger pressing the point down against my scalp, drew a quick line on my head and pulled it straight forward to the front, just like I knew exactly what I wanted to do. Whenever Mama did this there was a sharp straight line down my head, clear and definite. But now there were clumps of hair to one side or other of the line so it had little jags in it. I put the teeth of the comb along the line, pressed down hard and combed to the right, then did it again and combed to the left, but there were still little zigs and zags. A few more times and it was a little better.

This took too long. I had to hurry. I carved out a little rectangle of my hair at the front of my head. I looked in the mirror and did what Mama did. But my hand went the wrong way in the mirror and I couldn't make it go right. So I tried without looking. Then I looked and it was not a little rectangle, more like a circle lumped more to one side then the other and with zigzag lines all around its edges. So I tried again.

I had so much hair. I would never get done this way. So I took the lumpy circle rectangle and combed the hair up. I put the roller at the bottom of the length of hair right up against my head and pulled the roller up to the end of the hair like I was brushing with it just like Mama did. My arm hurt from pulling up my hair so the hair sagged instead of being pulled straight. Some hair escaped from the bunch, but I had to get done so I started rolling from the end. After two rolls the roller was only halfway up and the curler was full of hair. But I kept rolling and the curler was fat with hair. It wasn't tight but maybe I could clip it. I held it with my left hand and reached for a clip in the plastic bag. The hair was so thick the clip had to be too wide open to go over it so the clip slipped off. So I clipped it on the roller and just part of the hair so the clip was mostly hidden in a clump. I held the roller with my left hand again and got another clip. Then I held the roller with my right hand and tried to clip the left side of the roller with my left hand. That side was too fat also so I clipped it the same way. Then I let go. A big clump of hair came loose. I didn't have time to redo it, so I took the fallen out clump and combed it out and started another roller with it, but there wasn't room to lay a roller next to my head. So I just rolled it as close as I could. There was this lump of loose hair that didn't get wound as tight as the inside part. But I clipped it anyway.

Then I heard a knock at the front door and Mama said hello to Addy who lived downstairs and one building over. Addy was married but young and didn't have kids. She didn't talk with me much, but when she did she talked to me just like she talked with another grownup. Addy's hair was dark and short and straight and the bangs hung down along the top frame of her glasses and I didn't think she rolled her hair.

Mama would be busy with Addy and wouldn't come to see how I was doing.

I tried again to part off a new section but I knew it wasn't going to work even if I did get it parted straight, so when it was crooked after my second try, I just combed off a bit of hair and rolled it. It all fit on the roller but I couldn't fit the roller on my head without covering up some hair that hadn't been rolled yet, so I didn't roll it up all the way to my head but left it hanging some.

The next roller fit on my head OK, underneath the other roller. So I kept doing it like that, some rollers hanging from my head a little and some up tight. All of them had bulges of hair that wasn't wound tight and there were also loose pieces all over my head. I tried to redo the clips of some rollers to catch the loose pieces. Curlers hung all over my head, every which way.

Renee knocked on the door. "Are you done yet?" She asked.

"Almost."

There wasn't much more I could do without starting over. I found some more clips and stuck then into the rollers to hold the loose hair and clipped some rollers to other rollers so they wouldn't dangle quite so much. Then I decided that now was the time to try to make it to my room without being seen, while Mama was in the living room talking to Addy. So I put the comb back down on the back of the sink. I stuffed the rest of the curlers into the plastic bag and set it back down next to the faucet. As I leaned over to wipe off the tub the curlers swung around my head. They felt heavy on my hair. I wiped until the suds were all down the drain and there was no ring around the tub, then I rinsed the washrag, and laid it flat over the side. I hung up the towel. I picked up my clothes and laid them over my arm except my shoes which I held with one hand so I could open the door. Out in the hall I leaned against the bathroom door for a moment to shift the shoes from my left hand to my right. I faced the door to the living room but the couch was out of sight so I couldn't see Addy or Mama sitting there, but I hadn't heard Addy leave and there were noises like a cup sliding on a table.

Then Mama came out of her bedroom carrying something and she almost ran into me. She stopped and looked at me and her eyes and mouth scrunched together and stayed that way hard. This was the worst look. Mama reached out towards me and grabbed hold of my hair. She pulled me, from the cold linoleum floor of the hallway, yanked me forward through the living room doorway, onto the scratchy living room rug, then she yanked me again to the middle of the room, then once more so I was standing up against the coffee table in front of the couch on which the cups of coffee sat that my mother and Addy were drinking, except that Addy held her cup in her hand. The cup paused on its way to Addy's mouth. Addy put her other hand around it as well and lowered it slowly to the coffee table where she set it down on the saucer. She moved back on the couch like a little kid whose legs are too short for her feet to touch the floor and Addy set her hands down by her side on the seat and kept them there.

My head hurt but I didn't make any noise.

Mama said "Just look at how she rolls her hair for her mother."

Addy didn't say anything. She looked at the coffee table. I could see her even though I held my head down and my eyes were partly closed. I didn't move any part of my body. I felt the rug against my feet, the coffee table against my leg. Mama let go of my hair. She stood over on my left but I didn't look at her and I didn't know what her face looked like.

"Just get out of here. Get out of my sight." and I didn't need to see her face to know her look.

My feet moved quickly on the scratchy carpet, then quicker but not quite running on the cold linoleum, then through my doorway two steps to my bed; I closed the door behind me. Then I was on my bed, leaning back against the wall. The hard wall pressed the rollers against my head, and my shoulders moved up and down and my breath went in and out fast and I couldn't get enough breath. I cried and cried. Then the door opened and I tried to stop crying but my breath kept going fast and my shoulders kept moving and I couldn't stop them.

Leroy stood in the open doorway with one hand on the knob of the door that could only open halfway before it hit the head of my bed, and he spread his legs in the doorway and stood up tall. He wore his sailor blues because he had duty that night. "Your mom says you did a horrible job of rolling your hair. What do you have to say for yourself?"

One word at a time because I couldn't stop my breath, I said, "I ... never ... rolled ... my ... hair ... before."

Leroy had been holding his body all tight like he was at navy attention, but like the commanding officer not the sailor, but suddenly he changed. His body relaxed and his face went softer as he came and sat down beside me on the bed. It was as if he'd changed into another person. He put his hand on my back. My back was still moving and Leroy pressed on it lightly and said softly, "Its all right." He stayed there with his hand on my back until my breath came out slower, and he rubbed my back and squeezed my shoulder and said it would be all right. Then he said, "Why don't you just go ahead and go to bed now?" He stood up and I stood up and pulled down the covers and got into bed. Leroy pulled the covers up to my neck, and patted my shoulder. He turned out the light and shut the door behind him. Maybe it would be all right. Maybe he would talk to Mama and I wouldn't have to roll my hair anymore.

#

But after dinner the next night Mama said, "Take your bath now and wet your hair down and roll it and you just better make sure you do it right this time."

A couple of days later when I came out of the bathroom, Leroy stood in the hallway with the camera and snapped a picture of me with my hair all rolled up. He didn't say anything but the way he looked at me made me feel like the Leroy who had been kind to me for a few minutes had never really existed. I turned away from him and hurried away to my room as quickly as I could.

A few nights later he called me into the living room where everyone else was watching television, "I have something for you to see," he said. He sat on the couch next to Mama and tossed a photograph out on the coffee table.

"See here," he said, "Kids look at this." He waited for Renee and Danny and Sammy to all come over by the coffee table, so they could see. Leroy looked at the photo, then he looked at me. I looked at the photo of me in my summer pajamas with the short sleeves and the bottoms that were too short, the ones with the flower pattern. My ankles stuck out so my bare feet looked long.

In the photo I looked down and I had blinked so my eyes were half closed. The rollers looked like they did in the mirror, hanging from my head and laying against it at odd angles instead of lined up straight.

I couldn't leave, but I took a half step back. There was no place to hide. I could only stand very still.

Renee, Sammy and Danny leaned forward to see the photograph. Leroy picked it up and handed it to Danny.

"Quite a sight isn't it." Danny looked at the photo like he had to look at it. He looked in its direction but I couldn't tell if his eyes focused on it, then he laid it back down on the coffee table. Leroy picked it back up and handed it to Renee. He said, "See here how your sister rolls her hair."

Renee held the photo on its edge, with the tips of her thumb and her finger and turned it away from her just a little and nodded her head.

Leroy said, "I'm sure you could do a lot better than that, even being three years younger."

Renee didn't say anything. Leroy reached out and took the photograph from her. He handed it to Sammy, and Sammy looked at it and said, "Why does Annie have to wear those things in her hair?" Then he looked over at me and waited for me to answer.

I said, "I don't know," quietly, and looked down at the floor.

Leroy said, "To try to make herself pretty, if that were possible."

Sammy said, "Oh," then he looked at me, then he looked at Leroy, and he said, "Isn't Annie pretty all ready?" So Leroy pointed his finger at me in the photograph, and said "Look at this, does this look pretty to you?"

Then Sammy didn't say anything. He just put the photo back

down on the coffee table.

Mama hadn't said anything. She watched the television set. I looked that way too, at "Wagon Train," and when the commercial came on, listened to the jingle, "double your pleasure, double your fun, doublemint, doublemint, two mints in one."

Leroy went over to the side table and opened the drawer where the photograph album was kept. He pulled it out, along with an envelope of little black corners that hold photographs onto the photo album page. He took the album over to the coffee table. Mama moved to let him get around her to sit back down, but she didn't look at what he did. He laid the photo album open on the table and turned the page till he found one that was totally blank He put the photo of me in the middle of the page, and said, "There, now everyone will be sure to see it on a page of its own." He pulled a little black corner out of the envelope, licked it and slipped it onto one corner of the photograph. He pressed the corner down, very carefully, so the rest of the photo didn't move, then reached for another. I tried to watch the TV show, but I saw his fingers instead, as he held the photo down and slipped on each new corner, pressing each corner down carefully making sure the photo was straight, no rush. He finished the last one, then he looked up at me where I was looking at him. He looked straight at me.

He closed the album. He stood up. Mama moved her knees to let him get by, and he walked back over to the side table and pulled open the drawer and put the photograph album and the envelope of little black corners back inside the drawer.

21 The Magnificat

The school cafeteria had long rows of tables pushed together, with benches on each side. Several tables were grouped to the left and another several to the right of the big room, with an open space in the middle where we entered the cafeteria and went up to the serving area to get our food. I sat near the middle of a table on the left facing the center, so I could see all the tables on the other side. Sister Veronica, our religion teacher, walked through the doorway angrily, marched over to the right side and grabbed some kid by the hair pulling him away from his bench into the center of the room. The way she talked he must be a kid in her class, "I'll be calling your parents. Did you study at all for that last test?"

She'd got him by the hair, but she's wasn't yanking hard but just using it to get a grip on him. He was cute with black hair with tight curls and a sweet looking face, like my cousin Ronnie. The boy was crying, but Sister Veronica still yelled at him. And I was so scared for him, at what his parents would do to him after Sister Veronica talked to them.

Sister Veronica taught us religion because our regular teacher wasn't a nun, but a lay teacher. Sister Veronica's veil and robes were all black except for a little white section in the front where her blouse would be, and the white piece across her forehead.

Not long after this scene in the cafeteria she dropped a stack of papers on the desk in our classroom, her face red and angry. "These tests are a disgrace."

Everyone sat so still in their desks that there was no sound when Sister Veronica stopped talking and looked around the room at everybody's face. She said, "You couldn't have studied. Nearly all of you have failed this test."

A couple of chairs squeaked.

"You don't know how lucky you are that this test didn't go on your report cards that are coming out at the end of the week. If they had most of you would have failed religion for the quarter. Instead what is going to happen is that each of you is going to take your test home and have one of your parents sign every single page."

But I couldn't do that. Instead I waited that night until everyone was asleep. Then, by the light of the street lamp through the window, I wrote Mama's name on every page.

I don't know what I would have done if I had flunked religion, but it was bad enough when the report cards came out. Like always I had gotten out of the building and out on the black top as soon as I could after the bell sounded. The big yellow Christ the King school buses were pulling up to the curb way across the blacktop playground. The blacktop was wet with drops of rain and the sky looked like it might rain more any minute, but it didn't rain now. My hands were bare and red from cold. It hadn't been cold that morning so I'd only worn a sweater.

On the report card stuck into my history book were four D's. One in English, one in Grammar, one in Handwriting, one in Homework.

But a B in Religion.

On the street next to the black top the buses filled with kids. The lines outside the buses were getting shorter and I needed to decide. Should I just go, start walking the other direction, away from the bus and never go home again.

The rain began to come down, not too hard, but enough to wet my clothes and make it colder. It might be really cold overnight.

If I'd gotten an "F" in Religion I would have run away. Instead I went to the bus, almost the last to get on, and got in the seat behind Danny and Renee.

"How did you do?" Danny asked me; he looked unhappy.

"Four D's," I said.

"I got 3," Danny said, his face grim. "I wonder what they'll do."

But it wouldn't be as bad as it would have been if it had been only me. Now the worst would be a licking with a belt.

#

"Put your report cards on the coffee table," Leroy said. "Your mother and I will look at them after dinner."

I put mine down, and Danny put his down and looked at me. Then we just had to wait.

Through helping with dinner, through eating dinner, through doing dishes after dinner. Wait until Leroy called us into the living room where he and Mama sat on the couch and Leroy had an open report card still in his hands.

Danny went ahead, and I followed. Renee held back after me even though she was the only one who didn't have anything to be afraid of.

Mama said, "These are the worst report cards I've ever seen from you two. I'm ashamed of you."

Leroy coughed. He said, "I guess I forgot to mention that I'm giving a prize for the best report card."

He dug his hand into his tight jeans and pulled out two quarters.

"Here, Renee, here's 50 cents. Good work."

That was all. Even in the worst of times something can save you. The B in religion, Danny's three D's.

There was every morning when I told my teacher that I lost my homework on the bus, and she never once asked how I could lose my homework on the bus every single day. I just couldn't have explained how I would sit down to do it but I'd start thinking about something else and it just wouldn't get finished before it was time for me to help get dinner ready.

Even on that morning when Mama got so angry because I missed the bus, there was the quiet that came between us afterwards, and how I got the whole day alone in my room to read.

There was my birthday in November when I got the new blue car coat, my favorite color, with the soft fake fur inside that felt so soft and warm, even in the middle of all the cold hardness, something soft and warm against your skin. And there was the Magnificat.

During every religion class I expected Sister Veronica to yell at me, but even though she yelled at the black-haired boy with the sweet face, she didn't yell at me. Instead, one day she asked me if I wanted to memorize the Magnificat, to say it for the Monsignor when he came to visit.

She said, "It's kind of a long piece to memorize, but I think you can do it. Will you try it?"

"Yes," I said. She thought I could do it. I didn't know why but she thought I could so I wanted to.

By the third time I said it for her in the practice that we had every day, I knew all the words:

My soul magnifies the Lord and my spirit has rejoiced in God my Savior.

For He has regarded the lowly state of His maidservant; for behold, henceforth all generations will call me blessed.

For He who is mighty has done great things for me and holy is His name.

And His mercy is on those who hear Him from generation to generation.

He has shown strength with his arm; He has scattered the proud in the imagination of their hearts.

He has put down the mighty from their thrones and exalted

the lowly.

He has filled the hungry with good things, and the rich He has sent away empty.

He has helped his servant, Israel, in remembrance of His mercy.

As He spoke to our fathers, to Abraham and to his seed forever.

Mary said this when she visited Elizabeth the mother of John the Baptist, who had been barren but now was six months pregnant with John. Elizabeth's husband Zacharias was mute because he didn't believe right away when the angel Gabriel told him that Elizabeth was going to bear a son. Then John was born and Zacharias could speak again.

It was me who was to say the words of Mary, the mother of God, blessed among women, like I was special too.

#

The monsignor sat in a desk in the front row next to the one in which Sister Veronica sat.

When Jeremy said his piece the monsignor didn't smile or clap, but he nodded his head and he said, "Very Good."

He said, "Very Good," after every speech, and Sister Veronica didn't smile either, but she nodded at each boy or girl after the monsignor spoke to them.

All week I hadn't missed a word, then I said, "My soul magnifies the Lord and my spirit has rejoiced in God my Savior." And I couldn't think what came next.

Sister Veronica waited, then she said, "For he" and I remembered.

Then I was okay until almost the last line.

"He has helped," Sister Veronica said.

She must have been angry at me to be forgetting it in front of the Monsignor, just when everything is supposed to be at its best. Her face didn't look angry. Her voice didn't sound angry, but she must have been angry.

"He has helped his servant, Israel, in remembrance of His mercy.

As He spoke to our fathers, to Abraham and to his seed forever."

I got the rest of it out, but I worried what she would say to me next day in religion class because I wasn't perfect. In class beforehand I was perfect. I knew it.

The monsignor said, "Very good," and nodded at me, and I thought from his voice that he liked it okay, but I wished he could have known that I really knew the whole thing. Sister Veronica nodded at me also.

Then the monsignor left and Joe said, out loud, without even raising his hand, "Annie did good on the Magnificat, didn't she."

"Yes, she did it very well," said Sister Veronica and she wasn't grabbing my hair and telling me she was going to talk to my parents. *Very well*.

22 The Mental Health Clinic

"What seems to be the matter?" the psychologist asked from his brown leather chair in front of the window. He picked up a pad from his desk to his right. He leaned back in the chair, then sat back up and moved up to the edge.

My chair was wooden, with a seat and back of padded vinyl. "Nothing," I said like I always did.

He had beads of sweat on his white forehead underneath his hair that was blond turning to white. He looked like a kind man but I didn't know what to say to him.

He said, "Are you having some trouble at home?"

But I couldn't tell him that I was punished because I was bad. I didn't want him to know.

"I'm not having any trouble."

His hands fumbled with his pad, and he laid his pen down on his desk, then picked it up again. The sweat poured off his forehead.

It was a Thursday, the day when my mother picked me up from school to take me to the Mental Health Clinic. She seemed nicer on the drive, just her and me in the front seat of the big empty station wagon, no other kids, no car load of groceries that had to be brought into the house. When I'd first seen the sign that said "Norfolk Mental Health Clinic" I'd thought that it made sense. There was something wrong with my brain. If I was mentally retarded that would explain why everything I did was wrong.

The psychologist said, "Your mother says you've been having problems with school."

"No," I said, "no problems."

I wanted to help him out but I couldn't. He seemed like a nice man and I didn't want him to find out there was something wrong about me.

On the other side of the room there were toys laying all about on tables and the floor. One day the psychologist asked if I wanted to see them. I headed to the dollhouse. In Yakima, I'd asked for a dollhouse every Christmas, but could never have one because the little kids might swallow the pieces. But when I stood in front of the dollhouse, the man's breathing got faster. I could feel him watch me. I couldn't play with it while he watched me do it wrong.

The miniature pool table looked safe enough.

"What's this?" I asked.

"It's a pool table," he said. "You hit the ball with the cue stick." He picked up the cue stick and showed me how to make a V of my thumb and forefinger to support the cue.

I tried it, but I didn't actually hit the ball. I just moved the cue back and forth.

"Oh," I said, "like that."

Then I stood there and looked at the pool table.

He stood too, then took a step back from the table and turned his head to look back at his empty chair.

I headed back that way.

He followed me. He coughed. He said, "Well, I guess our session is about over for today."

Out in the waiting room I read *HighLights* while he talked with my mother.

Sometimes I read the grownup magazines. One had an article about autistic children. It said that they were good at math, sometimes very good, idiot savants, but it turned out they were autistic. I wasn't an idiot savant but I was good at math so maybe I was autistic, maybe a little bit.

Another article talked about mothers who hit their children. It said the mothers treated their children like they were a lot older than they actually were and they expected way too much of them. Maybe that was it with my mother. She thought I could do a lot more than I could.

On her way out of the psychologist's office I'd hear them. Sometimes she said something about school, "She always did so well before." Mostly I couldn't quite hear. I thought she was complaining about me, and then he always said to her, "You'll just have to be more patient with her."

She would be patient on Thursday. The ride back to school in the car was peaceful.

Just once I saw a different psychologist. His office was bigger. His desk was bigger. He sat in front of it at first and didn't look at me.

In the other big chair, I sank down into the leather.

The man wrote something at his desk. His voice came out big and booming when he said, "What seems to be the matter?"

I didn't say anything.

He twirled around in his chair and looked down at me. He was tall. His face looked dark and displeased. "I said, what seems to be the matter?"

"Nothing," I said.

He stared at me and he looked very mean. His voice came out loud again and impatient, "Your mother hasn't brought you here because there's nothing the matter." He picked up a folder from his desk and rustled through some paper. "It looks like your school suggested that you come here. They don't think you are working up to your potential. What do you have to say about that?" He looked back around at me, accusing.

What did he want of me? He already knew everything.

He leaned forward, "Well?"

Nothing came to me to say, and I didn't care about helping him. I stayed as still as I could in the chair. He scared me.

He twirled his chair back around, picked up a pen and asked me a series of questions in a brisk voice, one after the other.

"What grade are you in?"

"What school do you go to?"

"How long have you gone there?"

"Where did you go before."

I answered those questions because I could.

When he finished he walked over to his door and held it open.

I got up from the chair. I had to scoot up to the edge of it first, then get out and I went to the door and stayed clear of his arm while I went through.

On the way back to Christ the King my mother asked me about the psychologist's questions and what I answered. I told her what I remembered. The next week I was back with the man who sweated a lot. Not long after that we moved and I never went back to the mental health clinic.

23 The New House

The new house felt spacious and welcoming after all the cramped rooms, like something better could happen there. It had a big front porch, the porch swing kind. The entryway was as big as some bedrooms. Except for the kitchen and bathrooms, the floors were dark, rich wood. Besides the two bedrooms downstairs, the upstairs had four more, and its own bathroom. For a while we kids, had hopes of us each having our own room, until we found out that most of the top floor was going to be made into a small apartment to rent out. The back yard was big enough for softball. The house was still in Norfolk, but in a different part, nearer to the ocean. Beyond the back yard, rowboats were tied up at a dock, on an inlet from the bay that came right up near our house. The sound of the water slapping against the cement dock was always there and the different smell of the air near the sea.

After the Christmas break, we'd be going to a new school, a public school, not Catholic.

A few days before Christmas, Leroy took us shopping. After finding presents for everyone, and chipping in a dollar for the punch bowl we'd decided to buy together for Mama, I still had $2 left. I spent that on an extra present for Mama, a sky-blue necklace that I thought she'd especially like.

In the new house we were celebrating Christmas a new way too. Leroy said we'd go to midnight mass and by the time we got back Santa would have come, so we could open our presents. All of us piled into the car. It was chilly out, but sitting there all together in the car, I was only a little cool. Leroy got into the driver's seat.

"Oh darn," he said. "I forgot my cigarettes." He went back into the house. Several minutes later he still hadn't returned.

"He must be having trouble finding them," Mama said from

the front seat.

But finally he came back out and we headed to mass.

Before we'd left, the only presents under the tree were the ones we kids had bought for each other and for Mama and Leroy, but sure enough when we got back presents covered the floor and were stacked high underneath the tree.

Leroy handed them out until everyone had a little stack next to them, then we opened them. While I opened mine, I watched to see if Mama had gotten to the little box that held the necklace I bought for her. I thought it would make her happy, and she'd realize I'd gotten her an extra present, a special one. But when she opened it, she looked at it a minute, her face blank. She laid the box aside on the floor and went on to the next present. I looked away from her and bit my lip when it started to tremble. I tried not to look at her while she opened the rest of the presents. I didn't want to see her smile and exclaim over them and know that I was the only one that couldn't make her happy. Why couldn't I ever make her happy?

One day when it was still Christmas vacation, some friends of Leroy's came over, with their son. All us kids played baseball in the back yard. I was up and I couldn't hit. I used to be good at it, but now I didn't seem to know how to do it anymore. I kept missing and crying and saying the ball wasn't thrown right. I knew I was behaving badly, but I couldn't seem to stop. My brother said I could try again, and when I did I missed again, and I cried again. It was too much, how even in this new place I couldn't anymore ever do anything right.

24 Late at Night

How we came to walk to school with Cathy and Laurie was that they lived down the block from us, so we'd start out walking to school and see them up ahead. They acted like they never noticed us behind them. They didn't slow down. Renee and Danny talked about how stuck up they looked in their bobby socks and saddle shoes, and about Cathy carrying a purse and looking all haughty. One day when we walked close behind them Renee said something loud enough for Cathy to hear. Cathy turned around and yelled something at Renee. Danny yelled back at Cathy and all the way to school the two of them yelled insults back and forth.

The next morning Danny hurried to catch up to them, and from then on we all walked together in the morning. In the afternoon, Danny got out fifteen minutes later, so only Renee and I walked with Laurie and Cathy.

Getting to be friends that way you didn't have to worry about what would happen if your friend got angry, whether they would stop being friends with you, because being angry was how you got to be friends. I went to Cathy's house as often as I could. During spring break, we were all over there every day. Cathy told us stories about the empty house in the middle of the block we lived on. She would see a face in an upper window, though nobody else ever did. One day Danny climbed up on the roof and looked down the chimney. He saw something, he said, it could have been a gun, and some blood.

One night Renee and I slept over in their yard in a tent, and Cathy told us about a boy who used to sleep in our room, how he woke up to see an old man standing at the foot of his bed. The old man didn't say anything. But as the boy watched, he started to shrink away.

The next night back in our room, lights already out, the wind blew cold through the open window.

"Close the window," Renee said, but I didn't want to get out of my bed and anywhere near that window.

"You close it," I said. But both of us just pulled our covers up over our heads and pretended that the wind was not so cold.

Cathy didn't tell Renee, but she told me, that on Friday night she'd be sleeping over at the house behind us that was right next to the wooden dock on the inlet. She was babysitting, and then she'd spend the night. She told me that she'd sneak out late that night, and I could come to meet her on the dock.

"Can we go out in a boat?"

"I don't know. Maybe we can find one."

#

Friday night I kept myself awake, listening to all the sounds of the night. I heard downstairs when Leroy and Mama went to bed, then I heard the noises from outside, distant cars, and the sounds of the water. It took a long time before I dared to get up and put my clothes back on, then creep down the stairs, pausing each time a stair creaked. I reached the front door and no one had woken, so I opened it and stepped outside. I took the path behind our yard to the houses on the dock. Cathy wasn't there yet. So I walked over to where she told me the house was that she'd be staying at. It was totally dark. Maybe she'd fallen asleep. I tried the door, and it wasn't locked. I went in, thinking I could wake her. But inside all the bedroom doors were shut and I was afraid to try one to look for her. So I left, and sat on the dock for awhile, listening to the lapping of the water, and hoping she'd wake up and come outside to meet me. When the wind began to blow colder, I went back home and crept back up the stairs to bed.

25 The Dress

It was getting late and I couldn't find a clean dress to wear to school. The pink one had a button missing. The skirt of the blue one with the puffy sleeves was torn away from the top. Renee had gone downstairs already.

Mama yelled from downstairs, "Annie, hurry up!"

I started again through the dresses in the closet: Too small, a stain so I couldn't wear it to school, missing buttons, ripped. Mama getting angry at me downstairs. Danny and Renee ready to leave for school. Nothing here to wear.

Mama's footsteps. I shoved hangers from one end of the closet to another, hoping to find something.

"Just what is taking you so long?" Mama stood in the doorway with her hands on her hips, glaring. No answer would be a good answer.

"I can't find a dress to wear."

Mama walked to the closet and I hurried to move out of her way as she reached large and moved hangers quick and angry. "What about this one?"

I showed her the missing buttons. She laid it down on my bed, said, "You can get those buttons sewed on yourself this afternoon. No need for you to be waiting on me to do it."

Mama found the ripped one, laid it on the bed on top of the missing button dress. She took out another, "What's wrong with this one?"

"It's too short for me."

Mama said, "Then put it over on Renee's side. No sense in having it over here if you're never going to be able to wear it," and she laid it over the foot of my bed. She kept looking for a dress. Then she yanked one out, a short-sleeved white dress covered with small blue flowers. I hadn't seen it. How did I miss it?

Mama smoothed down its skirt, checked the buttons. "And just what is the matter with this one."

I said, "I didn't see that one."

Mama said, "I don't see how you could have missed it, standing up here in front of the closet for the last half hour. Now you just better get this dress on and get downstairs in the next five minutes or you're going to wish you had." She walked quickly from my room, her footsteps on the stairs already.

Five minutes before I had to face her again.

The blue flowered dress was pretty. I didn't know why I never wore it. It fit just right. I wished I could stay upstairs away from Mama, in front of the dresser with the mirror, to look at myself in the blue flowered dress. Instead I got on socks and shoes, brushed my hair and teeth quickly, and ran downstairs.

Danny and Renee were still at the table, finishing up their corn flakes. Renee didn't look at me. Danny did, "Slowpoke." They sat on the outside of the table, the side that wasn't up against the wall, so I had to go around and squeeze into the back, and I squeezed at the end next to the living room so as not to be too close to Leroy. Leroy sat at the end of the table by the hallway door, an empty plate in front of him, waiting for food. Renee sat next to Leroy. Leroy wouldn't hurt her.

The chair at the other end of the table, next to the living room door would be where Mama would sit. But now she stood safely away at the stove, in her robe, making coffee and cooking eggs. She lifted the skillet up off the stove, the spatula in her other hand and walked over to where Leroy sat at the table. She lifted the two eggs with her spatula, and put them on Leroy's plate, all plump and white, no broken yolks.

Leroy picked up the salt and pepper shakers and shook them

over his eggs, both hands at once. Danny and Renee were done. Danny got up and picked up his book bag, and Renee took a last bite and followed him. Renee left the screen door to bang as she went through but Mama didn't say anything about it like she would have if I'd done it.

The toast popped up in the toaster and Leroy picked it up, buttered it and put in two more slices of bread.

When Mama looked at me, I wondered if I should have sat in the chair next to Leroy after all. I had poured my Cheerios and milk and now I ate as fast as I could.

She said, "Well, now, you just tell your teacher when she asks that the reason you were late was because you spent 30 minutes deciding what dress to wear."

But I wouldn't tell my teacher that.

Mama put the iron skillet back on the stove and carefully cracked and separated the half shells of two more eggs. Once done, she put the eggs on her plate. Leroy handed her two pieces of buttered toast. She poured both of them some coffee, put the coffee pot back on the stove and sat down.

Mama said, "And don't think you can lie about it either, because this afternoon I'm going to call up and ask her if you told her, and if you haven't you can expect a whipping when you get home."

Maybe she'd forget about it by this afternoon. If not, I'd just have to take the whipping.

Leroy said, "You'd better make sure you do what your mother says. Or you'll have me to answer to me." He cut his eggs into pieces with his fork, the yolk bleeding out. Leroy laid one piece of egg on his toast and took a bite.

I concentrated on my Cheerios and nowhere else. Once I finished I had to scoot behind Mama to get out, had to say excuse me. Still they might forget, might both forget. I wasn't going to tell, not my teacher, not anyone. I wasn't going to let one other person in the world in on the secret of how bad I was.

#

After school I went upstairs to change my clothes right away. I sewed the button on the dress on my bed so it would be ready for the next school day. I stayed upstairs with all my school books spread out on my green bedspread to do my homework, until Mama yelled up at me to come peel potatoes for dinner. She didn't say anything to me while I peeled the potatoes at the kitchen sink.

Mama said, "When you get done, wash those off and slice them up for mashed potatoes," but she didn't say it angry. So maybe she forgot. Leroy didn't have duty tonight, so he'd be home for supper. Mama cooked pork chops. She covered the pork chops with flour and laid them in the oil in the electric skillet. When Leroy had duty we'd have hamburgers or soup and sandwiches.

While the pork chops cooked Mama opened a can of green beans and put them in a pan which she set on a burner on the stove, but she didn't turn the burner on yet. She got a pan ready for the brown and serve rolls and turned the oven on but she didn't put them in yet. She started a pan of water boiling on top of the stove and she took the potatoes I had finished slicing and dropped them in. She got the big white plastic salad bowl out of the cupboard and while she had the cupboard door open she took out a stack of plates and set them on the table. Then she got a head of iceberg lettuce and two tomatoes from the refrigerator, and a knife from the silverware drawer and made the salad.

I finished the potatoes and Mama put the rest of them into the boiling water while I put plates, glasses, silverware, salad bowls, salt, pepper, and napkins out on the table. It felt peaceful. Maybe she forgot about the dress.

After dinner, Leroy scooted his chair back from the table and said, "That was a good dinner, Barbara."

Danny said, "Yes, that was good, Mom. Can I be excused?"

Mama said, "Yes, you can be excused, and so can Sammy and Renee," because they were both done too. I waited for her to tell me to hurry up and finish eating, but she didn't. Instead she lit a cigarette and by the time she had smoked it I was done. Mama put out her cigarette in the ashtray and looked up and over across the table at Leroy. Leroy put his cigarette out too.

Then Mama asked me, "Did you tell your teacher why you were late to school."

I thought, I bet she didn't call, but maybe she did. If I said I told my teacher maybe she would call her tomorrow. It would be worse.

"No," I said. "I didn't tell her."

I waited for her to yell, but she didn't. She looked at Leroy again and Leroy stood up. He had on his Navy whites and he wore a t-shirt. He folded his cigarettes into the sleeve of his t-shirt. He pulled his chair out from the table and pulled the corner of the table out from the wall a little, and said, "Get up from the table."

I got out on Leroy's end of the table. As I walked around Leroy took hold of my right arm and pushed me forward towards the living room door. Mama got up from the table and went through the door ahead of us, into the living room and then turned into her and Leroy's bedroom.

Leroy steered me into the bedroom over next to their big double bed. He said, "Lay on the bed, face down," so I did. He moved to the foot of the bed. Mama stood by the head.

Leroy said to Mama, "Well, I guess she needs a lesson in learning to obey her parents." He asked me, "Why didn't you tell your teacher what you were told to say?"

I said, "I don't know." I couldn't see what they were doing.

Then Leroy hit me on the top part of my legs, hard, so it made the bed bounce and me with it. It surprised me but it didn't really hurt. I kept my face down on the pillow, trying to stay quiet and not think, but maybe I moved my leg when the bed bounced because Mama yelled, "She kicked you. She kicked her own father."

Mama hit at me furiously, on my back and my head.

Leroy joined in. He slapped and hit at my legs. Both of them moved round to the side of the bed. They hit me all over my arms and legs and back and butt and head. But face down on the bed, I pretended it wasn't happening. I waited for them to get tired and stop. I wouldn't ever tell my teacher.

#

That night, I stayed awake again. There was something I needed to do. This time, going downstairs, I paused again at each creak of the stairs to make sure that no one woke. I carried one of the kitchen chairs into the living room. Carefully I stepped onto it to reach the high shelf where the photo album was kept now. High up there, I thought about my parent's bedroom, right next to the living room, how, if one of them was awake, they would be able to hear every tap or squeak of the chair. I sucked my breath in little short stabs, but I didn't stop. I pulled the photo album out of the shelf. Stretching, and the weight of it made me feel the soreness of my back and shoulders. Opening the album up to that page with nothing but the photo of me in the rollers, I pulled the photo out from its little black corners, closed the album and shoved it back in place.

I stepped off the chair, taking extra care not to fall, because of how trembly I felt. I put the chair back under the kitchen table, and sat on it. It was quiet then, very quiet, like the quietness that comes after you've been crying and crying, and finally there is no more crying left, only calm. Then I ripped the photo into tiny white pieces into the kitchen trash.

26 Like Stepping Into a Different Country

Renee, Danny, Cathy and Laurie were only a couple of houses away. If I ran, I could catch up. But I didn't want to run.

Renee wore her light blue dress with dark flowers, the one she liked to twirl in, her white sandals from last Easter and her white anklets. She and Laurie held hands and skipped.

Cathy was my friend, but school mornings Danny walked beside her. The two of them talked all the way to school.

Danny turned and yelled to me, "Hurry up." They all waited while I caught up. As soon as I got close Danny was satisfied and turned to talk to Cathy again. I slowed back down.

I watched their backs. Renee's curls bounced on the back of her head. Renee was the curly-haired one. "Look at those curls," Grandma and Aunt Sharon would say. My hair was curly too, but not like Renee's.

The sun shone bright like it would be hot later and already my thick white sweater felt too warm. But if I stopped to take it off Danny might notice and yell at me to hurry up again. I don't know why he was in such a rush to get to school anyway. He probably had a crush on the teacher or some girl in his class.

Coming up, the corner house had a low stone ledge around the yard. Danny and the rest of them had reached the end of the next block. Way too hot, I set my books down on the stone ledge and pulled off my sweater. I sat down for a minute. They didn't look back.

It was too warm and bright to hurry, but I got up and walked towards school again before the others were out of sight.

The next time I remembered to look up I couldn't even see them. Maybe they had arrived at school and gone off to their classrooms. Danny must have decided I'd have to get there on my own I was so far behind.

I stopped walking. Maybe I didn't need to catch up.

If I didn't go to school, if I went off in another direction, no one would miss me until school was out. Sometimes Renee and I walked home together with Cathy and Laurie, but not always. No one would worry about me until I didn't come home. They wouldn't start looking until an hour or so after that.

I could be far away by then. I could just go, and never go back home where they hurt me. I could go someplace where they didn't know me, where they didn't think I was bad.

I turned back in the direction away from school, and turned right at the corner so I was headed away from home as well.

The houses got older, bigger, with big front porches and balconies, and large shade trees in the yard. A few people walked by, school kids at first. A boy looked at me for a long time, but then he passed by. After awhile I only saw grown ups and little kids playing in the yards.

The houses got smaller. They didn't have big porches anymore, just little concrete ones or steps in front of the door. After awhile the houses disappeared, replaced by concrete everywhere. Up ahead the sun shone on water. It must have been the ocean, but there wasn't any beach.

The water touched several feet down from the top edge and the side of the concrete looked wet for a couple of feet higher than the water reached now. Little ripples of dark water slapped against the concrete but not like real waves. But what could it be but the ocean. It didn't look like a river. I looked across and couldn't see the other side, and that was how you could tell if it was the ocean. If you could see the other side it was a lake. If you couldn't it was the ocean.

Nearby, across the pavement, men moved things from place

to place. Sometimes they carried them on their backs, but mostly they wheeled them on long flat dollies. Someone might ask me why I wasn't in school, but I wanted to watch the men. Only one looked in my direction. He stopped, wiped the sweat off his forehead with his sleeve, and looked right at me, but he didn't say anything. His face didn't change. The man leaned against the handle of his dolly for a moment, then pushed it again.

I wanted to stick around, figure out what they were doing, but I needed to be a long way away before anyone missed me, so I walked away from the water back to a street. Before long, though, that street ended at the water, a concrete walkway right up against it, and more men worked there. They carted things from one long low concrete building to another, down towards the water.

I only knew the way from my house to Larchmont school, the way from my house to the corner store, the way to Cathy's house. Once I went with Edna to her house farther away.

From the house before this one, when we went to Christ the King school, I knew the way to the park and to the bus stop. But I didn't know how to get to our old house in Azalea Gardens. From the apartment where we first lived in Virginia I knew the way to the beach, but that was no good, even if I knew how to get there. Going towards the beach with nowhere further to go, was no use.

Every street I took ended up at the waterfront. What if I didn't make it anywhere. Already the sun was halfway up in the sky.

I started off in a new direction. This time I didn't run into the water. First I came to small houses again, then big ones. There were more trees here than in my neighborhood. They lined both sides of the street and shaded the sidewalk where I walked. The trees made shadows on the sidewalk, darker and lighter shadows and spots of bright sunlight. It felt cool beneath them. These were just the right kind of trees to climb, with big sturdy branches growing low off their trunks. Walking was easier. My body felt lighter, not dragged down like before.

My book bag with my school books was still under my right arm. I'd been carrying it without even noticing, but now that I did, my shoulder and arm ached with the strain of carrying it all this way.

Still I couldn't lose my books.

Could I? I'd never go back. I wouldn't need those books again. I imagined myself flinging the book bag away, but I didn't. Instead I set it down, right next to a U.S. mailbox, brightly painted blue. Then I ran, ran and skipped away with the thought that I wouldn't go back.

I went a long way before I felt tired again, and hot too. The trees didn't grow so thick. An empty lot appeared here and there. The houses, still big and old, looked more run down, the paint peeling off. The sun shone nearly overhead. I was hungry.

I came to a corner with a small neighborhood store that had advertising on the side, and a coke sign over the door. I went in to buy something to drink with my milk money. The store felt cooler, but it wasn't air-conditioned like a big supermarket. Pop cost a dime, more than my nickel for milk. Little bags of potato chips and popcorn hung next to the cash register. The popcorn cost a nickel so I bought a bag and went back outside. I sat on a curb on the opposite side of the street to eat, with my feet stretched out in the street.

No cars drove down the road. The salt from the yellow, cheese flavored popcorn made me more thirsty than before. Since there was nothing to drink I opened my paper sack lunch, and ate it all, the tuna fish sandwich, the banana and the cupcake. Then I remembered I should have saved some of it in case I didn't find anything to eat later.

The curb was next to a corner lot with a huge yard, and a house set way back. The house was painted dark green, and had a porch along the whole front side of it, shaded by a roof overhead.

A Negro woman, plump and comfortable looking, came out onto the porch. She called out to me, "Aren't you hot out there in the sun? What are you doing way out here?" Her voice sounded friendly. Her face looked friendly.

"No, ma'am, I'm not hot. I'm waiting for a ride," I said, in case she'd been watching me.

"Well, wouldn't you like to wait in the house for your ride? I've got some milk and cookies in here, if you'd like some." She smiled at me.

My throat was so dry. The woman looked nice and safe, but what if she called someone.

I answered, "No, I'm not hungry. I just had my lunch, and I think I'd better stay out here so they'll see me when they come."

"Okay, child, but if you change your mind, you just come right in and have some cookies." She walked back into the house.

Maybe she wasn't suspicious then. Maybe it would be okay to go and get something cool to drink. The house looked so big and comfortable and cool. I could relax there.

I got up and walked out in the street a little ways, trying to act like I was just taking a look to see if my ride was coming to pick me up. I walked further up the street like I was just checking to see if I could see a car coming from up there. I walked slowly until I thought I was out of the woman's sight if she was watching out a window, then I walked quickly, looking over my shoulder every once in awhile to see if the woman came after me.

I slowed down, a little bit tired and hot.

The woman was so nice, and she didn't try to push. Probably she wouldn't have called the police about me being out of school. Maybe that was what was different about Negroes that made white people dislike them so much, that they were good to children. The

Negroes might understand that children had feelings just like grownups. White grownups didn't. Maybe the woman would have let me stay with her.

I knew white people didn't like Negroes because of what I'd read in the *Saturday Evening Post*. The Negroes had marches, or sit-ins trying to be served lunch, and the white people came with clubs to beat them. The Negroes didn't fight back. They just curled themselves into a ball, with their arms up over their heads to protect themselves. It didn't seem like much protection when I looked at them in the pictures, and saw the policemen with their clubs, and blood streaming out of some people's heads.

After I read that story I imagined myself as a Negro, marching. We got beaten, but still we marched. So in the end the white people admired our courage and were ashamed of how they had treated us.

And I knew too that white people didn't like Negroes because we'd had a maid for awhile. When Amy was in the hospital, and afterwards when Mama got sick, the Navy had paid for a maid to help out. A boy from the neighborhood had come to play with Danny and he'd said something mean about Dorothy just because she was a Negro, no other reason. Luckily Dorothy wasn't there that day. Dorothy was nice to kids too. She didn't talk much, but one day when the ice cream truck came around, she asked us kids if we'd like a Popsicle, and bought all four of us one for a dime apiece. When Mama got home and heard about it, she was angry. She said, you don't let someone who makes five dollars a day buy you Popsicles.

A railroad crossing lay up ahead. Train tracks went places. I followed them. These tracks ran on and on, past the houses close together, on to farmhouses far apart set away from the tracks which ran through the fields. The tracks ran from the trimmed back yards and the sun straight overhead to grass growing wild and the sun lower down in the sky. I lay down on the grass, long and cool, made a dent so the long blades bent over my head and made some shade. The cool grasses pressed against my cheek.

On the track, I jumped from tie to tie, the ties a little farther apart than I could step without that little jump. I wasn't tired at all any more. Way up ahead I saw a river.

The tracks came round in a long curve then ran along the edge of the river on top of a high bank. Farther up the rails separated from the bank and turned into a railway bridge stretched out over the water. The other bank of the river was so far away it was just a blend of brown and green. The bridge for the cars, or for the people, was nowhere in sight.

There was a tiny space on the railroad bridge between the track itself and the railing. Probably the railroad cars stuck out that much. Even if they didn't I didn't want to be scrunched up there as the wheels screeched past, sparks flying. Below the bridge, there wasn't much of anything to get a hold of. I could get a hand grip on the bottom of the bridge where the railing was, but there was no place to wedge my feet to help me hold on. I didn't know if I would be strong enough to pull myself back up after the train had gone by.

The water looked very far down. The bridge was higher up than the high dive of a pool. It was higher than the bluff my brother and my cousins sometimes jumped off of into a deep part of a dammed up river in Missouri, lots higher. Sometimes they claimed to have plunged down so far into the water that they touched the bottom. From this high I might not just touch the bottom but hit it hard. I couldn't see past the surface to tell how deep it was.

But as long as I followed the railroad tracks I was going somewhere. I followed them out onto the bridge.

One step out, another step, another, still close enough to run back. I didn't jump. The bridge wasn't solid underneath. I checked each time to make sure that my stretched out front foot was on the tie before I shifted my weight onto it and lifted up my back foot. I reached the point where I didn't think I could run back if the train were behind me. I didn't see a train. Halfway, still no train. I could only run forward. I listened for the train now, more than looked and I walked faster, even though I was up there on the bridge, so far out, high above everything.

The river ended. The other bank rose to meet the track, and now even if the train came towards me from up ahead I'd be able to outrun it. A whole river lay between me and my old home. I stepped onto the bank like stepping into a different country.

After awhile the tracks turned and ran parallel to the river again, and now I could leave the tracks. The only road was a wide paved one with no sidewalks, really country now, plowed fields, mailboxes coming in clusters along the road far away from the houses.

I opened one of the mailboxes, nothing there. I tried another, pulled out several letters, and a big manila envelope. There might be money in one of the letters. People didn't usually send money through the mail, but there might be, and I tore open the envelopes, and looked through the letters.

No money.

I looked closer at one of the letters, read a few lines, someone's trip was going well. I dropped all the envelopes except the manila one. I kept it and the magazine I found inside.

At the next cluster of mailboxes a woman ran out of a house, and screamed at me, "You leave that mailbox alone." Her voice sounded so clear I ran for a long ways before I realized she was way across the field too far away to chase me.

It was getting into late afternoon, past time for children to be getting out of school. By now I might have been missed. The buildings changed from farmhouses to one story houses closer together, each looking pretty much like the rest, still with big yards but the grass mostly cut short. A store came up on the right and I headed for it.

It was bigger than the store from the morning, with several windows in front and a parking lot. But it wasn't a supermarket. Only one clerk worked inside.

I headed round to the back aisles where the woman couldn't see me. In baking goods I picked up a bag of chocolate chips and stuffed it into the manila envelope. I held the envelope with the magazine side out so the bulge wouldn't show.

From the next aisle I slid a bottle of Dr. Pepper down the envelope, and kind of hid it by putting my sweater in front of it and holding that up against my chest too.

I couldn't find a bottle opener, but I picked up several packs of matches and added them to the rest.

The candy and Hostess cupcakes were all right down where the woman could see me if she looked, but I moved towards then anyway. I picked up a package of Hostess cupcakes. Before I opened the envelope and stuffed the cupcakes in I looked over to where the woman was to see if it was safe.

The woman's eyes were right on mine.

"Get away from that candy rack." The woman's black hair was pulled back tight. She had a sharp nose and narrow eyes.

"What have you got in that envelope?" her voice accused, but she wasn't sure.

"Nothing, I just have a magazine that I got in the mail." I checked out the distance to the door in case she demanded to look in the envelope.

The woman glared. She motioned with her head towards the door. "You get out of here, and don't you ever come back again."

I walked to the door, kind of sideways so I could see what the woman was doing. The woman watched. Once I got outside I ran, in case she changed her mind and called the police. They'd take me back.

After a few blocks I saw a wooded lot. I sat down in a cleared area with a big sawed off tree trunk. I ate chocolate chips until they made me thirsty, then tried to scrape the cap off the Dr. Pepper against the sawed off edge of the tree trunk, and, when that didn't work, on a big bolder. Finally I broke the top of the bottle on the boulder and drank the Dr. Pepper, avoiding the sharp edges.

Maybe tomorrow, or the next day, when I was far enough away, I could get a job. Maybe I could sell newspapers, like Dan did in *Little Men* before he came to Plumfield, but I didn't know how to play the violin like Nat did, so I couldn't earn any money that way.

Later I was in a schoolyard swinging. Rain puddled beneath the swings, so I pumped with my arms and never touched the ground. Two girls played on the other side of the schoolyard. One girl came closer and I recognized her. She'd been in my classroom at Christ the King before I switched to public school. I couldn't have come very far then if she lived here. I let my swing slow down and stepped out over the puddle. The girl had been one of the popular kids.

"Hi," the girl said. She smiled, and skipped over closer to me, so her braids flew up then fell back down on her shoulders again. She had never been friendly at school.

"Hi," I said.

"What are you doing all the way out here?" she asked.

"I'm visiting a friend."

"Oh, where is she?"

The other girl came closer and shouted, "Let's go. We have to get home."

"Well, I guess I have to get going now," she ran to catch up.

At Christ the King school the only two people I used to speak to were Thomas Wright and Donald. They were easy to talk to. The three of us whispered together all day long in the back of the room until the teacher caught on and separated us. But at recess boys played only with other boys. I was on my own. None of the girls ever asked me to play. Every recess I walked around the blacktop of the playground, by myself. Every lunch I ate alone.

Now that the two girls had gone I tried out all the swings, hung on the monkey bars, slid down the slide. No one called me home to dinner. I moved back towards the swings, and, with a running start, leaped right into the middle of one of the puddles. It made a good splash.

No one yelled at me about my muddy shoes.

I stepped out of the puddle, then jumped back in again. The muddy water dripped down my legs.

Back in the swing, I leaned way back, pumped myself higher and higher. I stretched my foot out to reach one high branch of the tree that grew in front of the swings, then stretched to touch a higher branch just with the tip of my shoe.

No one told me not to swing so high.

No one told me to stop swinging and get home now to help my mother.

But I would need a job later on, so I'd better keep my clothes clean. I wiped my shoes off as best I could on the grass.

The air had turned crisp. Back in Missouri, on the Willis farm, sometimes out in the fields where young trees grew close together, we'd bend them down over one another to form a hut of trees. We sat in there, leaning back against the tree trunks, and told stories in the dark.

Past the schoolyard was another wood but the trees were

older trees and didn't grow close together like that. Maybe farther out in the country, there'd be a field of saplings so I could make a hut to sleep in.

At the edge of the wood a grassy bank sloped down to a two-lane highway. Hardly any cars came by on the road. It wasn't really dark yet, but some cars had their headlights on. A wind blew.

The soft grass would make a good place to camp if I moved a little further away from the roadside so I wouldn't be seen by the morning traffic, and if I could stay warm. I wasn't really cold yet, but I thought I'd try a fire, on the grass because I didn't want to start a forest fire. My first matches blew out, so I climbed down the bank where it was less windy. I lit the pages of the magazine. Flames shot up bright for a few minutes then went out.

A car went past. I got the fire going again and spread out the pages of the magazine over it like a tent. The car slowed down and stopped on the edge of the road. A man stepped out on the driver's side. He stood there by the car, next to the open door on the highway. He had kind of a soft face.

"Kind of cold to be out, isn't it?" He said, his hand holding onto the handle of his car door.

"Oh, I'm not cold. Anyway I'll be going home in a while."

The man looked at my fire, and I wished it was a better fire. He looked back at me and for a few seconds he didn't say anything, then he smiled and said, "I see you've got a fire to keep you warm."

"Yes."

The man looked at the fire again. He moved his hand off the car door handle.

He hesitated, then he moved his hand back, "Keep warm then." He smiled again, opened the door, slid back into the front seat and shut the car door. He started the car, and drove off.

Now I would have to leave. The fire had died down again,

and I stomped it out the rest of the way. I went up by the woods to find a stick to dig up some dirt to cover it with. I stirred up the dirt but I didn't have any water to pour over it. So I stirred it longer to make sure every spark was out.

Walking warmed me up. The man's eyes were brown, soft brown, like Professor Bhaer's eyes, but he didn't have a beard like Professor Bhaer. His skin was smooth. Maybe he had a wife and the two of them were like Jo and Professor Bhaer who took in Nat and his friend, Dan, at Plumfield. The man probably had other children too.

I walked now through some kind of development, rows of houses and yards all alike. Some of them had kids' toys scattered about the fenced yards; here and there a tricycle or a wagon. But no one played in the yards. The light was dim now. Where would I sleep? Maybe on the other side of the development there would be fields again, or a tree.

#

It was really dark. Another store up ahead was closed up tight. A telephone booth stood in the parking lot, and its fluorescent "PHONE" sign made a weak light, enough to see the painted "Coke" sign on the side of the store. Maybe I could break into the store and steal some money, or some food. The only window was high above my head. I walked around the building to look for a way in, but saw nothing but the locked door. Well, tomorrow then, as soon as it opened up I would go in and ask the owner if he needed any help. The owner might give me the job, then ask me if I'd like to stay with his family in their spare room. The storekeeper that I imagined had kind eyes like the man in the car, but he was older and wore glasses.

It was cold. I went into the phone booth to get warm. I shut the door and the light came on. It was warmer. This was probably the best place I would find to sleep tonight. I opened the door a little.

The light went off, but then the cold seeped in. I lay down, but it was very cold. The wind blew in. I got up and closed the door, then lay back down. The light shone right into my eyes. I took off my sweater, and put it over my head. I tried to stretch out the sweater so that it was over my eyes, and over my shoulders too. The air seeped in under the sweater and raised goose bumps on my arms. I put my sweater back on then lay down again, determined to ignore the light. The glare of the light shone right through my eyelids. I thought the cold must be better than that, and took off my sweater, to stretch it over my head, and then pulled it tightly around my arms. It was cold. I put my sweater back on and put my arms around my eyes to shut out the light.

#

Everything shook. Pounding. Something banged on the telephone booth. I opened my eyes. Outside was very dark. A big dark shape stood by the door of the phone booth. A man. The man shouted something. He wanted to use the phone. I stood up and pulled open the door to the phone booth. It folded inward and I slipped through the opening in the dark that happened when I opened the door.

The man stood beside the door, his hand on it.

I moved away as fast as I could. I thought the man was going to say something to me, but then he shrugged and went inside the booth. He closed the door. The man wore a sports coat and had slicked down hair. I moved away from the booth, around to the other side of the little store so I was hidden but could still watch the booth.

His car was parked there right in front of the booth. It looked dark, with fins. Danny would know what kind it was. Cars all looked alike to me. It was cold. I walked up and down the store length to keep warm. The man talked for such a long time. Maybe up ahead there'd be a better place to sleep, a field of long grasses, the bent grasses making a cushion, the tall grasses keeping off the wind. I was tired. The man kept talking.

He pulled the door open, and stepped out of the booth whistling, with a quick step. He didn't even look around for me, but got right into his car and drove away. I waited for the sound of his car to die away, then went back into the booth.

I woke up, warm, having to go to the bathroom. I lay there and thought about getting up, opening the phone booth door, going out into more cold, so I kept on lying there. There was no one to yell at me. My pants would dry.

#

The sound of a motor woke me. Was the man back? No, it was light outside.

"Get out of there," said the voice from the police car pulled up next to the phone booth. The policeman leaned over to the passenger side and opened the door.

"Get in," he said. I pulled in the folding door of the phone booth. The open car door blocked me from running to the right. The officer watched me closely to see I didn't take off in the other direction. He'd be after me.

"I told you to get in here." He sounded cross and impatient. I should have left the phone booth last night. That man who came to use the phone must have called the police and told them I was here. I slid into the seat.

"Shut the door."

It was probably best to do as he said, for now.

"Now tell me what you're doing out here." The policeman was bossing, not asking. He was about as tall as my stepfather. His belly stuck out.

"I came to buy some milk at the store." I said.

"At six o'clock in the morning?" He snorted. "And what were

you doing in that phone booth?"

"I was waiting for the store to open," I said.

"Yeah, what were you really doing?" I sat with my feet flat on the floor, my arms down by my side, and stared at the dashboard, while he tapped his foot and waited.

"I asked you what you were doing here," he said.

I stared at the dashboard. He couldn't make me tell him anything.

"Hey, kid, do you want to go to jail?" I didn't think kids went to jail, but I wasn't sure. I knew he was bluffing though. His voice was all bluster.

"No," I said.

"Well you better start talking then," he said.

Jail was just another place to be, and he hadn't threatened to hit me. I scooted back on the seat and looked out the car window to think how I could get away.

The policeman kept talking, *better talk*, *going to jail*, *who did I think I was anyway*. He started the police car. His big face was red and he kept his lips pushed together during the ride. He parked the car in front of a red brick police station. The policeman got out of his door and before I could get mine opened and try to run away, he stood by my door. He opened it and told me to get out now. He reached for my arm and I moved it away and he didn't take it but he kept so close behind me I couldn't go anywhere but up to the police station and through the station door.

The room was big, filled with tables and file cabinets: the file cabinets around the edges and two big long tables shoved together, papers scattered over it.

Two men sat at the tables. One had a typewriter, a big black one, in front of him and a fresh sheet of paper, rolled in, ready to type on.

"She won't say nothing," The fat policeman said.

Both of the men looked up but neither said anything to the burly policeman. It wasn't like the burly policeman said hello, and they said hello back. They looked at him like they might look at a piece of furniture just seeing what was there, considering it.

They weren't impressed by him.

These two looked nice. Both of them were younger than the cop who picked me up, but they weren't real young. They didn't wear uniforms. They wore dress pants, and white shirts. The one at the typewriter smiled at me and motioned towards a chair.

"Just sit down there a minute until we finish this report," he said.

"Ok, what do we got?" he asked his partner. I rested my head on my arm and looked out the window, while their voices droned on. The fat cop left. The sun shone bright into the center of the room. My eyes wanted to close, but I kept them open. The two men finished their report. The man at the typewriter scrolled the paper out, put it in a manila folder and laid it on the table.

"Well, hello," said the man who hadn't been typing, the one with the nicer face and more little wrinkles around his eyes. "I'm Detective Davies, and this is my partner, Detective Phelps."

Detective Phelps nodded at me.

"So what were you doing out so early in the morning?" asked Detective Davies.

"My mother sent me to buy milk," I said.

"Kind of early in the morning to be going out to buy milk," Detective Davies said.

"Our clock broke, so we didn't know what time it was," I said.

"I see," said Detective Davies. He spread his fingers out and ran them back through his hair a couple of times.

"Got any brothers or sisters?" Detective Phelps asked me. It was better to say no. Then I wouldn't have to answer any questions about them. The two men never said anything about what I answered. Detective Davies asked me a question. Then Detective Phelps asked me a question, or Detective Davies asked me another one, both of them friendly. The fat cop walked through on his way out of the station. He heard me talking and grunted disgust. Detective Davies grinned at me then and I decided I liked him. I couldn't decide whether they believed me.

"My mother will be worrying about me if I don't come back with the milk," I said.

"Where did you say you lived?" Detective Phelps asked me. I remembered the houses, all alike, that I had passed earlier, described them to him. "I don't know the address," I said, "We just moved there. That's why we need milk."

"You know where they are?" Detective Phelps asked his partner, and when his partner nodded Detective Phelps waved him on. He picked up a clean sheet of paper and scrolled it into the typewriter, while Detective Davies picked up a jacket and a hat and motioned me to come along. "We'll have a look for that house of yours."

#

"That look like it?" Detective Davies asked me. He'd asked the same about several other houses. I tried to figure out from the look of the yard and the house whether anyone was home.

"It could be, " I said, so he pulled the car over.

"Come on," he said, opening the passenger door for me. He pulled open the gate of the metal fence that surrounded a modern looking house on a small lot. He led the way up to the small cement porch and rapped on the door.

A woman answered, so I didn't follow him on up the porch.

"This isn't the house," I said.

But he didn't go back to the car with me. Instead he showed his badge to the woman, motioned towards me, and asked, "Have you seen this girl before?"

The woman was nice looking, a little old, older than my mother, not too old. Not tired looking like my mother. Too bad I didn't live there.

The woman said, "Why, that's the girl I saw walking in front of the house last night. I wondered what she was doing out so late."

"Does she live around here?" asked Detective Davies.

The woman looked at me longer. She shook her head, "No, I never saw her around here before last night."

"Thank you, ma'am." He walked back to the car with big long steps, easy steps. I followed after him. I waited for him to say something to me about my story, but he walked over to the passenger side of the car and opened my door for me. He stood behind the open door with his hand on the handle and waited for me to step up into the seat. Then he shut the door, but just firm enough to shut it tight, not hard, not angry.

We drove around some more. I still tried to guess which house would have nobody home. I decided to take a chance on a house with some kids' toys out in the front yard. A tricycle lay on its side.

"That looks like my little brother's tricycle."

When Detective Davies looked over at me I remembered that I'd said that I didn't have any brothers or sisters. But he didn't say anything, and when he parked the car I thought maybe he'd forgotten.

No one answered his knock.

"This is it," I said. "Those are our curtains." I pointed to the picture window. The detective knocked on the door again, and waited.

"They probably went to look for me," I told him. "They probably got worried. I can wait for them by myself. You don't need to stay."

But Detective Davies turned around and leaned back against the frame of the front door.

"I can't do that. I can't leave you anywhere unless we find your parents."

Then how was I ever going to be able to get away.

Detective Davies said, "What do you say, I take you back to the station now? We can come back here later and check if they've come back home."

"Ok," I said. I wanted to just sit down on the porch, lean back on the house in the coolness of the shadows, and close my eyes and rest, not think, just rest, just wait, see who came home, but Detective Davies wasn't going to go away, and even if he did I wouldn't be able to stay and wait. I would have to get going again.

Back in the police station, the two detectives asked me some of the same questions again.

"You sure you don't remember your address?" Detective Davies asked.

"No, I told you. We just moved here." Only now I knew he knew I lied.

There was no way to convince them to let me go, but I repeated my answers just the same.

"Where'd you move from?" This was from Phelps.

"Norfolk."

He dialed before I realized my mistake. He said into the phone, "Get the Norfolk police department."

"Hello, this is the Newport News police department. Listen, have you got any missing person reports, white girl, ten years old, blondish hair, blue eyes."

"Sure, I'll wait."

#

Detective Davies took me to a restaurant.

We sat across from each other in the booth with its maroon plastic seats and white laminated table. A waitress in a black skirt and white apron brought two menus.

Detective Davies said, "What would you like to eat?"

"I'm not hungry."

"After a day without eating you're not hungry," Detective Davies said. "Are you sure?"

I didn't tell him about the chocolate chips or the pop. He was a policeman.

Besides, that wasn't the reason I wasn't hungry. It was like, if I ate, I was admitting that it was over. I was caught. It was done.

Detective Davies ordered a big breakfast, eggs, bacon, hash browns, toast. He spread strawberry jam on the toast. "Sure you wouldn't like a piece?"

"No," I said.

"Okay, have it your way. I just don't understand how you could not be hungry."

On the way back to the station Detective Davies stopped the car at a two-story house.

"This is my apartment," he said. "I've got to pick up a few things. You'll wait in the car for me, won't you? You won't try to run away again?"

I said, "No."

He said, "I'll leave the radio on for you." Then he got out of the car and headed for the house.

He had an outside entry to a second floor apartment, up a flight of wooden stairs. As soon as he went inside I looked around for a place to run.

There were more houses on the side of this street. On the other side there was a field, but only grass, no trees. No place to hide.

What would happen if I just took off running down the street, and he came outside and saw me. Would he shoot me? I didn't think that they shot kids, but I wasn't sure.

They would take me back. This was my last chance to get away. Do it now. Run, just run as fast as I could.

But I felt so tired. It was too hard to try again. I leaned back against the seat, closed my eyes, listened to the music on the radio. I felt the sun through the car window.

#

The woman came in a small, black, old fashioned car. We saw her pull up in front of the station through one of the two big windows at the front. Detective Davies had pulled up the Venetian blinds of the left one, and when he saw her coming he said, "Let's go out and meet the social worker. She's going to be driving you back to Norfolk."

So we stood on the sidewalk outside and watched the woman as she opened her car door and walked around the car and onto the sidewalk. As soon as the woman saw me she hurried over.

She said "You poor thing." She put her arms around me and pulled me towards her. She was a grownup. I couldn't stop her, but I didn't move my body at all. This woman didn't even know me.

The woman let loose of me.

Detective Davies, said, "This is Mrs. Morley." He waited a minute, then he said, "Well, I'd better be getting back to work. Nice meeting you, Annie."

He took my hand and he shook it, and that was okay, having him shake my hand and I shook his hand back.

Mrs. Morley said, "You can leave her to me now, Detective," and Detective Davies touched the tip of his hat and said, "Yes, I'll do that." Then he said to me, "You take care of yourself, now." He turned around and walked back inside the station. Through the glass I saw him go back to the table and sit down with his back to us. He didn't turn around.

Then I thought maybe Mrs. Morley would be hugging me again, but she opened the passenger door and said, "Well we'd better get going," and I got in and she closed the door. She went round to the driver's side. She didn't put her arm on me or anything, just put the key in the ignition and started up the car. We drove off. I expected her to talk, but she didn't, just drove. She didn't ask me any questions. I guess she already knew the answers so I didn't have to give her any, and now I was going back and I was so tired.

I leaned against the door and leaned my head on the warm window pane, but I didn't close my eyes. I looked out at all the things I'd seen yesterday for awhile, then I couldn't tell anymore if they were the same I'd seen before or different because she was going some different way. Then we reached a downtown with stores and tall buildings, and definitely it was different.

At Norfolk, there were two more glass doors, and Mrs. Morley hurried out of her side of the car to be right next to me as we walked inside. But she didn't reach for my arm like the blustery cop. She was beside me all the same, but I wasn't going to try to run then.

Mrs. Morley stopped at the front desk, a high counter with a woman standing behind it. She wrote something in a book.

Mrs. Morley said, "This way," and led me down a hall of green plastered walls, through a heavy wooden door, into a room. In the center of the room was a metal table, the kind with the folding legs, with metal chairs placed around it, and in one of the dark metal chairs sat my mother.

Mama started to get up, to come towards me reaching one hand out in my direction, but Mrs. Morley said, "Annie is going to take a few tests now. I'll just take her down the hall to the social worker, then I'll come back and we'll have a chat."

So Mama sat back down in the metal chair, slowly, like she was tired too.

Mrs. Morley led me back out, down the hall to another room. Another woman was in there and Mrs. Morley said to her, "This is Annie."

"Okay," said the woman in the lab coat with the dark hair, and Mrs. Morley left.

The woman motioned me over to two chairs by a small table.

"Why don't you have a seat."

There were some toys in a box by the table, but I just sat down in one of the little chairs. The woman sat in the other. She had a thick stack of big cards in her hand, and a pad of paper.

She said, "I'm going to show you some pictures and I want you to tell me what is happening in them. OK?"

"Ok," I said. Whatever they wanted, stories, whatever. I was tired.

The woman handed me a card. "What do you think is happening in this picture?" she asked me.

It was a picture of a boy sitting at a table. A violin lay on the table and the boy looked at the violin. I didn't know what she wanted me to say.

I said, "It's a boy looking at the violin."

"Yes," the woman said. She wrote something on her pad. Then she looked up at me and waited.

"Maybe he wants to play the violin," I said.

She wrote down more on the pad. Then she waited, but I didn't say anything else. She took another card off the stack and laid it down in front of me. I told her something about it, and the next and the next. But the woman didn't like any of it. She didn't say a word about anything that I said.

At the end the woman said, "I'll take you back to where Mrs. Morley and your mother are."

She took me to the door and left. I sat in the metal chair that was empty, next to Mrs. Morley, across from my mother.

Mama was saying, "I took her to the mental health clinic, but I don't think they did her much good there."

Mrs. Morley said, "You know private psychiatrists aren't always as much as you think they might be."

Mama said, "Is that right? Perhaps we could find one for her then." It was her polite voice. Mama couldn't afford even a cheap one.

Then Mama said, "Actually, though, Annie didn't really seem to give the psychologist much of a chance. She didn't talk to him much."

Mrs. Morley said, "No, well sometimes it's like that. You have to wait until someone really wants to be helped. My niece was like that. She wouldn't take help from anyone. Then when she was eighteen she called me up on the phone, and broke down crying, 'Please help me, please help me,' she kept saying"

Mama wanted to get away, but she talked on like she had to talk with Mrs. Morley, even though Mrs. Morley wasn't being mean or anything. Mrs. Morley just kept on talking. Neither of them looked at me. They talked on just like I hadn't come back.

Finally Mrs. Morley turned to me and smiled and said, "Now I want you to promise me that if you ever decide to run away again you'll call me up first. Now will you promise me that?" as if she was someone I had some reason to trust.

I said, "yes," because I knew I had to, like Mama had to, and then maybe this woman would let us go. Of course I wouldn't call the woman up if I ran away, just so I would be caught right away. And I would never ever call anyone on the phone, crying, "Please help me."

27 Different

The first thing that happened between being brought back and everything being back to normal, was right after we'd walked out of the glass double doors of the police station. Mama put her arm around me and pulled me up close to her, so tight I was sure there'd be wrinkles where my head pressed against her black dress that she only wore for special things.

This time the special thing had been picking me up from the police station. Mama pulled me against her all along the walk to the car.

I didn't know how to act with her being so different.

Before we reached the car with Leroy inside, he got out and met us on the sidewalk. He put his arm around me too and pulled me over to him.

Mama pulled me back to her. She said, "She's my daughter."

Leroy wasn't in his Navy blues, or his Navy whites. He had on a suit, maybe the suit he wore when he and Mama got married. He said, "Well, she's my daughter too." When he said that he pulled me back over to him and into the suit, so it got wrinkled too, but then he stopped pulling and Mama pulled still so I stumbled back into her black dress. Leroy kept his arm on my shoulder though and we all walked back to the car.

Maybe they both forgot it was me because they acted like it was someone else they had squished between them like that.

It was hard to walk. My legs and feet kept bumping Mama. Normally she would have slapped at me to stop being so clumsy but now she didn't. At the car door it was a little easier because Leroy let go and opened up the passenger door for us.

I would have ridden in the back but Mama guided me into the front seat, then got in herself and shut the door.

At home, when we went in the house, Mrs. Wiley waited at the kitchen table. She was old and lived across the street by herself. She looked up, with a questioning look at me, but all she said was, "Well, I'll be getting along now."

Mama said, "Thank you for watching Sammy and the baby for me."

"Oh, it was no trouble. She went down for her nap after her breakfast and she hasn't stirred since. And Sammy's been in the living room arranging and rearranging his toy soldiers almost the whole time you were gone. "

"Well, thanks all the same," Mama said.

Mrs. Wiley touched Mama's shoulder, "Now, dear, you know I'm glad to do it, any time."

Leroy said he'd better be getting back to the base now. He went into his and Mama's bedroom and came out wearing his Navy whites. Normal, except that he came up to me and put his arm around my shoulders and squeezed again before he left.

After they were both gone, Mama said, "Why don't you go on upstairs and take a hot bath."

So I filled the tub really full with hot water and lots of suds. On another day I would have been afraid to run so much water. Today I soaked in it because no one waited to go next and Mama wasn't going to yell at me for taking too long.

Except Mama called up from the bottom of the stairs, and her voice was scared, like she never sounded. She said, "Is anything the matter?"

I called down, "No," and I got out then.

#

Another thing that happened between being brought back and everything being back to normal, was Mama asking, "Did you think we were too strict about the bike?"

At first I couldn't even remember what she meant, then I did.

"No," I said. The day before I'd run away, there'd been a bike registration at school. Everyone was supposed to bring their bike to get a number engraved on it. When I didn't have mine ready to go, Leroy said, well you don't need to get yours registered then.

That would never have made me run away. I was used to being left out. That wasn't even as bad as when Leroy and Mama told us all that we were going to the Giant Open Air market for a treat, then I sat in the back corner still and as far away as I could while Renee and Sammy and Danny ate their candy bars and I didn't get one.

It was silly to think I'd run away for that.

I didn't have a reason, not some one single thing that I could say caused me to decide. I didn't decide. I ran away when I saw I could.

#

At Saturday breakfast the day after I came home Mama said to Leroy how I'd been much more helpful getting things out for breakfast than I usually was.

Leroy said, "I think Annie has changed from her old ways."

But just like always I'd tried to think of everything that Mama would want on the table and I put it out. Only Mama acted different because when I started putting out cereal bowls, she didn't yell. She just said, "Why don't you put out some plates instead. I'm going to make eggs and bacon for breakfast this morning."

So then I knew to get out the salt and pepper, and knives and forks, as well as spoons.

Mama agreed with Leroy, "Yes, I think she has. So I don't think there's any need to be yelling at her and punishing her like we had to do before."

Leroy said, "Of course not, no need at all."

After breakfast he drove me around Norfolk while I tried to describe the place where I dropped off my books, *a place with big houses and trees, next to the mailbox on the corner*. His mouth got tighter each time after he asked me, *Does this look like it?*, and we looked, but the book bag wasn't there. Still he didn't say anything. He didn't punish me.

#

All during the next week Leroy told me how much better I acted and to keep it up and not slip back into my old ways.

Then later he told me he thought I was slipping back into my old ways, and I'd better be careful.

And I was careful, watching for it, waiting for it, the moment when he'd decide that I'd gone back to my old ways and I was just the same.

I just wanted to be ready.

Between being brought back and everything being back to normal I broke one of the little panes in the window next to the back door. I dropped the broom handle and it fell against the pane so it broke and the pieces of glass dropped down to the floor.

I was ready then. I almost wanted it to happen then, so I didn't have to wait any more.

Leroy got still and quietly angry. I waited for him to slap me. But he just said, "That'll come out of your allowance."

Which was nothing because I never counted on my allowance. My allowance was almost always taken away before I got it anyway.

#

But the last thing that happened between being brought back and everything being back to normal, was going to see the nun, Sister Veronica, the one who had me say the *Magnificat*.

Mama said, "Sister Veronica wants to talk to you."

I figured it was about running away, but I didn't know how Sister Veronica knew about that because I wasn't at Christ the King school anymore.

After church we all went over to the office building next door. Sister Veronica was already there inside a little office. It didn't have a big desk like the large outer office, only folding chairs, and she motioned at us to sit down in them. She was already seated.

Leroy said, "Thank you, Sister."

Sister Veronica turned to him and Mama. She said, "I guess you're wondering why I wanted to talk to Annie today."

"Oh, no ma'am," Leroy said, his feet flat on the floor. "Whatever you want to talk to her about, that's fine."

Sister Veronica said, "I just wanted to know what would make her choose to run away from home."

Mama's voice trembled. "Yes, we'd like to know that too."

Sister Veronica turned to me, and she wasn't like at school, where even though she gave me the *Magnificat* to say, she had also pulled the boy by the hair in the lunchroom, and chewed out the class for flunking the religion test. And when we talked too much she'd made us all stand with our hands behind our backs and stare at the clock for half an hour. Right now Sister Veronica didn't seem like she ever got angry like that. She just seemed a little sad.

She said, "Can you tell me, Annie, just what made you decide to run away from home?"

"I don't know, Sister." My hands held the side of my folding chair and I closed them tighter, and opened them back up again.

"But there must have been something, to make you leave your home like that."

"No, Sister" I said.

Sister Veronica said, "Don't you know what it was?"

"No, Sister."

"Maybe you were having trouble in school, and were afraid to tell your parents about it. Was that it?" Sister Veronica was a lot like the psychiatrist at the Mental Health Clinic then, but she wasn't sweating.

"No, Sister" I said. What did she want me to say?

Leroy sat quietly, looking at Sister Veronica. Mama looked at her knees and then she'd look at Sister Veronica too, and it seemed like she wanted to get up and move around, just like me.

Sister Veronica sat up and her black habit hung down straight instead of folding in the places where she bent over. She said to Mama, and her voice was so soft, so gentle, "Maybe it would be easier for her to talk to me if it were only me and her."

Leroy jumped right up, "Certainly, Sister."

But Mama wasn't so quick. She looked at her hands folded over her purse in her lap. She laced her fingers together, then unlaced them. Then she got up. Mama said, "If you think it would be better."

Sister Veronica said in her so soft, so soothing voice, "Yes, I think it would."

Mama walked out of the room, with her head and her shoulders bowed down, carrying her purse in her hands in front of her.

Then the chairs where Mama and Leroy had sat were empty and there was no one between me and Sister Veronica. She said, "I won't be talking to your parents about whatever you say to me. So, can you tell me now what caused you to leave home?"

"I don't know, Sister."

"Was it something that happened at home?"

"I don't know, Sister."

Sister Veronica said, in the soft way she talked to my mother, "But, there must have been something."

I didn't know how to tell her about Danny and Renee and Cathy being so far up ahead and thinking I didn't have to catch up, I could just go, and how that felt not to have to go to school and then back home again.

How it felt laying down my books by the mailbox, leaving all their weight on the sidewalk.

How I was the bad one always being punished.

It seemed like she was questioning me like my mother did, trying to get it out of me that I was bad, that there was this great badness inside that made me act as I did. I didn't want her to know, not Sister Veronica who let me say the *Magnificat*, the longest piece, for the Monsignor.

I said, "I don't know why I ran away. I just left."

Not even if it made her sad, and worried like the psychologist at the clinic. Maybe, if she'd known, she wouldn't have let me say the *Magnificat*. Maybe now she'd be sorry she had.

But she just sat quietly and waited. She didn't move at all on her chair, or change her position. Even now she didn't look angry at me. She didn't yell.

I didn't move either but I looked down at the wood floor, how the pieces were put together so the boards in one row started and stopped in the middle of the boards in the next row.

Sister Veronica's eyes were big looking at me and then she stood up and went to the doorway of the room.

"Mr. and Mrs. Bradford," she said, "You can come back in."

They came back in but Sister Veronica didn't sit back down and neither did Leroy or Mama. Mama held onto the strap of her purse in front of her with both hands instead of just one.

Sister Veronica came over and stood by my chair. She said, "You know you can call me here at Christ the King anytime you need someone to talk to."

Mama moved her purse from hand to hand and looked down at the floor.

Sister Veronica said to Mama, "Thank you for bringing her."

Mama said, "Yes, of course we're glad to have you talk to her. Anything you think might help." She talked like she had talked to the social worker at the police station, polite until she could get away.

#

In the car, away from Sister Veronica, I imagined I'd told her why I ran away. *No*, she'd answered. *You aren't bad. They made a mistake. I know you. You could never be bad. You're the one I chose to say the Magnificat, to play the part of Mary. You're good.*

I leaned back against the vinyl of the car seat. Maybe it really would be better now.

Leroy drove. Mama turned around in her seat. She said, "What did you tell Sister Veronica about why you ran away from home?"

"Nothing," I said.

"Nothing," Mama said. "You expect me to believe you said nothing when a nun spoke to you?"

No, I couldn't say nothing. It was rude to say nothing to a nun. It wasn't being a good Catholic. I said, "I told her I didn't know why."

Leroy looked back at me, a short look, then back at the road. His back straightened up more. He said, "The hell you don't. If you don't know why then who does?"

Mama eyes went into slits. She looked at the seat and at me. She said, "Answer your father."

"No one, I guess."

"You guess," Mama said, her voice louder. "You guess. Don't you know anything? Just where were you going?"

"I wasn't going anywhere."

Leroy turned his head and shoulders around again, letting his hand slide over the steering wheel without turning it. "What do you mean you weren't going anywhere? You walked 30 miles. You were obviously going somewhere."

"Were you going to your Dad's?" Mama asked.

"No," I said. I never thought of going there, or even of that being a place I might go.

"Then where?" Mama said.

"Nowhere," I said. "I wasn't going anywhere. I was just going away."

"I wasn't going anywhere," Mama said with her voice mimicking me, except her voice didn't sound like me. She made her imitation sound like a stupid person. "I was just going away." And Mama made that sound like a stupid impossible thing.

Leroy turned the car into the driveway.

Mama said, "You actually think I'm going to believe that you weren't going anywhere."

Leroy turned the car off, pulled out the key and got out his door, then slammed it. He opened my door, took hold of my arm and pulled me out of the car.

I got my feet under me so I didn't fall.

Leroy said, "Just like the old Annie, lying to her parents, thinks we're both just idiots to believe some lie like that."

Mama came around the back of the car up next to us. Leroy kept pulling me along, up to the front door.

We were home.

28 Teeth

Mama yelled down from upstairs, "Who the hell didn't put the attachments away with the vacuum cleaner? That attachment had better get found." Her voice carried loud and clear all the way down in the kitchen where I ate cheerios. I took a couple more bites, then scraped the rest of the cheerios into the garbage, poured out the milk and set the bowl in the sink.

Renee entered the kitchen. She looked like she'd been in the middle of brushing her hair and had just left it, one side mainly smooth, the other still with little wisps of hair curling apart from the rest like it was when she first woke up. She'd gotten dressed in her pink shorts, but the collar of her shirt was turned to the inside. She said, "Mama says to tell you to look for that vacuum cleaner brush and don't stop until you find it."

Renee got down on her knees and looked under the table. Then she stood back up and pushed in all the chairs. The kitchen was so cramped with the washer and dryer in there that we had to push the table up against the wall and shove the chairs in to be able to get through the doorway.

"Where do you think it could be?" Renee asked.

"Which attachment is it anyway?"

"The little brush one that she uses for sweeping behind appliances and stuff." Renee opened the cabinet doors under the sink, pulled out the garbage, then on her knees pulled out the Ajax, the bleach, the extra paper sacks all out on the kitchen floor. No vacuum cleaner brush.

"I don't remember seeing that brush in a long time, " I said.

"Oh," Renee stood up. She shook a little at her knees. "She's really mad."

She got back down on her knees, picked up one paper sack

and laid it back in the kitchen cabinet under the sink, wedged between the pipes and the side. She picked up another. But the attachment couldn't be hidden in the stack of sacks because it would have made a big lump and made the sacks fall, and there wasn't any lump.

"I'll go look in the living room," I said. Renee kept putting the things back under the kitchen cabinet.

Under the cushions of the couch were bobby pins and old popcorn but no vacuum cleaner attachments, and there was nothing wedged between the cushion and the side of the big beige chair that matched the couch. I checked the corners of the room, all around the edges of the rug. Mama always said, "Vacuum the edges. Don't just vacuum the center of the room." I looked behind the couch, behind all the chairs, under the foot rest, behind the drapes on the window sills, through all the magazines in the rack and on the coffee table. I looked through the ironing in the basket by the ironing board.

"Did you check the pantry?" I yelled in to Renee.

Renee looked close to crying but she wouldn't be the one who would be screamed at or hit. But she stood there with her lower lip trembling, and stared at the floor. "Yes," she said. Then she walked to the couch and pulled up a cushion. I moved on to the downstairs bathroom, the one off the living room.

Nothing under the bathtub, its claws holding it up, or behind the toilet, nothing with the cleaning supplies in the cabinet under the bathroom sink. No vacuum cleaner attachments hidden among the towels on the shelf over the foot of the tub. I opened the closet door. There were more towels on the top shelf. There wouldn't be a vacuum cleaner brush there, but I pulled out all the towels, all the sheets from the second shelf, all the dishtowels and dishrags and washrags from the bottom shelf. From under the bottom shelf, I pulled out the bathroom rug that went by the tub when you took a bath, and the rubber mat that went into the tub to keep you from slipping, and the plastic bucket that held the Stanley brushes for cleaning the tub and the toilet. When the closet was all cleared out I felt along the shelves and under the shelves for anything, but there was nothing except dirt and one marble, so I put it all back, except the marble which I put in my pocket so Mama wouldn't find it and take it as evidence that I hadn't looked there.

Renee was searching the ironing basket when I came out the bathroom door.

Mama yelled again, "You kids better find me that attachment before I run out of patience."

It sounded like she stood at the top of the stairs, her voice reaching all the way from the landing, down the stairs to the front entry then all the way to the back of the house where we were, still loud and angry enough to scare Renee all skinny and white and shaky. But no one would hurt her.

"You look in Mama and Leroy's room and I'll start on Sammy and Amy's," I told her. Renee nodded her head. We both went into our parents' bedroom off the living room, then I went through to Sammy and Amy's bedroom.

I took all the blankets off the mattress in Amy's crib. Then I took off the sheet. Who would put a vacuum cleaner brush in a baby's crib? I looked through all the blankets and sheets anyway, then put them all back together. Sammy's bed was half a bunk bed taken apart, and I pulled it away from the wall, checked behind it, checked under it. Sammy and Amy had gone to the store with Leroy, Amy in her car seat. Sammy would have ridden beside her in the middle seat of the station wagon to keep her entertained. Danny must have been looking for the attachment upstairs. Mama probably sent him from room to room to look, upstairs bathroom, Danny's bedroom, Renee's and my bedroom. The other three rooms were empty. Mama was turning them into an apartment to rent out because otherwise this big house was too much for us to afford.

Mama yelled again from the top of the stairs, "If I have to find that vacuum cleaner brush myself somebody is going to be very sorry." Her voice hadn't gotten louder but it had gone colder. Next she would be coming down.

As fast as I could I looked through Sammy and Amy's closet, then through all the stuff on the shelves of the changing table. I went out the doorway to the hallway and quickly to the kitchen. I stayed on the side away from the stairs in case Mama had not left the landing. I remembered I'd found an attachment once behind the washing machine stuck in there with the big stiff washing machine hoses and wires.

There was only a little space in that corner where the sink was on the same wall as the living room door and the washer jutted out from the wall between the kitchen and the outside. Higher up there were cabinets above the sink and they continued around the corner over the washing machine.

I got in the space between the kitchen sink and the washer and turned to look behind the washing machine. I couldn't see anything so I bent down and reached in the space behind the washer to see if anything had fallen back there. There was nothing there, and I didn't know where to look now. I straightened back up as I turned away from the washing machine.

My head cracked against the cupboard. I pulled away from the pain, down, still turning, and hit my teeth on the sink.

"Ow," I yelled. I grabbed my mouth and sat down on the floor between the sink and the washing machine.

Renee ran in through the living room doorway. "What happened?"

I couldn't talk. I pulled a chair out from under the table and crawled over to it. I raised myself up onto it with one hand while I held my mouth with the other. After a few minutes I felt for the broken pieces of teeth in my mouth and spit them out on my hand. My front teeth felt jagged to my tongue.

Renee saw the pieces of teeth and ran for the stairs, yelling, "Mama, Mama, Annie hurt herself. Annie broke her teeth."

Mama came down, into the kitchen, Renee behind her. She said, "Here, what is it?"

I showed her the broken off pieces of teeth in my hand. I didn't want to open my mouth. But she moved over to the front of my chair, said, "Let me see," and put her hand on my chin.

When I opened my mouth the air hurt my teeth all over again.

Mama finished looking and I closed my mouth. Mama pulled out the chair at the end of the table. She got her pack of cigarettes, lit one up, took a puff then set it on the ashtray. She stood up and took a coffee cup and saucer from the cupboard over the sink, set it on the table and filled it with coffee from the pot on the stove. She sat back down and took a puff of her cigarette. She sat smoking, looking around at the walls.

"We'll have to get you to a dentist now, " Mama said. "One more thing we can't afford." She set her cigarette down. She picked up her coffee and sipped it, then blew on it and put the coffee cup back down.

My teeth throbbed and the thought of the hot coffee made them throb more, but I tried moving my hand and opening my mouth a little. The air still hurt but not so bad.

Mama tapped the ash of her cigarette on the ashtray, didn't look at me, but at the ashtray, and then around at all four walls. "You'll have to get crowns."

"Oh," I said, "Are crowns expensive?"

"Oh yes," Mama said. "They'll be expensive. And they'll be gold and ugly."

#

My two front teeth each had a corner broken off in the center so it looked like a half moon gap.

The dentist talked over me to Mama on the other side of the dentist chair. "Crowns would be a waste of money," he said. "You could get her temporary caps, but at her age her teeth will grow and we'd have to replace them every year or two." The dentist had white doctor pants and a short sleeve white doctor shirt. He had old fashioned glasses with thin metal frames and a pinkish round head with thin straight hair that laid down flat on his head.

"How long should we wait?" asked Mama. She wore her Navy blue dress-up dress, with the thin white stripes and the belt.

The dentist bent over towards me, and said, "Well she's ten now, so…." Then he said, "Open up your mouth for me a minute will you, and after I did, he pointed to my front teeth. "Here, see how long these front teeth are. What we need to do is watch them until she's about sixteen and by then they may have grown enough so that instead of putting caps on them we could just file them off even. There's no way to know for sure, though, until she's older." The dentist took his finger away from my mouth.

I expected Mama to look happy at hearing that it might not be so expensive, but she still had creases on her face. She said, "If she does have to have caps, would they have to be gold ones?"

"Oh, no, " the dentist smiled. "Gold caps are almost never used anymore on front teeth. We have some nice enamel caps nowadays. They wouldn't look much different from her natural teeth."

#

The kitchen counter was piled high with dishes from Sunday

dinner. I ran hot water into the dishpan, adding dish soap while the water ran.

"You make that wash water good and hot now, you hear, " Mama said.

Mama sat at the table in the Grandy Park kitchen. We'd moved but the furniture was the same, the kitchen table with the hard vinyl top, chrome sides, hollow metal legs, flecks of gold color in the white and silver top. Mama was still finishing off an after dinner cigarette. She tapped off the ash and laid the cigarette in the notch of the ashtray then picked up her coffee cup and took a sip. She stared off into space or at a wall while she drank her coffee and smoked. She pressed her lips together like she was holding the cigarette with them or smoothing her lipstick after she put it on and her eyes looked angry. Then Mama looked at me and her eyes hadn't changed. She waited.

"Yes," I said, "I hear."

I turned the hot water up higher and then added cold a bit at a time until I could stand to put my hand in the running water. If it wasn't at least that hot Mama might check it and dump it out and fill the dishpan with even hotter water, burning hot, but it didn't seem to bother her. I added a little more dish washing soap to the running water until the dishpan was full of soapy water. Glasses still remained on the counter after I put as many as I could fit in the dishwater. I lowered the dishrag down into the dishwater by a corner. Then I pulled it out and wrung it out as quickly as I could but my hands still burned and turned red.

The sink was on the opposite wall from the kitchen table at the end of a narrow aisle made of the space between the washing machine and dryer on the left wall and the refrigerator and stove and counter on the right. I turned around from the sink with the wrung out dish cloth and walked over to the table hoping Mama wouldn't pay attention to me washing it off.

Mama looked up, "Get those crumbs on the edges of the table too. Don't just wash in the center."

I gathered the crumbs and the dishcloth in my hand. I opened the cupboard door under the sink where the trash was, and shook the dishcloth a little to get most of the crumbs into the trash. Then I rinsed the dishrag in the sink, the water now just a little cooler, almost not too hot to bear, but my hands were still red after I washed and rinsed the dishrag out again.

I stepped as quietly as I could to the table and maybe Mama wouldn't look up this time. This time I concentrated on the dirty spots, the sticky food that had to be scraped and rubbed hard with the dishcloth to get it off.

Mama looked over to the other end of the table, "What's that over there? Some egg yolk from breakfast? Get over there and wash that off."

I scrubbed at the dried egg yolk, used my fingernail through the dishcloth. It came off and I finished the rest of the table. The water wasn't too hot when I rinsed the dishrag again. Mama didn't look up when I walked over the third time, and washed the table one more time all over just to get anything that I might have missed before.

Back at the sink I washed a glass. I held it by its rim so I could keep my hands out of the water as much as possible. Then I turned on the hot water to rinse it. If I could leave the water running I could adjust it with a little cool so it would be hot enough for Mama and not burn me so much, but I had to turn it off between to save water and if Mama came and felt it and she didn't think it was hot enough she'd be mad. So I just turned on the hot water. I held the bottom edge of the glass to rinse the inside. It burned the tips of my fingers as the hot went from the inside to the outside. Then I held the rim to rinse the outside quickly before I set it in the drain. After I'd washed and rinsed all the glasses in the dishpan the dishes were still barely started. I put in all the rest of the glasses and cups and saucers and silverware to soak.

During the second dishpan full Mama left. I could hear the television turned on in the living room. Everyone was there but me. I turned on the cold water to rinse one saucer, but I couldn't keep using cold in case Mama came back. I finished the second pan full and filled the dishpan up again with most of the plates.

Now I stopped washing and dried all the glasses and cups and saucers so there would be room in the drain board to hold the plates. But the glasses were mostly dry already so I just put them up in the cupboard.

Plates were the easiest to wash and rinse. Our plates weren't glass so they didn't get so hot from the rinse water and I could hold them by the edge and rinse the rest.

The plates were done. Now the bowls, the bowl for the mashed potatoes, the salad bowl, the big serving plate for the chicken, the bowl for the peas, the shallow bowl that held the rolls, the bowl for the gravy. I stacked them up high on the drain. Then I filled the dishpan up with pans to soak while I dried the plates and bowls and put them away in the cupboard.

I washed the pan for the peas, the pan for the mashed potatoes, the pan for the rolls, the electric skillet. The hot metal of the electric skillet burned my fingers when I turned it around to rinse the soap off the handle.

Mama walked in. "Aren't you done yet?"

"Almost," I said. "I just have the silverware left." I washed the silverware then rinsed it with Mama watching me. I dropped a fork when it burned my fingers, but I picked it up and got it rinsed off and in the drain.

Mama said, "Don't you empty that water until you've washed off the stove and all the cabinets."

I washed off the cabinet to the left of the sink where the drain board and rack were.

"Do that again," Mama said, "and get under the edges of the drain board this time." She came over and stood right behind me.

I did it again, lifting up the edges of the drain board, trying not to tip out any of the dishes.

Mama said, "You could have dried off some of those pans as you went along."

I finished with the counter and the drain board.

"Rinse that rag out now," Mama said.

I rinsed it in the dishwater.

"Rinse that rag out in some hot water," Mama said.

I turned on the hot water. It was very hot and I tried to keep my fingers out of the water while I rinsed the dishrag.

"Wring that rag out. Don't use it all sloppy wet like that."

I turned off the hot water and wrung out the dishrag. The hot water burned my hand and my skin was red, but I wrung it out until it wasn't dripping at all anymore. Then I wiped the counter to the right of the sink where the dishes had been.

Mama slapped my back. "Don't just wash the middle. Wash the counter around the edges."

So I started again around the edges. I picked up the objects around the edges one at a time, washed under them and then put them back, the salt and pepper shakers, the toaster.

Mama hit me on the back again. "There's no reason that you have to take so damn long to do any little thing," she said. "Here, give me that." Mama washed the cabinet. Then she rinsed out the dishrag under the hot water again and wrung it out and it didn't seem to burn her. She began to wash off the stove. The pressure cooker sat on a burner. She took off the lid and looked inside. "This pressure cooker is not clean. How, long were you going to leave this pressure cooker on the stove dirty like this?"

"I thought it was clean," I said.

"How could you think it was clean when you're the one that washed it and left it dirty like this?" Mama asked, her voice getting very loud, her face red. She banged the lid back down on the pressure cooker and twisted the lid back on. She picked up the pressure cooker by its handle and said, "Here, you wash this again," and she flung it out with her arm towards me.

The pressure cooker hit me in the mouth. My head went back. I felt my teeth breaking. I took a step back to keep my balance.

Mama looked at me. Then she closed her eyes just for a moment, then opened them and looked back away at the stove.

My top lip swelled on the inside. The edges of my teeth felt sharper.

Mama said, "Now, if you've gone and made me break your teeth again, I'm going to really be angry." She didn't look at me. She went on washing the stove, around all the burners except the one that still had the coffee pot on low. Then she dropped the dishrag into the sink.

My teeth didn't hurt as bad as the first time. I put the pressure cooker into the dishpan, twisting the lid back off. First I washed the lid and put it in the drain, then I washed and washed the pressure cooker with the steel wool scratch pad and while I did I felt the broken pieces of my teeth on my tongue where I held them against the roof of my mouth so I wouldn't swallow them.

Mama went over and sat down at the table. She started a cigarette.

I finished the pressure cooker, rinsing it in the hot water and burning my fingers when I turned it to rinse the soap off the handle. I dried the pressure cooker with the dishtowel because there was no room left on the drain, then I set it back on the stove. I dumped the dishwater out of the dishpan. This time I used cold water to rinse out the dishpan, because you can use cold water for the dishpan. I took the scouring powder from under the sink and sprinkled it around the sink and the dishpan and scrubbed them both clean, then rinsed it all away with the cold water. I pushed the pieces of my teeth back towards the front of my mouth so I wouldn't swallow them. I put the scouring powder back under the sink. I made sure the faucet was nice and shiny and rinsed out the dishrag, wrung it out, and wiped up all the splashed water around the edges of the sink. I rinsed and wrung out the dishrag again, and folded it in half, then in half again and laid it over the faucet. I turned the dishpan upside down in the sink.

I turned around from the sink, walked past the stove, the washing machine, the refrigerator, and turned left before I reached the table where Mama sat with her cigarette. She didn't stop me. I turned again to go up the brick stairway. I walked up the stairs, into the upstairs bathroom.

In the bathroom I spit out the pieces of my teeth into my hand, then I threw them in the garbage, making sure they slid to the bottom, under bits of paper and other trash so no one would see.

29 On the Docks

Danny already stood over on the dock with his pole set on the railing. The dock jutted out from the cement of the Navy yard, connected but floating, so it bounced up and down when the waves came and slapped the cement. But the water stayed calm in the harbor, not real waves, just ripples on the top, and a little more movement when a boat came by and created a wake.

Danny leaned over the railing, looked down at the water, at his line, set his elbows on the railing and wedged the end of his fishing pole into his chest. A light wind whipped Danny's hair to the left. Danny had on his jean jacket and looked warm enough. I wished I had worn something warmer, because already, even though it was still daylight the air felt colder and goose bumps rose up on my arms under my sweater.

Leroy helped Renee with her pole. He'd brought worms and he threaded one onto Renee's hook.

I put the worm on my own pole, although it was a waste because I never caught anything. Neither had Renee, but Danny had once.

Well, I had once too, when I was little and we were out camping with Daddy. We fished in a little stream off a bridge, and when I got a bite this older boy helped me with it and pulled out a catfish. But he threw it back, said it was too small, and there was nothing I could do about it even though he shouldn't have because it was my fish. But Daddy must have agreed with him about the size because he didn't say anything about it to the bigger boy. So that didn't seem to me to count for catching a fish. More like an accident.

Danny caught a real fish that didn't get thrown back.

The harbor smelled like fish. Salty.

Leroy handed Renee her pole with the line still wound up

most of the way, only a couple of feet hanging down with the hook and the worm. Renee poked the pole out in front of her steering it carefully along to avoid hitting it on anything or swinging it anywhere so the worm might come back and touch her. Renee just had a sweater on too, and it was a white sweater she wouldn't have wanted to get messed up.

Leroy wore jeans and a Navy pea coat. He must have realized it would be cold, but he didn't tell us.

Renee and I went up to where Danny was, but not so close so we'd get our lines tangled up with his. Once we had our poles balanced on the railing we let out the line so the worms went down a few feet into the water. The water was dark so I couldn't see the line after it reached the water.

Leroy had come to crab. He went off the cement ledge down onto a square dock without a railing, where the edge was more sunk down into the water. It sunk down even more when Leroy stepped on it. At one corner he lowered the crab cage. Then he got down on one knee with his own pole. He tossed his line out by flicking his pole and pushing on the button to let the line go out. The line slid sideways along the surface of the ocean, on the smooth water of the bay by the Navel Yard docks.

Even though I was cold, while the sun was still out it felt good to be on the dock and feel it bounce up and down a little with the small waves, or a little harder with the wake of a motor boat.

But then it got dark and a little windy and a lot colder. My hands turned red with the cold. I reeled in the line and set down my pole so I could put my hands into my pockets.

At the other dock Leroy pulled up the crab cage. Empty. Maybe we'd go, but no, he lowered it down again. He picked up his pole.

Leroy had brought a bucket too, to put water in to hold the

fish in case we caught any, but that was empty too.

When I stepped on that dock, Leroy looked up.

"I'm cold," I said, "Can I go back to the car."

Leroy looked away, "Go on if you want. We might be awhile yet." Then he slid his line back out like before.

The car was parked in the lot just a short walk away back from the concrete at the edge of the water.

I didn't want to ride back in the front seat, next to Leroy, but now I got in there. I slid over to the driver's side and put my hands on the steering wheel and turned it a little, just a little, to the left, then back to the right. It was still cold in the car, but at least there wasn't any wind.

So many knobs and things on the dashboard, I pushed a lever to the right, then back left again. I pushed in the cigarette lighter then pulled it out and looked at the red hot coil. The palm of my hand got warm when I held it up close.

The windshield wipers turned on when I twisted a knob, so I twisted it back. I twisted some other knobs and punched some buttons on the dashboard, but nothing happened.

Pretty soon now Leroy might be coming, or just Danny and Renee, so I tried to remember how everything was and put it back that way. Then I climbed over the seat to the back. I slid over to window seat on the left, laid my head on the door and closed my eyes.

The light came on as the back door opened and then the front door opened. Renee climbed into the back and pulled her door shut. Then Danny in the front slammed his door and the light went off again. Danny looked like a black shape in the front seat.

"Is he coming?" I asked.

Danny said, "He's coming in a minute. He's pulling up the crab cages."

Renee said, "He didn't catch any crabs. We didn't catch any fish either."

I said, "That's good about the crab, so we don't have to smell that horrible smell when the crabs are cooking."

"Yeah," Renee said.

"It's so cold," Renee said, and I could see her shivering even though it was dark.

Danny said, "Yeah, wish I could have taken the keys and got the car started and the heater on."

I said, "He doesn't think about how we might be cold."

Danny said, "No, not him."

Then I heard the sound of Leroy's work boots on the concrete. Renee heard too, because she said, "He's coming."

Danny slid way over to the passenger side window.

Leroy pulled open the door with a jerk, got in behind the steering wheel, and slammed the car door. "Who the hell turned on the lights?"

"What?" Danny said.

"The lights," Leroy said, "The god damn brights are on."

"I didn't do it," Danny said. Danny didn't actually move, but his body leaned, just slightly, away from Leroy. "Renee and me just got here."

Leroy turned the key in the ignition, and the engine started. He pushed himself back in his seat.

"Whoever it was is pretty damn lucky they didn't wear down the battery."

Leroy steered out onto the street. "Annie, did you turn on those lights?"

I said, "No." I thought I'd put everything back.

Leroy twisted around to look back, but he turned back forward before he got far enough to see me right behind him. He changed lanes and drove faster. He said, "Are you trying to tell me that Renee or Danny turned those lights on?"

"No."

"Well, if they didn't you're the only one that could have, aren't you?"

"I guess so," I said.

Leroy said, "So, did you?"

"No."

"Then who the hell did?"

I said, "I don't know."

Leroy said, "You were the only one who could have, you were the only one alone in the car."

I didn't say anything. Leroy was quiet too. I laid my arm on the car door and tried to go to sleep. If I was asleep he might not ask me any more questions.

It got warm in the car and Leroy was quiet so I felt better. It was a long ride from the Navy base to Grandy Park, and I thought maybe Leroy would just forget about it by the time we got home. Maybe I could go to sleep.

A long time later, the car stopped, a door opened and the light came on. It took me a little while to get myself out of the car. On the way to the door Leroy brushed against me in the dark. He whispered, "I'm going to find out who turned that light on. Don't think I'm not."

So he wasn't going to let it go.

But then he went on up ahead and into the house first. He didn't say anything to Mama, though, nothing about me, just that we hadn't caught anything.

Mama said, "Kids, you get on up to bed."

So I went up, changed into pajamas and got in bed. Maybe Leroy would let it go.

In bed, I did what I always did, imagined I was at Plumfield, that Jo and Professor Bhaer had taken me in. Only now someone had stolen a dollar. Jo thought it was me. But it wasn't me.

Just like Dan when he smoked and almost burned the house down, I got sent away to Mr. Lane. Then I ran away and came back home to Plumfield like Dan did, and broke my foot on the way, and walked on it anyway just to get back. Of course, by the time I did get back, they found out who really stole the dollar, and it wasn't me.

Jo said, "I don't know how we could ever have suspected you."

Of course I would never have done such a thing.

But then Leroy was in the doorway, standing there against the hall light looking in, filling up the space of the door frame.

He came over and sat on my bed by my side.

I put my arms up over my face.

Leroy didn't hit me though, he put his hand on my arm and he talked to me softly, like he had that time when I rolled my hair wrong. He said, "What's the matter? I'm not going to hurt you. You don't need to put your arms up like that."

Leroy pulled one of my arms down off my face. He said, "I'm not going to be angry at you. I just want to know the truth. I won't be angry if you turned on the light." Then Leroy's voice sounded so sad like it hurt him that I would be scared of him, "You don't need to be afraid."

Leroy pulled my other arm down, and I let him do it because I believed him that he wasn't going to hit me.

Leroy said, "Did you turn the lights on? You can just tell me. You won't get in trouble."

"No," I said.

Leroy's arms on me turned all stiff, and it wasn't like he had lied when he said he wouldn't hit me. It was like he changed completely right in that moment when he reached back his fist and punched me hard on the side of my face, when he hit me again on the same side, then one more time on my mouth. So I felt my skin on my teeth and tasted my skin and my blood

Then Leroy got up and walked out of my room, and I went to sleep without thinking any more about Plumfield or Jo or Dan.

#

Sometime later, I woke up. The light through the window was like in the morning before it was really light out, but past the dark of the night. But the hall light was on too, and that light came in and made a bright shape on the foot of my bed, with a harder edge than the light that came in through the window.

Leroy stood by the side of my bed, that was what woke me, and Mama waited out in the hall, just outside the door. She had a belt in her hands, a leather belt. She held it with one hand and rested the other end over her arm. The way she looked at me was like she never felt anything for me except to hate me.

Leroy had his arm on my shoulder, shaking me awake, then grabbed and pulled me by the shoulder. He said, "Get up and get out here." He grabbed and pulled me out of the bed and into the hallway to the top of the stairs. He took the belt from Mama, and Mama held onto me by my other shoulder.

Leroy said, "Did you turn on the lights?"

I said, "No."

Leroy hit me with the belt, swung it once on my back and once on my legs.

Then he asked me again. "I said, did you turn on the light?"

I said, "No." Somehow I couldn't not say no.

Leroy hit me a few more times with the belt. When he hit me the belt made me lean towards the stairs and I concentrated on staying upright to keep myself up away from the stairway. If I concentrated on staying upright then I could just think about that and not about the metal tip of the belt hitting my legs, through my thin cotton pajamas.

Anyway I didn't want to fall down the brick stairs.

Leroy was in his T-shirt and jeans, but Mama had her robe and underneath, a nightgown. Her hair was pressed out of shape like hair is when you just get up. She had her eyelids half closed and she glared out through them at me. Her mouth was a little open but with her jaw held tight.

Mama said, "He asked you if you turned on the lights?"

I said, "No," because I couldn't not say no. I held onto no, like I held onto keeping my body up straight, so I didn't fall down the stairs.

So Leroy hit me again.

Then Mama said, "Give me that belt."

Mama hit me with the belt. She hit me on my back and on my butt, and on my legs, again and again. My pajamas felt like they weren't even there, not like jeans that kept it from stinging as much.

"Did you turn on the lights?" Mama asked.

"No."

It was hard to stay straight with her behind me, with him behind me. Their bodies so close, and then hitting me with the belt, and sometimes their hands, attached to the belt. Trading off, Mama with the belt, then Leroy, then Mama again. Mama asked if I turned on the lights. Leroy asked. Mama asked while Leroy hit me. She asked while she hit me. And Leroy asked and hit me.

"Did you turn on the lights?"

I said, "No," because I couldn't not say no. Because I wasn't going to admit to it, whatever it was. It wasn't me. I didn't do it.

It wasn't the lights.

Every time I said no, they hit harder, hit longer. I went

forward, closer and closer to the top of the stairs, with the hard brick steps.

Maybe it was an hour, maybe longer, when Mama finally said, "Did you turn on the lights?" and she had the hand with the belt already raised up, ready. She looked at me like she hated me, and she would go on hating and hating me forever.

There was nothing I could do to change it.

Nothing I did would matter.

"Yes," I said, "I turned on the lights."

Mama's hand dropped down. She looked tired then like she lost all of her energy. She looked at the belt, and she looked over at Leroy. Leroy looked at her and he looked at the belt.

Like they just realized what they were doing.

Mama looked at me. Her eyes lost that hating look then.

Mama said, "You could have just told us instead of lying."

Leroy said, "We wouldn't have gotten angry if you hadn't lied about it."

Mama said, "We spanked you for lying, not for turning the lights on."

They looked worn out.

"Go back to bed," Mama said. She went down the stairs, Leroy after her.

I went back to bed.

I pulled the covers way up over my head and I didn't try to go to sleep. I didn't think about Plumfield. I just lay there under the blanket as still as I could.

30 Navy Whites

Leroy came whistling into the kitchen where Renee and I did dishes, me washing, Renee drying. Off work, after duty last night at the Naval base, Leroy went to the washing machine where he pulled his Navy shirt up over his head. It was the shirt from his Navy whites, his everyday work uniform. Underneath, his T-shirt moved up a little on his belly and showed his belly muscles. Leroy pulled the bottom of the T-shirt back down to his waist and tucked it into his pants. Before he dropped the Navy shirt into the washing machine he took a pack of Salems out of the pocket. He rolled up the short cuff of his T-shirt shorter still, up around the pack of cigarettes so they were held in place. Leroy's muscles bulged out there so the T-shirt cuff stretched tight over his muscles and the pack of cigarettes.

Renee and I were boxed up next to the sink at the end of the kitchen because Leroy blocked the small passage from the dining room area to the sink, the passage made by the counter and refrigerator and stove on one side, and the washer and dryer on the other. He didn't move out of the way once he'd put his shirt in the washer and closed down the lid. He whistled.

I scrubbed on the silverware, scrubbed a fork, then laid it to the side of the dishpan to be rinsed with hot water. I didn't want to stop washing and look to see what Leroy was doing because I didn't want to be yelled at. I didn't want to rinse the silverware because I'd have to turn the water on so hot it'd burn my fingers or have Leroy yell at me if he noticed it wasn't. So I washed the silverware piece by piece, while Renee stood impatient with the dish towel ready, spread over her two hands. That was risky too, because if I took too long Leroy might tell Renee to go ahead and go play, that it wasn't fair to her that I took so long and I could just dry the rest of the dishes by myself. But that wasn't so bad so I kept washing slowly, while Renee rocked back and forth on her feet. Then she turned to face Leroy, because Leroy still whistled, and he hadn't moved away from us.

I didn't stop washing silverware, but I did look back over my shoulder.

Leroy stopped whistling. He put his hand in his pocket and pulled something out, a little book, purple. He held it out flat on his hand. In capital letters on the front: ADDRESSES.

"A guy at the base gave me this," Leroy said.

I stopped washing since he was talking to us, and turned around. Renee wadded a corner of the dish cloth in her hand.

"Yeah," Leroy said. "And of course I thought of you, Renee. Thought, I could bring that home and give it to my good girl." He held his hand with the address book out to Renee, then he turned his head so he looked at me. He kept looking at me and I couldn't look away. I could only keep my face from changing by looking past him at the washing machine lid. Finally Leroy turned back to Renee.

Renee dried her hands on the dishtowel and didn't look at Leroy's hand. She didn't smile or look happy. She just stared at her hands while she wiped them. Then she reached towards the book with the hand that didn't hold the dish towel.

"Thank you," Renee said, like she had to say. She glanced quickly at me, then back at the book in her hand. She laid the book on the counter by the dish drain and spread her dish towel out on both hands again.

"No," Leroy said. "Don't put it there. You go ahead and take that address book up to your room. Annie can finish up with these dishes."

Renee folded her dish towel in two, lengthwise, then laid it over the towel bar next to the sink. She faced the sink then with

Leroy behind her and she looked at me again, like asking me something. I turned back to the silverware and I didn't change my face. Renee picked up her address book and headed towards Leroy.

Leroy had to move out of the little passageway between the stove and the washing machine, so Renee could get through, and he went off to the living room then, whistling.

#

A week later the address book lay on the top of the dresser that I shared with Renee. I had the top two drawers. She had the bottom two. Besides the address book, Renee's teddy bear sat on the dresser, along with a couple of pencils and the ballerina dancer music box I got for Christmas.

On my bed, back in the corner against the wall was my place to hope no one remembered me and called me to do something, when they'd get angry if I wasn't fast enough or did it wrong. I had my book, *Little Men*, but I couldn't keep my mind on it. Such an awful part anyway, when Mr. Bhaer told Nat to hit him with a switch on Mr. Bhaer's bare arms, because Nat had told a lie again.

I laid down *Little Men*, the switch in Nat's hand, to walk to the dresser and pick up the address book. None of the pages had any addresses or phone numbers. There was no name on the first page: "This address book belong to:" blank. Renee hadn't written anything in it all week. Maybe she didn't even remember it, just tossed it and forgot.

Leroy could have given it to me.

My finger against the edge of the pages, on the tabs, "AB," "CD," down to "XYZ" at the bottom.

I picked up the pencil. "This address book belong to:" I wrote "Annie."

It looked good. Leroy could have given it to me and said I was his good girl. My name looked like it really belonged there. The address book was mine.

All those spaces, four to a page, to fill up with names and addresses and phone numbers. I could put the address book at the back of my underwear drawer, or under my mattress, on the side next to the wall, and Renee wouldn't even miss it.

My thumb on the tabs, opened the book on the "MN" tab. Who could go on that page? No one for "MN," no one I could remember. Becca could go under "RS," Rebecca, or "CD," Christenson, but I couldn't remember her address and I couldn't remember her phone number.

Besides, Becca was in Yakima. I couldn't call her even if I had her number.

I put down the pencil, and tossed the address book back onto the dresser. Renee could have it. I didn't want it.

#

Leroy, in his whites, in his T-shirt, his outer shirt off, his cigarettes rolled up in the cuff of his T-shirt, over his muscles, next to the washing machine, stood behind me at the sink. He took off his belt.

"Look here," he said. Leroy held out the white belt. He pulled it and it stretched. It had a metal clasp but not the triangular metal tip that most belts had.

"It doesn't look like it would hurt much, does it?" Leroy said.

No, not so bad. It wouldn't be so bad.

Leroy laid the belt down on the washing machine. He reached in the tight pocket of his whites and pulled out Renee's address book. He opened its cover.

"Why look here, " he said. "'Annie'," he said. "Right here in the front of the address book that I gave to Renee, it says 'Annie'." Leroy laid the address book down on the lid of the washing machine.

He picked up the belt.

"Yes, " he said. "It doesn't look like it would hurt much, but you see, you can fold it like this," Leroy folded the belt in two, pulling the folded end and the end with the clasp tight between his two hands. "And when you fold it you can snap it so it will really sting." Leroy let go of the looped end, brought the belt back and snapped it on the top of the washing machine so it made a loud noise that made me jump, even though I tried not to.

Leroy didn't hit me then.

"Turn around and wash those dishes," Leroy said.

I put the dishwashing soap in the dishpan. I turned on the hot water, some cold water, so it made a pan full of sudsy water. I put the glasses in the water, not all of them because they wouldn't all fit, but most of them. I put the silverware in too, so it could be soaking while I washed the other stuff. Glasses first, so they wouldn't be greasy.

"Why did you steal Renee's address book?" Leroy asked.

I started to turn, to look at him.

"Turn around and wash those dishes." Leroy said.

"Why did you steal Renee's address book?"

I held a glass. With the other hand I put the dishrag inside the glass. I got my body ready for the belt, "I didn't steal it."

But I did, for a minute. For a minute I'd wanted something from him, and pretended that he gave it to me.

The washing machine lid rattled when the belt snapped down.

Leroy shouted, "Your goddamn name was in the book. Are you going to lie to me and tell me you didn't steal it? He said, "You'd better not lie to me."

I set down the glass. I held on to the edge of the sink.

Leroy said, "You'd better be washing those dishes."

I held the slippery glass tight and tried to stop my hand

shaking. I picked up the dishcloth again.

"Did you steal it?" Leroy said.

"I just wanted to see what my name would look like. I forgot to erase it."

Leroy said, "You really expect me to believe that?"

The belt did sting when it snapped on the back of my legs and I dropped the glass into the soapy water.

"Wash those dishes," Leroy said.

"Did you take the address book?"

I got ready for the belt, held my body still, closed my eyes. "No, I was just pretending."

Leroy didn't hit me. Maybe he believed me.

Leroy said, "Pretending. You really think I'm some kind of fool to believe that."

But he didn't hit me.

Leroy thumped the belt on the palm of his hand. Leroy's eyes moved up to mine.

I turned back to the sink and grabbed a glass. I moved the dishcloth in and out of the glass. I pressed up as close as I could against the sink.

Leroy said, "I'll get the truth out of you," still thumping the belt.

Then the thumping stopped, and I held tight to the glass.

The belt didn't come, so I took a breath, a short breath, and still it didn't come. I washed the glass again, breathed again.

Then it came.

It hit me just under the edge of my shorts; not ready.

"You meant to keep it, didn't you?"

"No," I said. The glasses were done. I started the plates.

"Didn't you?" he said.

"No."

Washing plates, the whole rest of the house silent, except Leroy thumping the belt, not thumping the belt, him breathing, pausing, me breathing, holding my breath, breathing short breaths, trying to hear him about to move.

The belt surprised me again, snapped across my back. It stung under my blouse. I almost dropped the plate that I rinsed under the hot faucet.

"You stole it, didn't you?" he repeated again and again through the plates, the pots and pans, the silverware. He repeated it while I washed, then dried them all; while I washed the stove, the counters, wiped out the dishpan, scoured the sink.

No, I didn't, I wouldn't, ever, admit to that moment, wanting.

31 Meanness

Rows of connected houses made up the Grandy Park housing project. Each block of houses stretched about a city block long. The blocks faced each other so in the front there were two sets of front yards together, then another block, then two sets of back yards together, these separated by wire fences and each with a clothes line for hanging out laundry.

Three doors down from us on the left lived a family of mother and father, an older girl, nine years old, maybe ten, and her little sister, six or seven years old. The older sister had something wrong with her. Maybe she was retarded, seemed like it. It seemed like her arms and her legs and her bobbing head didn't quite go together as her body. It didn't flow in one piece. Parts of her got in the way and stopped unexpectedly.

Only the little sister talked much like a regular person. The older sister almost never talked. She said yes and no when her parents yelled at her or asked her something. That was most of the talking the parents did: they yelled at the older sister, because the older sister never did anything right.

The other talking the parents did was before they went somewhere and left the two girls alone. Then they talked quietly to the younger sister, like they were telling her how to handle things while they were gone. They told her even though she was the younger sister; even though the older sister stood close by listening, with her eyelids pressed tightly closed. Her tanned brown arms swung and hit, then bounced off her tanned brown thighs poking out skinny from her shorts. Swing, hit, bounce, swing, hit, bounce the whole time her father talked and her mother talked to the younger sister.

The street that came into the housing project didn't break off into side streets to divide the long rows of project apartments into real city blocks. It came in along the edge, and ended in a circle to turn around. So only one end house on each housing block was near the street. Mostly people didn't own cars, weren't allowed to unless they were a Navy family.

We were a Navy family, so we had a station wagon, blue-green, long. I stood on the curb and leaned on the back car door.

The older sister walked down the sidewalk between the front yards of the housing blocks. She saw me when she turned onto the sidewalk next to the street. She walked over by the hood of the car, then to the front door. She didn't lean like I did. She stood with all her body wrong, lifted the heel of her foot, then set it down, touched her cheek with her fingers and patted it with her stretched out fingers over and over.

"Stupid," I whispered, "stupid. You're stupid."

She heard me, like I meant her to hear me. She turned her face my way, her hand next to her cheek, not patting. She didn't say anything. The look in her eyes wasn't surprise. She had never spoken to me and these were the first words I ever spoke to her.

Nothing in her face fought back. Nothing angry, nothing that asked me why I treated her that way. Nothing said she didn't deserve to be treated that way.

Only a small hurt, almost not a hurt. Like an experiment on the science TV they showed at Larchmont school, how you hear. The difference between zero bells ringing and one bell ringing is very loud. The difference between nine bells ringing and ten bells ringing is hardly loud at all.

The barely hurt spread through me, through my arms, made them heavy and tired on the car door. The older sister opened her mouth and I waited for her words, but she didn't talk, never talked. She patted her bottom lip up on her top lip. She closed her eyes then opened them in slits opening to the sidewalk, not to me. She walked away from the car. The older sister didn't need to tell me how I'd wanted to hurt her, hurt her bad, because she was like me. We were the older sisters, the ones who did everything wrong.

She walked on the grass, not the sidewalk, on the way back towards her house. Her feet were bare and every time she lifted one of them she held it first over the top of the grass so the tips of the grass blades just touched the bottom of her foot, before she bent the blades down.

32 Worthless As The Dent In My Car

Our station wagon pulled up to the docks at the Navy Yard. I sat in the third row of seats with Danny. The second row had Sammy and Renee with Amy in her car seat with the movable beads on the front.

Mama and Leroy planned to catch crabs. They had a crab cage in the way back of the station wagon on some newspaper - black and steel. I didn't understand how it worked, how it let the crabs in but wouldn't let them out. Bait was worms, but better than that was to use the worms to catch some fish and use the fish to catch the crabs. Use some hamburger. Leroy did that sometimes.

The car stopped and we got out. Last thing, Mama got in the seat with Amy, unstrapped her and pulled her out of the car seat. She had trouble getting Amy's legs out as her shoes and legs got caught on the seat, and Mama was careful not to not to twist the baby's leg or foot when she pulled.

Mama took Amy to the back of the station wagon. We parked way up close to the docks. At this dock you just had to step down onto the wooden part. And then go out on the wooden part a ways to get to the water. The water looked all black from where I stood. Sometimes it looked like it had an oil slick on it, but not today. Today it just looked deep and black.

Mama waited for Leroy to open up the back window of the station wagon. She didn't pull open the tailgate. She lifted Amy over it, and set her down to crawl back there.

Mama said, "Annie, I want you to stay here with Amy. You watch and you make very sure that she doesn't put anything in her mouth. If anything happens, if she starts to choke or anything, you yell for me."

I kind of wanted to walk on the docks, on the wooden part

that went down with your weight, then lifted back up when you stepped off. But I didn't care about fishing or crabbing. Staying with Amy was better than that. Especially better since I wouldn't be near Mom or Leroy where they'd find something wrong with what I was doing, even when what I was doing was fishing, not even housework or chores, but something that was supposed to be fun.

They went off in a group. They looked like a regular family without me, with the mother and the father and the three children, all walking close together, and Mama resting her hand on Renee or Sammy. If I'd been along they wouldn't have looked like a family because I would have been hanging back, trying to stay out of the way. And nobody's hand would have pulled me in.

Once they went down on the dock I couldn't see them anymore, but I knew they were nearby. I knew I could see them if I took five steps over to where the ground sloped down to the docks, but I didn't go over there because I didn't want to take my eyes off Amy. I had to make sure she didn't pick up anything in the back of the car to put in her mouth and choke on.

All Amy did was crawl around, sometimes up towards the seat back, and sometimes near me at the back, where she'd put out her arm and lift herself a little on the closed tailgate. When she did that she always looked up at me to make sure I watched her do it and her face, her mouth and her cheeks, got rounder, when she laughed at being able to lift herself up and be right next to me.

Amy just did the same things over and over, crawled over to the back of the third seat, crawled in circles around the way back, came up to the tailgate and lifted herself up, and sometimes reached right out to touch me on the chest. Every time Amy was just as delighted, her hair fell over on her forehead, and her eyes got very bright blue when she laughed.

When she came around to me, I did the same things over and

over too; put my hand out so she could touch it, or clap it and laugh. Stand close up to the tailgate to make sure she didn't get up too high and fall out. And laugh when she laughed. Every time, I laughed when she laughed. Every time, I looked at her blue eyes that looked at me.

#

Amy crawled near the seat back, and she started choking. But she hadn't put anything in her mouth, because I watched every second and she never picked anything up.

I ran towards the dock yelling, took one step down on the slanted ground and yelled. I didn't want to leave Amy, but I thought I might have to get close for them to hear. I ran back up to Amy, and she still choked, so I ran back again towards the dock yelling, but then Mama came up.

"She's choking," I said.

Mama ran to the back door on the side, got in the seat and reached back over it and pulled Amy out. She stood up with Amy outside the car and held her over one arm and pounded on her back.

Leroy came up during this, while Amy was still choking.

Mama said, "Did she eat something?"

I said, "No, she didn't eat anything."

Amy stopped choking. She leaned against Mama like she was all tired out.

Mama held her and then she asked me angry, "Why was she choking like that if you didn't let her put anything in her mouth?"

I said, "I watched her every minute. She never even picked up anything"

Leroy came over right next to me. He shoved me on the arm, then he got up close to me and he whispered.

He said, "You're as worthless as the dent in my car."

Leroy walked up by the driver side door. He said, "Get in the car."

Danny, Renee and Sammy had all gotten back by then. They got in the back seats along with me.

Leroy put something in the front seat. Mama got in the front seat with Amy. Then Leroy told her he was going to go get the crab cage and the rest of the fishing gear.

I cried, not very loud. I tried not to be loud, but I couldn't stop crying.

Mama said, "Will you shut up that crying. What have you got to be crying about?"

I said, "Leroy said I was as worthless as the dent in his car."

Mama looked surprised. Her voice got softer. She said, "Well, it must have been those peas she had at dinner. The hull of one must have got caught on her teeth somewhere. Then it got in her throat and she choked. That must have been what it was.

"Hush now," Mama said.

Leroy returned. He set the crab cage and the other things in the way back, then turned up the window.

When Leroy opened the front door of the car and got in behind the steering wheel, Mama said right away, "It must have been the skin of a pea that she ate at dinner that got caught in the baby's throat and caused her to choke. I don't think she picked anything up off the floor of the car at all."

Leroy said, "Annie probably wasn't paying attention to her at all back there. Probably she was just daydreaming like always."

Mama said, "No, the baby didn't pick up anything to cause her to choke. It must have been just the shell of a pea that's all."

I got myself to cry less, and I kept my head down in the arm of my coat so it didn't make much noise. Then my crying would just start up again, swell up.

Mama didn't say anything about it again if she heard.

By the time we got home it had pretty much stopped.

#

The next day Danny, Renee and I sat at the kitchen table, Danny in the chair to my right, and Renee on my left. Mama and Leroy had gone shopping taking Sammy and Amy along.

Danny told about a boy down the street. "You know what I heard Steve did, spray painted all over the school."

"Yeah," Renee said, then she nodded towards me, "but that's not as bad as what she did." Just like I wasn't even there. She meant that I let Amy put something in her mouth that made her choke. But I hadn't. I waited for Danny to say that I hadn't, to defend me.

"Yeah" Danny said. That's all he said. I had no one.

33 Babysitting

The little girl, Patty, stood by the screen door. Her hand reaching up for the hook that kept it closed. The hook was just higher than she could reach, except that if she stood on her tiptoes she could just manage to touch it and push at it. If it had been high on the door like most screen door hooks were, I wouldn't have had to be watching her every second, because even though she was tall for her age she was still not even two years old. Patty looked at me now like she was waiting for me to turn away for a moment so she escape.

But when she pushed at the hook a couple of times and it stayed wedged in the eye, I thought she wouldn't be able to get it unhooked even if I did look away for a bit. If she could do it at all it would only be after pushing and pushing it for a long time.

I walked to the door and made sure that the hook was pressed completely down into the eye.

The little girl looked like she might hit me or kick me, but all she did was lean against the screen door and start pushing harder on the hook.

Before she left Patty's mother turned on the TV. She said that Patty sometimes liked to watch and would forget about escaping outside for awhile. So I said, "Look, there's Bugs Bunny again," and Patty looked but then she turned back to the door.

I said, "Don't you want to sit down and watch the cartoons?"

Patty didn't say anything.

Then I said, "Are you hungry? Do you want your bottle?" and she nodded. Her mom had shown me where the condensed milk was that they mixed with water to fill her bottle. Amy already drank real milk and she wasn't even a year old yet, but this girl still had to have mixed up stuff for some reason.

I got her bottle from the kitchen. Then I came back and checked that she hadn't worked the hook out any. Back in the kitchen I got the condensed milk from the cupboard. I put the bottle and the can of milk on the kitchen table where I could look into the living room and see the little girl still standing there by the door. Then I went to the kitchen drawer for the can opener, the kind that has a punch can opener on one end and a bottle opener on the other. I took it back to the table, and I could see the little girl still standing by the door.

When her mother got back she was going to pay me fifty cents. And I didn't have to do anything except watch her and fix her a bottle of milk.

I ran the bottle half full of water, and took it back over to the table. At the table I punched a big hole and a tiny hole in the can of evaporated milk, the tiny hole to let in some air so the milk poured smoother. Then I screwed the top of the bottle back on.

The little girl was old enough that her bottle didn't need to be heated, just like Amy was, so I brought it in and handed it to her.

I said, "Would you like to sit down on the couch to drink it?"

But the little girl didn't like that. What she liked instead was to stand next to the screen door with one hand on the handle of the screen door and the other tipping her bottle up over her head so she could suck it out. But at least with her hand full of the bottle she was not knocking at the hook trying to get it out.

I kept looking over at her, but she was drinking her bottle now. If I was lucky maybe it would make her sleepy, and she would lay down and go to sleep. Then I could move her over to the couch.

I looked at the TV. I didn't get to watch TV much any more By the time I finished the dishes I had to take a bath and go to bed.

Patty leaned back sleepy against the screen door. She still had her bottle tipped up drinking it, about two-thirds gone. Her eyes closed some.

It was nice to watch the cartoons and not have anyone asking me when I sat down if the dishes were all really clean. Or taking me back in the kitchen to inspect them, and, finding one dirty fork, taking out all the dishes in all the cupboards for me to wash again.

Patty still stood by the door. Her bottle was almost empty, but she still sucked hard on it.

The next time I looked up Patty wasn't there. The screen door was still closed so at first I didn't even see that the hook was hanging loose now instead of in the eye, and I looked around the room to see where Patty could be. Then I saw the hook. I stepped outside and looked all up and down the front yards of all the connected apartment. Patty wasn't anywhere.

That couldn't be. I hadn't looked away long enough for her to get out the door and then out of sight. So I thought maybe she went somewhere in the house after all and I looked in all the downstairs rooms, the kitchen and downstairs bedroom. Then I went up the stairs, just one bedroom and a bath up there. Our apartment had two bedrooms. I checked the closet in the bedroom, even opened up the linen closet. She was nowhere.

So then I went back downstairs and back out the front door. Even though I knew she hadn't had time to get there, I went around the block of apartments into the back and walked down the path between the back yard fences of two blocks of apartments. I walked quickly, almost running and I got up to where our house was and Mama was out on the path too.

Mama said, "What are you doing out here?"

"The baby ran out," I said. "She ran out and I went after her and she didn't have time to get anywhere, but when I got out I couldn't see her anywhere."

"What," Mama said. "How could that have happened if you

were watching her?"

"I don't know," I said. "It was just a second. She didn't have time to get anywhere before I was after her."

Mama said, "You just keep looking."

So I did. All up and down the blocks of apartments, running through them, and then I started back to our row and to the ones on the other side. But then I met Danny on the sidewalk and he told me Mama found the baby, and now she wanted me to come back to Jean's house.

I couldn't understand how Mama could have found her when I couldn't. But maybe she found Patty close by and so she'd know I told the truth about it just being a minute and not get mad at me.

I went in the front door and Mama had the little girl in her lap and now Patty really was going to sleep.

Danny came in the door after me.

I was scared to say anything, but I said, "Where was she?"

Mama didn't answer right away, and before she answered she kept her lips pressed together so I knew there was no chance of her not being mad now that she found out the little girl was okay.

Mama said, "She was right next door."

I said, "But I looked next door in the yard. That was the first place I looked."

Mama said, "You God damm, good for nothing. She was inside next door."

"How did she get inside?"

"Mrs. Abramson let her in, that's how." Mrs. Abramson was an old lady who lived in the project and sometimes babysat for the little kids. And I knew I couldn't ask or say anything about why would Mrs. Abramson let the little girl come into her house and not even tell anyone about it.

Mama laid the little girl down on the couch.

She said, "Danny, you stay here and wait for her mother to come home. Just tell her that Annie needed to go."

So Danny would get the fifty cents.

Mama said, "You get yourself home."

I walked ahead of her and she said, "I come back with her and the TV is on. What were you doing, just watching TV and not paying any attention at all to that baby? Who the hell told you that you could turn on the television set anyway?"

I said, "Her mother turned it on. She thought Patty might watch cartoons and stop trying to get out the front door."

We reached our front door, and I opened it.

"I was watching her," I said. "I only looked away for a moment."

Mama came close and shoved on me so I went through the front door. I started over to the stairs and Mama went past me into her bedroom, then she came out with a belt in her hand.

She said, "Get up those stairs."

I started up, but the belt came down onto my head and I fell down so my knee hit on the second step. I couldn't get up because Mama kept hitting me over the head with the belt, so I hunched down to try to stay away from the belt, to keep it from falling over my head into my face.

Mama breathed hard and she hit down with the belt between the words, "You .. are .. never .. going ..to do ..anything .. like ..that again. Never, do you hear me."

"Yes," I said, "yes."

But she kept hitting me with the belt. I knelt on the hard brick steps and waited for her arm to get tired enough so she finally stopped.

She said, "Just get out of here, get out of my sight before I murder you."

Then I went up the stairs, hunched over, into my room and onto my bed in the center of it, face down, my forehead on my arm so the back of my head didn't touch anything. And if I were lucky, I'd just be able to stay there by myself and not be hurt for awhile.

34 The Things I Did to Get Through

To get through I tried to see saints, especially Mary, the mother of God. I tried to see Jesus.

If you saw saints, if you saw Jesus, it meant you were good.

I never saw the saints but I imagined seeing Mary and how she held me and stroked my hair. How Mary said, "You are good. You have never sinned."

Even though I told lies and stole candy from the drug store, still Mary said that I had never sinned.

#

To get through every night lying in bed I imagined myself at Plumfield. Maybe I came by Plumfield selling newspapers, and Jo invited me in for lunch then asked me to stay. Or she spied me on a trip to town.

The story always went the same. Jo and Professor Bhaer were so good to me, and I did all my work and did well at school. They were proud of me. But something always happened, some money stolen, something wrong. And because I was new and it had never happened before, everyone blamed me.

Jo was sad, but she thought it must be me.

Sometimes they sent me away, like Jo sent Dan to stay with Mr. Lane after he taught the other boys to smoke cigars and gamble. Sometimes I just went off on my own because I was so hurt that they believed that I was the guilty one.

But the stories all ended the same way too. Maybe I made my way back with a broken foot like Dan had, or somehow Jo found me after I had gone away. But by then they knew who had really done it, whatever it was.

Jo would always say, "How could I ever have suspected you?" and hold me close.

To get through, in the morning, when it wasn't a school morning, I laid in bed as long as I could. I pulled the covers up high so I was as hidden as possible, and I thought, no one will yell at me until I get up. No one will look at me like I'm nothing, or dirt or scum, until I get up. So I didn't get up.

Not until someone yelled up the stairs.

One morning I heard the family talking and I knew they were sitting around the kitchen table eating breakfast.

Maybe Mama made her voice louder than usual, but I couldn't tell because I heard her voice above everything else always.

Mama said, "That lazy Annie. Renee gets up, changes the baby's diaper, gets the baby up out of her crib, and all the while Annie is lying up there pretending to be asleep, not doing a damn thing."

Then it didn't matter that she wasn't looking at me like I was nothing, or dirt or scum, because it was all in her voice.

So I got up. I got dressed in my clean underpants and my shorts and my T-shirt. I had to move fast, but at the same time I got myself ready because I had to go into the kitchen and sit down with the family to eat breakfast. What I got ready for was to not show them that I heard them talking, to act like I just got up and came down and I didn't know anything about Annie, the lazy, Annie the dirt, Annie the scum, Annie who was nothing.

This meant I had no look on my face.

I was braced to enter the kitchen with everyone there: Renee and Sammy in the chairs up against the wall. Mama at the end next to the toaster on the table. Leroy on the other end so I had to pass him to reach my seat. Danny to Leroy's right on the side of the table that was not up next to the wall, so I passed by him too. Mama looked up, so I looked down at the back of my chair, just before I pulled it out. When I pulled the chair out I tried to do it without making any noise, so that when I sat down it wouldn't be like I just sat down, maybe like I'd already been there a long time and they just didn't notice. Even though I knew that they did notice, because they were talking about me before I came in.

I sat down. I looked at my plate. I looked without looking at the dishes on the table.

Mama looked away from me and she didn't say anything but her bottom lip pulled in, then she stared at the wall over Renee's head, and tapped her cigarette on the ashtray, tap, tap, tap until she picked it up and gave it a draw then blew the smoke out, and her jaw was tight while she held her mouth open until all the smoke was out. Then she closed it.

I got through by not looking at her. Not looking at Leroy at the other end of the table where he put more butter on a piece of toast, used his knife to slice off little bits of the pat of butter and spread it around evenly.

I dished up some scrambled eggs, took a piece of buttered toast, and ate it slowly so I'd have something to do until I could leave the table.

When Mama looked at me, when Leroy looked at me, I got through by keeping my face smooth like I didn't know they were looking at me, like it wasn't me that they looked at that way.

#

And when Mama stood in front of me, close, and started to slap me in the face, I tried to get through by putting my hands up in front of my face to protect it. Then when she wouldn't let me, when she said, "Put those hands down by your side," in her hard voice, I got through by looking away, but not at anything, and by feeling her slap cut the inside of my lip, noticing it from far away, just like the inside of my lip and the taste of my blood was not me.

Until I couldn't get through any more.

That's when I laid awake in my bed, my eyes closed so nobody knew, in the dark house, quiet now.

The baby's breath changed to how it sounded when she was really asleep, when you could put her down if you were holding her and she wouldn't wake up.

That happened after Renee was asleep and after I couldn't hear Danny or Sammy over in their room, moving or turning over in their beds, but before Leroy and Mama finally went to bed. Then Leroy and Mama's bedroom door opened and closed, and their noises got quieter and then were gone.

Even after that I laid in my bed and listened.

A long time after the last rustle I got out of my bed. I stood with my bare feet flat on the cool floor to hear if anything changed from the noise that I made getting up.

Earlier that evening I'd found my dress, the one I wore the first time I ran away. I'd placed it in the closet apart from the others. So now my hand found it easily even though I couldn't see the dress, white with short sleeves and little blue flowers. I put on the dress, then I waited again for the sounds of anyone awake.

My tennis shoes were the last thing before I tiptoed downstairs.

This time I was going to be prepared with food and a can opener, so I went to the right into the kitchen.

The light through the kitchen windows was enough to see the shape of the table. But I had to feel through the silverware drawer to find a can opener. Down on my knees I felt through the cabinet under the counter, and tried to guess what was in the tin cans by their size. Tuna fish I was sure of. I tried to read the labels on the others through the light from the window, but I couldn't. Lots of things wouldn't be any good, creamed corn, chicken noodle soup. I hoped for fruit cocktail. But, I guessed anything would do if I were hungry enough. Just a few things though, I didn't want to be weighted down.

Two of the cans banged together and I stopped moving and listened, but there were no sounds from anywhere inside the house.

Mama and Leroy's bedroom was right off the hall that I had to cross from the kitchen to the living room, and their door was not all the way shut. I tiptoed across the opening. I could outrun them if they woke, and maybe even hide if they called the police and a cop car came after me. There were woods and fields out in the back of the projects, scraggly with long grass and cattails. A wire fence separated some of it from the project and a cop car couldn't go back there.

But I held my breath anyway when I stopped at the coat closet in the living room and took out my blue car coat. I'd be ready if I had to sleep in a telephone booth again. Even though now it was summer and warm even in the middle of the night, I'd have my blue car coat with the soft fur lining and the hood if I needed it; the one I got for my birthday, that was exactly the kind I wanted.

I turned the knob and pulled the front door open. I waited for it to creak, but it didn't creak, and I stepped outside into the dark. Even though I closed it very slowly there was a little thump when the door shut.

But I didn't hear anything from inside the house and already I felt away from it and out in the safety of the dark. I needed to be a long way gone before morning when they would miss me, but this time I knew how to make sure I was going in a straight line.

There was a railroad crossing about half way between Grandy Park and a little store where we bought candy sometimes. I'd never seen the light flash or the wooden bar come down but there was a track and the track went somewhere.

Before I came to the tracks I walked a long way through the

project, until I reached the last of the long row house apartment buildings of Grandy Park. After that there was a stretch that wasn't on the water, but was near it. The water didn't look open like the ocean. The shape of it was more like a river, except that it didn't have a current like a river, so probably it was just some little inlet from some bay or something where the ocean got still.

I couldn't exactly see the water. It was just a different kind of darkness, and where there were street lamps, a different kind of reflection than the light on the road.

I could hear it more than see it, little slapping sounds. Then in one place I saw a long dock built out into the water and it bounced up and down. If I hadn't been running away I would have gone and sat out there and listened. Night is the best time to listen.

Night is the safest time, in your bed, safe to think, and imagine living at Plumfield with Jo and Professor Bhaer, and if there was somewhere like that in the world today maybe I could find it and live there. I hadn't found it the last time, but I didn't have very long to look.

The railroad track lay up ahead. The ground under the track was built up to be a little higher than the ground all around, and flat on the top where the tracks were. I walked on the flat part but not on the tracks. There weren't street lamps by the tracks, but I could see them a little ways away and they kept it from being really dark, that and, here and there, a neon sign from a business.

I could see the metal of the tracks, the weeds that grew between the cross ties, but I didn't think anyone could see me walking along there if they looked by the dark by the tracks, not unless they came close.

#

The ground had already been shaking. The noise had gotten loud before I realized there was a noise. By the time I could see the train, it was just a light, brighter and brighter, until I had to close my eyes. It was a noise louder and louder until I felt the noise was crashing down on me, and I moved down the mound of the tracks even though I was nowhere near where the train would come.

Then the train beside me churned so loud against the track that it rattled everything. It felt like my bones shook even though the only motion was the vibration through my legs. As the train rushed past I looked up ahead to the end of it. The long tail of the train seemed to be coming off the track, whipping off like crack the whip, coming right towards me.

My body shook, my legs shook, then I got ready, just like I got ready for Mama's slap, going still.

Then the train went past.

All that was left was me and the dark.

Everything left behind. I wouldn't see Amy again, wouldn't see anyone, but she was my baby sister. She could walk if you held her hands. Amy liked it when you picked her up and helped her walk and I did it when I could.

Maybe I'd find her again when I grew up.

Another train came and flew towards me with all its loud noise. Now I knew it was an illusion that the train's long tail of cars came hurtling at me, but my body still got scared like it was real, shook, got rigid, and after the train passed, felt just as empty.

This was how it would be for me. I wouldn't be able to make friends. Anyone I met might find out that I had run away from home. They'd wonder where I lived, where my family was. The only way to be safe was to stay a stranger.

There along the train tracks everything stretched out dark ahead. If I followed these tracks they would spread out to more tracks, but no one would be waiting at the end of the tracks.

Up on the mound I was high enough I could see ahead on the

streets nearby. Straight ahead of me the land looked flat and stretched out endlessly, but the street to the left was divided up into city blocks, human size. Mostly there were empty warehouses with dark windows, or buildings with blank outside walls, but two, no three blocks ahead, was the big neon sign of a diner, "Bob's" and beneath it, the light flashing "Open."

Maybe the truckers stopped there on their way to deliver things to the docks. Or maybe a family stopped for a coke and coffee on their way from one part of the country to the other.

I wouldn't go in. Everyone would wonder what a kid was doing up so late, all alone. But I could walk by. I could look in through the windows at the people lit up inside. Afterwards, I'd go back to the tracks where I couldn't talk to anyone. I'd go on following the train tracks, where I'd definitely be getting somewhere.

Getting down from the big mound that held up the tracks, I had to feel with my feet because I couldn't see well right in front of me, and the side wasn't kept as smooth as up on top. I tripped over little dips in the ground and over weeds that got in the way.

The street started right on the edge of the mound. The ground felt hard under my feet. Almost like when you've been roller skating with the heavy skates on your feet and then you take them off and everything seems so light for a minute. It was like it was too easy to take a step, everything being so hard and even.

The diner sat there almost all by itself on the dead end street, with cars and a big truck with a long trailer parked diagonally in its parking lot.

I walked over to the edge of the curb that was next to the diner. The street light just ahead of me made a big round spot of light on the street, the curb, the grass and sidewalk in front.

I started to the edge of that circle where it ended right across from the diner's front window, so I could see in without being lit up by the street lamp. Just at the point where I stepped out of the circle a new light lit the ground in front and all around me. I stepped right to get out of the headlights, expecting the car to pass, and it did, a white car. But instead of continuing the car pulled in to the curb and stopped just ahead of me. Before I could react a hand reached over and opened the right front door. The hand held out a wallet with a badge clipped on. After I'd looked at it, the man patted the passenger seat. "Have a seat," he said. "We need to have a talk."

It hadn't even been as long as the first time.

"Where are you going?" the cop asked me. And he wasn't like the mean, blustery cop who picked me up the first time. He wanted to know.

"Just away," I said. "I just wanted to get away."

It was dark in the car, but he seemed to have dark hair and dark eyebrows. His face appeared softer than the detectives in Newport News, more waiting, not so alert for what he would hear, for some particular thing. Not so much knowing what he wanted.

"Running away from home, huh?" He said, and he looked back at his steering wheel and the road and then back at me.

I nodded my head. I didn't want my voice to say it, not now, when I hadn't even lasted half the night.

"Have you ever run away before?" he asked.

"Once," I said, and I looked away from him, out the window. Outside, the darkness was there anytime. It just didn't seem like I could make it away again anytime soon into all that aloneness.

"Why did you run away?" He looked at me, then ahead, then at me again, like he really wanted to know.

Here, on my way back, in the car, the vinyl of the seat cover rubbing on the back of my knees, I didn't know how to get through.

So, I said it, "My parents don't love me."

He answered too fast, his eyes back on the road.

He said, "I think they do love you, and you'll find that out when you go back."

I didn't tell him he was wrong. But he was wrong.

"Where do you live?"

I could refuse to tell him. If I didn't tell him I'd be saved from going back until the morning when they woke up and found me gone, but then I'd have to face them all the same.

I gave him my address.

If I had to go back maybe I could get back without them knowing.

"Could you just drop me off there and let me go back on my own?"

He said, "I can't do that."

"I'll go right inside," I said. "I promise. I'll just go in and go back to bed."

He held the steering wheel tighter, then he said it again, "I can't do that." He rolled up his window a little. "But it will be okay," he said. "I'm sure you'll find that your parents really do love you, and they'll be glad to see you back safe."

I shook my head inside myself. They won't be.

If they are, it'll be like last time and it won't last. Then it will be worse again.

He parked on the street next to our block of row houses. There was plenty of room for his car.

"Ok," he said and put his hand on the door handle.

Instead of opening my door I tried one more time.

"Couldn't you just let me go in? No one would ever need to know I was gone. I'll stay inside. I won't try to get away if you just let me go in and go to bed."

"I need to talk with them," he said. He took his hand off the door handle. "And I should tell you, if you run away a third time most likely you won't just get brought back home. You'd probably have to go to court and there's a good chance you'll end up in reform school."

We walked across the grass. The grass felt wet even though it hadn't been raining. My shoes turned dark where they got wet in the grass.

I walked slow, but the policeman was right behind me.

I'd read a magazine article about boys' reform schools, about the bad ones. One boy had to walk on his knees over a floor covered with peanut shells, his knees bleeding. Girls' reform schools might be different. They might not hate me. I might get by.

But we reached the door. He stepped up next to me and knocked.

No one came.

I said, "There's no need to wake them up. The door is unlocked. I could just go in."

He shook his head.

I said, "I won't run away again."

But he shook his head again. He raised his hand and knocked again, three loud raps.

There was a noise inside, then walking.

Leroy opened the door. Mama stood across the room. When she saw me she slumped against the wall.

Leroy looked right at the policemen and he seemed annoyed.

The policeman said, "I've brought your daughter back."

Only then did Leroy see me too.

"Oh, Annie," he said. And then to the cop, "Thank you." Then to me, "Where have you been?"

The cop said, "She was running away from home."

Then Leroy was going to be like the first time I ran away, his face all understanding the way it was when he was the nice

Leroy.

First he said, "Come in." He held the screen door open for the policeman and then for me.

Leroy said, "You ran away again. What happened to make you feel you had to run away?"

So maybe I was going to get off easy, at least for the night, except that Mama yelled at Leroy from across the room, "Doesn't it matter to you that I almost collapsed?"

"What?" Leroy said, turning.

Mama said, "Doesn't it matter to you that I almost collapsed with the shock of her doing this again?"

The policeman started to say something, but he stopped while Mama kept on, "How many times are you going to let her get away with this?"

The policeman stepped back.

Leroy's face changed.

Leroy looked back at her, then at me, and he wasn't the nice Leroy. His voice came out hard. "How could you do this to your mother again?"

Mama said, "Because she doesn't care who she hurts. She only thinks about what she wants to do."

The policeman waited in the corner by the door. He held his policeman hat in his hand. He didn't twirl it. But he moved it in a circle, about an eighth of a circle, so his fingers held it in a new place. He looked somewhere between Leroy and Mama. He said, "I'll need your phone number. Someone will be calling you tomorrow. They'll probably want you to come down to the station."

Leroy was the one who answered with the number, voice crisp like he responded to an order, his body stiff, 2nd class petty officer at attention.

The policeman pulled out a pen and pad to jot it down. "And

your name, sir? And your wife's name?"

Leroy said the names.

Mama said, "Dragging us through all that again."

Leroy's attention left the policeman, pulled back over to Mama, then to me. His body got stiff in a different way. "There are going to be some changes around here, young lady. You better get it out of your head that you can do any damn thing you choose."

The policeman began to open the front door again, so there was a gap. He stood in front of the opening with his hand back behind him on the edge of the door.

Mama said, "It's no use trying to treat her like a normal child. She doesn't even have feelings like a normal child. She doesn't care about anybody."

The policeman broke in. He said to me, "I'm sure you'll find that your parents really do love you."

Mama didn't stop talking. "I've never seen anyone so selfish and so hateful."

Leroy took the sack from my hand. "You just get yourself upstairs and into bed."

The policeman left through the door, then he closed it. He closed it almost as softly as I had closed it earlier that night, when I wanted to make sure that no one would hear.

35 Going To Missouri

Mama and Leroy came in the front door, back from the police station. I waited for them to yell, but neither of them said anything to me. They were angry, though, I knew they were angry. It was the way Leroy didn't slam the door, how he so carefully closed it so it made almost no sound at all, as if it were important that he close it precisely right. They didn't say anything to anybody, not then.

Then they called me into the kitchen. "Sit down," Leroy said, and I did, in my usual spot. Leroy sat at one end of the table, and Mama sat at the other end. Leroy took his time sitting down, and then he waited even longer. All the while he acted like he was doing something important. Finally, he asked, "Why did you say we didn't love you?"

I couldn't explain. How could I if they didn't already know. Every single day they yelled or screamed or hit me, or looked at me like I was a piece of trash that disgusted them. But I couldn't say any of that. So I said, "I don't know. It just doesn't seem like you love me."

Then Mama leaned forward, her elbow on the tables, impatient and irritated, "If we didn't love you, why would Leroy be trying to adopt you?"

Like that was a reason to think they loved me, like that was proof. I couldn't tell them I knew that the adoption didn't mean anything. I didn't know their reasons, but I knew it didn't have anything to do with loving me.

"I don't know," is what I said. I don't know. I don't know. They got angrier and angrier, both of them yelling. Mama jabbed her cigarette butt in the ashtray and screamed at me that I should know that they loved me. But they didn't say they loved me, just said that I should know they did, like it was something more that was wrong with me.

They didn't get up. They each stayed at their end of the table, but the ends felt closer. I tried to take up less and less of the chair. Still, every time they asked, like they wanted me to say that I was wrong, and, of course they loved me, I didn't say what they wanted. I kept saying, I don't know. I said it as quietly as I could. Sometimes I didn't say it out loud at all, so the words sounded only inside my head. All the same, they were the only words I had.

After awhile they let me go.

#

The next time I was too slow washing dishes, Mama said, "That kind of behavior is why you're going to Missouri to live with your grandparents."

I didn't say anything. I never said anything, except, "Yes, Ma'am," "Yes, Sir," answered questions. I knew she was telling me I was being punished, so I wasn't supposed to feel happy. I wasn't supposed to feel all of a sudden that maybe I could make it through that summer. Something must have shown on my face.

"That's right," Mama said, "Your grandparents are coming for a visit, and when they leave, they're taking you back with them. Maybe, then you'll learn to behave."

So then, when it was bad, really bad, I'd think, just hold on, and I'll be going to Missouri. That's how I made it through.

#

It was almost the end of August, late one evening, when Grandma and Grandpa came. Renee and I had finished our baths. Mama told us to get clothes from our room. We'd be sleeping in sleeping bags in the boys' room for the next few days so our grandparents could have our room. There was a stack of clean clothes that hadn't been put away yet on top of our dresser. I took some clothes from the pile for the next day and put some more in my drawers. I picked up a pair of socks from the pile.

Renee said, "Hey, those are mine."

"No, they're not. They're mine. Yours are smaller." I kept them with my pile of stuff.

"I know they're mine," Renee said. "I had a pair just like that."

They were plain white socks, anklets. Mine were just a size bigger than hers. I didn't have any others for the next day. "They're mine," I said. "They're the only ones I have clean."

Renee went out of the room to the to the top of the stairs. She yelled down, "Mama, Annie stole my socks and she won't give them back."

Mama's footsteps came to the bottom of the steps. If she came up she might see they were mine. Probably she wouldn't look close enough. I tensed up, waiting, but the footsteps stopped. Mama yelled up in her harsh voice, "Annie, you'd better give those socks back before I have to come up there. You're nothing but a liar and a thief."

Renee came back into the bedroom, triumphant. Liar and thief, I tossed the socks on her bed. I didn't even dare to throw them at her. My mouth stayed closed and my eyes stayed fixed on the pile of clothes on my bed.

#

The day before we were to leave, after lunch, when everyone was still gathered around the table, Mama said, "Annie, Grandma and Grandpa want to know if you want to go back with them to Missouri. Do you want to go?" It was her company voice, cheerful.

I was puzzled that she seemed to be giving me a choice, but I said, "yes," quickly to take away any doubt, because how could I not go now when thinking about it had been the only way I'd managed to hold myself together. When I said it, Mama's face changed a little, like she was hurt that I said it, or hurt that I said it so quickly, but it was only a moment. Then she told me I'd need to get all my stuff packed then because they'd be leaving the next day.

After dinner Danny, Renee, Sammy and I were all together in the boys' bedroom, sitting around on the two twin beds.

"You're lucky," Danny said. "You get to leave."

Renee and Sammy each nodded.

"We have to stay here with Leroy."

"Yeah," said Sammy. "He's mean."

This was the first I knew of how it was for them. They weren't getting hit, and I thought it was okay for them. As far as I knew they thought I was bad and that it was justified the way our parents treated me. But all three of them, even Renee, the favorite, looked downcast. We'd talked so little that whole year. We knew so little about each other.

Part Three: Fall 1962
36 Not Afraid

It seemed like we'd barely been driving any time at all when Grandpa said to me, "Well, how about taking that exit up ahead and getting ourselves some lunch?"

"Ok," I said.

He took the exit and, after checking with Grandma, "This okay with you?" pulled into the parking lot of a Denny's. When I got out of the car Grandpa put his arm around my shoulder, and Grandma went to the other side of me and took my hand. Grandpa said, "Well, this is pretty special, all right. It isn't every day that Grandma and I get to take our granddaughter out for lunch."

"That's right," Grandma said.

We got a rounded booth, and I slid in so that I was between the two of them. Grandma handed me a menu and told me to order whatever I wanted. I checked it over, thinking to get something that didn't cost so much. But then Grandpa said, "I think I'm going to get the chicken dinner, something like that sound good to you, Annie?"

The chicken dinner was one of the most expensive things on the menu. I didn't want it but then I felt like I could get whatever I wanted, so I said, "I think I'd like some spaghetti, and a coke." That was fine with them. Afterwards Grandma asked me if I'd like some dessert. When I didn't she told Grandpa to get us some gum and some Lifesaver candies for later.

Back in the car in a little more than an hour we were driving down a highway high up with a view down to a canyon. Grandma said to me, "Just look at that view." So I did, across the canyon where I could see the sharp drop on the other side. Then she added to Grandpa, "Let's keep an eye out for a lookout point."

Pretty soon one came up, and Grandpa pulled to the side of

the road. The viewpoint was a rounded area with a concrete surface that jutted out a little over the canyon. It was fenced with benches up next to the fence. Grandma sat down, and Grandpa pulled out a cigarette, which he had a little trouble lighting. I stood against the fence and looked out over the canyon. Down below I could see the tops of pine trees and a river or stream. It was so far down I couldn't tell which. It was just a snaking shape with sunlight reflecting off it. I looked all around while Grandma and Grandpa watched me. It was quiet, except for the rushing of water far below, and every once in awhile a car that passed us by. High up here, it was like the noise dropped away. I looked at my grandparents, and I was just their granddaughter, nothing else. I didn't have to rush to figure out what they wanted of me. I could just look over the canyon and feel the light breeze. And then, there it was, what I didn't feel. I didn't feel afraid.

37 St Agnes School

I slipped into a pew, and sat and kneeled with everyone else as the mass moved from song or prayer to gospel or epistle, or communion to sermon. The songbooks had the Latin words and the translations beneath: *Kyrie Eleison, Christe Eleison,* Lord have Mercy, Christ have mercy; *Agnes Dei, que tolis peccata mundi,* Lamb of God, who taketh away the sins of the world. This was my favorite time at St. Agnes school, early morning when my grandmother dropped me off on her way to work in time for the special early mass which every sixth grader could sing. I loved to sing the mass, the words solemn and clear, and I loved the quiet in the church. I tried to feel myself close to God, to think of actually talking to God. It was a feeling I had singing, and I could feel it in church on Sunday if I concentrated, and at night before I went to sleep. I'd say a prayer then, too, and afterwards I could sleep.

We wore uniforms of plaid skirts and white blouses – the boys had gray pants, white shirts - but it was singing the mass together that made me feel part of this new Catholic school. Other sixth graders took seats in the pews around me as they arrived. Then, at the end of the mass, the priest said in Latin, "Go the mass is over," and we replied, in Latin, "Thanks be to God." We all rose together, filed out in a long line, then marched to the school half a block away and up to the second floor where we had a few minutes to gather in the hallway before Sister Margaret Mary called us into our classroom.

"Open your math books to p.236," said Sister Margaret Mary. "We'll do drill 31."

St. Agnes was harder than my last school, more tests, more homework. The math drills were hardest because you had to answer fast before the person behind you yelled out, "Too slow," and took your problem. I couldn't predict what my problem would be so I was ready with the one being answered, and the next, and scanning a couple more ahead. Today everyone was fast. "Thirty," I yelled out on my turn. But you could get two or three problems in a drill with forty-eight kids in our class and a hundred problems in each drill. Sister Margaret Mary timed us with the second hand of her watch. Under three minutes was good. "Two minutes and fifty-eight seconds," she said.

Good, no lecture today.

School was hard, but now my brain worked again. When report card day came, the monsignor had come into our class to hand them out. He'd stood at the front of the classroom, kind of a round man, like our Pope, John the XXIII, in his brown robes with the rosary draping down one side over the cloth. He'd called the name, then taken a quick look at each report card as the student walked up. Each time he handed it over, he'd said a few words, a "good work," or "excellent," or sometimes something quiet, only for them. Sister Margaret Mary looked on from her desk, and sometimes the two of them exchanged a glance. Or she added something, like, "her work has really improved since the beginning of the year."

The monsignor called my name, and when I came up, said, "Well, this is very good, all A's." He'd fished in his robes and he came out with a quarter that he handed to me, "Congratulations."

Sister Margaret Mary beamed at me from her desk as I took the quarter and said, "Thank you, Father."

And sometimes you really think you are going to win, when the fear is gone, and your mind works fast like this morning with the math drills so you can say all the answers quickly. And when your responses in religion class are good enough so that Sister Margaret Mary calls you "my little Theologian," then you think, maybe you could be somebody.

But now Sister Margaret Mary jumped up from her desk. "I've had some good news," she said. "The diocese is going to be able to send me to take art classes at the University of Missouri in St. Louis again next summer." Her black robes flowed from her arms as she moved them excitedly. "I didn't think there would be enough money, but God provides." She settled down, but her face kept that smile, just a little calmer, that told us this was an amazing thing.

She'd taught us watercolors, how to do a wash, use wet paint for the large shapes, then go in with a dryer brush for the outlines and details. She showed us with a bowl of fruit, so I painted bowl after bowl of fruit. And I drew. I copied pictures from books and could do the outlines exactly.

"Today, we're going outside to paint the fall flowers."

We grabbed our watercolors and cups of water and followed her out to the flowers that grew on the strip of lawn between the sidewalk and the street.

A light breeze jostled the flowers, so I couldn't see the edges and didn't feel the control I had with the careful pictures. I didn't know how to do it, but somehow I did, dabbing in splashes of color.

Back inside, she told us to pin our paintings up on the bulletin board at the back of the classroom. "We're going to grade them together," she said. She pointed to one. What's this, a B, a C?"

"B," someone yelled, but she didn't say anything.

"C" someone else said.

"Yes, that's about average." Sister Margaret Mary wrote the grade on the back then pinned it back up.

Students continued to yell out grades, sometimes even D's and F's, until they'd settle on one. Most of the time you could tell what grade she wanted. Sometimes, she seemed undecided.

I didn't yell anything, but dreaded the moment when they would reach mine.

It was almost the last. There was something I liked about my painting, bright, lively and colorful, but not what I thought of as good drawing. I expected to be humiliated, but she said, "How about this one? An 'A'?"

And the class agreed.

Maybe that was what grace meant, when you aren't studying or memorizing or doing something that you know will be thought good. Maybe when you try something, that you'd like to hide for awhile, because you kind of like it, but you aren't sure of it. But someone sees it, and they see you. And they think it is good too. Then you can feel it, the grace that is in you, that you didn't have to do anything to get.

#

Sometimes, you really think you are going to win. You'll make it, be the hero, the one to save the day.

There was the day of the girls versus boys softball game. Nearly all the boys and several of us girls played softball at recess nearly every day. Kay always played and Laura, sometimes Janie, usually at least ten or twelve girls per recess. I played every day. But it was Sister Margaret Mary who proposed the girls versus boys softball game.

Next to art, and maybe next to God, I thought, what Sister Margaret Mary loved was baseball. That fall, every afternoon that the world series was on television, lessons dropped, the portable TV was perched on Sister Margaret Mary's desk and all 48 of us were gathered as close as we could on chairs, in desks, on the floor, to watch. Sister Margaret Mary sat in a desk right up front, the black folds of her habit spilling out into the aisle. It was the San Francisco Giants versus the New York Yankees. Sister Margaret Mary favored the Giants.

"I guess I'm just naturally for the underdog," she'd said.

That last game, it wasn't looking too bad for the Giants. The games were tied 3-3. Right now the Yankees were ahead, 1-0 at the start of the ninth inning, but the Giant's pinch hitter had made it to first on a bunt. Then the Yankees' pitcher struck out the next two batters.

Sister Margaret Mary leaned forward, looking tense. "Come on, McCovey. He can hit," she said. And he did, hard. We all started to cheer, but the second baseman stepped to the left and reached high. Somehow he snagged the ball, and the cheers died in our throats. Sister Margaret Mary was out of the desk with a gesture of disgust. She turned off the TV set.

She didn't even mention baseball for a week or two.

But then, even though she still didn't mention the Yankees or the Giants, Sister Margaret Mary starting talking about how she had loved to play baseball. In her small school the boys and girls had played together. There wouldn't have been enough to make two teams otherwise. She didn't say it, but I thought I knew that she was a good player.

"What do you say, we have a boys versus girls softball game on Friday afternoon?" she proposed.

There were shouts of "Yes," and "We'll whup them," and it was set. It was an extra recess for us, and who would be against that? All the rest of the week, several times a day, someone would say, "I can't wait for the game."

Friday afternoon, we swarmed out to the far field on the right of the school yard.

The girls were up first. Sister Margaret Mary would pitch for each team.

One after one, the girls struck out, or hit short balls and were put out at first base. I watched horrified, because it wasn't only the girls who never played. Kay, our hardest hitter, went up to bat. She struck at the first two balls and missed. She stepped back then and let the third pitch go by.

"Ball," said Sister Margaret Mary, "one ball and two strikes."

Kay struck at the fourth pitch, and connected but only with a piece of the bat. Tommy Lambert made an easy toss to put her out on first.

Then we were out in the field. The boys hit hard, and we made a lot of errors. The score was 30 to nothing before we got back up. I would bat third.

The two girls who batted before me struck out. When I was up, my knees shook. This was new for me, so I understood what had happened to Kay. Still, I told myself to watch the ball, and held the bat back ready to swing. When the pitch came I swung, and I hit that ball straight on and harder than I ever had before. It went so far it was beyond the last row of fielders and into one of the other baseball diamonds. I had rounded third before the right fielder even reached the ball. Still, I ran as fast as I could home, as though something might still happen and the ball would reach home before me. But it didn't. I ran across home and scored our first run before the ball even reached the infield.

But the girl after me struck out, and we headed in.

Inside Peter McCauley said, "We sure whipped them, 30 to 1."

But Neil, one of the twins said, "Yeah, but what about that home run Annie hit. That was sure some home run."

38 Christmas

I stood on the sidewalk next to the parking lot right outside the school. Every morning when my grandmother dropped me off there, she'd remind me, "Be waiting here for me this afternoon." But she was often late. She was late now.

Then, Sister Francesca, the choir teacher, came out of the school. She walked slowly, burdened down by a big stack of books. I ran over to her, "Can I carry those for you?"

She was one of the oldest nuns. In choir she made us practice over and over until we got it right. She'd stop us in the middle of the line, and we'd start again. Again and again. We were practicing now for the Christmas program. My favorite song was "Oh come, oh come, Immanuel / and ransom captive Israel / who mourns in lonely exile here / until the son of God appear." It was a new song for me. It sounded so solemn, so yearning and Sister Francesca wanted us to get it right. She talked to us sternly until we did.

But now she smiled at me, and handed me her stack of books, "My old back does get tired. It's nice to have someone with a young, fresh back to take the burden off me."

I stood up straight with my young, fresh back. It wasn't so many books really, and it wasn't so far, only across the parking lot and up the walk to the Nuns' house right next to the rectory where the priests lived.

"You're doing well here, aren't you?" Sister Francesca said. "I heard you made straight A's."

"Yes," I said.

"You live with your grandparents?"

I nodded.

"What did they say about you doing so well?"

I'd handed my report card to my grandma when we'd gone

into the house after she drove me home from school. She'd told me to put it down on the dining room table and she'd look at it and sign it later. I set it down, feeling glad that I didn't have to worry about what would happen when Grandma and Grandpa looked at it. Then I thought they might act pleased or surprised because I'd heard Mama telling Grandma I'd had trouble with school in fifth grade. In the morning the report card was next to my plate. Grandma said, "Don't forget to take you report card back. I signed it for you." That was all.

"They were happy," I told Sister Francesca.

"Of course they were," she said, and we were at the door to her house. She thanked me, took her books and went inside. I hurried over to the parking lot, running the last way when I saw that Grandma's car was already there.

"Where were you?" she asked. "I've been waiting."

I told her. I thought she'd be pleased that I was carrying Sister Francesca's books, but she was irritated.

"I'm tired. I had a long day, and now you make me wait to go home."

After that I watched for Sister Francesca, but while I walked along with her, or carried her books, I made sure to glance over at the parking lot, and, if I saw Grandma's car turning into it, I told Sister Francesca I had to go, and ran to get there before my grandmother stopped. But most of the time Grandma still wasn't there after I'd walked Sister Francesca home.

It was getting dark earlier now.

By the time we'd had dinner and I'd done my homework, and dried the dishes while my grandfather washed, the light was fading. When I asked if I could visit the girl who lived across the street, Grandma said, "It's too late to be walking around by yourself."

"But, it's just across the street."

"I don't care. No granddaughter of mine is going to be

running around the neighborhood after dark."

It wasn't even that dark yet, but I knew it would do no good to argue. She'd made up her mind. Instead I found a new book to read off the long shelf in the living room.

#

Back at the Willises' there'd been a thick Sears-Roebuck catalog Renee and I used to thumb through. On each page we'd pick out the things that we'd buy for ourselves or our kids one day when we were grown up.

When I found the Sears toy catalog lying on the arm of the easy chair in the living room, I thought maybe Grandma or Grandpa had left it there for me so I could tell them what I wanted for Christmas. This was the first time I'd seen a whole catalog of just toys, so I settled up in the chair and pored over it. Then I saw the chemistry set. I read through the description, all the experiments I could carry out if I had it, how I'd be a budding young scientist.

I was sitting in the big green chair near where Grandpa was making sandwiches in the kitchen.

"I'd like a chemistry set for Christmas," I told him.

Grandpa seemed irritated. He said, "Chemistry sets cost ten or fifteen dollars."

I checked quickly, and he was right, $12.95.

Grandpa talked like he was arguing with someone. "We spend five dollars on each grandchild for Christmas. We have sixteen grandchildren, and we can't afford to spend more than that."

Grandma came into the living room while he was saying this, and must have agreed because she didn't say anything. I wanted to say, but this year I'm living with you. It should be different. My parents would probably send me only a small present because they'd think my grandparents would get me lots of things. I wanted to say that I was special, but it looked like I wasn't.

But they might've changed their minds by Christmas. Grandpa could even have said that so I'd be all the more surprised when I got just what I wanted.

So on Christmas morning, I woke up excited, ready to rush out and open presents. At home we always did that first thing, even before breakfast, except for last Christmas when we opened them up in the middle of the night after we came home from midnight mass.

Grandpa was up already and offered me sweet rolls for breakfast.

"Are we going to open presents now?" I asked. He sat down opposite me at the small table in the kitchen. He was still in his plaid pajamas and slippers like he was most mornings. He'd leave his slippers on through most of the day unless he went out.

He said, "We'll have to see what your grandmother says about that." I sat in the living room, just waiting at first, and then found a book to read. I was halfway through it before Grandma even came out of her room. Then I waited for Grandpa to ask her about opening presents, but he didn't. I wanted to ask, I don't know why I didn't. If Danny and Renee and Sammy were here, one of them would have blurted it out by now, "Hey, when are we opening our presents?" but something held me back. It made the day feel so long and lonely and empty, waiting for something to happen. I just wanted someone to say something that made it special, turn on the radio to hear Christmas music, just to make it Christmas and not just another day. But nobody did.

Grandpa made us sandwiches for lunch and still no one said anything about the presents under the tree.

Grandma sat on the arm of a chair in the living room, not even reading, just sitting there, pushing her lips out and sucking them in again the way that she did. She was dressed up. She seemed discontented, and, like me, she seemed to be waiting. She kept checking her watch, and after awhile she told Grandpa that he'd better be getting ready. We were going to see Uncle James and Aunt Sharon and my two little cousins, Cindy and Jack, for Christmas dinner. Ted, my uncle who was in high school, wasn't here, and maybe Grandma was waiting for him. He was usually out with his friends when he wasn't working.

Then the phone rang, and Grandma got it and I could tell it was Sharon. Grandma's voice brightened up. After the call she seemed cheerful again, and she said, "Well, let's open presents, then get going."

Grandma and Grandpa each unwrapped presents but they just thanked each other and didn't take the gifts out of their boxes.

"Well, go on," Grandma said to me. I opened the present from them first, a set of bath powder and bubble bath.

I thanked them. Then I opened the other box that came from Norfolk. I thought I knew what it was. Mama asked me in a letter what I wanted, and then in the next letter she'd said she thought I was getting old for dolls, but she'd got the Barbie doll for me anyway. I just had time to unwrap it, before Grandma was urging us into the car so we could get over to Sharon's. Well, that would be fun. I especially liked my little cousin, Jack. He was such a cute little guy.

39 Hell

You had to believe in hell, didn't you, because the children of Fatima had seen hell. The Virgin Mary showed it to them. It was like a great sea of fire under the earth. Jacinta, the youngest of the children was so affected by it that she did everything she could to rescue sinners from hell. She would do penance by wearing a rough, knotted rope around her waist. She would give up her lunch or refuse to drink water in the heat of the day when she was out with her brother, Francisco and her cousin, Lucia, watching sheep. All the children did penance, but Jacinta seemed the most affected by the sight of hell.

In church I tried to be devout by concentrating on feeling God in the quiet when the priest called us to kneel down to pray. Instead of thinking about Plumfield before I went to sleep at night, I said a prayer and concentrated on feeling what the words said.

The shelves of our classroom library had three books on archeology, and all the rest were stories of saints. I read them all, and I wondered if I would be able to die for my faith like the martyrs. I wondered if I could touch the sores of the lepers like St. Francis of Assisi had. I would try to imagine it, hot coals in my mouth, flames coming up around me.

But, hell? Did I really believe that God would put anyone in hell forever? Wasn't God all merciful, and all knowing? Sure people did bad things but that didn't mean that they were bad, did it? God could see into them and know all the reasons why they did what they did.

My mother did the worst things that I knew about. She looked at me like I was scum, so all I wanted was to disappear, and I never knew what it was about me that made her hate me so much. She'd slap me or pull my hair or break my teeth, and it was because I didn't do the dishes fast enough, or I couldn't figure out what she wanted before she told me. But my mother wasn't bad. I knew it. I didn't believe that God could look at my mother and not know that she wasn't bad. I didn't believe that God would send my mother to hell.

Even Sister Margaret Mary did bad things sometimes. She didn't talk much about herself, but a few times she did, usually during religion class. There was the time she'd talked about her challenges. "I have a temper," she told us. "I have to work on that."

We'd seen it.

"Sit down now," Sister Margaret Mary had said to Brent, the red headed kid. But he kept on arguing.

"It isn't fair," he said. I didn't hear what it was about, a grade maybe. But when he said it, Sister Margaret Mary jumped up from her desk and started slapping his face.

"I said, sit down now," she yelled, and he went to his desk, but he was still yelling, yelling louder now, that it wasn't fair. His face was red with anger, and he sat down, but Sister Margaret Mary just kept slapping at him, his back, his arms, and then he got up and he pulled his desk over on its side and all the while he was yelling. And Sister Margaret Mary was hitting, and saying, "Pick that up." And he wouldn't.

I wanted him to stop. I was afraid for him.

Sister Margaret Mary was still slapping. Finally Brent stopped yelling, set his desk upright and sat down. Then he just laid his head down on his desk over his arms that were grabbing it, and she finally stopped hitting him. He was so angry. I didn't know why he was so angry. He didn't even seem to feel it when she hit him. It just made him angrier.

His face had gotten so red, and his veins pulsed. Finally he just laid on his desk and cried.

It was wrong of Sister Margaret Mary to hit Brent like that, but Sister Margaret Mary wasn't always wrong when she got fierce and angry. A few days later our class was outside. The recess was nearly over and the group of us girls who played softball every day had stopped the game and were heading in from the field. Sister Margaret Mary was out on the blacktop. Janie, who was Filipino, was crying and Sister Margaret Mary held her. Janie was enveloped in the black folds of Sister Margaret Mary's habit.

"What happened?" Sister Margaret Mary asked.

Janie struggled to get loose from her, but Sister Margaret Mary wouldn't let her go, just held her tighter up against her.

Janie just cried and struggled, her long black hair twisting around her as she aimed her body from one side to the other, like red rover, trying to break through. Then she said, "They said, say 'black eyes' backward."

So then I had to think, 'black eyes" backward, "eyes black." Next about Janie's eyes and how they weren't black, but deep brown that met black in the center. Only after that got the "I's black." Got that someone wanted to hurt her for no reason.

Sister Margaret Mary was angry like she got angry, when she was really angry, her face getting red. Looking around, at all of us, like any of us might have done it, said, "Who said that?"

Her eyes went around the circle of us huddled around Janie, and when they reached me I felt bare and raw and guilty even though I hadn't done it, wouldn't have. Sister Margaret Mary's eyes kept going and they didn't stay on anyone very long. Janie said, "Two girls in another class."

"Who?" asked Sister Margaret Mary, but Janie shrugged, and she wouldn't say anything else.

Sister Margaret Mary looked like she wanted to shake Janie, but she didn't. Instead she kept holding her tight like that. She said,

"Everybody's color is right with God." She looked round again and this time when she settled on me I felt different, like she knew I wouldn't hurt Janie, like she knew that I knew that everybody's color is right with God.

God knows everything, so God knew about Sister Margaret Mary's temper and her slapping hand, but he also knew how she held Janie so tight, and told us all that everybody's color is right with God. I couldn't believe that God would send Sister Margaret Mary to hell.

So I didn't believe in hell, not really. Well, it had to exist because the children of Fatima had seen it. But I didn't believe that God put anybody in it. No, hell was just to scare people.

#

Ted hollered through my door, "Hey, you gonna watch this movie with me?" My uncle Ted wasn't around much. He was in his last year of high school and was usually working to pay for his car, or off in it somewhere with his best friend, Walker. But tonight Grandma and Grandpa had gone out to dinner and they were seeing a movie afterwards, so they must have asked Ted to stay with me even though I'd be just fine on my own.

I came out of my room, and watched the start of Friday Night at the Movies.

The movie was *The Hoodlum Priest*. "It's based on a true story," Ted said.

"But I'm supposed to be in bed by 8:30." Even though it was Friday night, and even though my bedtime in Norfolk had been 9 on school nights, and later on weekends, Grandma insisted on 8:30.

"Well, they aren't getting home until late tonight, and I'm not telling anyone," Ted smiled at me. He tipped back the dining room chair. When I thought it was going over he let the front feet settle back down, then scooted it back to rest his feet on the dining room table.

I guess he just wanted some company. We talked during the commercial, but while the movie showed I was absorbed in it. The main character, Billy Lee Jackson, didn't seem much older than Ted (who was 18). He'd gotten in trouble, but now he was trying to go straight. Father Clark was the Hoodlum Priest who tried to help Billy and some other young men stay out of trouble. But Billy got involved in a robbery. He didn't mean to hurt anyone, but the man being robbed came at him with a crowbar, and he killed the man trying to protect himself.

Then it seemed like all the cops in the city were after him, and he was holed up in a empty house. He had a gun, and he said he wasn't going to come out, and he'd shoot anyone who tried to come in.

But then the priest was there and he rushed past the cops and into the house. He persuaded Billy to give up the gun and come out.

"That was a big embarrassment to the St. Louis police," Ted said. "All those cops with guns couldn't get him to give himself up, and then the priest just walks in and gets him to come out."

Then later, after Billy had been sentenced to death, the priest walked with him to the electric chair and stayed with him as long as he could. He kept telling him to think about the good thief and how Jesus said, "This night you'll be with me in Paradise."

"I didn't know you could be sentenced to death for killing someone in self-defense," I said.

"Yeah," Ted said, "but the rules are different when you kill someone while you're committing a crime, no matter how it happened."

"But he wasn't really bad, not bad enough for the electric chair."

"Naw," Ted said. He took a drag off his cigarette, then put

out the stub. "Lot of things aren't fair in this world. Sometimes it doesn't matter what someone deserves."

#

The next morning I woke to Ted and my grandmother's voice. I dressed quickly and went out to the dining room where they were eating breakfast. I went to get dishes from the kitchen and poured myself some cereal and milk.

Ted and Grandma continued talking to each other for awhile. Then Grandma turned to me.

"You're up late," she said. "When did you go to bed last night?" So I wondered if Ted had told her, but he said he wouldn't.

"8:30," I said. Then she and Ted exchanged a look, like, as if Ted were saying, *See, she lied about it.*

Grandma looked down disgustedly at her bowl, and just ate for awhile and didn't say anything to me. Did he tell her, too, that he promised me he wouldn't tell? Did that lie matter to her, or only the ones that I told?

I finished my cereal as soon as I could and went out to the living room, where I'd left a book. After a little while I heard their voices brighten up like they'd been when I'd woken up, but I couldn't hear what they said.

40 Fire

Grandpa smoked so there were always books of matches laying about. And my uncle Ted smoked. Sometimes he'd smoke while he watched TV in the dining room. After he lit a cigarette he'd play with the lit match, bringing his fingers together over the flame of the match, then apart again, before he'd blow it out. So I tried that and found it didn't hurt, but it wasn't as much fun as staring at the flame, seeing all the colors flicker about and change from moment to moment.

My room was the small utility room off of the dining room. It didn't even have a door, but most of the time there was no one in the dining room. When I first tried burning paper, I'd taken a piece straight from my notebook and lit it. I held the paper in my hand as long as I could, watching, until it got so hot my finger felt the burn. A flat unfolded sheet of paper burned with a big flame that reached my fingers so fast I'd dropped it and had to stamp it out quickly into thin black sheets and dust. I rubbed away the black soot marks and cleaned up the burnt paper.

Then I tried wadding the paper first. A crumpled piece burnt fast too, but with a smaller flame, so I could hold one edge almost until the end. Fanfold worked best, especially if I went to the sink in the kitchen or the bathroom to wet the handle end. When I lit the fan end there'd be a large flame first, then a smaller one as the fire crept towards the tighter folds, dying to embers as it reached the wet handles.

When you burn a candle you see all kinds of colors, blue at the center, yellow and finally red on the outside, but on the paper the flame was mostly just red, almost orange, and even looked a little clear right next to the paper. Though, after it had burned for awhile, it began to look blue at the bottom edge of the flames nearest my fingers. At the same time the paper turned a dark gray and curled over gracefully. As the flame crept past the gray, the color changed and became an even lighter gray, and small bits of the paper fluttered down on the floor. As the flames reached the wet part of the paper, the flames became smaller and then went out altogether.

The grayed paper looked soft like soft leather, and when I felt it, it felt soft as well, delicate and flaky. Then I heard grandpa coming towards the dining room, and I hurriedly swept the paper and ashes behind the hot water heater.

Grandpa's steps stopped in the kitchen with the sound of water running from the faucet. He said, loud, so I could hear, "About time we were getting ourselves some lunch, isn't it." So I went into the kitchen and sat at the little kitchen table while he got out bread and cheese, and made us sandwiches. I'd have to clean up the ashes later.

#

"Jesus, Mary, Joseph and all the saints and sinners. What is this?" Grandma turned to me where I lay on my bed reading. Grandma was pointing to a pile of charred paper behind the water heater.

"Nothing, it was just a piece of paper." That one I'd dropped and stomped out. I'd meant to clean it up later, but I forgot.

"I guess we're lucky the hot water heater didn't leak gas," she'd said.

That was all she said, but next afternoon she arrived early at school, parked the car and had me follow her up the stairs back into my classroom. Up in my classroom, she pointed to a desk, "Wait here."

She and Sister Margaret Mary talked for awhile. Sister Margaret Mary looked my way sometimes, and I felt some dread, because sometimes you think you are winning, but then there was that look between Grandma and Uncle Ted, *she's lying*. I wondered if I'd see that look again. Then they both came over. Grandma sat across the aisle. Sister Margaret Mary sat in the seat ahead of her, but she didn't face ahead, but put her feet out in the aisle so she was facing me. I waited for the yelling, but when she talked it was in a normal voice, friendly, "Your grandmother says you've been lighting fires."

I looked down, "Just little ones."

I was afraid she would ask my why, or something else I wouldn't be able to answer. But she just said, "You know you can't be lighting fires, not even little ones."

Was that it then?

She reached over, and put her hand on my chin to tip it up. "Do you have any more matches now?"

I dug them out of the little pocket of my plaid skirt.

Sister Margaret Mary put them in her pocket hidden in her long black habit.

"Now, I'm sure they'll be no more problem with that," Sister Margaret Mary said confidently to my grandmother.

I didn't light any more fires. I wanted to, but now I knew the water heater could blow up, and I didn't have any other place besides my room to light them secretly. Still, as soon as I could I got another book of matches just to carry around. I liked having them near me.

#

Grandma sat up so straight in the hard wooden chair. That's what I noticed first, how straight she sat, how dignified she was, and her face, hard and disappointed. The chair was in my room on the far wall from the door. I'd just come home from the park and had gone into my little room, and there she was.

What I noticed next were the presents on my bed. They'd

been under it, hidden there until my brothers and sisters would come with my parents to pick me up. All their birthdays were in the summer, July and August, and they were coming in August. It was important to me that I be able to give them presents, and I couldn't ask my grandparents to buy them.

My grandparents didn't give me an allowance, but I soon noticed that when my grandmother gave me money to pay for the school lunch, that she always gave me more than it cost. One day I kept the extra money instead of turning it in to the two 8th grade students who had come to collect it. Then I waited before I spent the money in case Grandma asked for her change, but she never did. After that I kept it all the time.

But that wasn't enough to buy presents. Grandpa often sent me out to the nearby grocery store for bread and milk. On the same block was a drug store that sold toys, and household items as well. One day, after I got the bread and milk, I slipped into the drugstore and sat my bag of groceries down on the floor and started looking through the toys. The toy section was back out of sight of the clerk. I found a model, and I decided to slip it into my sack. It was easy. I pulled out a lot of models and looked at them one by one. Then as I put them back on the shelf, I picked up a few at once, and I let one slip into my bag. And if anyone had said anything it would have been an accident, but I picked them all up and put them on the shelf, except for the one in my bag. Then I looked around a little more, finally came back and picked up my bag and carried it away.

I took something from there nearly every time I went. Soon I had presents for everyone. Other times I'd go into grocery stores and take candy. No one ever stopped or questioned me.

Not until Grandma found the presents under my bed.

She pointed over at them, "What are these?" and her voice accused me.

I felt like crying. "Those are birthday presents, for my brothers and sisters. I was hiding them until their birthdays." I saw how she hesitated a moment then, like she was uncertain, but then she continued.

"How about those candy bars in Ted's drawer?" Uncle Ted had left to join the Air Force just a couple of weeks ago. I thought he'd just forgotten about those candy bars in his drawer. "Ted said I could have those," my grandmother said, "but I went to look for them, and they were gone."

I didn't say anything. I couldn't think of anything to say. So then she said it.

"When your mother called you a liar and a thief, I thought that that was the worst thing I had ever heard, but now I know that it's true."

Then she got up, her back still straight, and she left without looking at me or saying anything more.

I picked up all the presents and shoved them back under my bed. Then I lay there on my bed, sank down into it, and held every muscle just as still as I could. As if I could just lie there, and everything could just sweep over me, the way I was ashamed, the way I was alone.

#

I used to tell myself that I'd pay the stores back when I grew up, when I had money. But the stores had so much stuff. It didn't seem like they'd even miss it.

In the spring my grandfather had started driving around Springfield selling ice cream from his truck. Sometimes he left his money belt lying around, full of coins, and I'd take just a few from each of the holders. He never said anything. I thought he never noticed.

On a day when I'd taken some money, during recess none of

the girls wanted to play softball. I was alone in the big open field behind the school when an ice cream truck drove near the fence. It wasn't my grandfather's truck, so I yelled to the seller, and I bought several ice creams, then I yelled at some girls that I had ice cream for them. A bunch of girls came, and they started grabbing the fudgesicles and ice cream bars. I thought they'd stay and we'd laugh and talk and eat it together. But they grabbed the ice cream and ran off again. I was left alone in the middle of the field feeling lonelier than I had before, and empty.

But then a couple of days after that day when my Grandma had sat so straight in the chair in my room, I saw my grandfather's money belt on the counter. But this time he was right there at the stove putting on a pot of coffee, instead of in another room so I could sneak a couple of coins without him seeing. There wasn't even anything that I wanted money for, but I felt like I had to have it. So even though he was there I moved over by the counter where his money belt lay. As I reached for it Grandpa's voice surprised me, "Get away from that."

He sat down at the little table in the kitchen. As he made his breakfast, he talked out loud, "I thought I was missing some change. I just wasn't sure."

He put toast in the toaster. As he did, I sidled over to the counter again. Somehow I felt I had to reach the money, even though I knew that he knew.

Grandpa looked up, yelled, "I told you, get away from there!"

I moved back, then moved forward again. He yelled again and I moved back.

But I tried again and again, the more he looked at me, his face calling me a thief, the more I felt I needed to get to the money, until at last he finished his breakfast and headed out to the ice cream truck with his money belt around his waist.

41 Janie

I walked into the store casually, not focused on anything in particular. I headed first to the magazines and spent a little time thumbing through. Janie wanted a movie star magazine. That's what she said after I told her I'd shoplifted. She didn't say "Prove it," but it was like that a little. I looked at several of the magazines, and when I finished I still held one in my hand, loosely, as if I'd forgotten that I even had it. Then I moved to another aisle. This time it was the candy aisle, mostly candy, cookies back at the other end, and across from them crackers.

I picked up a half pound bag of M&M's. I held the bag in my left hand for awhile, and then, as if I wasn't really thinking about it, shifted it, so now it was in the same hand as the magazine, actually inside the slightly rolled up magazine out of sight held next to my body. If anybody had asked about it, I could have said I was trying to decide which I wanted. Then I could put them both back and just leave.

But nobody did ask ever, and this store even had a back door, just at the end of one of the long aisles. I continued looking over the shelves until I was at the back, then lingered back there awhile, before finally just walking out the back door. Sometimes I even walked out the front door. If you acted like everything was okay, nobody questioned you. Who was to say you had not already paid for your purchases, and you just didn't need a sack. But this time I went through the back door, and once outside looked around to see if anyone followed. By that time I had crossed the street to the field next door, and could have taken off running if there was anyone, because it was a longish field, and it was a ways to where Janie and her little brother and sister were sitting waiting for me. And, though they weren't near the trees, there were some that I could have climbed if I needed to. But I knew I wouldn't need to. Nobody had taken any notice of me.

Taking things never make me feel scared. I never thought about what would happen if I got caught.

"Here," I said to Janie, handing her the movie star magazine. Janie looked it over searchingly. I couldn't see why she would waste her time on them. I held on to the M&M's. What is that? Janie asked, and I offered her some. She looked scornful but took a few. I took some and gave the rest to the kids. The two of them ran around the field playing, and their fists on the inside got that candy color you get from clutching a fistful of M&M's until they are melty. After awhile Janie called to them to bring her some more.

Weekdays while my grandmother worked I went to the park program. Mrs. Beloit helped us with crafts, and we played games like miniature golf. At noon there was a break, and I ate lunch with my friend, Della. Afterwards we'd swim in the public pool before we went to the afternoon session. I'd been at the park when Janie had come by. I hadn't seen her since school got out. Even then I hadn't seen her much. At the Girl Scout campout and after, she'd started hanging out more with the older girls, the ones who'd turned twelve by the end of the school year. At the campout we'd been going to meet on the trail and go hiking. She said she'd wait for me at the clearing at the start of the path, since I was on cleanup. But she wasn't there. Another girl told me Janie had gone ahead with a group of girls. When I saw her later she'd told me that she waited and finally decided I wasn't coming. I knew I hadn't been late, but I let it go.

But she hadn't been with those other girls today, when she came to the park with her brother and sister, and she had nothing to do but swing slowly in the swings while the two little kids went down the slide and played in the sandbox. When Della was ready to go back up the hill to the afternoon session of crafts, I told her I'd stay with Janie since I hadn't seen her in such a long time. Della seemed uneasy.

"I might come up in a little while," I told her. Maybe I could persuade Janie to bring her brother and sister up to the craft program. Della hesitated, but then said ok and left.

But Janie wanted to go and suggested I leave the park and come with them instead. We went to the field across from the Kroger's super market parking lot. I started telling Janie about the shoplifting I'd done. While I told her, it was like I was a cool kid, like one of the girls she'd hung out with at the Girl Scout camp.

"I stole five dollars once from a family I was babysitting for," she said.

I was a little shocked. That seemed different from stealing from a store, or from my grandfather's money belt that had lots of change in it. What if they needed that five dollars?

But I didn't say anything. I wanted to stay cool. I told her I could steal her something from the store.

"Get me a movie magazine," she had said.

A movie magazine. That had seemed so boring, but I got her movie magazine. When I'd handed it to her, she'd looked disappointed so I worried I'd gotten the wrong kind, but now she lay on the grass, absorbed in the movie stars. I watched her until it was time for me to start walking home.

As I was walking away, she shouted after me, "Why don't you ask your grandmother if you can spend the night on Thursday?"

"I will."

#

I was surprised how easy it was to get Grandma to let me go to Janie's house. She agreed I could leave from the park program and then come back home the next day when I usually would. That afternoon when Janie came to the park program to get me, she was by herself. She explained that her mother was at home with the younger kids, but tomorrow she would have to work again. Janie didn't seem in a hurry to get back home. We went down to the swings and swung on them lazily for awhile. Janie got out suntan lotion and rubbed it on herself. As she rubbed her legs, she said, "I'm getting too dark. I have to watch that."

I didn't say anything but wondered why. Most people wanted to get a sun tan. After a whole summer in the sun my arms had turned a light russet color that was still lighter than most people in the middle of winter, and I wished I could get darker. But I didn't say anything because I was afraid it might be because of that "Black Eyes backward" joke from school, and I didn't want to hurt her feeling again by saying anything that made her think of it.

We took our time getting back to Janie's house. The day was cooling down, and we walked slow, relaxed. Janie told me it was her mother's birthday the next day, and it was too bad that she had to work, but Janie planned to clean the house the next day, so at least she'd have a nice clean house to come home to as a present.

"I wish I had some money to get her something."

I'd have given her some if I had any, but I didn't. We kept walking then, quietly. The cool of the evening felt soothing.

I was walking barefoot, carrying my shoes, and I stepped on something. It was some kind of ticket, no, two of them. I bent and picked them up, looked at it. "Rain check" they said, and "Springfield Speedway."

"What's that?" asked Janie.

I handed it to her, "I don't know. Looks like some kind of tickets."

"Springfield Speedway," she read. "That's a racetrack."

I said, "Do you think you could get into the race track with them?"

"Maybe," she said, then she got all excited. "I know," she said, "tomorrow I can clean the house, and you can go out and try to sell the tickets. If you could get two dollars for them, I could buy my mother a birthday present."

"Ok," I said. "I'll try anyway."

"It's probably worth more," Janie said. "Someone will want it."

I met her mother at dinner, but right afterwards we went up to Janie's room. Janie had a catalog that we looked through deciding what she would get for her mother if she had two dollars.

Next morning she started cleaning, and I left to try to sell the tickets.

42 Caught

It was horrible, but it was familiar, running, scared. Running without tracking where I was going, so now I didn't know the way back to Janie's house. Because that would be best, to reach her house and go inside where I would be hidden. My chest hurt as my breath came hard. And then I was in a totally unfamiliar place. The street had broadened. Trees lined it and softened the light that filtered down.

The day would be hot, but it wasn't yet. The sidewalk was full of flittering shadows that moved with every breeze. All the quiet and calm reached me, until I was out walking on a beautiful morning. My heart slowed down, and I began to think that I was far enough away, even if the woman had called the police.

The car moved so quietly, it was beside me before I saw it. It eased in to the curb, and then there was the hand that felt familiar now, that reached over and opened the door to the passenger side of the police car, and the voice that wasn't familiar, but what it said was familiar, "Get in."

I wanted to run, but too scared, I scooted into the passenger seat and waited.

He looked okay, not mean. "You been taking letters this morning?" he asked me, but without much energy, as though he wasn't really expecting an answer.

I stared at the dashboard, "No."

"Yeah, well what are you doing out here then?"

"I went for a walk. Then I couldn't remember where my friend's house was where I spent the night. I've been looking for it."

"That so." He swung the patrol car into the driveway of the house where I took the letter. Another patrol car was parked in front, and two cops stood on the porch talking to the woman who'd yelled at me.

"Hey," she'd shouted. "What do you think you're doing." She'd stood there in the doorway in her brown hair and her house dress. She looked sixtyish, older even than my grandmother, and you could see the shape of her under the dress, her stomach poking out a little, not like she was fat, not even plump, but her body filled the dress.

"Hey, what are you doing? Why'd you take that letter?"

And I ran and ran, down to the corner and then around the block. Then on and on until I was too out of breath to run anymore and had to walk.

Now the woman stood in the doorway of her house, her hand holding the screen door part way open.

The cop who drove me opened my door and walked me up to the porch.

"This her?" he asked the woman, who stood up straighter and pushed her glasses up on her nose before answering, "Yes, it is."

"Tell us again what happened," he leaned back against the house, on the side with the second door.

"I heard a knock," the woman said, "but I thought it was the neighbor's door."

I'd knocked on her door first. Maybe if she'd come I wouldn't be in this mess.

"Then I heard another knock. The neighbors asked me to keep an eye on the place while they were gone, but it took me awhile to get to the door. I was going to tell whoever it was that the neighbors were away for a few days. But by the time I got outside, all I saw was this girl, about fourteen years old heading down the block. While I watched she tore an envelope in two, throwing half to one side and half to the other. I looked at my neighbor's mailbox because I knew they had put out a letter to mail before they left for their trip, and that letter was missing. So I yelled out to the girl and she took off running."

"And this is her?"

"Yes, it is," the lady said.

"I'm eleven," I told the cop. He did a little flick of his head, like my words were a fly he'd brushed off.

"Think now," the officer said, "did you take that letter out of the mailbox?"

"No, I didn't."

The woman leaned against the door railing, looking concerned, "Honey, they can check your fingerprints."

Oh yeah, fingerprints.

"You sure you didn't take that letter?" the policeman asked again. They all watched me, the woman, the cop who'd picked me up, the two cops who'd been talking to the woman when we'd pulled up. The pot-bellied one scowled at me.

"There wasn't any letter in the mailbox. It was lying on the ground. I picked it up to see what it was."

"She's lying," the tubby cop said.

But my cop silenced him. "How do you suppose it got over there?"

"The wind must have blown it."

"You sure you didn't just take that letter over there?"

"No, I didn't."

The tubby cop shook his head, repeated, "She's lying." But my cop glared at him until he left the porch, although he leaned against it and held onto the railing. Then my cop asked me if I didn't know I shouldn't open other people's mail even if I found it on the ground.

"I didn't know whose it was."

"Could have looked at the address, couldn't you?"

"Imagine the people it was sent to," said the woman. "They wouldn't get their mail and they wouldn't even know what happened."

I hadn't thought about that.

Then they ignored me, while my cop said something to the pot-bellied cop, who took off. Then he talked to the lady for awhile. While they were still talking, yet another police car parked on the street in front of the house. A young looking cop got out and walked over to the curb side, where he leaned back against the car like he was waiting, completely relaxed.

After awhile the cop at the porch told me to get in the police car. He motioned to the one where the young cop stood.

"Can we stop by my friend's house to let her know where I am?"

"Just get in the car."

The young cop held the door open for me, so I knew to get into the front seat.

It was familiar, doing what I was told, in trouble, going somewhere I didn't know. But I tried again, asking if we could stop so I could let Janie know what had happened to me.

"I can't," he said. "You'll have to phone her later."

So I just sat there, silently. He looked nice though, like the young cop on *Car 54 Where Are You?* The TV cop was always nice to the people they picked up, and expected the best of them, not like his partner, who was tough but professional.

The young cop asked me where I went to school.

"St. Agnes."

And he grinned, "You don't say. I went there too when I was a kid." He looked at me again then, and I thought he looked at me just like I was any other good Catholic kid, like we had a bond being Catholic.

It was horrible, but it was familiar, to be riding in the cop car with the young cop, but it was different that he looked at me like I was a good Catholic kid, just a regular kid.

"What were you doing this morning anyway?" the young cop asked me.

I told him how Janie and I had found some tickets on the ground on the way to her house, and how Janie had thought maybe I could sell them and get some money to buy her mother a present for her birthday the next day. That morning I'd gone out to sell the tickets, while Janie cleaned up the house for a surprise for her mother. I told the young cop how I didn't take the letter, just picked it up off the street then dropped it again. I waited for the look, the horrible but familiar look of him finding out about me. That look that told me he knew how worthless I was.

He said, "Here, let me see those." I handed the tickets over to him.

He studied them, driving with one arm. "These are rain checks. They aren't worth anything." He handed them back.

I tore up the rain checks, but he stopped me, "Wait, that's your alibi."

So I stopped. But he never gave me the look.

Now I had these little pieces of paper in my fist, "Will you keep them for me?"

He laughed. He said, no, he couldn't do that, but I should hold onto them.

He kept looking at me like I was a regular kid.

He believed my story.

And then I wanted so badly for my story to be true.

#

I'd thought he was driving to the police station, but he stopped the car in front of a hospital.

"Come on, we've got to find your grandmother."

I'd never been to my grandmother's hospital. I just knew she worked with the preemies, babies born too soon. Some of them died.

He asked at the reception desk for my grandmother, and then upstairs motioned me to sit in the waiting area while he asked for her again. She came to the reception desk in a fluster. The cop talked to her quietly for a few minutes. She disappeared again for awhile, then returned with her coat and purse and both of them came over to where I was. The young cop just said to me, "Now you take care of yourself, and don't be selling anymore rain checks. Bye now." Then he left first.

"Come on," Grandma said, and hurried out. I had to walk fast to keep up with her. She didn't speak to me as we went through the corridors.

We got to the car before she said anything. Then she said, "I've raised seven children, and not once have I had a policeman tell me I would need to appear at a police station, not once before today." She didn't seem to expect me to answer.

When we got home I went to my room, but I heard her say to Grandpa, "I told them at the hospital that she'd gotten lost, but they knew. I've never been so embarrassed in my life."

#

Next day on the ride to the station she didn't talk. When the car stopped I was surprised that she'd parked it in front of St. Agnes Church. Grandma got out on the street side. She came over and opened my door, so I got out, and followed her into the church. Inside Grandma stood by a pew and motioned me to enter it, then she said in a hissing whisper, "Get down on your knees and pray to God that they don't send you to reform school."

I didn't even know if not going to reform school was what I wanted. It was hard to decide between my parents coming to pick me up, hearing what I'd done, how they'd look at me and what they'd do, and reform school. Reform school might be better. But it was clear what my grandmother thought, and I prayed not to be sent to reform school. There was no use praying that my parents wouldn't find out, but I prayed that somehow it wouldn't be too bad, that it would be something I could get through. Even after I was done praying I stayed kneeling, my eyes mostly closed. My grandmother knelt beside me. When she got up and started out to the car I followed her. She moved swiftly in her anger. She seemed taller.

At the police station, she sat at the table with me and the police chief, but she didn't say anything while he questioned me.

The police chief wasn't blustery, but he wasn't anything like the young cop. He told me that robbing the mails was serious, a federal crime. But the main thing was I needed to tell him the truth, to put it behind me. If I did, I'd be given another chance. My grandmother pursed her lips and then began pulling them in and pushing them out the way that she did.

First he asked me to tell him what I'd been doing at that house yesterday morning.

I told the same story.

"Now," he said, "the important thing is for you to tell the truth. You won't get in any more trouble if you tell the truth. If you tell me right now that you took the letter out of the mailbox you won't be in any trouble. The only thing that can get you in more trouble is if you took it, and then you lie about it."

He looked straight at me, "Do you understand what I'm saying?"

"Yes," I said. I knew I had to say yes.

"Ok, then. So tell me, did you take that letter out of the mailbox?"

"No."

He looked away with a frown and he clenched his hands together. His voice was quiet like he was trying hard to keep calm. "I think you're not understanding me. If you tell me now that you took the letter out of the mailbox you won't be in trouble. There's no reason at all to lie about it. Do you understand me?"

"Yes," I repeated.

"So, did you take that letter out of the mailbox?"

"I found it on the ground."

He wasn't exactly yelling, but his voice got louder. "Do you really expect us to believe that? Just how do you explain how that letter got from the mailbox to the ground?"

"I don't know. Maybe the wind blew it."

My grandmother looked at the table with no particular expression on her face. She'd been like that the whole time. The police chief looked angrier, and he asked me a couple more times and repeated what he'd said about not getting into trouble if I admitted it. I didn't really think about whether I believed him or not. He could have been telling the truth. Even if I'd thought he was, I wouldn't have said anything different. Whether he was lying or not, I didn't trust him. I didn't care about telling him the truth like I did with the young cop. I didn't care if the police chief knew that I was lying.

Finally, he said, "Ok, you can go. But if I ever find out that you've been lying today, I'll find you, wherever you are, and make sure you go to reform school until you are 21 years old."

We left then, my grandmother still quiet, but she didn't walk so fast as before, or stand so straight. In the car she said, "Lucky they didn't know about you running away in Virginia."

Then she drove back to the church. I followed her in. She whispered, "Get down on your knees and thank God they didn't send you to reform school."

43 After

You think you're really going to win, and then there is the lonely schoolyard when it seems you have no friends at all. Then there is the Christmas when the whole day is one long wait, and you realize that you aren't the one that anyone is waiting for.

And it gets worse, Grandma sitting on the chair, straight and stern, telling you how she realizes it is true, you are a liar and a thief.

But then, a reprieve, and maybe, even if you aren't winning, maybe you are doing okay. Janie comes to the park and wants to be your friend again. You're helping her plan her mother's birthday. And something starts to go bad, but maybe not. You might be okay. You're walking on a tree lined street full of flittering shadows that calm you, and maybe this time you have gotten away far enough. You start to relax. And that's when it hits you.

That's when the police car glides up and you hear the familiar words, and you are back, and it is horrible, but it's familiar, feeling worthless and ashamed.

The next week I wasn't allowed to go to the park program or anywhere else. The only time I got out was when my grandmother took me to Janie's house to pick up my things.

Grandma knocked, then stood stiff at the door, while she waited for someone to come. One of the kids came first, not Janie.

"Could I speak to your mother?" Grandma said, and she didn't say it in a friendly way, not mean either, just separate, and going to stay separate. I hoped Janie might come, but I couldn't even see through the screen door into the dim house to know if she was even there. She might have been mad at me, just taking off, for all she knew, because I didn't have her phone number and couldn't call. I didn't even remember seeing a phone.

Janie's mother came to the door, and said, come on in, but

my grandmother said we just came for my clothes, and we didn't need to come in. Now I saw Janie, but her mother sent her up to her room to get my clothes.

Janie's mother said, "I treated her just like my own child." She kept repeating it as though she thought someone was going to accuse her of something. She had been there in the evening, but Janie and I went upstairs for most of the time, and then the next day she had to go to work. So I didn't really understand what she meant about treating me like her own child. Why would she?

Grandma didn't say anything back to her, but it did seem a little as if she blamed her, but for what? Then that was just another reason why Janie might feel mad at me. All sixth grade I wanted Janie to be my friend. Then she finally did, and now it was over. I wouldn't see her again, and I couldn't even explain. Janie's mother stood in the doorway while we waited for Janie to bring my things. Janie's mother seemed so lively now, when the other night she had seemed quiet and tired. The moment Janie handed me the clothes Grandma walked off the porch and back to the car so I had to follow along, though I turned back to wave at Janie, and mouthed, "Sorry," at her, but I couldn't say it loudly or my grandmother might hear. I made a gesture, but I don't know what Janie thought it meant.

That week Grandma and Grandpa barely spoke to me. All day I was alone in the house except for when Grandpa stopped in from his ice cream selling route for lunch. I came out when they called me for meals, but mostly I stayed in my room when either of them was around. At the end of the week my parents and brothers and sisters would be coming, so this would change, but I didn't know if the change would be bearable. At least my grandparents didn't hit me. They had been something to look forward to once, and now they weren't, but they hadn't hit me.

I'd already read most of the books in the house. Now I started in on the ones in the bookcase in my bedroom, which had seemed like boring grownup books when I'd looked at them last. I had nothing else to do. So now I looked through them again.

One of the books had a short story by O. Henry. It was told by a man in a city jail. At first he waited, not knowing what he'd done. He'd been drunk. Maybe he was just there to sleep it off. But something else gnawed at him like he should remember. He vaguely recalled having a gun and that he'd been firing it into the air. Then the detective came in to talk to him, and a sense of dread came over him. He looked worriedly at the detective, who asked him what he knew about the man who'd been shot. Someone was shot? He knew he hadn't shot at anyone. But the bullet belonged to the gun with his prints on it according to the detective. It must have ricocheted. He kept repeating this to the detective.

"How is he?" he asked.

"It's not looking good."

The detective left, and the dread settled into him, and the waiting.

The way the dread settled into me, waiting for my parents to come.

If they'd hit me before for washing dishes too slowly, or not getting every single one of them clean, what would they do to me now? The fear of that was all I had to think about. Well, almost all. Because the other thing I thought about was the young policeman and how he'd looked at me like I was just a regular kid, a good Catholic kid even. It had seemed like I was so bad that anyone could see it, my parents, my grandparents, but he hadn't seen it. Funny, I hadn't known how much I agreed with them, until the young cop talked and laughed with me like that, as if the badness wasn't so clear at all. It was the surprise of it, almost a shock, and beginning to see myself the way he saw me that made me realize how I'd been seeing myself just before.

I started thinking, maybe I could get through it, whatever they did to me. I'd made straight A's all through sixth grade. I'd been Sister Margaret Mary's "Little Theologian" in religion class. I thought I could quit lying and stealing, and be the kid that the young cop thought I was. Maybe I wasn't lost for good, if I didn't look any different to him than a regular kid, then maybe I could change.

I'd get through it, whatever it was. I'd been through as bad, or worse. I'd stop lying, stop stealing, I'd make straight A's. Maybe my parents would love me then.

Even if they didn't, I'd be the person the young cop thought I was. I'd have that. I wanted to be that person. It would get me through.

Sometimes you think you are winning. You hit the home run. You think you can be the hero. And then you're not winning. Everything seems to be slipping away, but there's something you can hold onto, not being a hero, just being a person, just being a regular kid, worth as much as any other kid. That was what I'd be.

#

It was evening when their car pulled up. We'd been expecting them by dinner time, but dinner was over, and it had begun to get dark. Soon the fireflies would be darting among the bushes like they did on warm summer nights about the same time the cicadas stopped their chirping. I sat on the porch, and since I'd decided what I was going to do I was almost looking forward to the beginning, even if it was bad, to get through it. Then the car slowed in front of the house and came to a stop.

I could hear Mama's voice right away, as she opened the door. "Hand me that bag," she was saying to someone in the back seat. Then car doors opened and everyone got out, Danny and Renee, then Leroy with Amy asleep against his shoulder, Mama with the suitcase, then Sammy, and I knew it as soon as I saw him. He was different. It wasn't even like at the Willises'. when he was scared of the strap. He was different, a year older, but that wasn't it. His body was different, the way he walked, an awkwardness, like he was separated off from it a little, and what I knew then was that he had taken my place as the bad one. I knew that someone was picking on him.

But Sammy wasn't bad. He was my sweet baby brother.

It was late enough that the rest of the evening was spent getting things brought in from the car, and settling where everyone would be sleeping.

When I woke the next morning Mom and Leroy had gone to the police station, and I felt instant relief at not having to see them yet, and fear at what would happen when they came back. I kept telling myself I could get through it. What could they do, but hit me, or look at me, like I was worthless, but they'd done that before. What I needed to remember was how the young cop saw me, like I was a regular kid, and that I could be what he thought I was.

Then they came back, and they didn't say anything to me at all. Nothing. They didn't exactly not talk to me, but it was little stuff, would you hand me that, where's the park you've been going to swim at? Then I decided it was like those Thursdays when we'd gone to the mental health clinic and the psychiatrist had told my mother she needed to be more patient with me. It was hard to imagine that police chief telling her to be more patient. But it didn't matter. I had a chance and I was going to take it. They were going to visit in Missouri for a week and then we'd go back to Norfolk. I'd make a fresh start in Norfolk.

Only I messed up. Danny and Renee and Sammy and I were going to the park and Mama gave me four dimes so we could buy sodas to have with our lunch, but somehow I left them behind.

Everyone complained that day about how long the walk was, and how hot it was, and they didn't want to do anything with the crafts program. Mrs. Burletti, the counselor, seemed annoyed at me. Maybe she heard what had happened. I wanted to stay, but no one else did, and so we went off to the playground and sat on the swings. They weren't happy there either. They were really just waiting around for the pool to open, and that wasn't until the afternoon. We had lunch, and when I couldn't find the dimes, Renee started complaining about how it was so hot.

Then when we were back home, Mama asked, "How was the park?

"It was hot, and Annie forgot the money for pop."

"What, all day out in that heat, and you didn't even get anything to drink." She gave me a look like I'd heartlessly deprived them. I hadn't lied. I hadn't stolen anything, but still Mama looked at me that way.

Grandma was there, and I thought for a moment she might say that I'd been going to the park all summer without having money for pop. But then I didn't really expect it. There'd been that time early on when I'd gotten lost on the way home and she'd been understanding about it when I told her, but then when Grandpa starting saying he didn't see how anyone could get lost and I was probably doing something I shouldn't, she hadn't defended me. She just nodded her head at whatever he said.

But I just had to hold on. What would the young cop say? Kids forget things sometimes. I did when I was a kid. Just hold on. They'd see. I wouldn't lie or steal. I'd make straight A's.

And it did get better with my brothers and sister at the park. Next day Mama gave the money to Danny to take care of, and we left later, so we got there just about in time for the pool to open. Renee and Sammy stayed in the shallow end, but Danny and I spent the week diving. Danny taught me how, and I dove off the low dive and then off the high dive. He showed me a back flip and I landed on my back a couple of times. I could hear grownups commenting, "That must have stung." But I kept it up and I got it after awhile. Danny could do back and forward flips, sometimes a double somersault off the high dive. He could do a cutaway, but I was just too scared of hitting my head on the board, so I wouldn't start coming forward soon enough. I landed once with a big belly flop that really hurt. I did do a forward flip off the high dive though, even though it was harder for me than the back flip.

Danny and I got to be friends again.

#

Friday afternoon we came home, and the moment we walked into the dining room, before we had even had time to hang up our towels and suits, Leroy rushed up and waved a paper in my face.

"What is this?" What now? What could I have done? He finally stopped waving it, and I took a look, and even then, it took me awhile to remember. They must have been packing up my room and come across it. It was a permission slip to be a candy striper at the hospital. My friend, Angie was doing it for the summer, and she wanted me to as well. I'd gone with her once. My Grandma said I could do it, and to leave it on the table for her. Then she'd gone off to work without signing it. I was supposed to go with Angie and turn it in that day. Angie said it would be okay to sign for Grandma, since she'd said I could do it. So I did, but the woman in charge of the volunteers said I had to be fourteen. I forgot I still even had that form.

So I told them what it was.

"What are you now, a forger?" my mother said.

"Grandma said I could do it," I said.

"But you signed her name."

I didn't understand, "But she said I could do it. She just forgot to sign it."

Leroy said, "Young lady, you are going to write a letter of apology to your grandmother."

Danny said to Mom, "But she didn't know. Isn't that too much?"

"Do you want her to be a criminal?" my mother asked him, and he backed down.

"Sit down at the table here and start writing," Leroy said, and he took some paper out of my school notebook that was lying with a pile of things on the dining room floor. He handed me a pen.

I wrote, "Dear Grandma," then I sat staring at the paper and my thoughts were somewhere else when Leroy said, "Aren't you done yet?"

"No."

"Well, put that stuff away and help set the table for dinner. You can get right back to it after dinner."

But after dinner, Mama told me to pack up the rest of my things in boxes, we were leaving the next morning. Leroy didn't mention the letter. I didn't want to write it. I hadn't meant to do anything wrong. I knew he'd bring it up again, though. Anytime he'd get mad at me he'd ask me again if I'd written the letter. But that didn't mean that I'd ever get it done.

#

Next morning I woke to Leroy's voice. "Six years old, almost seven, is too old to be wetting the bed." So he was wetting the bed again. I wondered when that started. By the time I got up Mama was sitting at the dining room table smoking, and I could see Sammy out in the side yard in his underwear trying to wash out his pajamas under the spigot for the hose. Mama looked angry. Sammy hurried like he was scared, crying then trying not to.

The pajamas hung on the clothes line while we finished packing everything else. Grandma cooked up fried chicken for the trip. Mama made bologna sandwiches. She packed it along with a half gallon of milk and ice into the cooler. That went into the trunk, but the fried chicken was set in the front seat.

We were all in the car and Grandma and Grandpa were standing near Mama's window to say their last goodbye. Finally, Grandpa said to me, "Well, goodbye, kiddo." And Grandma hugged me through the window, and said, "Take care of yourself." She waved again as we left.

We had two days ahead on the road. Leroy started complaining early in the drive, "We could have left a little sooner. You know I have to be back at the base for duty. Now we'll have to drive straight through."

Mom's teeth were clenched, "Like it was my fault we got started late. Did you help at all to get going, or just start shouting like always?"

Leroy stared ahead, didn't answer, just drove. We didn't stop at a motel that night, but Mama took over driving and sometime when I woke in the night we were over on the side of the road.

#

Mama said, "You tried to kill me." She was driving again.

Leroy leaned back against the right side door. "I didn't try to kill you."

"I woke up and your hands were around my neck. Keep your eyes on him kids. Don't let him kill me if I fall asleep."

"Ok," said Danny, and Leroy glared at him across the seat back.

"I did not try to kill you. You were dreaming. I didn't try to kill your mother," he said into the back seat.

I couldn't read Danny's look, not completely. He didn't say

anything, but he looked angry. Still I didn't know whether he believed it or not.

I couldn't ask Danny or Renee what had been going on while we were all sitting in the back seat where Mom and Leroy could hear. Neither of them acted like this was out of the ordinary. Then later when we stopped to dig the milk out of the cooler so we could have cereal for breakfast, Leroy told Danny to go get his cigarettes from the car. Danny didn't move. Leroy looked towards Mama, and she didn't meet his eye, but just acted like she hadn't heard a thing. Leroy walked over to the car to get his own cigarettes. And I thought, things won't be the same.

44 Norfolk

Mama laid a tin can on the edge of my hospital bed and opened the lid to show me oatmeal cookies. She said, "We made them for you, the girls and I. They miss their big sister."

It seemed to me like they'd barely had time to get used to me again before I got sick the second week of seventh grade, but it made me feel good to think they might be missing me.

Ever since that night when my fever spiked Mama had been so nice to me. It wasn't until the second trip out to the base hospital that they admitted me. We'd waited for a long time for the doctor and Mama held my head in her lap because I could barely raise it to sit up. Mama told the doctor she gave me aspirin and left the car windows open while she drove to the base so the cool night air might cool me down, but my temperature was still 102.

The doctor had a technician take my blood, and we waited again in the little examining room, Mama sitting in a chair holding my hand while I laid on my side on the examining table.

When the doctor returned, he said, "We're not quite sure what is going on with her. We're going to admit her and do some more tests." He talked some more to Mama, and I heard something about "liver involvement." I didn't care. I just wanted to lay down, and soon Mama was helping me into the pajamas she'd brought along and tucking me into the hospital bed. It was the nicest she'd ever been to me.

Besides the cookies, Mama had brought a new list of school assignments, and a stack of library books, because I felt a lot better now, just weak when I got out of bed and tried to walk further than the bathroom. Practically all the books Mama brought were teen romances, but I read them anyway. My science textbook was the coolest. It had colored pictures of an internal combustion engine, and it started off with a chapter that told how the sun released energy when helium got broken down into hydrogen.

"Leroy's coming up in a minute," Mama said. "He's just parking the car." Leroy hadn't come before. Mama changed the subject, asking me if I'd spent the dime she gave me to buy candy off the cart that came round every evening. She dug through her purse for another one.

Leroy came a few minutes later. He said hello and stood by my bed while Mama talked, then he asked about my schoolwork. I handed him the stack of it. He looked it over, and said, "It seems like you could have written this a little neater."

Then Mama got angry. "It seems to me that you could be a little less critical of everything." She took the papers away from him, and said, "It looks just fine to me."

Leroy started to defend himself, "I'm just trying to teach her that neatness is important," and Mama kind of turned away from him, then he said he was going down to the gift shop for a minute. Mama didn't mention him while he was gone. He came back just before the end of visiting hour, and handed me a book of paper dolls.

"Here," he was kind of sheepish.

"Thanks," I said. I liked paper dolls. I spent most of the next day cutting them out, and trying on the outfits.

#

Leroy had stitches on his head when I got out of the hospital. I couldn't go back to school yet and Mama had set up the couch bed in the living room for me. Danny would perch on an arm of the couch to talk and he told me about the stitches. Leroy and Mama had gotten in a fight in their room. The rest of them had heard from outside the door.

"Mama was saying, 'you're trying to kill me'. I was about to rush in, when I heard a crashing sound. I got in the door and Leroy's head was all bleeding, and the radio was yanked from the wall, and on the floor. "

"Served him right," Danny said.

"Do you really think he's been trying to kill her?"

"I don't know. He might. If she was asleep, he might. He'd never have guts enough to do it if she was awake." He made a look of disgust. Danny whispered, "He's a coward really. You just have to stand up to him."

I saw what he meant one evening when Mama had gone to a friend's house. Leroy told Danny to go out to the car and get him his duffle bag that he'd left out there.

Danny was watching TV and he didn't look up, until Leroy came to stand right in front of him. He stood like he did when you felt his breath sucked in and his muscles tight. Then Danny looked up, and he sat taller in the easy chair, but he didn't get up. Leroy said, "I told you to go out to the car and get my duffle bag."

Danny glared right at Leroy, and he didn't look scared even though Leroy stood over him. "You can go get your own duffle bag," he said. And I was scared for him. I was afraid that Leroy would hurt him and Mama wasn't even here to stop anything.

But Leroy didn't move forward. He glared at Danny, but when Danny just glared back, he didn't do anything. He finally said, "Well, when it comes time for allowance, I wouldn't be expecting anything if I were you." He went and got his own duffle bag.

Leroy didn't bother me while I slept on the couch and stayed home from school. After a month Mama took me to the base for a follow-up. While we waited a woman first, and then a boy, asked me if I was an albino even though my hair was blondish, not white, and my eyes were blue instead of pink. When we saw the doctor, a different one, he said, "Is she always so pale?" with a worried look that made me afraid I'd have to go back to the hospital. But he told me I could go back to school, but I shouldn't run or get too tired.

#

Instead of acting scared around Leroy like I used to, I made a point of standing up straight, and looking right at him. He didn't yell at me when I looked at him like that. He didn't hit me. Mama had stopped being so nice once I'd gotten better, but she hadn't hit me either.

Mr. Laufer, my seventh grade teacher at Chesterfield, had visited me while I was home, talked to Mama, and told us both that I was doing great in my schoolwork, working on my own. Once I was back in class he'd say in front of the whole class that he'd only run into two geniuses among his students, and I was one of them. When report cards came out I'd made straight A's. I hadn't stolen anything. I hadn't told lies. I'd kept the promises I made to myself.

#

Renee and I had just gotten Amy into her pajamas and into bed, then gotten into our own beds, mine the top bunk, when Leroy came into our bedroom. He sat on the side of her bed. She'd have been asleep in a moment, but he startled her and her eyes opened.

"Shut your eyes and go to sleep." His voice wasn't mean, exactly, more soft and cold, and Amy closed her eyes quickly. She laid still, but I could feel the tenseness in her body with him there beside her. Still he didn't go away. Every time she'd move even a little or start to turn over, he'd tell her to "lay still" or "go to sleep" so she couldn't relax because of the nagging voice that wouldn't let up. I wanted to tell Mama, but I didn't know what to say, when I knew he'd say he hadn't done anything, just told her to get to sleep.

#

It was late on a Friday and Danny and Renee and I were all still up watching TV in the living room. Mama started yelling from the kitchen, "Kids, Leroy is hitting me." We all rushed in. Leroy

- 374 -

stood near Mama, but if he was hitting her, he had stopped now. Mama said she was going to call the police. She had the receiver in her hand. Leroy started pulling on the base to keep her from dialing. Danny grabbed him round the waist to pull him away. Mama grabbed the base from Leroy, lifted it and brought it down on Leroy's head. Leroy staggered back, his forehead bleeding. He sat in a chair, and laid his head on his arm. Mama tried to plug the phone back in, but then she couldn't get a dial tone.

Leroy lifted his head, "Never mind, I'm leaving." He went to their bedroom and came out after a few minutes with his bag.

"Bye," he said, and headed out the door.

He came back next day at dinnertime. Mama didn't speak to him. She made dinner but didn't bring him a cup of coffee or tell us to pass him the dishes of food the way she usually did. Leroy went and got his own cup of coffee and stayed at the table just as long, as if he were making a point that everything was just the same.

#

We were up in our room, Renee and I and Amy standing between the bunk beds that Renee and I slept in and the single bed where Amy slept. We were in our pajamas and getting Amy ready for bed.

Leroy came in, impatient, "Haven't you got her pajamas on her yet?" He got between me and Renee, next to Amy.

Renee snapped, "No, we haven't. We're going as fast as we can. Why don't you just leave us alone?" But, she made a mistake then, because she had started to turn away, and Leroy used all his strength to slap her in the face. I rushed towards him. Renee recovered and started towards him too, but he grabbed up Amy and held her in front of him, so we couldn't hit him without hitting her. He backed out of the room with her, before finally setting her down and hurrying down the stairs.

We didn't follow him. I got Amy and we went back in the room, and that night he didn't bother Amy while she was trying to go to sleep.

#

The phone hadn't been fixed yet the next time Mama shouted to us that Leroy was hitting her. Though we were undecided about whether he'd tried to murder her, we all knew that Leroy was too much of a coward and our mother was too fierce for him really to have hit her the way she said he did. But we all rushed into their bedroom, next to the living room. Leroy was hunched over, and Renee and I hit Leroy on his back. Danny started swinging and managed to hit Leroy's nose which started bleeding. Renee and Danny cheered, so I did too, although it made me uncomfortable. I saw Mama looking at me, and I was afraid she was thinking that I wasn't really trying to protect her, but after looking at me for a few minutes while I tried to pound harder, she just said, "Annie, run down to the Scotts' and tell them to call the police."

I ran out the front door and down the block. I was glad to be out of the house and felt my body trembling as I ran. Mr. Scott had his door open and stood behind the screen door as I ran up. Mrs. Scott stood a little further back in the dark.

They'd invited us for dinner once. They'd been worried about their daughter who was barely three and they'd just found out she had epilepsy. All I knew about Mr. Scott was that he was comforting to his wife when she was upset, and that he did the dishes. "She cooks the meals," he'd said. "The least I can do is the dishes." He was the first man I knew who did that.

Now I shouted out, "Can you call the police? They're hitting each other and everything."

He was calm, and seemed quietly angry, "We've already called them. Come on in for a minute."

Inside, Mrs. Scott put her arms around me, and I managed to calm down. It wasn't long before we saw the lights flashing as a police car moved down our street. I went back home while it was still parking. I could see Mama at the kitchen table smoking a cigarette, but I couldn't see Leroy anywhere. Danny and Renee sat on the couch, and I went to sit beside them. "He's in there," Danny motioned to their bedroom. "I don't know what he's doing."

Mama talked to the policemen in the kitchen. I heard her asking if they could keep him out of the house, and they said that they couldn't, not legally, because it was his home, but then they went into the bedroom, and later when they walked out, Leroy was between them with his duffle bag, and they were telling him he'd better find somewhere else to spend the night.

Next day Mama told us he'd be staying on the base for awhile.

He came by several days later. I was in the kitchen washing the breakfast dishes, when I heard him knock and moved to the kitchen entry where I could see the door. I just stared at him a moment, then I looked at Danny and Renee sitting on the couch with hard looks on their faces, and Mama, who looked at him, and then away with her mouth tight.

Like he was feeling all our looks and disapproval this time, he said, "I've come to wash my uniforms."

Mama had been vacuuming the living room, but now she turned the vacuum off. Then she went into the kitchen, sat down at the table, and lit a cigarette. Leroy watched from where he stood next to the front door where he could still see into the kitchen. When she sat down, he moved closer to the kitchen entry where the table was.

Mama said, "Something wrong with the Laundromats on base?" There was a hard edge to her voice, and Leroy shuffled from one foot to another, then stood up straight, and said, "No, but I didn't think I ought to be wasting change on a Laundromat when I could better spend it on my family."

"Your family?" Mama voice was sarcastic, and she tapped her cigarette on the ashtray to dislodge the ashes.

Then she said, "Don't think anyone is going to be doing your laundry for you."

Then, Leroy reached into his pocket and pulled out an envelope that he laid on the kitchen table. "Here," he said, then hurriedly went over to the washing machine and loaded it with his duffle bag full of clothes and then the duffle bag itself. He started up the washing machine, said, "I'll wait outside," and went out the front door again. I heard the door close, but I didn't look after to see where he went.

Mama opened the envelope, spend a couple of minutes reading it, then tossed it back on the table.

Danny and Renee had come in the kitchen. "What is it?" Danny asked.

"Read it for yourself." Mama went back to smoking.

So he took it out to the living room, and Renee followed him.

Later, Leroy had come back in, taken his clothes to the back and hung them up, then gone out again while he waited for them to dry – it was hot so that didn't take so long – then come back and made a point of standing with the pile of clothes on top of the closed lid of the washer, shaking out each piece and then folding it crisply, and finally packing them all back up, saying, "Well, goodbye then," and having no one respond, as Mama had gone to her bedroom and the rest of us just ignored him, he just left again out the front door. Then Danny and Renee brought the envelope into the kitchen to show me.

"Last Will and Testament," Danny read, and he read some

more, and laughed. Leroy had written about feeling like no one cared about him and no one ever had. They were making fun of it, so I did too, for that reason, and because he had hurt me so much, but even so I read the words and felt sorry for him.

#

Leroy didn't come back. Mama got a job as a ward clerk at a hospital. Renee and I were supposed to rush home from school to pick up Amy from the neighbor's house on the end, Mrs. Steward, so Mama wouldn't have to pay any extra for babysitting. Mama worked the swing shift so she wouldn't have to leave Amy until the afternoon, and she wouldn't get home until 11:30 at night. We'd miss her altogether except for Friday nights when we stayed up later, and the weekends. Mama had stopped being so nice to me after I'd gotten better, though it had never gotten so bad as it had been. Still, it was a relief to come home and not have to feel her disapproval of me, even though it meant that I made supper, shared the laundry and vacuuming, washed dishes, and gave Amy a bath every other night.

We hadn't seen Leroy in so long, it was a surprise when Mama called us all downstairs, saying she wanted to ask us something. All of us, even Amy, came down to the table. Mama sat in her usual spot at the end by the back door. Danny took the other end. Renee and I sat on the outer side with Sammy standing next to Danny and Amy sitting in my lap.

Mama said, "I need to know what you want to do about something." She was smoking, and drinking coffee, the two things she usually did at the kitchen table, and she took a puff while she thought of the next words.

"I could stay with Leroy, and we could move out of here into a better house."

We waited. That did not sound good.

"Or, I could get a divorce, and we would have to stay here."

For weeks now we'd been washing dishes both before and after eating, because even after the project row house had been repeatedly sprayed with DDT – forcing us to wash all the dishes in the house before using them again – there were still roaches so thick that the table was black if you got up at night and turned on the light in the kitchen. The bedrooms were tiny and Renee and Amy and I had to share one. The walls were all brick painted with an institutional green, not smoothly but with drips on the porous brick. The refrigerator barely kept things cold so milk couldn't be kept more than a couple of days. Mama would buy a few gallons of milk when she got to the Navy commissary every couple of weeks. That's when we all got to drink milk. But once that was gone she'd buy a half gallon at a time from the store nearby where it was more expensive, and we had to leave it for Amy and sometimes Sammy.

Danny said, "Get the divorce." It was what we all felt, and, except for Amy, we all nodded with a sigh of relief. Later, I had to think about it, because I was a Catholic and divorce was wrong according to the church. But I just couldn't see how something could be wrong when it felt so much the right thing to do.

"Ok," Mama said. "I'll get a divorce." I don't know if she would have taken our advice, if she hadn't already decided. Perhaps she worried that she would be hurting us, depriving us. She seemed to relax then, leaning back in her chair and breathing deeply.

45 Yogi

A loud pop went off in the lunchroom, like a paper bag popping. It was my job to track it down and make them stop. Being lunch monitor wasn't my idea. My mother set it up when she'd called the junior high school to see if there was some way to get my bus tickets paid for. She told me I'd be working for my lunch and the bus tickets. Lunch monitors left for lunch five minutes early and that was good, because the first day when I showed my paper for a free lunch to the cashier on the girl's line she told me I had to go over to the boy's side where the cashier handled that. I'd have been too embarrassed to go through the boy's line if everyone were there. It was bad enough with just the other two lunch monitors. They both brought a sack lunch, so I knew my mother made it up about paying for my lunch by being a monitor.

I went over to the table where all those girls smiled and laughed after every pop. They looked older – ninth graders who thought it was fun to tease an eighth grader. One girls showed me her empty arms. She didn't have the paper bag. But she probably did. I wanted to play too, or at the very least, forget about it, but I felt responsible. This was my job whether or not I got the free lunch and the bus tickets for it.

But I gave up and sat back down. Then another bag popped. I went back over to the table, gave up, sat down. This was repeated several more times. Then I saw a bag with its popped bottom in the hands of a slightly chunky looking girl with glasses, light brown medium length hair flipped up in back stiffly. She wasn't pretty. She looked intelligent, but she was tormenting me.

"Come over here and sit," I told her and pointed to the table where I sat with the other monitors. If she refused I didn't know what I would do. I was supposed to keep order, but I didn't have any power. The girl looked familiar though. She was in some of my classes, not a ninth grader.

She came to our table and sat down. She spread all her lunch things out like she was making it her place, not embarrassed at all.

"What's your name," I asked her.

"Yogi."

"Yogi?"

"Well, that's my nickname." She laughed at my look, "Because I do yoga."

I didn't know anybody who did yoga. It was some eastern meditation thing. I imagined a Buddha-like person in a pose. "What's your real name?"

"Cassandra Fuchs."

No wonder she changed it to Yogi. She could have gone with Cassie though.

"Do you still do yoga?"

"Sure, but I don't have time to take classes now. I have guitar lessons, and school keeps me too busy."

"Yeah, school."

Some days we'd get something for lunch like chicken with gravy on it. We didn't get knives and the forks wouldn't cut the chicken, so I'd get self-conscious about how I was supposed to eat it. Luckily today's lunch wasn't a puzzle. But I still felt awkward eating in front of her. She didn't look like she ever felt awkward. I poked around in the mashed potatoes a little.

I asked her, "You're in my Latin class, aren't you?"

"Yeah," she grinned, "Latin, algebra and U.S. history. You're so serious. You don't look around much."

I felt my face going red.

"I'd like to be able to play guitar," I said. Then I thought she was going to ask me why I didn't, and I'd have to make up a reason that wasn't that I didn't have a guitar, or money to get one, or to pay for lessons. So quickly I said, "Latin takes a lot of time. I could handle the declensions and the conjugations, but the long marks kill me."

She agreed.

When the bell rang, we bussed our garbage and trays and headed up the stairs to history class together. As we walked Yogi called out hello to kids we passed. It seemed like she knew everyone in school while I had no friends at all.

I said, "I thought at first you were a ninth grader like those other girls."

"My birthday is October 3rd, and the cutoff for being 6 to start school was September 30, so here I am, fourteen years old, and still stuck in eighth grade."

I didn't tell her that I wouldn't be thirteen until November.

"I'm trying to think of something to do for the science fair," Yogi said. "I won it last year, but this year I'm having trouble thinking of something interesting to do."

So she did yoga, played guitar and won the science fair. We hadn't had a science fair at Chesterfield. And if we had, I couldn't have entered. It would take money for materials to build something.

Yogi said, "Maybe I'll build a model of a cotton gin. You know the cotton gin probably caused the civil war, don't you?"

Now that I did know. It was in our American history book. It made growing cotton more profitable, and cotton took more labor to pick it than another type of crop. "Sure," I said.

Yogi waited.

I said, "It made cotton more profitable. And slaves were cheap labor to pick the cotton."

Her assigned seat was in the row to my left and almost even with mine. I should have noticed her before now. But she didn't answer questions in class. I did. Other than answer questions the students just sat and listened while the teacher talked and made notes on the board. I didn't take notes, because I found I could absorb more if I just listened. Now I also paid attention to Yogi. She wrote in her notebook from time to time, but not like some kids who scribbled furiously.

Afterwards I caught up with Yogi to walk with her to algebra. Only a few of the kids from that history class went to algebra. Most of the rest probably took modern math. The kids who took regular math were in different history and English classes, but some of them were in home ec. or P.E. with me. None of the kids from Chesterfield were in any of my classes. No one except me took algebra, or even modern math, not even Stanley who, along with me, was voted "most studious." But a couple of Larchmont kids were in our class, including Grace, the smart kid in fifth grade. She probably didn't expect to see me since I hadn't been doing so well in school back then. The kids from Larchmont, and most of the kids in my classes, were better dressed than the others in the school. They had sweaters and skirts that matched, unscuffed shoes.

My clothes were all hand me downs from someone I didn't know. I'd figured out how to mend my loafers with heavy thread where they were falling apart. I wanted to wear knee-high socks like the rest of the girls, but I had to wear white anklets.

Yogi wore white anklets.

#

Before long Yogi and I and a boy named Neil were moved together so we could work through the book at a faster pace. And Yogi sat beside me at the monitor table every day, and she sat behind me in Latin where we didn't have assigned seats. With Yogi I didn't feel self-conscious about my clothes. She never said a word about them. Hers were new enough, but not stylish.

In PE class while the students waited for everyone to finish dressing, the girls gathered into little groups and chatted about people they knew. I'd want to join a conversation, and sometimes I stood on the edge of a group, but I didn't know anyone they talked about and I didn't know what to say. But with Yogi I could talk nonstop. All through Latin class we'd whisper. In the hallway between classes we'd talk until the last minute.

She'd tell me about politics too.

"Do you know who the Secretary of Defense is?" She asked.

"No."

"Well, it's McNamara, and Dean Rusk is secretary of state, and Udall is Secretary of the Interior."

I was impressed. I started trying to read the newspaper to keep up with her. I read editorials on whether Johnson could have guns and butter. I read accounts of battles in Vietnam, but they didn't make a lot of sense to me. I supposed you had to have kept up from the beginning. Yogi and I both had the same ambition, to be the first woman president.

#

"Do you want to read a poem I wrote?" Yogi asked. We were in the library, with the history class, supposed to be finding books for our reports. Yogi and I had already decided on a topic and found our books.

"Sure, " I said, but she seemed kind of shy then, and just looked at the notebook open in front of her.

Then she pushed it over. I read to myself.

"Wow," I said. Her poem was so strong and passionate. Three lines jumped out.

My tongue swells with the words I cannot speak.
When I try to sleep it is as if hard stones press against my

spine

> *like their hard words bend my spirit.*

I read the first lines again.

Hell
Is where I live, and
I would leave if I could, but
instead I burn in flames of fear
and dread. Oh I want
to lay it all down, to stop
trying for their love,
If there were a God he wouldn't have left me here in the fire.

I wanted to ask her about what made her feel that way. Were her parents mean to her? Did they punish her like mine had? But I said, "It's cool that it doesn't rhyme, and how 'Hell' is the title and part of the line at the same time."

Then I asked, "So, you don't believe in God?"

"No, I don't."

"Why not?"

She didn't answer but instead went to a library shelf and searched for a book. She pulled it out, handed it to me, "Here, read this."

The book was *This Believing World*. I checked it out and started reading it on the bus. Then I couldn't stop reading it, except I had to, to do homework and make dinner. I stayed up late reading and got into bed just before Mom was going to be home.

The book was all about different people and different religions all over the world and how everyone was searching for the same thing. After I read it, it didn't make sense to me that the

Catholic Church was the only true church and everybody else was wrong. I couldn't be a Catholic anymore, or even a Christian. But I couldn't say that I didn't believe in God.

Next day I told Yogi I was an agnostic, not an atheist. I was afraid she might decide I wasn't smart enough to get it, so I said it like I was expecting her to argue with me.

But she just looked at me with a kind of questioning look, and said, "All right."

46 Return

I ate my last piece of toast. Danny and Renee were moving about upstairs. From the living room I heard Sammy say, "Roll the ball back to me, Amy."

My mother stood at the bottom of the brick stairs, just outside the door to her bedroom. She was in her housecoat still, but her tinted red hair was combed and sprayed into place.

"Why are you always the last one to finish?" she asked. "Are you waiting for your sister to finish all the chores before you get off your butt to help?"

My mother held her white ward clerk's uniform. She looked over at her ashtray, a couple of stubs already inside, then behind me. The ironing board rested in the corner. When the kitchen table was pushed up against the wall as far as it would go with all the chairs pushed in, there was just room beside the back door to fold out the ironing board and stand beside it.

"You know I want to get this house swept and mopped before I go to work. Don't think you're going to get out of any work by taking your sweet time."

"Can't I even eat my breakfast?" I said.

"What did you say?" My mother pulled a chair away from the table. She laid her uniform over the back of the chair. Then she started towards me.

"What did you say?" My mother asked again, now in front of my chair. I put up my arms to protect myself. My mother told me to put them down. I thought, *No, I am not going to be treated like an animal any more.*

"Put your hands down." My mother slapped towards my face, but hit my arm. She pulled back her arm for another shot at my face, but I moved my arms as well and she slapped hard on the bone of my forearm. "You hit me. You hit your own mother," she said, but I hadn't hit her.

"Put your hands down!" my mother shouted but I kept my hands in place, so she turned and shouted towards the stairs, "Danny, come down here. Come help me." When he didn't come, she went upstairs.

"Come hold your sister for me, so I can hit her." I couldn't hear Danny so clearly, except that my brother was saying he wouldn't do it.

"She hit her own mother. Doesn't that matter to you?"

"No, Mama, I won't," Danny said.

#

I left the house while they argued. I walked out the back door. I stepped over the low wire fence that surrounded the tiny back yard, into the common space between our house and the next block of row houses in the project. I walked toward the street, to the sidewalk. I held my arms by my side. I walked fast. I felt the blood rush up and down my forearms.

I reached a busier street with no sidewalks. The ground was damp from rain the night before, so my tennis shoes sunk slightly into the dirt. A railroad track ran parallel to the road but no trains came. The neon sign of a diner blinked up ahead.

I kept walking, fast. My body couldn't settle down. I had gone a long ways before I began to think about what I would do. If I went to the police, if I told them how my mother hit me, what would they do? Would they believe me? Would they take us kids away from my mother? When I ran away from home when I was ten they hadn't done anything, but I never told the police that she hit me.

Amy was only three. If they took us away, what would happen to Amy? My mother didn't hit the other kids. Amy wouldn't understand. Amy would lose her mother and she wouldn't understand.

But probably, they wouldn't do anything, or they'd put me in reform school. All my good grades would be for nothing. How could I get to college from reform school? But there were nearly five years to get through before I could leave home.

I slowed down a little, took a deep breath. I passed a tree in front of a house set way back on the lot. An inner tube swing hung from its thickest branch. A kid's plastic truck lay on its side in wet grass.

When I was ten I thought I might find a place like in *Little Men*, someone like Jo, someone like Professor Bhaer, but this wasn't Plumfield. There was no place to go, no place for a kid. I walked. I knew I would have to go back, but I wasn't going to do it yet.

I saw a white car. The last time there was a white car, it had picked me up when I ran away from home. This car turned into the driveway of a restaurant across the street. Had it come for me? Had my mother called the police? There was no sense in putting it off. I crossed the street and walked over to the car. The driver sat there. He was looking at a map spread over the steering wheel. He didn't look up when I came over to his open window. I started to turn away. Then he noticed me, looked right at me.

"Are you a policeman?" I asked.

"No, why, is something the matter? " His hair was thinning and partly gray. His eyes were crinkled at the corners. He opened them wider. "Are you in some kind of trouble?"

"No, I just thought you were a policeman."

"What's the matter? Can't you tell me about it?"

"No, it's nothing, I've got to go now." I backed up.

The man leaned on the door, his eyelids closed a little. The collar of his raincoat was flipped up against his neck. He turned it back down. I crossed the street again, headed back in the direction of home. I looked back over my shoulder to see if he followed, to see if anyone followed.

I walked quickly, but I wasn't breathing so fast as before. I reached the sidewalk of the dead end street that went into the project. I passed the sideways blocks of brick row houses, with their front yards facing on one side, merging into each other, their back yards facing on the other side, the back yards separated with little fences. I stepped over the back fence into our yard.

I opened the back door of our house and entered the kitchen. My mother's white uniform lay flat and ironed over the center of the ironing board. A man's leather belt hung over the narrow end. My mother sat at the table with a cup of coffee and another cigarette. She took a puff then laid the cigarette on the ashtray. She got up and closed the back door. She picked up the belt, doubled it, then let the end fall free again. Her arms and legs were skinny, but her belly poked out. I was three inches taller than my mother. Once she said that she used to be an inch taller, but she had shrunk.

"If you ever walk out of my house like that again, don't bother to come back," my mother said.

I turned around as she drew back the belt. I looked out the back door window: the back yards with their grass cut short, the little fences, the little yards, the row houses lined up like Monopoly hotels, the streets, the cars, the railroad tracks, the city, the whole wide world, and the kid's plastic truck lying on its side in the wet grass.

47 Wanting

Could you hate someone so much if you didn't love them? Could they hurt you that bad if they didn't matter to you? I stood in my bedroom, and my arms trembled as I clenched my fists to my side. I hated her, my mother, I hated her so much.

"How come you're so smart at school, and so stupid around here?" she'd asked me. And why? Because I didn't know that she'd wanted me to put out saucers when I set the table, because Ed would be there. She hadn't said anything about putting out saucers. We didn't usually put out saucers, but I should have known that since he was coming, we'd have our salad on saucers instead of on our plates. I should have known, and if I didn't, it meant I was stupid. It didn't matter that now I was good at school, or how well I did anything else, to her I was stupid, just stupid. Nothing else counted besides knowing exactly what she wanted me to do, whether or not she let me in on what it was that she wanted. How I hated her. I felt my heart pounding. It was like I could feel the blood surging up and down my arms, I was so angry.

I paced the floor back and forth, but there wasn't much room in the little bedroom with the bunk beds and another bed that took all the floor space. It took a long while before I was able to calm down.

#

On a Sunday near Christmas, Mom had come up the stairs, and was out in the small hallway when I'd come out of my room to go downstairs. She'd surprised me. She didn't often come up, except for the bathroom, but she seemed to be waiting for me.

She said, with a strange look on her face, "That two dollars you earned babysitting yesterday, I was wondering if you'd give it to me so I could buy some fabric to make Ed a robe for Christmas."

Then she waited, like I had a choice, but I didn't think I had a choice.

Still I hesitated, although I knew I wouldn't be able to refuse her, and I could see that she hated to be asking for it. It was humiliating for her, I could see that, to be asking her daughter for money, but she didn't have any extra money, none. My hesitation wasn't saying no, it was just one more moment of thinking what I would do with the money, maybe buy a new skirt, or a pair of shoes to replace the loafers that I had stitched up with the thick piece of twine and then colored over with shoe polish to make it match the shoes.

But she must have thought I'd say no, and she wanted me to agree. She didn't want to force me. So quickly, she said, "You know it was Ed that paid for your sewing machine."

So I said it. I knew I had to, and probably I would have anyway, because I couldn't stand it to see her asking that way, and see how it humiliated her to ask her daughter for the extra money that she couldn't earn because she'd dropped out of school in the tenth grade, and no one wanted a high school dropout for any kind of a decent job.

"Yes," I said it quickly. My hesitation hadn't lasted more than a couple of seconds. It'd been just long enough for her to think she needed to press me and feel all the more humiliated because of that. And I couldn't stand that, and yet, and yet, I just wanted to be able to keep some small thing for myself, and I couldn't, not even what two dollars would buy.

#

One weekend morning, we were all sitting at breakfast, and there was one slice of toast left on the plate, and no more bread left in the loaf that my mother had been feeding into the toaster. Mom turned to Danny on her right, and said, "Go ahead and have the last piece of toast." But Danny knew she was hungry and said that he'd had enough. Then Mom asked the rest of us, "Who wants this piece of toast?" And all of us said that we weren't hungry, although I was hungry. Since school started I'd grown four inches and I was always hungry, and from the way Renee and Sammy looked down at their plates, I knew that they were hungry too, and Mom knew too, because she started crying and said, "I never thought I'd have to watch my children go hungry."

She made Danny eat the toast. So he took it then, and it was gone in a second. He ate it cheerfully, and by the time it was gone, Mom looked a little better.

#

Mom asked for my help to make the robe. This was something that I didn't understand, that my mother who was always criticizing how I did almost everything, who stood over me and made me so nervous I couldn't do anything, that somehow she had it in her head that I was good at some things, that I didn't do often and didn't know that much about. She believed that I was good at sewing. We had sewing in home ec, but I had trouble with sleeves, which was the only hard part.

When she asked me to spell something and I didn't know, she thought that I just wouldn't tell her. Why did she think I must be a better speller than her? I was in 8th grade, and she had been valedictorian of her 8th grade and got through tenth grade before she dropped out. But it didn't matter, just because she dropped out, she felt stupid. She thought I was taunting her, pretending not to be able to spell something, but I'd never taunted her. She'd taunted me, *I thought you were so smart,* she'd say if I told her I didn't know how to spell a word.

Still we worked all day Saturday on the robe, because she thought I was good at it and had asked me to help her. I did my best. I knew the steps for pinning and cutting, at least, and together we made it so it seemed to look like a robe. Then it was late, past ten, and we were both in the hallway upstairs as she came out of the bathroom and I was waiting to go in before going to bed. For a moment it felt like a year ago, when I was sick with mono, and she was nice to me. I was a kid then, almost twelve, but still a kid. Now I wasn't. I'd hoped it would last back then, but it hadn't. She'd turned hard and critical again. So when I felt close to her, I also felt that I couldn't just trust her, and something in me resisted moving towards her, something that wanted it so bad I had to stop wanting, and now I'd let my anger keep me apart. Though anger wasn't what I felt now, just protectiveness. I said goodnight. Her shoulders were stooped and she looked tired, old even, although she was only thirty one. For a moment I wondered what I would do if she moved towards me, but then the moment passed, and she said, "Goodnight," and went on her way down the stairs.

48 My Mother's Stories

Mom told her first story when she unpacked the barbells she'd asked Grandma to send. My sister, Renee, wanted to play an instrument in the school band, and Mom had no money to rent one. Mom sat at the kitchen table in her old house robe, smoked a cigarette and drank a last cup of coffee. She drew in a drag of the cigarette, and her eyes looked wet, but she held the rest of her face, her chin and her mouth, rigid.

"I wanted to play the clarinet," Mom said. "My parents went out and bought me those barbells." She tapped her cigarette on the side of the ashtray to flick off the ashes. The sleeve of her robe slid down on her arm. "For the same money they could have bought me the clarinet I wanted." Mom finished her cigarette and drank the rest of her coffee without saying anything more.

#

Her second story came at Christmas, right after I unwrapped my basketball. I wasn't expecting it. Whenever Mom asked me what I wanted for Christmas, and I said a basketball - I always said a basketball - she'd say, "Don't you think you're getting too old to be out there with the boys playing basketball?" or "Wouldn't you rather have a hair dryer?"

Besides we were so poor, even with Ed around now, I only expected one real present. Already I'd gotten a skirt, a sweater and a hair dryer. Still Ed reached behind the tree for one more box, and held it out. "The last one's for you, Annie."

It wasn't likely anything else was that size and shape, but I couldn't be sure even when I saw the Voit box underneath the wrapping paper. Mom was always reusing old boxes. So I opened the box and pulled out the basketball, feeling around it with both my hands. It wasn't one of those cheap rubbery ones that bounced wildly off the rim when it should have sunk inside, or one of the heavy ones you could barely dribble. The weight felt just right.

Mom watched me with the ball. She turned to Ed sitting on the arm of her chair. She said, "One Christmas I saw this pair of gloves in a store window. I wanted them so much I told my parents the gloves were all I wanted for Christmas. I thought I'd be sure to get them."

She pulled out a cigarette from the pack on the coffee table. Ed picked up his lighter and lit it for her. "I opened all my presents on Christmas morning, and they didn't get me the gloves."

#

I figure, everyone has their one story they keep telling themselves over and over again, about who they are and what their life is. My mother has two stories, but they are really just one. Her story is: "I never got what I really wanted."

And my story, maybe it's the one about having a mother whose story is, "I never got what I really wanted," and how she took out all her hurt and pain on me. But I wonder what could happen if I told myself a different story, or even more than one. Sometimes I even think my story could be the one about Christmas and a basketball that I didn't expect but got anyway, and how that basketball felt so right in my hands.

49 An Adventure

I went with Yogi to pick up her things before she rode the bus home with me. Her house was so big. From the entry I could see down a half flight of steps into a big carpeted room with a few pieces of furniture around the edges. We walked up another half flight into a wide open living room with high ceilings. A full flight of stairs took us up to a passageway or balcony that circled around the middle. To the outside of it were several doors. On the inside you could look over the railing to the living room. All that space and it felt so empty.

Yogi led me to her bedroom where she started tossing clothes into a bag. It was so quiet in the house. I couldn't hear anybody.

Then all of a sudden an old woman ran into the room. She pulled out some money and handed Yogi a dollar bill. She had a kind of mischievous look like she was doing something naughty. "Have a good time," she said.

Yogi smiled, happy like a little kid. "Thanks, Grams," she said, and her Grams hurried away as if she couldn't risk getting caught.

"Grams always gives me extra treats," Yogi said, still kidlike.

I liked her Grams. I was happy to see Yogi cared for. Because I'd got an idea of Yogi's parents, that might be wrong, but they felt like emptiness. Yogi talked about suicide sometimes, about how she'd do it if she was brave enough.

#

My mother worked most week nights. At first she'd worked days, but it cost too much to pay for a babysitter for Amy. Even Mrs. Jenks who charged a dollar a day was too expensive for my mother who only made $1.25 an hour, minimum wage. So she worked the 3PM to 11PM shift and Mrs. Taylor on the corner watched Amy just until the first of us arrived from school. This Friday, though, Mom was off and she was making dinner so I didn't have to. I took Yogi up to the bedroom I shared with Renee and Amy. We'd sleep on the living room floor in sleeping bags that night, but now we just tossed her bag and my books on my bed. Renee and Amy slept in the bunk beds now with Amy on the bottom.

Danny came in. He was holding the comic he'd been reading.

"Hi," he said.

"This is my brother, Danny," I said.

"What are you reading?" asked Yogi. Danny showed her the comic book.

"Do you have any more?" Yogi asked, and I went to the closet and pulled out the cardboard box filled with our collection of comics, mostly Superman, Batman and the Fantastic Four, but a few others. Yogi started reading, and Danny settled on Amy's bed and read along with us. It couldn't have been too comfortable with the middle of Amy's bunk sagging down, so he had to lean forward with his long legs stretched out into the space between to keep from falling backwards.

"I never had comics," Yogi said. How strange. It fit with her house, though. It didn't seem the kind of house that people would read comics in.

"We always have comics," Danny said. We'd bought a few new, but also people would sometimes give us boxes of old comics, or we'd get a box from a garage sale. We had so many it was easy to find one you hadn't read, or read so long ago that you'd forgotten. Danny only half read between making suggestions to Yogi about the best ones to read, but Yogi got totally absorbed reading one, then another.

Mom called me to set the table, so I went down. Yogi stayed in the bedroom with Danny, until everyone came down for dinner.

Ed was there that night too. He was there a lot now. The chicken was for him, and maybe partly for Yogi. Usually we had soup and sandwiches, especially on nights when Mom worked and I was the one fixing dinner.

"So, what are you taking in junior high?" Ed asked.

"Oh, Latin, algebra, history. I'm in those classes with Annie. Then I have to take P.E. and I've got Science and English. It's not bad."

"So, you're taking algebra in the 8th grade too," said Ed. "When I went to school we didn't start algebra until the tenth grade, and it was tough for me then."

"It's not easy," Yogi said, "but we have a good teacher. She lets us work ahead too."

"Oh," Ed said, knowingly, "you're one of the smartest even in the smart class." He took a bite of chicken then set it down and wiped his hands on a paper napkin. "Who else gets to work ahead?"

Yogi answered, "Oh, it's just me and Annie and this boy named Neil," and Ed looked as though he hadn't expected me to be on the list. I never talked about things like that at home, although I brought home good report cards.

Danny said to Ed, "I thought you knew Annie was smart." Still, he paid more attention to Yogi than he did to me.

I'd have been awkward at Yogi's house, with her parents, but Yogi kept up a conversation with everyone, even Mom and Ed. She was the center of all the talk. They all liked her.

After dinner Yogi went back upstairs while I did dishes. Mom said, "Why don't you call her back down here to help you." But I wasn't going to do that. I knew she'd probably gone back to reading the comics. I doubted she had chores at her house, certainly not as much work as I had. She might not even have realized that I had to do dishes. Once I was back upstairs, I joined in the comic books.

"This is great," Yogi said. We barely moved until it was time for the Friday night *Out of this World* film. It was *The Day the Earth Stood Still.* Yogi and I were sleeping downstairs so we rolled out our sleeping bags, got in and leaned back against the couch. Mom and Ed had gone to Mom's bedroom. Sammy and Amy had already gone to bed, and Renee was soon asleep on the couch. So it was just me and Yogi and Danny who made it to the end. I kind of remembered seeing the movie before in Yakima at the drive-in. We used to go a lot, especially the one with the playground down in front where kids could go play while their parents concentrated on the movie.

I was ready to sleep, but Danny said, "What do you think we'd do, the earth would do, if that really happened? Do you think we'd make peace with everyone?"

Yogi was yawning, but she struggled up on her elbow, "Not a chance. Probably, they just would abandon the space race, and put even more money into weapons." She snuggled back down, "Until they forgot," she said. "Then we'd all die."

"But how could the aliens really bring themselves to kill a whole planet full of people, if they aren't violent?" I asked.

"Like in that sci fi novel, *The Chrysalids,*" said Yogi, sleepily. "Maybe they would look at us like we were another species, like an animal, too primitive to matter."

"Except he got to know them. He got to know Bobby. He liked him."

"Yeah," Danny said. Then no one said anything, and I snuggled down in my bag and fell asleep.

Next morning Yogi and I walked to the schoolyard of Chesterfield grade school. There weren't many places to go around Grandy Park. We could have climbed over the chain link fence into the marshy forest where there were hardwood trees and pussy willows in some places that were hard to get to because of the spongy ground and thick roots, but I didn't know how Yogi would be with chain link fences and I didn't want to embarrass her.

I could say anything to Yogi, about algebra, or Neil who'd been her boyfriend the previous summer, or about how hard Latin was, having to remember all those long marks. We competed over who'd be first to get an A. Tough to get 94% with a quarter point off for every one you missed. One long conjugation or declension, and there went the six points, nominative, accusative, dative, genitive, ablative, past present, progressive, what was the use of all those endings? We talked about the ancient Greeks and about God. Only I didn't know if she could climb a tree or over a chain link fence.

"Your house is an adventure." Yogi said.

An adventure, not how I thought of it. We were almost to the school yard. The air was a little cool, with a feel of dampness in it, but it wasn't cold. We wore jackets, though. Now her house, all that space, that would be an adventure.

Luckily Yogi didn't seem to expect an answer to her comment about my house, because I didn't really know what to say. In school I was self-conscious about my clothes, and never having money. But I knew Yogi wasn't putting me down.

We got to the schoolyard. I went to 7th grade here, Chesterfield. Yogi and I tried out the swings awhile, then we went to the tree.

And I shouldn't have worried, because Yogi could climb a tree. Only she climbed it like someone who had never climbed a tree before. I would have chosen a low branch and pulled myself up on it. I could have gotten higher right away, then continued up on the branches. But Yogi didn't look for branches she could wrap her legs around and pull herself up, or look for knots or dents she could rest a foot on. It was like a problem she was figuring out. She went to the center of this tree, which split early, and shimmied herself up between the two big branches that stayed pretty close together. She did it awkwardly, then she stayed wedged about halfway up the tree with her legs in her black stretch pants spread out to brace herself lower down on the tree. It was like Spider Man might climb up in the narrow space between two skyscrapers. I followed up after her and stopped when she did. She didn't go any higher as I expected her to, so we stayed that way.

The morning had a chill to it that you felt when you stopped moving, but I felt the warmth of her around me as I rested within the space made by her legs.

Then there was something I couldn't say, more a feeling than words, about that silence I had felt in her house. I wanted to tell her. *It's not your fault that they all have something to do other than you, even though you work so hard to be clever and to charm them. It's not your fault.*

Instead, I said, "I want to run away from home, but I don't have any money."

She said, "I know," as if I'd told her already. She said, "I could get you away." Where would we go? "South", Yogi thought, "where we wouldn't stick out so much."

But we had to go to school, I thought. I couldn't be poor like my mother who didn't finish high school, stuck being a ward clerk for minimum wage. I had to go to school. But I didn't say that then. After awhile we barely talked at all. Then we walked back home, again almost in silence, as if not to change that feeling between us. We were friends. We could talk about anything, so we didn't have to talk. And we would be running away together.

#

The next morning we rode the bus together to school. I don't know why it was in my mind, but there was something in my mind.

It was something I'd always known, but only just realized.

"My mother wasn't married when she got pregnant with Amy," I whispered to Yogi.

"Really?" she was shocked by it. I wasn't sure if she would be. Yogi didn't think like most people. But I was shocked, and I had always known, because Mom had told us that Amy wasn't Leroy's baby. Anyway they'd only been married a week when Amy was born. It just hadn't clicked, that that was what it meant, that my mother had an "illegitimate child," What kind of an ugly thing was that to say about my sister?

"My mother had an illegitimate child." I tried out the sound.

"Wow, holy wow," said Yogi.

"Yeah," I said.

"How'd that happen?"

I told her about it, about Todd, and then Leroy, and my mother getting fatter and fatter, and she laughed at how I hadn't known.

The whole bus ride we talked and laughed about it. Funny thing is, after I told Yogi and we were shocked together, we never talked about it again, but I started thinking, what was it that was so wrong? My mother had a baby, and she took care of her, and she was my sister who I loved. There's nothing wrong in having a baby, if you take care of the baby. That night my mother was crying with Lorene and Rita, that's what that was for, because of people saying it was shameful, when my sister was a good thing. She was the best. I loved her.

Maybe Yogi came to the same conclusion once she thought about it.

50 The Vice Principal

The history teacher talked on and on, as she often did. I'd sort of listen. If I read through the assignment once, and just listened without taking notes during class, I could ace her tests without studying at all. This was good because algebra and Latin took a lot of time, and every day I had to make dinner, do dishes, do laundry or sweep the house, give Amy a bath and get her to bed. Amy would insist that I lay down beside her, "I'm not going to sleep unless you do."

Sometimes I'd wake her up again, climbing out of her bed.

I'd sit down at the kitchen table to do homework as soon as the dishes were done, and Amy's bath was over. Then I'd keep an eye on the clock so I'd make sure Amy was asleep before time for my mother to be home at 11:30. Sometimes I'd barely make it, and I'd have to get to bed too, unless it was a Friday night. I'd have to be up again at 6AM to catch the bus.

But sometimes I only half listened in history class, so I missed whatever it was that got Yogi so angry, or I didn't understand. But I could see her fuming.

"What's the matter?" I whispered, but she waved me off. Her hands were clenched. She stared ahead at her book. Then she was packing her book bag, and she had gotten up and was walking towards the door even before the bell sounded. But it rang before she got far, and I jumped up and hurried after her. She was walking fast, and I just walked behind her. We had algebra next, but she wasn't headed to algebra, and I didn't know what to do exactly, but I wasn't going to leave her.

She walked down a stairway, and, in a moment she walked back up again, and I thought, good she'd go to class now, but she didn't.

"The stupidity," she said.

"What?"

"Stupidity."

Then she walked down the stairs again, me following, and she paced up and down the hallways. She was going back and forth, so I waited by the stairs for her to talk. All the other kids had disappeared from the hallways now, and I was really worried about what kind of trouble we were going to be in. I couldn't leave her, though. I just had to wait until she started talking or something.

But before she could, a teacher came up, "What are you two doing out here?"

And Yogi just strode right past her, charging to the door.

She got out before the teacher, or I, had time to react. Then I headed towards the door to follow her, but the teacher got in the way. She blockaded the door.

A few minutes later, she told me to come along to the office, and then I was too scared to try to get out again. I just followed along.

She took me to the assistant principal's office.

"She was out in the hall after the bell rang," the teacher told the assistant principal who sat at his desk which took most of the space of his office. "And another girl who was with her just went out the door without permission."

"Thank you, Mrs. Sawyer. Don't worry about the girl who left. We'll figure that out later. Hopefully she'll return on her own and avoid getting into major trouble."

He motioned me into the chair on the other side of his desk.

"Tell me now, what was this all about?"

I didn't really know what it was all about. There was no way I'd have done something that I knew would get me in big trouble if my mother found out. She hadn't hit me again after that day that I walked out the back door, but that didn't mean that she wouldn't.

I'd been reading about the Greeks, though, Archimedes, Socrates, about Pythagoras, and how he started by paying a boy for each theorem he'd learn. Then, after awhile he turned it around and started charging them to teach them more, and they'd pay because they were hooked on learning by then. Why couldn't school be like that, I'd said to the vice-principal, a place where you went because you wanted to learn, instead of a place where you were almost locked up, scared to walk out the door?

He started talking about how I was superior. Maybe he just meant smart, but there was something I didn't like about it, not exactly what he was saying, but something that he meant, only I didn't know what it was.

He said, "You know you're superior don't you?" and I shrugged because I didn't like the word. Then he said, "Well, then, maybe you're not as smart as I thought you were."

I felt a little put down, but it wasn't like someone I really looked up to or cared about had said it. It was just odd, because I was in the office, supposed to be getting in trouble and instead he was talking like I was somebody special.

At one point he asked me if he needed to call my home, and even made a move towards the phone, which made me wonder if he knew who I was. If he did, I didn't know how. And if he didn't, I didn't understand how he came up with that superior stuff. He started asking some questions then, and I was worrying what I'd say if he asked for Yogi's name. Eventually, he did ask, and I told him that I couldn't tell him. But then Yogi walked in and sat down in the other chair near me.

The vice principal said, "Well, hello. Your friend here was just telling me how you think school should be more like it was in ancient Greek times. Was that why you left the school grounds?"

"No, " Yogi said. "That wasn't it. I didn't actually leave school. I was right outside."

"Well, maybe then you can enlighten me about just what the reason was."

Luckily, Yogi seemed calm now. "I just got upset over something, was all," Yogi said.

"I see." Then I just sat back and listened to the two of them talk. The vice principal kept us the whole rest of fifth period, then told us to go on to class. At the end of it, I still didn't know what had made Yogi so upset. We had different classes, so I didn't get to ask her about what was going on.

Nothing happened to us because of it, except the next day the algebra teacher asked me where I had been. I told her I'd been in the vice principal's office.

"Was it an excused or an unexcused absence?"

"I don't know," I said.

She said in a calm voice, "Well, I'll just give you an F for the day, then." She marked it in her black grade book, but it didn't feel like a punishment. She wasn't angry.

#

When Yogi hadn't said anything about running away after a few weeks, I just decided she was working it out. She'd seemed so confident, I felt she knew more about the practical side of things. So for a long time, I didn't bring it up either. Then we were together in the library again, another research day. The teacher was around somewhere, but Yogi and I were off in a section of the library by ourselves. It was the most privacy we'd had since the day she stormed out of history class. I'd been thinking a lot about it, because Mom has said that she and Ed were planning to get married. He was a sailor like Leroy, and in June he was going to be relocated to a naval base in Sanford, Florida. We would be going with him.

I was at the head of the library table, and she was on one side. I talked low. I said, "Have you thought any more about running away together?"

She kind of nodded.

"When do you think we can go?" I was ready to go now. And I thought Yogi would be glad to get away, but she said this really weird thing.

She said, "I could take you away to die."

And I just stared at her. I didn't know what to say, so I said, "What?"

She repeated it, "I could take you away to die."

I just looked at her. She started taking notes from the pile of books she had on the table. I opened a book, too, because I just didn't know what to say. Was that what she'd been thinking all along, that I wanted to die? Did she want to die? I didn't ask her. Maybe she did. She'd said that she'd kill herself if she wasn't so afraid of her parents. But I didn't want to die.

Finally, I told her, "We're moving to Florida, Yogi. Ed and my mother are getting married, and he's being stationed in Florida."

She looked miserable then. "I'm sorry," she said. "I wish we could escape."

51 Summer, 1965

"Don't swim in any rivers, hear," my mother said and waited to see us nod. We did, Danny and I did, hoping that then she'd let us get going. We all stood in Grandma Keenan's living room. It'd been two years since I'd stayed with them for a year. Now we were visiting before moving to Ed's new base in Florida.

Mom looked over at my father, and said, "You promise not to take them swimming in any rivers. You never know what diseases there are in those rivers."

Danny and I waited over by our suitcases. My father had started to pick up a suitcase, but stopped when my mother began to speak. He stood between her and us. *Just don't argue with her*, Danny and I both watched Dad to see what he would do. Only Sammy wasn't tense. He kneeled by the couch playing with his little green plastic soldiers, building formations on the couch pillows.

"I won't take them swimming in any rivers," Dad said. He sighed and looked down at the floor. Mom had already agreed to let the three of us go. Renee didn't want to come. Dad didn't look too much different from when he'd visited us in Virginia over a year ago, near my twelfth birthday. I'd been surprised then how old he looked. I hadn't seen him since I was nine. His hair was thinner, and had gone white like his father's, Grandpa Mills'. He was heavier too. Afterwards, my mother had said the least he could have done was bring me a birthday present. She was never very happy with him.

"I want them back by noon on Sunday, not a minute later," my mother said. She wasn't wearing the shorts she had worn all week. She'd put on a light summer dress, and her hair was combed the way it was when she went out.

"Don't worry, Barbara, I'll get them back on time," my father said. His voice stayed the same, no louder, waiting.

Dad was in Missouri visiting his family too. Grandma and

Grandpa Mills lived near Salem and Dad's brothers and sisters were all close by. Mom must have told Dad we'd be here. But now she treated him like an intruder. Her body was rigid, her hands almost clenched. Any minute she could get angry and tell Dad she wasn't going to let us go.

I was on edge, but Dad stayed calm. He wasn't going to do anything to blow it.

"I don't want them to come back and find out they've been swimming in any rivers," said my mother.

Ed walked in from the dining room. He put his arm around my mom's shoulder. "He'll bring them back on time, Barb. It's okay."

"He damn well better," my mother said, and she didn't relax into Ed's arm, but she didn't knock if off either. Then she went back into the dining room with Ed following her.

Danny and I each picked up a suitcase and Dad got the other. He told Sammy to pick up his soldiers and come on out to the car, so Sammy put all the green soldiers into their box. Just before we left, my mother came out the front door. She hugged Danny and me and Sammy before we got in the car.

She said to Danny, " You watch out for your little brother, now, hear. Don't you let him go swimming in any rivers." I didn't know why Mom was so worried about rivers. We'd swum in the creek at the Willises', but maybe she'd read something about contaminated rivers in the newspaper.

Danny said, "I'll watch out for him, Mom."

Mom turned away and went back into the house. Ed had been standing in the doorway, and he reached for her hand, but she pulled it away from him, and walked through the doorway on her own.

Danny got in the front seat. I followed Sammy into the back. When Dad got into the driver's side, shut the door and turned the key in the ignition, I stopped worrying that my mother would come running out and say we couldn't go. Because now, if she did, somehow I knew my father would take off anyway and pretend not to see her.

#

It was dark by the time we turned into the dirt road that led to the farm. I'd been eight the last time I'd been here, but even in the dark some things were familiar.

Twice Dad stopped the car for Danny to open a cattle gate, then drove the car through, and Danny closed the gate behind the car. The gates were just the wire of the fence continued from the fence post on the left side of the road, attached to a narrow post, which slipped into place on the fence post on the right side of the road, with two loops of wire to hold it. The gate post was stuck into the bottom loop, then the top loop was pulled down over the top. I knew that the gates kept the cows in the field away from the highway and also away from the house. When we got through the last gate and pulled up to the house, I could see several trucks and cars parked up next to it. There wasn't a garage, or even a real driveway because the road stopped before the house, so the cars were parked every which way around the house just avoiding a small patch of grass in the front.

My father explained that the relatives knew we were coming and had come down to see us. The last time I'd seen my father's family was when we'd stayed here on the farm for two weeks while Mama looked for an apartment in Springfield. That was the month before I started third grade. I remembered running around barefoot and eating ripe tomatoes straight from the garden.

The door was open, except the screen door, and Dad walked in without knocking. Someone said, "Clifford's here." Someone else said, "Howdy, Clifford." It was a summer night, but there was a chill and the wood stove was going, blasting out heat. The living room was lit only by the sparks of the wood stove, and light spilling over from the kitchen. Grandpa Mills sat in a rocking chair near the stove. Other people sat on the big high bed that Grandma and Grandpa Mills slept on in the living room, and still others sat on the wide ledge of the window. A few people sat on wooden chairs that must have been moved in from the kitchen.

Grandpa raised himself up in the rocking chair to look at Danny and Sammy and me. He said, "Hi, kids, sure is good to see you." He looked like Dad, but his hair was thinner, softer, curlier. Grandma Mills brought a bench out of the kitchen, and set it up between the living room and the kitchen, near where Grandpa sat by the stove.

Grandma said, "It's a shame your sister didn't want to come."

She looked sad, and Dad looked like he wanted to say something, to tell her never mind, and finally, he said, "Well, I got the three of them anyway."

Grandpa laughed, "Sure enough." He kept rocking.

Then someone told a joke. Everyone chuckled, then there was quiet so you could hear the fire of the wood stove crackle, then again someone had a thought and told another joke. It was the men mostly that told the jokes, Uncle Ryan and Dad and Uncle Joe. If Grandpa told a joke it was usually an amusing story about something that had happened back when my dad and his brothers and sisters were still young, or something about one of my cousins, not a punch line joke.

A girl looked at me from the window ledge and smiled, and I thought I recognized my cousin, Carol. She was just a couple of years older than me, fifteen or sixteen, but she'd been about ten when I saw her last. Between her and Aunt Karla was a boy who seemed to be about seven or eight, and I thought he must be Aunt

Karla and Uncle Ryan's son, Derek, but he'd been a toddler when they'd come out to visit us while we stayed with Grandma and Grandpa Mills. I kept looking at him, thinking I saw something familiar in his face, and also at the other kids and teenagers, who must have been my cousins, trying to sort out who they all were. All of us cousins just sat in the warm room and got sleepy. Nothing was expected of us. Nothing was expected of anybody really. It didn't seem to matter to anyone how long the pauses were between the jokes. It didn't matter if the jokes were good. I don't know if they were good or not. Everyone laughed at everything, and I enjoyed the jokes, but I don't remember what any of them was about. It got late, and after awhile I leaned against the wall with my eyes half closed. Everyone had a drive to get home but no one seemed in a hurry to go.

It was hours and many jokes and stories later when people started to leave. As they left, most stopped where Danny and Sammy and I sat, and said, "Sure is good to see you kids again," or "Don't be a stranger so long again," and some of them I barely remembered, or didn't even recognize, but they seemed to know me. Then their motors started up. Headlights shined through the front window while they warmed their engines. The last car turned onto the dirt road, then soon I heard them stop, and I knew they were opening the cattle gate. They started up again, then stopped, and they were getting out to close the cattle gate. By the time they got to the next one they were too far away to hear and I was up in the attic crawling into one of the quilt covered beds, the same beds my Dad and his seven brothers and sisters had slept in when they were all at home.

#

Next morning I came downstairs to see that Uncle Ryan and Aunt Karla had come back with Derek. Grandma was up, and she handed Dad a cup of coffee, then she went to the stove and brought

- 414 -

over a frying pan with fried eggs. There were fried potatoes already on the table.

"Have some breakfast," Dad said. "We're going up to a lake in the mountains in a little bit." He headed to the stairs, and yelled up, "Danny, Sammy, are you awake?" There was no answer so he went on up.

"They'll be down in a minute," he said to Grandma when he came back.

Next Aunt Karen arrived.

"Well, good morning," she said to me and gave me a quick hug. On our last visit we'd ridden the bus from Springfield. Karen had picked us up at the Greyhound station after her shift waitressing in town and driven us out to the farm.

"Are you still a waitress?" I asked her.

"No, I've got a job in an insurance office now," she said, and grinned, "pays a little better."

"Have a seat," Grandma told her. "I've got eggs for you too."

"Don't mind if I do," Karen said.

Grandma and Grandpa didn't come with us to the lake. I rode sitting next to Karen in the front seat of her car. It was warm riding in the car, and nice sitting beside Karen. She was ten years older than me and ten years younger than Dad, my only aunt who wasn't married.

When we reached the lake, it wasn't just a lake. There was a bathhouse to change in, picnic benches and barbecue pits. Uncle Ryan had set a cooler on one of the tables.

Out on the lake there was a rope marking out a swimming area, and way out, a platform to swim to. For awhile I swam closer to the shore where Sammy and our cousin Derek played together with Aunt Karla watching over them. By the time I swam for the platform, Dan and Dad were already out there.

I touched the edge of the platform. Dad reached down to help me up. He pulled on my arm as I grabbed the platform, with my other hand trying to pull myself up. Then Dad kind of lifted me the rest of the way, and set me down on the platform. There was something so familiar about the way he lifted me so that after all this time it brought back memories of camping trips, when we swam in lakes, and he must have held me or lifted me like that. It was like my body remembered and my body wasn't worried anymore.

Later, on the ride back, I remembered something. It was back when we lived in Yakima when I was little, probably about six because Renee was there. But we must have been on vacation, because Daddy was walking us into the lake. I think it was Great Salt Lake. We headed for a rope that was so far out in the water, farther out than I'd ever gone before. Daddy was between us so we each held one of his hands. Looking out all I saw was water and sky, not the other side. The water felt warm and it wasn't the sea but it had that sea smell. We got to where our feet no longer touched the bottom, but we weren't sinking. Daddy's strong arms held us up so we didn't sink. I could feel the tension of his arm that held me up. I felt so safe there held up by the water and Daddy's strong arms.

When we got back Grandma made us a late supper. I was helping her set the plates on the oil cloth table. She stood across the table from me, short, a little heavy, and her skin was brown and rough. She hadn't said much during our visit. She was just there in the background, handing out food, blankets, whatever was needed. But now she looked up at me and said, "You know you were born the day after my birthday. You were my birthday present, just a day late." And her face had a look of such delight. I thought I could remember some other time, too, when she'd told me that same story before, and she'd had that same look.

But now her face got serious. She said, "I heard you were

having some trouble in school." But she wasn't scolding, instead she was reassuring me, "Just remember good grades aren't the only thing that matters."

For a moment I was going to tell her that it was a long time ago that I had trouble with school, that now I nearly always got A's. I even got an A in the Latin class that gave Yogi and me such trouble. But then I stopped myself. I knew it didn't matter. I didn't have to prove myself to her. I didn't have to explain or justify anything.

I was her delight. I always had been.

#

That evening was our last with them before we went back to Springfield, but there was only Danny and Dad in the living room with Grandpa. Sammy had fallen asleep on the way back from the lake. He woke for dinner, fell asleep again and Dad had carried him upstairs to bed. I sat at the kitchen table with Grandma. We'd just been sitting there in silence and the half dark for awhile.

The light in the kitchen was off, but some light spilled in from the doorway of the other room, from a reading lamp, and the glow of the wood stove. Dad came into the kitchen and sat down at an end of the table so I was to his left and Grandma to his right. Then Grandma began to talk. I'd never heard her talk so much. That night she told about everyone she could ever have known. Most of the names I didn't recognize. A few I did, Delia's boy, or Ronnie. Maybe my father knew who they all were. So many names, where they'd been, where they were now, who was in school, how they were doing, who was sick, or better, or had died, or married, or divorced, or had a new baby, or lost one, or was off in the service. Dad sat quietly, his arms stretched out, elbows on the table, making shadows on the oilcloth. He didn't say anything.

Grandma's words were like a chant, and she seemed to be

weaving something as she spoke. I followed along even though I didn't know who all those people all were. It was like their names got woven into the glow from the wood stove, or the way the light from the other room spilled onto the floor – a cat's cradle of voices inside her one voice. It was like I was fixed there too, in my place, in the kitchen with my Dad, his arms elbowing the table, and the way he'd lifted me onto the platform, the relatives who'd waited for us, and missed us, when I barely remembered or thought of them.

Grandma stopped talking, but her voice remained for awhile, like with a fourth of July sparkler when you wave it around in the dark and it leaves a trail that burns bright for a moment after the sparkler has gone. And even after that the three of us remained there at the table in the dark. A little later Danny came through, heading for the attic stairs to go up to bed, and I roused myself to follow him up.

#

We left the next day. In the car on the drive back I had the same feeling as at the lake, the feeling of not being afraid, like I'd left the tightrope I was always on at home, of being afraid I'd do something wrong. I could picture it, Mom, sitting at the kitchen table, with her coffee and her cigarette, tapping it on the ashtray, and all of us being careful around her, not to annoy her, not to set her off, never acting normally except when she was at work. But now I was headed back. I felt my body tensing up and I concentrated on keeping the feeling of the last couple of days.

Sammy fell asleep after awhile, and I laid my head down on the seat, and had fallen asleep too, or almost, when I heard Danny's voice up in the front seat.

He said, "I'm coming to live with you."

Then I knew it, and my body relaxed with my certainty. It wasn't a decision, I just knew. "I'm coming too," I said, up to the front seat. Somehow I knew, too, that it would happen. Mom might object, or get in the way, or make conditions and then act like she'd change her mind. But in the end, I knew it would happen. It was like an evening when I'd sat on a dock in Norfolk in the dark, dangling my legs over the water, and just feeling the waves and the tide pulling out. I felt all the things going out from that dock, the water itself going out, and connecting to something over on the other side of the ocean. I felt myself then too, moving outward from where and what I had been.

I knew. As certain as getting older, as the tide moved away from the shore, I was going too.